"A unique novel of forensics and fanaticism. A good story on timely subjects well told. For me, these are the ingredients of a successful novel today and Carrie Stuart Parks has done just that."

—CARTER CORNICK, FBI COUNTERTERRORISM
AND FORENSIC SCIENCE RESEARCH (RET.)

"Parks's real life career as a forensic artist lends remarkable authenticity to her enthralling novel, *A Cry From the Dust*. Her work is a fresh new voice in suspense, and I became an instant fan. Highly recommended!"

—COLLEEN COBLE, *USA TODAY* BEST-SELLING AUTHOR OF
ROSEMARY COTTAGE AND THE ROCK HARBOR NOVELS

"In *A Cry from the Dust*, the novel's courageous protagonist—a forensic artist recovering from cancer—finds herself facing "blood atonement" when she investigates the death of a young woman. This superbly researched mystery, based on actual events, shows what can happen when lack of education is combined with religious fanaticism."

—BETTY WEBB, AUTHOR OF
DESERT WIVES AND *DESERT WIND*

"Things I loved about *A Cry from the Dust*: the fascinating and painstakingly researched historical tapestry into which the story is woven, the frantic but intensely believable arc of events that makes you hold on extra tight, the compelling and flawed heroine who has absolutely no idea she's the heroine. Part *CSI*, part *Lie to Me*, and all relentlessly original, *A Cry From the Dust* blends rich characters, little-known history, and a dose of conspiracy into a very modern storytelling style. Can't wait to tear into Gwen Marcey's next adventure."

—ZACHARY BARTELS, AUTHOR OF *PLAYING
SAINT* AND *42 MONTHS DRY*

"With a strong heroine and suspense that keeps the pages flipping, *A Cry From the Dust* is full of twists from the past, secret societies, and a sinister race against the clock. Highly recommend!"

—ROBIN CAROLL, AUTHOR OF THE JUSTICE SEEKERS SERIES

A CRY FROM
THE DUST

A CRY FROM THE DUST

CARRIE STUART PARKS

THOMAS NELSON
Since 1798

NASHVILLE   MEXICO CITY   RIO DE JANEIRO

Published in Nashville, Tennessee, by Thomas Nelson. Thomas Nelson is a registered trademark of HarperCollins Christian Publishing, Inc.

Thomas Nelson, Inc., titles may be purchased in bulk for educational, business, fund-raising, or sales promotional use. For information, please e-mail SpecialMarkets@ThomasNelson.com.

Scripture references are taken from the KING JAMES BIBLE and *Holy Bible*, New Living Translation. © 1996, 2004, 2007 by Tyndale House Foundation. Used by permission of Tyndale House Publishers, Inc., Carol Stream, Illinois 60188. All rights reserved.

Publisher's note: This novel is a work of fiction. Names, characters, places, and incidents are either products of the author's imagination or used fictitiously. All characters are fictional, and any similarity to people, living or dead, is purely coincidental.

Library of Congress Cataloging-in-Publication Data

Parks, Carrie Stuart.
  A cry from the dust / Carrie Stuart Parks.
    pages cm
  ISBN 978-1-4016-9043-4 (paperback)
  1. Mountain Meadows Massacre, Utah, 1857--Fiction. 2. Mormons--Fiction. 3. Utah--Fiction. I. Title.
  PS3616.A75535C79 2014
  813'.6--dc23
                                    2014006456

Printed in the United States of America

14 15 16 17 18 RRD 6 5 4 3 2 1

To Frank,
who taught me to fish.
—Grasshopper

FOREWORD

BEFORE I MET HER, CARRIE STUART PARKS WAS already a forensic artist with years of experience in reconstructing crime scenes, drawing composites of bad guys from witness descriptions, recreating faces of the dead on—shudder!—their original skulls. Once she was interviewing a witness to a murder when she realized he was the murderer. She still has photos of people she's had to draw the way they used to look before they were shot, clubbed, stabbed, drowned; you name it. Consequently, every dinner my wife, Barb, and I had with her and her husband, Rick—my banjo-picking buddy—included stories, some hilarious, some astounding, some a little difficult to hear while eating a rare steak.

At least twelve years ago, she said, "I've been working on a novel. It's just in the first stages. Would you like to take a look at it and tell me what you think?"

And she said all that to Barb!

Well, Barb read it and passed the pages to me as we lay in bed. *Hmm,* I thought. *Not bad. No, you lost me here. Ah! I like this! Ohh, Carrie, don't do that. Now* this *works.* Finally, I responded to the question Carrie never asked but . . . you know . . . sort of did.

Okay. I'd help her. (It was a no-brainer.)

From then on, every few weeks she hollered at the back door, "Knock, knock?" then brought in a case full of pens, highlighters, Post-it notes, her computer, and pages of manuscript—her homework—a copy for her, a copy for me. She read aloud; I followed. I commented; she listened and scribbled notes all over her work. She dubbed me "Master" and herself "Grasshopper" after that old *Kung Fu* TV show, but we were both new at it: she'd never written fiction and I'd never taught it. The learning was mutual.

And I guess it worked out.

Her perseverance alone was deserving of success, but she became a writer because she knew—and I knew—she could do it. She had the flair, the imagination, the whimsical, inventive, sometimes zany ability to go to other places in her mind and come back with the unexpected. She was a creative explosion sure to go off somewhere; all I had to do was aim her.

So . . . *Ka-Boom!* Here it is, Carrie's first novel of the unexpected, mysterious, and shocking, drawing (pun intended) upon the highly specialized world of forensic art and featuring a heroine very much like herself. Hang on for the ride.

Oh, and, Carrie? Well done.

Frank E. Peretti
October 16, 2013

PROLOGUE

1857

THE BULLET EMBEDDED INTO THE DUSTY WAGON wheel, sending wood slivers flying.

Heart pounding, Priscilla James whispered a prayer through cracked lips. "All I have to do is stand, Lord. The next shot'll kill me dead." Her death would be fast and preferable to this parched agony.

She willed her muscles to push her off this blistering earth, to face the Indians who'd kept the wagon train pinned down for the past four days. Without food. Or water.

She tried to keep her gaze off the small row of crudely made crosses near the edge of the circled wagons. Seven men dropped like buckshot quail with the first hail of bullets. Three died right away, and the other members of the wagon train gave them a proper Christian burial. The preacher read the Bible and every-thing. She'd felt all tore up inside. Then.

Stand up. Do it now. One shot. It'll be all over.

The breeze shifted, wafting the stench of rotting flesh.

Priscilla shivered in spite of the heat. Lying like small mounds of snow out on the prairie were the two little girls. The men said not even heathen savages would hurt children dressed like tiny angels, waving white flags and toting water buckets.

That had been two days ago.

They gave up burying the dead yesterday.

She tried to swallow past the lump in her throat. No tears formed in her burning, dry eyes. The September sun lashed the reddened earth.

The child's whimpering started up again.

Priscilla sighed, shifted farther into the buckboard's meager shadows, and pulled the tiny girl into her lap.

Jane Baker settled down and muttered in her sleep "'. . . I shall not want . . .'" Priscilla gently worked a snarl out of the girl's hair. *Poor lass. Who'd take care of her if I were dead?*

Though Jane was nearly ten, she was runty and looked half her age. She lost her ma only four weeks ago, birthing. The baby scarcely took a breath before it, too, died. Her pa, an old man with a scarred face and slight limp, said they'd leave the wagon train at Salt Lake City, but he took sick just before they reached their goal. He must have had brain fever, 'cause he ranted like a madman for a week. He was just getting better when the Indians killed him; he now rested under one of the three crosses.

Priscilla's uncle was buried next to Jane's pa.

Priscilla figured that sort of made Jane her ward. None of the remaining settlers would have anything to do with the child.

They said she was wrong. Touched. Some even said the Devil was in her.

Another bullet smacked into the buckboard.

Priscilla jumped.

Maybe that's the solution. They'd both try fetching water. They'd die heroes.

The murmuring of voices roused her from the sooty black thoughts. The grumbling grew to excited calls. "White men!"

"Praise God. We're saved!" Mrs. Dunlap waved a hankie. Settlers poured from the circled wagons, pointing.

Goose pimples broke out on Priscilla's arms. *Thank You, Lord.*

In the distance she spotted several men on horseback, waving flags. They'd come! Mr. Fancher's plan worked. Last night he'd sent three of their best scouts to find help.

She'd soon be out of Utah Territory, in California. Home with her folks. She wrapped grubby fingers around the locket holding pictures of her ma and pa. Little Jane had her own treasure, a small packet never far from her. Priscilla peeked once when Jane was sleeping, but there wasn't any money or jewels, just a journal and photo of her pa.

Jane would get better in California. Priscilla would take care of her.

Jane jumped to her feet to join the milling throng. Priscilla followed, squinting at the two men waving white flags and slowly riding toward the camp.

"Mormons," a man standing next to Priscilla said and spat on the ground. "Don't never trust 'em."

Priscilla nodded. Mormons refused to sell them fresh supplies since they entered Utah Territory, and food was all but gone even before the Indians ambushed them. Priscilla even thought she saw white men driving off their livestock after first slaughtering some of the cattle.

"Maybe so," she said. "But they be lookin' like saviors right now."

One stranger dismounted, handed the reins of his bay horse to his companion, and continued forward. The settlers crowded around him. Priscilla caught the words "Indian agent," but she couldn't get close enough to hear more. The weary smiles around her spoke of good news. The agent waved, jumped on his horse, then spurred it to a gallop. The two men quickly disappeared.

Funny. The scouts weren't with them. Maybe they were waiting up the trail. The tiny hairs on the back of her neck prickled. *Stop fussing now. We're safe.*

Jane stood motionless, gazing after the retreating men, her eyes wide and unseeing.

Priscilla touched her on the shoulder and shook her sleeve. "It's over. Come on, Jane."

Jane's lips moved. Priscilla bent closer to hear.

"'. . . cry from the dust . . . ,'" Jane said. "'. . . for vengeance—'"

Priscilla cupped the small child's face in her hands and stared into her unfocused eyes. Heavens t'be, the last of the girl's mind was going.

After grabbing Jane by the wrists, Priscilla twirled her in a circle. "Come on, we're going to California. You can come to my party."

Priscilla stopped spinning, stood motionless, then touched her hair. "I must be a sight." She pulled Jane to the Conestoga where she retrieved a comb and mirror. The mirror's image shocked her. She'd lost weight and her skin was brown from dirt and the sun.

With no water to wash up, she contented herself with brushing and braiding her hair.

Jane continued to mutter, "'. . . vengeance . . . destroy . . .'"

The thud of hooves and creak of wood announced the return of the man, this time accompanied by two wagons.

"Surrender your weapons," the Indian agent shouted. "Put them in the bed. Wounded go into the second wagon. We'll walk you out of here."

Grinning broadly, Priscilla took Jane's hand. The rescuers marshaled women and children first, then the men. Slowly, like the Israelites leaving Egypt, they followed their Moses. Priscilla hummed and swung Jane's arm. A crisp breeze brought the smell of sweet prairie grass, and Priscilla breathed deeply.

"'Yea, though I walk . . . shadow of death,'" the young girl whispered. "'I will fear no evil . . .'"

The valley narrowed, with rocky outcroppings and sagebrush hemming in the straggling group. The agent reined in his horse. He was near Priscilla, and she smiled slightly at him.

He didn't seem to notice. He rose in his stirrups, looked around, and shouted, "Do your duty!"

The rocks seemed to burst into life as Indians hurtled down upon them, shrieking, shooting, chopping, slicing through the women and children.

Priscilla froze.

Mrs. Dunlap, walking beside Priscilla and carrying her baby, fell dead with a bullet piercing her forehead. Eight-year-old Sarah Fancher's scream was cut short as a crazed Indian sliced her throat.

Heart pounding, unable to breathe, Priscilla bolted, yanking Jane with her.

They ran like jackrabbits, dodging the rocks, shrubs, bodies, and frenzied killers. The air filled with the reek of copper and screams of anguish. A huge man stabbed a bayonet into young Henry Cameron, screaming, "For Jehovah!"

Not Indians. Mormons.

Something punched her, and a million scorpions stabbed her side. Priscilla stumbled and lost her grip on Jane. The child flew through the air as one of the bloodied men grabbed her up.

The landscape blurred and she glanced down. A red stain spread up her dress. Her legs refused to hold her. She spun, slamming into the earth.

The sun blinded her for a moment, then a man blocked it. The big man.

"Please, spare me." Priscilla raised her praying hands toward him. "I'll do anything. Please . . . oh, please . . . I'll be your slave . . ."

"For Jehovah," he shouted, and thrust the bayonet.

CHAPTER
ONE

MOUNTAIN MEADOWS, UTAH, PRESENT DAY

"ARE THESE FROM THE THREE BODIES THEY DUG up?" The question came from my right.

The first of the early-afternoon tourists gathered just outside my roped-off work area. More people charged toward me, ignoring glass-fronted display cases holding historical articles and docents in navy jackets hovering nearby.

You can't beat disembodied heads on sculpting stands to draw a crowd.

The open, central structure of the Mountain Meadows Interpretative Center featured towering windows that overlooked the 1857 massacre site. The architect designed the round building to resemble the circled wagons of the murdered pioneers. Exhibits were below the windows or in freestanding showcases, allowing visitors an unobstructed view of the scenery, with directional lighting artfully spotlighting displays. In the center of the room was a rock cairn, representing the hastily dug mass grave where the US Army interred the slaughtered immigrants more than two years after the attack.

A woman in a lime-green blazer with the name of a tour group ushered silver-haired couples past the welcome banner to a tidy grouping on my left. Neatly dressed families with a smattering of dungaree-clad teens joined the spectators and advanced to my cluttered corner.

Out the window I could see another surge of visitors scurry through the late-summer heat from the tour bus parked on the freshly paved lot.

A hint of sweat, deodorant, and aftershave replaced the odor of fresh paint and new carpeting. I double-checked to be sure the two finished, reconstructed skulls faced toward the vacationers. The clay sculptures rested on stands looking like high, three-legged, wooden stools with rotating tops. I'd nicknamed the three Larry, Moe, and Curly. Larry and Moe were complete, resting on shoulders made of wire covered with clay. Once I finished Curly, all three would be cast in bronze for permanent display.

The questions flew at me from all sides. "Who are they?"

"Are real skulls under that clay?"

"Doesn't it bother you to touch them?"

I opened my mouth, but before I could deliver the memorized greeting, the chunky director pushed through the visitors. "Hello, ladies and gentlemen. Welcome to the Mountain Meadows Interpretive Center. I'm Bentley Evans, the director." He waited a moment for that important piece of information to sink in.

Most of the crowd ignored him and continued to pepper me with questions. "I thought all the bones were busted up."

"I heard Brigham Young was responsible."

That last comment got the attention of two young men in short-sleeved white shirts, black ties, and badges designating them as elders.

Elders? I studied their fresh, adolescent faces. I had older shoes in my closet.

"Ahem, yes, well," Mr. Evans continued. "This is Gwen Marcey, world-renowned forensic artist. She'll explain this project."

He turned toward me, tilted his head back, steepled his hands in front of his mouth, and raised his eyebrows.

His body language screamed arrogance.

A trickle of sweat ran down my back. I could have used a vote of confidence right about now. Sometimes I wished I didn't know so much about nonverbal communication. *Remember why you're here.* This could open the door to that new position for a regional, interagency forensic artist. It wasn't the title I wanted so much, but a steady paycheck—and the first step toward returning my life to normal. Whatever "normal" was now.

The crowd shifted and rustled like a hayfield stirred by the wind. A new set of tourists joined the throng, bunching together on my right and pushing against the hunter-green velvet ropes.

My heart pounded even faster as I placed the wire-tipped tool on the sculpting stand. Speaking in front of people had never fazed me, but it had been a year since I'd done a presentation. A year since my divorce. A year since I was diagnosed with cancer. *Just keep thinking it's like riding a bicycle . . .*

"So, do you, like, always work on dead bodies?" A shaggy-haired young man in front of me ogled the display.

I breathed easier. A simple question. "Sometimes. These three"—I caught myself before calling them Larry, Moe, and Curly—"are historical cases, so I'm using plaster castings done by a company that specializes in reproductions. The real skulls were reburied with the bodies over there." I pointed to a small cemetery outside. "On forensic cases, I would use the real thing. I also work on court exhibits, crime scene sketching, and composites—"

"But isn't all that stuff done on computers now days?" A young girl snapped a photo of me with her iPhone.

"Well, you know the old saying, 'garbage in, garbage out.'"

"Huh?" She lowered the phone and scrunched her face.

"The idea that computers can replace artists is the same as computers replacing authors because of spell check. You need the knowledge. The computer is just the tool."

"So you still use a pencil?" The girl pointed at my head. "Is that why you have two behind your ear?" Several people chuckled.

"You bet." I self-consciously tugged one out and placed it on my stand. "Anyway, the National Park Service and Mountain Meadows Society hired me to reconstruct the faces of the only three bodies formally buried at the site and recovered intact." I took a deep breath and released it. Outside of the pencils, no one stared at my face or commented on my appearance. I picked up a chunk of clay and began to form an ear.

"Why only three?" one of the young missionaries asked.

Before I could frame my answer, a woman jammed a guidebook under his nose. "Didn't you read this?"

I stiffened. Her sarcastic tone reminded me of my ex-husband. I squeezed the clay ear into a shapeless blob.

4

"It says right here." She had everyone's rapt attention. "Most of the bodies were chopped up and left out to rot and be eaten by wild animals."

"*Ahem*, well . . ." I cleared my throat. The director's voice echoed in my brain. "*There might be people upset about the interpretive center. Mormons who don't believe it really happened, anti-Mormons looking for any excuse to bash the church, descendants of the survivors who think the whole event was buried as a coverup, Native American activists who are angry that the Indians were blamed for the slaughter, you name it. The Mountain Meadows Massacre is a relatively unknown part of American history. We don't really know how visitors will react to learning about it for the first time. Just remember: remain neutral.*"

A man in Bermuda shorts standing next to her added, "It was the worst domestic terrorist attack in America."

I dropped the blob of clay. "Well, technically, the Oklahoma City bombing—"

"They blamed the Indians." The woman's voice went up an octave. She looked like a freeze-dried hippie from the sixties, complete with headband holding her long gray hair in place.

I wiped my clay-covered hands on my jeans. "After the—"

"Go ahead: say it." The woman wouldn't give up. "After the *massacre.*"

"We don't—"

A young man with a long chin, wearing a yellow CTR wristband and a button-down shirt, now waved a similar guidebook. "That's right. Over one hundred and forty innocent people—"

"Unarmed men, women, and children, brutally slaughtered!" finished a chunky woman spilling out over a too-revealing, sleeveless T-shirt stating *as/so.*

The protesters surged forward, crunching the blue plastic tarp protecting the carpeting from stray clumps of clay. I moved to the front of my display and tried to speak again. "The—"

A tiny woman in a plain, black dress adorned only with a silver pendant piped in. "The killers were Mormon fanatics calling themselves Avenging Angels."

The voices flew at me like wasps. An older woman with a cane stumbled slightly as Button Down shoved against her. I caught her arm before she could fall and glared at the man. He blinked at me, then slunk off, followed by several fellow agitators.

"Thank you," the woman said. "A most unfortunate individual. Why do you suppose they are so upset? The Mountain Meadows Massacre happened over a hundred and fifty years ago."

"People still fight over the Civil War. I guess anger and revenge don't have a time limit." I was tippy-toeing on the edge of neutrality. Bentley Edwards would have my hide. I glanced around for the man, finally spotting him overseeing the refreshments.

"How did you know what they looked like?" a man on my left asked. A new set of tourists now stood in front of me.

I moved closer to Curly. "Your skin and muscles are on top of your bones, so bones are the foundation. If you feel here"—I placed my finger on the outer edge of my eye socket—"the tissue is very thin and you can easily feel your skull. Here on your cheek"—I poked the spot—"it's very thick."

Half the listeners began touching their faces.

"I cut tissue-depth markers to precise lengths and glue them on the skull. Then I build up the clay." I was probably rubbing clay all over my face so I dropped my hand. "Any more questions?"

"How about the nose? How do you know what that will look like?"

"I measure the nasal spine." I placed my finger at the base of my nose and pushed upward. "You can feel the bottom of it here."

Several people poked at their noses.

"The tip of your nose is three times the length of your nasal spine, and on Caucasians, the width is five millimeters on each side of the nasal aperture."

"Any survivors?" asked a spiky-haired girl with black lipstick.

I nodded toward a nearby display. "Yes. The information about the survivors is over there. Seventeen children were spared, all under the age of eight."

"Why eight?" asked a young man wearing a North Idaho College T-shirt. Numerous other teens, all wearing similar shirts, surrounded him, though most appeared riveted by the electronic devices in their hands. The image of my fourteen-year-old daughter, Aynslee, swam into my mind, and I glanced at my watch. Her classes would be wrapping up for the day. Maybe today she'd talk to me on the phone. She'd refused since I'd sent her to the academy. My eyes burned and my nose threatened to start running.

"Ha!" The left-over hippie woman stepped from behind a post. "The Mormons figured they were too young to remember."

"For crying in a bucket, don't you have somewhere else to go?" I slammed a piece of clay into Curly's cheek. I sighed, then wrinkled my nose at her.

She stuck her tongue out at me.

Well, that was mature. I turned my back on the visitors and concentrated on smoothing the clay.

An overweight man wearing a Hawaiian shirt stretched the

barrier around my work area inward, as if to physically intimidate me. I could now easily read the button he wore: *No More Mormon Cover-Up!*

"I suppose you're one of *them*," he whispered.

His stale beer breath made me gag. I glanced around. "No," I whispered back, pointing at my reconstructions. "I can't be one of them. They're made of plaster and clay." I checked around again. "They're not *real*, but I understand there's a huge government cover-up in Nevada. Area 51 . . ."

The man reared back, mouth open, giving me one last whiff of bad breath, and waddled away.

I really needed to study the definition of neutral. And the grumpy protesters needed to go home and form a bowling league.

"Nice job," a male voice commented to my left.

I turned. Craig Harnisch, a deputy in my hometown of Ravalli County, Montana, stood next to me. I'd worked with him on numerous cases over the years. "Hey there, stranger! You're a few miles from home."

"Hey, back. I have family not far away in St. George. Thought I'd drop by and see what Ravalli County's favorite forensic artist was up to. Heard about the preview opening from my in-laws."

"We actually open in a week and a half or so. A bunch of poo-bahs and folks with deep pockets wanted to see everything before the opening. Director Edwards figured the visitors wouldn't mind using temporary vending machines and Porta Potties to catch a preview of the new center. Thought it would bring extra publicity. Bet he didn't count on the protester cartel."

"I liked your snarky comeback," Craig said.

"It'll probably buy me a formal reprimand." I picked up a dab of clay. "I'm supposed to stick with the scripted answers."

A flat, slightly nasally female voice announced through the loudspeakers, "Refreshments are being served by the north wall." The ever-hungry teens drifted toward the offering of free food while the adults continued to admire the displays.

I noticed Button Down, Hippie Lady, Chunky Woman, and Black Dress all gathered around Beer Breath, listening intently. Their body language indicated he was their leader. "Craig, is there a chance these people"—I jerked my head at the group—"could be professional agitators?"

Craig turned to look in the same direction. "You think someone could be paying them to cause problems?"

"Yeah, I do. Director Edwards said resurrecting the past like this might stir up trouble. And, well, technically, there was a cover-up. Of sorts."

"What do you mean?"

I checked to be sure the director was out of earshot. "Back in 1999, a backhoe was digging some footings for a new monument and accidentally scooped up the remains of at least twenty-nine bodies. Under Utah law, it's a felony to rebury any human remains discovered on private land without a scientific study, so a forensic anthropologist started to examine some of the bones. She'd just started to report on the brutal attack"—I moved closer and lowered my voice—"and stated that white men, not the Paiute Indians, committed the massacre. But before the study was completed, the governor, a descendant of one of the Mountain Meadows killers, demanded the bones be reburied and all research stopped. The families were furious."

"Okay. What's your point?"

"Just look at the people causing the uproar." I nodded in their direction.

"I am. So?"

"So, Director Edwards mentioned the people who might be upset by this center: Mormons, anti-Mormons, Native Americans, and families related to those killed."

"And . . . ?"

"That group is totally mismatched."

"And you can tell this because . . . ?"

"*Look* at them. The woman in the black dress is wearing a pendant with a sego lily, the symbol of the LDS Relief Society. And the man in the button-down shirt has a CTR—Choose the Right—wristband. That's the Mormon version of 'What Would Jesus Do?'"

"All you've proven is that you're observant, which I already knew."

"I'm not done. The guy in the Hawaiian shirt was drinking. Mormons don't drink. And the chunky lady's wearing a T-shirt with a shortened form of 'as above, so below,' a Wicca saying that everything is balanced. Except for that guidebook and *Cover-Up* buttons, they have nothing in common. They sound like they're reading from a script. And they just seem . . . wrong."

"Ah, yes, your famous antenna." Craig's mouth twisted into a skeptical grin. "You're always analyzing. You let things get to you. Finish your work and hurry back home. I've got a cold case I want you to look at."

"Does Ravalli County finally have the money to pay me?"

"Are you kidding? You'll get your usual reserve deputy salary."

"It's a voluntary position."

"Yup."

"I need a paying job now. Child support doesn't stretch very far."

"Talk to the sheriff." He grinned. "In the meantime, I want to walk around a bit more."

"Sure. See you."

A few families and the *Cover-Up* crowd returned and surrounded me. I looked again for the director and spotted him eating a piece of cake by the refreshment table. Maybe it was time I took a coffee break. I could slink out of sight and let someone else be neutral to the *Cover-Up* crew. And lose my job because I was hiding.

"What happened to the children?" A young woman hugged her baby tighter.

"They—"

"I'll tell you what happened," a grizzle-haired man wearing biker gear answered. "The killers parceled them out to Mormon families and tried to get the government to pay 'em to get the kids back."

Terrific. Where are a couple of neatly dressed, respectable Mormon missionaries when you needed them? The crowd now glared at me, and Button Down stared intently at my penciled-in, nonexistent eyebrows. Could I make a citizen's arrest of the cranky quartet for being annoying in public?

I smiled without showing my teeth and fell back on my memorized presentation. "These three settlers were killed on the first day of the four-day standoff, and the remaining settlers buried them. The rest of the bodies were left out in the elements for two years. By the time the US Army arrived, the bones were scattered. The army interred the remains in a mass grave." I pointed outside. "The original rock cairn was rebuilt by the Mormon Church—"

"Tell them why it had to be rebuilt." The biker lifted the brass post holding the restraining ropes and shifted it closer to me, knocking against one of my stacked plastic boxes. "Brigham Young and his followers tore it down in 1861."

The hippie woman deliberately bumped a stack of reference books. I stared at the books, then at her face. She met my gaze with a challenge in her eyes.

The anger *was* fake. They were here to cause trouble.

I gritted my teeth. "The purpose of this center is to heal the past—"

"Nah. People like you are covering up for the Mormon Church." The biker jabbed a finger at me.

The finger did it. "Back off and get outta my face!"

"I knew it!" The man gave a triumphant grin and stalked off.

He was probably heading to Mr. Evans to complain. The thought triggered a hot flash. I took deep breaths, trying to convince my body I was fine. *This is an air-conditioned building.* For some reason I kept thinking I could talk my body out of turning into a furnace whenever I was stressed. And whenever I wasn't stressed. My pep talks hadn't worked yet. *Keep your head down and look busy.*

Mr. Evans would understand. The guy's finger had practically impaled my nostril. He'd assaulted me with a deadly digit. Self-defense. The guy wasn't even a true visitor. He was a paid thug.

Mr. Evans was probably scribbling out the pink slip at this moment.

"Did you do the skulls from the Battle of the Little Bighorn?" a sweet voice asked. "We saw them a few days ago."

"No, I didn't work on those." I turned to face the woman and fought the urge to hug her.

There was something familiar about her. It took me a moment to figure it out. She was slender and dressed like me—in a denim shirt and jeans. We had the identical pale blond hair color and cut. Her hair, unlike mine, was real. We could have been sisters, assuming sisters could be twenty and thirty-five.

I patted Curly's cheek. "Once I finish, these sculptures will be cast in bronze and placed on display. The entire anthropological excavation and reconstruction will become a permanent exhibit. Are there any other questions?"

"Could we see the third man?"

"Sure. I have to sculpt his other ear and finish the rest of the hair, neck, and shoulders, but you can see the face at any rate." I gently pivoted the stand.

The blond woman blanched and crumpled to the floor.

CHAPTER
TWO

A YOUNG MAN DOVE TO HER SIDE. "BEKKA—"

"Call a doctor," someone yelled.

"Oh dear!" I knelt beside the fallen girl. The crowd lapped around us like a human ocean.

"Miss? Are you hurt?" I picked up her limp hand and looked around for help. "Please, someone call 911."

"Bekka? Oh Lord, is she dead?" the young man asked.

Dead? I touched her neck and felt a reassuring *thump-thump-thump.* "No."

An older woman with short gray hair pushed through. "I'm a nurse. Please, everybody move back and stay calm."

I slid out of the way as the nurse took my place and checked her carotid pulse.

"What's wrong with her?" the young man asked.

"She probably just fainted. Please, everyone move back." The nurse gently rubbed the girl's face.

I stood. "Did someone call 911?"

"Yeah. They're coming," Craig answered.

The young woman seemed to be in capable hands, so I trotted to the entrance to direct the EMTs. They soon arrived in a flurry of lights. Two men carrying medical cases charged through the door and raced in the direction I pointed. I slowly followed, not wanting to get in the way.

Did the girl faint because of a medical condition, or did my reconstruction have something to do with it? She had been staring right at the sculpture when she collapsed. But nothing about my work was gory, just clay over a plaster casting.

The voice on the loudspeaker announced the center would close in thirty minutes. The visitors meandered toward the exits, and I could see the EMTs talking to the young woman, now sitting cross-legged on the floor.

I felt a rush of relief that she wasn't hurt.

"I'm so sorry," the girl said. "I feel so embarrassed." She smiled when she saw me. "I guess I gave you all quite a scare."

"As long as you're okay." I nodded to the apparent boyfriend. "Are *you* all right?"

"Yeah."

I glanced at the offending reconstruction. Someone had shoved the stands holding Curly and Moe against the wall. The third stand lay on the floor, Larry's sculpture smashed.

Bile rose in the back of my throat, and I covered my mouth to keep from crying out. Five days of labor lay ruined.

I moved closer and picked up a plastic container holding the backup skulls. The ominous rattle made my stomach turn. The castings were in pieces. No way could I finish by the opening. Though the Utah work was satisfying, I'd been looking forward to returning home soon, picking up Aynslee from boarding school, and starting fresh. Now I'd be here another week at least. And Aynslee would be another week more resentful. The academy seemed like such a great solution when this job opened up. Robert was traveling and couldn't, or wouldn't, take our daughter, and I couldn't have a rebellious teen hanging out at the motel while I worked. And I desperately needed this work.

I could hear my best friend's, Beth Noble's, voice in my head: *"Everything happens for a reason."* The problem was I could never figure out the reason. *Just once, God, couldn't You show me why?*

No use whining. Maybe I could sculpt a smile on the settler's face the next time.

I turned away. The EMTs helped the girl to her feet, and the young man wrapped a protective arm around her waist. I caught up with her. "Excuse me?"

"Yes?"

"Are you okay?"

"Yeah, sure."

"Well . . . uh . . . good, that's good." I glanced at the sculpture. "I sometimes forget folks aren't used to watching CSI-type work."

"I love those shows."

"But most of that is make-believe. Maybe seeing real forensic work—"

"Oh, that. I found it fascinating." She looked away. A moment passed. "It's just, well. Actually, I was, uh, not feeling well." She leaned on her boyfriend and drifted toward the exit.

She'd just lied to me.

Just before the door shut behind her, she glanced back.

Getting the vapors had gone out of style in the Victorian era along with whalebone corsets.

The protestors had left, as well as the biker. Some families and the tour group still hovered around the refreshments. I sauntered through the rapidly thinning crowd to where Craig leaned against a display case. "Craig, can you do me a favor?"

"What?"

"If I get you a name, would you check on it for me?"

"Is it a case you're working on?"

"Maybe—"

"The center will be closing in five minutes." The loudspeaker echoed.

Craig looked toward the exit. "Don't tell me. You want to check out that fainting girl. You're doing your Superman Syndrome routine again."

I clamped my mouth shut on a nasty retort. Superman Syndrome referred to forensic artists who overstepped their duties and tried to solve a case single-handed. "Never mind." I probably didn't need his help. These days, once I had a name and a little information, I could do more research about someone on a social network.

We said our good-byes as the last of the people strolled toward the exits. Bentley Edwards gathered his docents, four gray-haired women newly hired for the job, and escorted them out.

Someone had kicked the neon-blue tarp under my work area into a pile, and the tan plastic boxes lay on their sides. I tugged the tarp flat, replaced the brass posts holding the velvet ropes, and straightened the books. The sculpting tools appeared unharmed, but even with expedited service, the new skull casts wouldn't arrive until tomorrow. Plus, I'd probably have to pay for that out of my own pocket until the insurance company reimbursed me.

I picked up Larry's smashed face off the floor. The soft oil-based clay used in the reconstruction now had embedded plaster chips. A clear footprint, made by a woman-size shoe, mashed down the facial features.

I dumped the work into a nearby trash can. Larry'd been the first reconstruction I'd completed, and it was like losing a buddy. I gripped the edge of the bin. *Good-bye, m' friend.*

One final bit of cleanup near where the girl had fallen yielded a maroon backpack with a broken latch. I carefully turned it over. No name appeared in the clear plastic holder sewn into the flap. I should turn the backpack over to lost and found.

I should.

But if it belonged to the fainting girl, she'd be leaving town soon with her college group. A quick peek at the wallet would give me an identification of the owner.

That's snooping.

No. Identifying the owner was just being thoughtful. I was heading to town, and if there was a clue to the owner, I could return it. I opened the backpack. The pink fake leather wallet gave me the name of Rebekah Kenyon, c/o North Idaho College. *Rebekah. Bekka?* The college address matched the logo on the girl's shirt. I returned the wallet and placed the backpack with my purse and lunch cooler.

Maybe if I spoke to her alone, she'd tell me why she fainted. And why she lied.

After sitting on the high work stool, I stared at Curly's face. The blue eyes gazed upward above pronounced cheekbones and a slender jaw. The anthropologists described him as a man in his late forties to fifties, with a chip in his front tooth and left zygomatic bone, suggesting old injuries. I created a scar across the cheek, but, like all forensic artists working on unknown skulls, I guess at the parts of the face consisting of soft tissue: the eyelids and exact shape of the nose, lips, and ears.

I patted the clay cheek. "Well, Curly, you and Moe survived the day. Looks like you're still making the ladies swoon. Just wait until I give you more hair." I smoothed the clay on his temple. "You have to admit the girl's reaction was strange. It was like she saw the face of someone she knew."

Minuscule tentacles of unease tripped across my shoulders. I shrugged them away. "I'm sorry to break this to you, but you've been dead for over a hundred and fifty years." I squinted at my work. "Although you don't look your age—"

"Excuse me? Is someone still with you, Gwen?" George Higbee, the elderly security guard, peered around the room.

"Just talking to my buddy here."

George shoved his thick tortoiseshell glasses up the bridge of his nose and shuffled over. A widower, he was jockey-small, with a full head of ginger-and-white hair. "You'll need a permit and pass if you're having someone stay after hours."

"See?" I addressed the skull. "Now you need a green card."

The guard stopped, then scratched his head. "Are you talking to that . . . that thing?"

"Careful, George, Curly's got ears, you know. Well, okay, one ear. I'll give him another one tomorrow." I smiled at his expression. "Never mind. I'm leaving for the evening." I checked my watch. It was much later than I thought. George usually ushered me out long before this. "Thank you again for the slice of banana bread. It was delicious." *Maybe he'll invite me to dinner again sometime soon.* He was a marvelous chef.

George ducked his head. "'Twas nothing." He squinted at the two heads. "They give me the creeps, you know. Like they are still mad or want revenge."

"They're harmless, George." I took out my digital camera and photographed the day's work, jotted the progress in my notebook, and loaded my oversize purse. George moved closer and stared at my work. I couldn't read his expression.

"George?" He didn't seem to hear me. "George?"

Like a man waking up from sleep, he finally looked at me. "Oh. Sorry. Say, missy, I didn't ask. How did today go?"

"Interesting. Quite the drama."

His gaze seemed to sharpen. "How so?"

"Several arguments. A lady was almost knocked to the floor. A young woman fainted—"

"Fainted?" He nodded. "That would explain it."

"Explain what?"

He glanced away and cleared his throat. "Nothing. Ready to leave?"

I nodded. He followed me to the exit and opened the door. I strolled past him to my car, parked in the employee's lot next to George's Jeep and someone's blue pickup. I dumped everything in the trunk and slipped into the driver's seat. The interior was oven-hot, even with the windshield cover. I cranked up the air-conditioning and let it run a bit while I called the casting company.

"Skull-Duggery. How may I direct your call?"

"I'd like to place an order." I pulled my credit card from my wallet as I waited for the sales rep.

"Customer service, how—"

The roar of the truck's diesel engine drowned out her words. George's Jeep was in the way, but through the Jeep's dusty windows I could just make out a figure in the blue pickup. "What's he doing?"

"What's who doing?" The voice on the phone sounded suspicious.

"Oh, sorry—" The engine roared again.

"—can't hear you." The woman's voice was irritated.

"I'd like to place an order."

The truck revved again, belching diesel fumes, and backed up. I turned to see if I could read the license plate, but the truck shot from the parking area before I could see anything. It was probably just someone talking on the phone like I was.

Maybe he was looking for something. Or waiting for someone . . .

"I missed your answer. Have you ordered from us before?"

"Yes." I quickly placed the order, and she assured me I'd have the skulls the next day, quoting an expedited shipping fee that made me wince. I hung up and tossed the phone in my purse.

Mountain Meadows was a verdant paradise in 1857, but I now drove through a God-cursed, arid wasteland toward the community of Fancher, named after the leader of the doomed wagon train. The new businesses forming the town were as colorful as the surrounding landscape was desolate. Fancher was one street wide, sprouting less than a mile from the Mountain Meadows site.

The only hotel, the Baker Inn, was my residence for the past few weeks. Except for the occasional dinner invitations to George's home, I'd subsisted on restaurant chow. I'd memorized the menu. As I never mastered even the simplest cooking skills, I'd enjoyed that part of the stay. The room was clean enough, and I'd made a game of seeing what housekeeping would forget to replenish each day: plastic-wrapped cups, hand towel, or shampoo instead of another bottle of conditioner to go with the three already there. I gave up on hoping they'd leave me regular coffee packets instead of decaf. I bought my own.

A silver-and-red bus with a North Idaho College logo straddled the motel parking area. I parked and slipped from the car. My cell phone rang as I approached the lobby. I rummaged in my purse. "Gwen Marcey."

"You have an obstreperous dog." Beth sounded breathless.

"Is that your word of the day?"

"Yes. It means unruly, but also noisy."

"Ah. What has Winston done this time?" The clerk approached from the rear of the building. "Hold on, Beth." I pulled the phone from my ear. "Hi, Joyce. Any messages or packages?"

Joyce shook her head. "FedEx hasn't come yet. No messages. How'd the preview opening go?"

"Quite the drama. A young gal fainted by my display. I need to return her backpack. She's probably with that college group."

"I think everyone's at dinner." She nodded at the cafe on the side of the building.

"Beth? Still there?"

"What fainting woman? Are you doing some sleuthing while I'm stuck here taking care of your dog? Don't you realize I'm going crazy bored without you here telling me about your cases? Where would Sherlock be without Watson?"

"Smoking opium and playing the violin."

"Correction. Watson knew Sherlock smoked opium and was often around when Holmes played the violin."

"I should never try to be funny with a research software engineer."

"I'm retired and that wasn't funny."

I reached the door. "I'll call you a bit later for a blow-by-blow account. Do we have a dog emergency?"

"No."

"Good. I need to try to catch up with this girl before she leaves town."

"Promise you'll call?"

"Promise." I dropped the cell into my pocket. I once made the mistake of playing Scrabble with Beth. She thoroughly stomped me, using words like *zwieback*.

A blue pickup trolled past on the main street, speeding up as I watched. It looked like the same pickup I'd seen parked at the interpretive center.

I headed over to speak to the girl. I couldn't wait to get to my room, relax, take off my incredibly itchy wig, and veg out.

Crossing to the restaurant, I folded my arms to ward off the cool gust of high desert wind. Though still August, the fragrance of autumn was in the air. So was the smell of steak and garlic. My mouth watered. Maybe I'd order the number seven. Or the number two. Roasted chicken with garlic mashed potatoes.

I nodded at the hostess and glanced around the spacious room. The college students occupied almost every table and half the counter, all trying to talk over their neighbors. Dishes clanked, silverware clattered, and waitresses leaned close to hear the meal orders. I didn't see Rebekah. The only person I recognized was the young man sitting alone against the wall. He would know how I could get in touch with the fainting girl. I strolled over. "How's your friend, Bekka?" I had to speak up to be heard.

"Uh, she went to her room . . . to change . . . and said she'd be down soon." He wiped his hands on a napkin.

"No injuries from the fall?"

"Said she was okay."

"Did she say why she fainted?"

"She said she was hungry and sick."

"Oh." I waited to see if he'd offer any other information. "I'm Gwen Marcey, by the way." I tugged out a business card and handed it to him.

"Ethan Scott."

"Okay, Ethan. I just wanted to see how she was doing. I have something of hers. Will she be long?"

He glanced at his watch. "She should have been here by now."

Unease pricked my neck. "Maybe we should check on her. She might have fainted again."

The young man lurched to his feet. "I didn't think about that." His eyes widened, and he clutched the napkin in a white-knuckled fist. "She's in room twenty. All the way at the far corner. I have a key."

Hmm. More than a casual boyfriend? I raised my eyebrows, and the man's face turned lobster red. He threw some bills on the table to cover his cola.

The rooms of the two-story building faced the densely landscaped parking area and formed a U shape around a pool. The lobby and meeting rooms faced the main road and completed the top of the U. Breezeways allowed access to the center of the complex, and sliding-glass doors opened to the pool area from the ground-floor units. No traffic sounds drifted to this part of the motel. Coincidentally, my room was directly above Rebekah's.

I rapped sharply on the door. "Bekka? Rebekah Kenyon?" My voice sounded loud in the still air.

No answer.

I raised my fist to knock again, but a large fly hummed past my face. I swatted at it. The bug landed on the window, then tapped against the glass. A second fly buzzed around me before landing by my foot and sliding under the entry.

The tiny hairs on my arms rose. I grabbed the key card from Ethan and shoved it into the lock. After glancing at the boyfriend's pale face, I used the edge of my shirt to gently turn the knob, then nudged the door open with my elbow.

The metallic stench was unmistakable.

CHAPTER
THREE

THE SWIMMING POOL LOOKED SO PEACEFUL.
The lapis-blue water danced with tiny flashes of silver glitter. I
squinted, making the sun-sparkles merge.

Her bent fingers clutched the carpet.

Stop it. I yanked my attention from the motel pool and continued my sketch. Rebekah's image took shape under my steadily
moving pencil. I'd tilted her face, added diagonal shadows, and
now worked on her hair. I wanted to capture the expression
she had as she asked me the questions. Eager, intelligent, and
inquisitive.

Her open mouth in a soundless shriek—

I shifted in my chair. *Concentrate.*

I could smell her blood.

No! I'd soon speak to the detective assigned to interview
me. I'd need to be clear and concise if any of my information

might be a clue to finding Rebekah's killer. I'd already written my notes.

It was quiet here. On this side of the motel, I couldn't hear or see the bustle of law enforcement officers, curious onlookers, or Rebekah's weeping classmates.

My ears still rang with Ethan's scream.

I snapped the tip of my pencil.

The young uniformed officer assigned to stay with me perched on a lawn chair nearby, swallowing loudly and frequently to keep from throwing up. Again.

Poor, poor Rebekah.

My eyes brimmed with unshed tears. She probably wasn't much older than my own daughter. What will her parents say when they find out?

How would I feel if it were my own child lying on the floor?

I stopped sketching and blew my nose. Did her murder relate somehow to the center? Or did Fancher have a crazed killer running around murdering young women? Neither thought was reassuring. What about the protesters, or the biker? I leaned my head back and pictured the crowd around the girl. Hippie Lady with her pulled-back gray hair, the two missionaries in short-sleeved white shirts, the guy with beer breath, an older man in a Stetson . . . I could easily picture their faces. I was blessed, or cursed, with an almost photographic memory of faces. None of the people closest to Rebekah had looked at her until she fainted. Only me. So, had someone followed the bus back to the motel? Had they waited until she was alone?

I'd finished the first drawing. I turned the page and started on the faces of the crowd.

The officer jumped to his feet. A burly man wearing a beige

suit and tie approached with the unmistakable stride of a detective. The sun glinted off his lapel pin and gold badge attached to his belt.

"Mrs. Marcey?" he asked, extending his hand. "Deputy Howell, Washington County Sheriff's Department."

I closed my sketchpad, shoved my sunglasses up, and shook his meaty paw.

Pulling a chair next to me, he gave a dismissive nod to the patrol officer. "I understand you found the victim and called it in. How did you open the door?" He tugged a notebook from his pocket, then opened it.

I handed him my notes. "Here's my statement."

His eyes narrowed. "I didn't ask you for an alibi—"

"I thought I'd save you some time. I'm a forensic artist, Deputy Howell, and also a reserve deputy for Ravalli County, Montana. You can call Sheriff Dave Moore. He'll vouch for me."

The detective studied me, then rubbed his top lip with his finger. "You look familiar. Have we met?"

"I don't think we've been formally introduced. I'm working at the Mountain Meadows site. I have something—"

"Deputy Howell?" A uniformed officer waved. "Sorry. We need you."

Howell stood and folded my notes into his pocket. "We'll get back to you. Don't leave town until we've had a chance to talk." He hastened away.

"—belonging, I think, to Rebekah."

He was already out of hearing range, leaving me alone by the pool. A slight, ash-scented breeze created tiny waves on the water and flung desiccated leaves across the surface.

I felt a tingling between my shoulder blades, that slithery

feeling that someone was staring at me. I was alone. I slipped my sunglasses over my eyes, stood, then carefully surveyed the rooms overlooking the pool. Most had white sheers drawn over the windows.

Wait. There. Movement, a twitch of fabric in my periphery. I counted over from Rebekah's room on the ground floor. The seventh unit.

I strolled to the corner pass-through where two buildings met. If the suspect was hiding out, I didn't want to spook him. I also wanted to be out of sight.

Crime scene tape outlined the end units of the structure. Blue-and-white strobes blazed out the open door as the technicians photographed the room. Cars pulled in and out of the lot, but no ambulance or morgue vehicle stood waiting, so the coroner must have transported Rebekah's body to wherever they conducted autopsies. Deputy Howell wasn't in view. No one even looked in my direction. *Not very observant around here.* Then again, how many homicides had Fancher, Utah, ever had? The town was less than ten years old and built to take in big tourist bucks. Of course, a brutal murder could dry up those dollars.

The watcher's room would be in the middle of the wing.

I advanced until I stood in front of the door, allowing my gaze to track over every inch. *There.* A tiny drop of rusty red just below the knob. I stepped back, then trotted toward the bustling crime scene, glancing over my shoulder every few seconds.

A uniformed officer holding a clipboard stopped me. "Sorry, no closer."

I checked behind me again. "Is Deputy Howell here?"

The officer pointed with his pen at two men standing beside a patrol car. Ethan Scott was a frozen statue in the backseat.

"Excuse me." I raced to the two men.

Deputy Howell turned, eyes narrowing as I approached. "I told you I'd talk to you later.

I took a deep breath. "Your killer may still be in the motel." I nodded at the unit.

"Impossible." Deputy Howell shook his head but placed his hand on his pistol.

"Someone watched me, and blood is on the door. Room thirty-two." I hoped I was right. They could arrest the murderer within hours. And I could sleep tonight.

Howell turned to the second man. "I thought you checked all the rooms?"

"We did. That is, we knocked and—"

Howell swore. "Get a pass key." He jerked his head at the other man, then pulled his Glock from the holster and dashed away. Several uniformed officers leaped after him, taking up positions around the perimeter.

Heart pounding, I ducked behind a wide ponderosa. Apparently they weren't waiting for a SWAT team from St. George, assuming the small farming community needed a resident SWAT team.

Howell waved two uniformed officers to the pool side of the building and waited until he had radio confirmation. He took the short interval to examine the tiny drops of blood. His radio crackled. He nodded and thumped on the door.

Bam-bam-bam!

I jumped.

No answer.

"This is the sheriff's department. Open up!"

The second man brought the key and took his position

against the wall. Standing on the other side, Howell swiped it, then opened the door, keeping his body out of the opening. They took turns quickly peering into the room. Howell slipped in. After a moment, his voice rang out. "Clear!"

He reappeared, pointed at a man in overalls with CSI on the back, waved him over, then marched over to several of his officers. He kept his voice low, but from the men's expressions, it was clear he was dressing them down for sloppy police work. He turned and saw me. He took a moment to wipe his face with a handkerchief, then crossed to me. "Good call. The perp used the room to clean up. Might get something, though." His tone held a little less of his gruff detective veneer.

"You're not arresting Ethan, are you?" I asked.

"Police business." The Voice was back.

I sighed. It was so much easier working with a department that knew me, where growling was because they liked me, not on general principle. "Whatever. One last thing. I think I have Rebekah's backpack. She dropped it when she fainted."

"Why didn't you say so before?"

"I . . . Forget it. It's in my car." I strolled over and unlocked the trunk. Before I could warn him about the broken latch, he yanked out the backpack, sending the contents careening into the trunk and onto the pavement.

Howell let out a few well-chosen cuss words and looked at me as if I were the one who'd made the mess. I helped him collect the miscellaneous items and jam them back into the bag: a hairbrush, eye shadow, wallet, digital camera, pink sweatshirt, and water bottle.

He slammed the trunk closed and stalked over to the crime scene van.

I trailed after him, but peeled off when I spotted Ethan. "Wait up."

He'd apparently not been charged with anything and was wandering about like the walking wounded. He drifted toward me. His eyes were bloodshot and shoulders hunched forward. "Yeah?"

"Here." I handed him the drawing I'd done of Bekka. "I'd like you to have this."

He stared at the sketch for a moment, then rubbed his eyes and nodded. "Thank you. I . . . she . . . oh, never mind."

I waited a moment. "What?"

"Uh, what if . . . what if I had some stuff of Bekka's?"

"Like what?"

"Her jacket. A paperback. Stuff like that. The latch on her backpack didn't work."

"Well then, you should probably give it to Deputy Howell."

"Deputy Howell is a jerk!"

"Then send it to her parents."

"How? I'm staying here. Mom and Dad are driving down, and I doubt they'll let me out of their sights."

"Go into the business center here." I nodded toward the office. "Get on the computer and print out a shipping label from FedEx. Give the package and the right amount of money to Joyce at the front office. Be sure you put enough insurance on it. She'll see that it's shipped. Okay?"

"I guess . . . so . . . Where are you going now?"

"Home. Finally." I patted his arm, then turned away, suddenly bone-tired. My feet felt like I'd walked barefoot on sharp gravel. I trudged to my room, pulled the blinds, and cranked up the air-conditioning unit to block the sounds of the investigation just below.

After yanking off the wig, I inspected my head in the bathroom mirror. Everyone told me that, after chemo, my hair would grow back thicker, a different color, and wavy. Somehow I'd assumed it would also sprout quickly, like a lawn after fertilizer and a good watering. Not so. Pale peach fuzz, barely visible, represented two months of growth.

I rubbed the soft stubble and grinned at my reflection. All I had to do was take off my breast prostheses and I would look like a young man. Being bald wasn't all bad. I didn't need to pack a brush, curling iron, hairdryer, hair spray, or conditioners. The motel's tiny bottle of shampoo lasted over a week, and I could get ready for work in minutes. Not to mention I could get my hair styled at the salon and go shopping at the same time.

After changing into beige cotton shorts and a clean T-shirt, I pulled back the covers on the bed and checked for spiders. *All clear.* The pillows equally free from insects. I stuffed them behind me, then wiggled until I was comfortable. I dialed Beth's number.

"How are you feeling?" Beth said before I could speak.

Another leftover from battling breast cancer. Everyone always asked how I was feeling or how I was doing. "Good."

"Still getting as many hot flashes?"

"I can't tell yet. I seem to get more when I'm stressed, and this job is stressing me. And why do they call it a flash? More like a sustained burn. Maybe I can get a job testing deodorants' staying power."

"Ha. Tell me about your fainting woman." The background noise of a forensic television series suddenly ceased.

"I'm interrupting your show."

"I'm recording it. You're more interesting. Go on."

"Well, she did more than faint. Someone murdered her."

"You're kidding!" She was silent for a moment, finally muttering a quiet, "Amen."

"Beth?"

"I'm here. Are you the lead investigator? How was she killed? Do you need an associate? Who murdered her? I want you to divulge everything!" The words tumbled over each other.

I ran my fingers over the fuzz on my head. "Right. No. Knife or something sharp. No. I don't know. I just did."

"You're so droll. Why was she murdered?"

"I don't know much of anything. We just found her. It was . . . pretty gruesome."

"Who is 'we'?"

"The girl's boyfriend and me."

"Did it have anything to do with—" Winston's deep bark drowned out her words.

"So what's the problem with my dog?" I pulled my knees up and wrapped an arm around them.

"Oh no. More details first."

I sighed. I loved Beth, but sometimes her addiction to forensic shows, mysteries, and the dictionary wore me out. "Remember our agreement."

"Right. Everything you say about your work is confidential. I am sworn to secrecy."

I filled her in on the case. "I wouldn't want to be the crime scene technician working that mess."

"What do you mean?"

"Ripped mattress, blood everywhere. Think Jack the Ripper kind of stuff. Maybe even ritualistic." I described her wounds.

She gave a slight gasp. "Ritualistic? I'm going to do some research."

"Just remember, it's not my case, and I doubt the police will appreciate your work the way I do."

"I'll send you my findings anyway. You never know, maybe the police will be so impressed that they'll have you help them investigate her murder. Then I can drive down and assist you. Norm's going on a fishing trip to Alaska."

"Aaaaaah, no. That's not the way it works. About Winston?"

"He excavated my dahlias, but only the peach ones. I did some probing, operating on one of several theories. The choice of flower is interesting, so perhaps the scent disturbs him. One article on the Internet mentioned that Great Pyrenees notice shapes, so the shape of the leaves or petals might trigger him, however, as he seems determined to just dig up the peach ones—"

"Beth."

"I thought I'd—"

"Beth!"

"Yes?"

"He's getting revenge on you."

Silence for a moment. "Dogs get revenge?"

I tugged the blanket over my legs. "Great Pyrenees do. What did you do differently?"

"I was trying to train him to track criminals. Then we both could help you. A team. Like the Three Musketeers."

"He's not a bloodhound, you know. And I don't, personally, go after criminals."

"Details. When do you anticipate returning?"

"Soon."

"Keep me informed on your progress, and you know what I always say. Everything happens for a reason."

I hadn't yet figured out the reason my life was such a mess, except to make my ex-husband rich. Maybe I just didn't get a reason. "I'm beat, so can I call you tomorrow?" It took some convincing, but Beth finally hung up.

I turned off the lamp and curled up under the covers. Light seeped through the curtains and under the door. I closed my eyes, but the glow remained. The sheet bunched under my legs, and I rolled over. Something was swirling around in my brain. *Bekka?* The pillow seemed lumpier than usual. I pounded it and flipped it over. The alarm clock's red digital readout clicked out the minutes. *College . . . something . . .* Dead? No. I've seen dead people before. I flopped on my back. Passing headlights pirouetted across the ceiling.

Sisters!

I jerked upright and turned on the light. Bekka and I had been dressed alike, with the same build and hair. My room was just above the young woman's. I got out of bed. Did someone see her from behind and think it was me? Had she been the real target . . . or was I?

My hands felt icy, and I rubbed them together. I double-checked that the door was locked and then peeked out the window. I wedged a chair under the doorknob. Who would want to kill me? Robert? No. He was indifferent. I'd simply been a good subject for his thinly veiled novel about my cancer battle. If he hadn't already been a best-selling novelist, no one would have even read that stupid book.

36

Why would anyone want to eliminate a forensic artist from Montana? The serial killer in my last case had gotten away, but that was more than a year ago. Was it connected to the work at Mountain Meadows? Some of the folks seemed mad enough to murder.

I went to the tiny bathroom, filled a glass with water, and took a gulp. But why would someone want to butcher a young college student? I made a mental note to talk to Deputy Howell about the possibility that I'd been the target. If the killer grabbed Bekka from the rear and cut her throat, he wouldn't know he had the wrong woman . . . no . . . she'd answered the door. Hadn't she?

I shivered as my brain tumbled the possibilities around like a tossed paper cup in a brisk wind. Did Bekka have something the killer wanted? I picked up the phone and dialed Deputy Howell's number. It rang six times, then went to voice mail. I hung up without leaving a message.

I tugged out my suitcase, reached into a side pocket, and lifted out an amber prescription bottle. *Just this once.* Post-traumatic stress disorder. That's what the doctor had called it. I figured I'd earned PTSD. I was diagnosed with cancer, divorced, the pathetic subject of Robert's book, and working on a serial killer and bombing case all at the same time. I shook out a pill, downed it with another slurp of water, and slid under the covers.

It seemed as if I'd barely closed my eyes when I heard someone bang on my door. "Mrs. Marcey?"

I glanced at the time. It was 4:23 in the morning. I'd throttle that deputy if he'd decided to interview me this early. I crawled from the bed and peeked out the window. A uniformed officer.

I opened the door as far as the chain would allow. "Yes?"

"Mrs. Marcey?"

"Yes. We've established that."

"The sheriff wants to see you right away."

"What—"

"Someone trashed the Mountain Meadows Center."

"I'm not—"

"George, the security guard, is dead."

CHAPTER
FOUR

RAVALLI COUNTY SHERIFF DAVE MOORE GLARED
at the steaming liquid swirling in the delicate pink cup on his
office desk. "What. Is that?"

Louise, his matronly secretary, folded her hands neatly in
front of her. "My special tea. For nerves. I blend it myself. Some
St. John's wort, peppermint, lemon balm, lavender, and just a
hint of raspberry leaves." She pivoted and left, gently closing the
door behind her.

"I don't have nerves," Dave said. "And I hate tea."

He sighed and glanced out the window overlooking the
parking lot for the patrol cars. Late-afternoon shadows stretched
across the lot from the pines along the perimeter, and chain-link
fencing imprisoned the vehicles.

He pushed the cup and saucer away. He'd inherited Louise
from his father, the former sheriff of Ravalli County, Montana.

She was well past retirement, but showed no sign of surrendering her job or of giving up on bringing him tea.

He checked his watch. Almost seven thirty. He piled the last report onto the out-box and placed his pen back into the marble award holder proclaiming him the Jaycee Distinguished Service winner. After tearing off the top sheet of a yellow legal pad, he reread the grocery list his wife, Andrea, called over earlier. *Lettuce, carrots, celery, apples, skim milk, coffee.* He sighed, stood, and was about to leave when the phone rang. Probably Andrea calling back to add more to his list. He guessed she wouldn't be adding ice cream with fudge syrup. So much for watching the Grizzlies play their first football game on television. He snatched up the handset. "Sheriff Moore. Make it fast."

"Uh, yeah, sorry. I didn't look at the time. This is Deputy Howell, Washington County Sheriff's Office, here in Utah. We have a homicide—"

"Gwen . . ."

"So you do know her."

"Is she . . ." Dave slumped into his chair. He couldn't say the words.

A pause. "Oh. No. Gwen Marcey isn't the victim. She found the body and stumbled across the suspect's hiding spot. Didn't catch him, but we were close. She gave us a pretty thorough police report. I'm just following up."

Dave exhaled. "Yeah, so how can I help you?"

"Just wondering about her."

Dave scratched his cheek. "She's the best. Like a sister to me."

"She's your sister?"

Dave shifted in his chair. "Practically. She lived with my family. My dad got her interested in law enforcement. She taught some classes for the police academy."

"Sketch classes?"

"Yeah. Also cognitive interviewing and signs of deception."

"I took some of those classes recently," Deputy Howell said. "Never heard of her."

"She's . . ." Dave rubbed his chin.

"Yes?" Deputy Howell said.

"She took some time off."

"Why?"

"A lot . . . a lot of personal things. She's fine now. More than fine. She can sketch anything you need, conduct interviews, do statement analysis—"

"Statement analysis?"

"Yep. Catching lies by people's words. She's good at it."

"I thought she just drew pictures."

"Yeah, but she has to draw from the surviving victim's memories, so she has to be good at interviewing. And she has to know if they're lying."

Another long pause from Howell. "I see. Well, thanks." He hung up.

"You didn't tell him," Louise said from the door.

"I didn't hear you knock."

"I didn't. I was getting ready to leave. Why didn't you tell him about Gwen's troubles?"

"What's to tell? Gwen's fine now. And she needed that job."

Louise's lips settled into a frown. "But you said she was *like* a sister to you. I thought your dad actually adopted her."

41

"He told everyone that, but Gwen never disclosed her background to anyone. You were here. You remember how hard he searched for any of her family members."

"Harrumph. I would think you'd at least warn him."

"About what? What's past is past. She's in remission from cancer. Her divorce is final, and Robert is at least paying child support. Her daughter is out of trouble and in a good school—"

She shook a finger at him. "You told Gwen to send her daughter to that school."

"It was the only solution."

"But it's a school for juvenile delinquents!"

"And for kids who need some extra guidance, which Gwen couldn't provide while working in Utah. And Robert—"

"Don't even get me started on that man. That . . . that . . . monster blamed her and Aynslee for his writer's block." Louise sniffed a final time and left the room.

Dave had never liked Robert either and would have loved to have had a reason to arrest him and put him away for good. But now that Gwen was working on a homicide investigation, maybe her life was turning around. As long as Deputy Howell didn't read Robert's stupid novel where he painted Gwen as a self-centered nutcake.

Dave looked at the cup of tea. Nerve tea, Louise called it. It wasn't *his* health, or nerves, he was worried about.

CHAPTER
FIVE

I RECLINED IN THE SEAT, CLOSED MY EYES, AND longed for a large mug of steaming coffee. The stupid pill made my brain feel like swirling dust bunnies. I debated about asking the officer driving the patrol SUV to swing by a convenience store before leaving town. Glancing at his name tag, I changed my mind. R. Young. Undoubtedly a descendant of Brigham Young. Mormons didn't drink coffee. Or tea. Or any strong drink. Just my luck.

Like a replay of last night's light show, the interpretive center swarmed with law enforcement vehicles flashing blue, red, and white strobes. Khaki-clothed deputies bustled about looking serious and a bit lost. Harsh fluorescent lighting streamed from the center's windows.

Deputy Young escorted me past fluttering cadmium-yellow crime scene tape toward Deputy Howell, who was directing the action just inside the door. He turned as we approached. "So, we meet again. Did you call me from the motel?"

"Is that why I'm here?"

"No. Sorry about the early hour."

He didn't look sorry. "I just wanted to tell you that Ethan has some of Bekka's things. He doesn't want to give them to you, but you might follow up anyway."

Howell pulled out a small notepad and jotted something down.

I stared longingly at the break room. Maybe someone had started the coffeepot. I tried to stifle a yawn. Unsuccessfully.

"I know you've been working here and thought you'd be able to help us. Your sheriff vouched for you."

I stared intently at his face. Nothing twitched. Dave must have kept silent about the past year. I glanced around the room. It looked like a tornado had touched down: cold air whipping through broken windows, graffiti spray-painted over newly installed pine paneling, overturned trash containers, ivory papers from ripped books, and two legs poking from beneath a shattered case. *George.*

My muscles tightened. I'd never worked on a case where I personally knew the victim, let alone had been a friend. *Don't act like a rookie.* I cleared my throat. "Is this related to the other murder?"

Howell narrowed his eyes at me. "We'll ask the questions, if you don't mind. When did you leave work yesterday?"

"Around five thirty. Later than usual. George saw me out—"

"Did he lock the door after you?"

I folded my arms. Bad interview technique. Never interrupt a witness. Instead of snapping at him, I slowly counted to four, letting the deputy cool his impatience. "I don't know. I was focused on my c—"

"Were any other cars in the parking lot?"

I could add *leading questions* to *interruptions*. "No."

Howell rubbed his chin. "We'd like—"

"I did see a pickup."

"You just said the parking lot was empty."

"You asked if I saw any cars. My answer was no. There was an indanthrene-colored pickup." *Don't bait him. Just answer and go back to bed.*

He stared hard at me for a moment, then, unexpectedly, grinned. "Yeah, yeah. Your friend Dave said you were good. What's an Indian-anthem, uh, . . . pickup?"

"Indanthrene. Dark violet-blue, leaning more toward blue. Like navy, but with a richer, warmer tone . . ."

Howell frowned at me.

"Anyway, late model."

Howell nodded. "Can you tell me more about the argument at the opening?"

"A bunch of protesters showed up. Do you think they came back and did this?"

"We're exploring every possibility."

"I could do composite drawings of the four of them: Button Down, Black Dress, Chunky Woman, and Beer Breath."

Howell pursed his lips. "Beer Breath?"

"Oh, sorry. That's how I remember them."

"I've never used a composite artist before. Let me think about it."

"Sure. Just let me know. Who . . . uh . . . who found . . . the body?"

"We got an anonymous call from a pay phone. Could you look over your area and tell us if anything is missing?" Howell scratched his hastily shaved chin.

I nodded. "Are you done taking photographs and measurements?"

"We're still processing the body. If it isn't too upsetting, could you take a look at George and see if you notice anything unusual?"

"Sure." *Being dead is unusual . . .*

"Deputy Young will stay with you so you won't step in the wrong spot."

Young puffed his chest out and lifted his lip in a slight sneer.

I sneered back. He blinked rapidly and glanced around. Turning, I started a triumphant march to my area, but flames rushed to my face as the hot flash took over. I knelt down and pretended to tie my shoe until I figured my face no longer had a sweat sheen. I hoped he didn't notice that I didn't have any shoelaces.

After pulling a small notebook and pen from my pocket, I drew a line down the center of the paper. On one side I wrote, *Known,* on the other I wrote, *Unknown,* then stepped away from the officers and slowly surveyed the room. My gaze lingered on the break room. No light showed under the door. No coffee. In the early-morning gloom, I saw only my reflection in the windows and the room behind me.

Is someone still out there, watching?

I approached George's body but found the closer I got, the more I had to pry each foot forward. Once again the rank, metallic odor of blood burned my nose. I couldn't feel my hands, and bile seared my throat. *Be a pro.*

He was sprawled across an exhibit. His slacks bunched under him, exposing white athletic socks poked into heavy-duty work shoes. A large pool of deep-maroon blood created a moat around his feet, his glasses forming a plastic island.

I put my hand over my nose and mouth to block some of the smell. Something glittered on his hand, and I leaned forward slightly.

"He fell backward," a deep, male voice said.

I spun, losing my balance, and windmilled my arms to keep from cascading onto my dead friend. The man grabbed my arm and yanked. I catapulted forward, clutching him in a parody of a lover's embrace. The woodsy-spice scent of Brit cologne enveloped me.

"Nice to meet you too," he said.

Heat rushed up my neck as I pushed away from him. "You . . . um . . . what's the matter with you?"

He took a step backward. "Sorry. I thought you knew I was here." His raised eyebrows seemed to imply I was acting like an amateur.

"Obviously I didn't." I turned and crashed into Deputy Howell. *Didn't these guys believe in personal space?*

"Ah, Gwen, I see you've met Mike. Special Agent Mike Brown, FBI."

Special Agent Mike Brown, FBI, held out a neatly manicured, tanned hand.

I took it and sized him up. Under umber-brown hair, his eyes were the brilliant, peacock blue of my favorite tube of watercolor, framed by black lashes a model would covet. His shoulders were barely contained in a federal-blue suit, with a starched dress shirt and maroon-striped tie. No wedding ring. My gaze drifted back to his face.

He nodded at me slightly.

I let go of his grip and quickly looked away, hoping I wouldn't suffer another inopportune hot flash. "So. FBI. At a homicide. What brought you here?"

"Deputy Howell gave me a call." Mike nodded at the man. "I was in the area."

I folded my arms and stared at Howell. If I was lucky, he'd jump in with more information to fill in the silence.

"I met Mike at the NA," Howell said.

National Academy. Ten weeks of training at Quantico offered to select law enforcement officers. My opinion of Deputy Howell rose. "Classmate or instructor?"

"Instructor," Howell said. "Domestic terrorism and crime scene." He smiled at Mike. "Now he's the senior resident agent in Salt Lake."

I looked at my shoes. An expert in domestic terrorism just happened to be in Utah, and there just happened to be two murders within twenty-four hours? That put a different filter on the events.

"Blood spatter." Mike pointed to George. "Before terrorism, I was an expert in bloodstain pattern analysis. That's why Deputy Howell invited me over."

Yeah, right. Or he could be checking out some local group of fanatics. "So, what does George's blood pattern tell you?"

"Like I said, before you jumped into my arms—"

I glared at him, but he didn't seem to notice.

"George fell backward into the case. They may not have intended to kill him, but he severed an artery and bled out in a matter of minutes. He has a nasty bump on his head, so he was probably unconscious and couldn't call for help."

I sincerely hoped George was unconscious when the glass

sliced him. *Deep breath. No tears.* I deliberately turned and studied the body. "How could a fall shatter the glass like that?"

"One side was open, so it had less reinforcement."

"Open? But the display had nothing of value in it. Just copies of survivor accounts."

"Survivor accounts?"

"You know, documents, diaries, newspaper articles, and some letters. Was—"

"No." Mike obviously anticipated my next question. "This was the only open case." He caught Howell's attention and stepped away.

Under *Known* I wrote, *Survivor display case open* and sketched the deadly tableau. I could see the mark on George's temple along his graying hairline where someone had struck him. I stopped drawing and concentrated on his hand. The glittering object was a ring. It had an enameled American flag with two eagle wings on either side. I sketched the ring and avoided George's empty stare. He was wearing the same neatly pressed, beige pants and steel-blue work shirt from the night before. I closed my eyes and rewound the previous evening, then jotted some notes.

Mike and Howell were talking as I walked over. "I appreciate the offer to take over, Mike," Howell was saying. "But I think I can run a homicide scene."

I poked the pencil behind my ear and cleared my throat. "He's dressed the same. I didn't notice that ring." I recalled the day I'd arrived at the center. George helped unload my car, then invited me to dinner with his grown children. I could taste the meatloaf with the surprise of raisins, along with corn pudding, homemade bread, and parsley new potatoes.

I quickly moved away from the body before I made a fool of myself. Someone had spray-painted "LDS Liars!" and "Brigham Young is a murderer!" on the walls. *Interesting.* LDS: Latter-day Saints. The correct name for the Mormon Church. Not Mormon, the name of the original author of the Book of Mormon. Put that together with the presence of Mike, domestic-terrorist expert, and you could have someone pretending to be anti-Mormon. I glanced at Mike. He was watching me.

I ducked my head and wrote, *Mormon connection? Check violent splinter groups* under *Unknown* and headed to my work section.

The sight stopped me dead. Someone had used what appeared to be an ax to smash into every box, container, and sculpture stand. They'd shredded books, ripped photographs, and stomped the remaining plaster reconstructions into clay and dust.

I stifled a cry. This was the center of the violence, which had rippled outward. How could I know if anything was missing? Nothing was left undamaged. Weeks of work . . .

I waved Deputy Young over. "I'd need to see if anything is still intact."

"That'll have to wait until they release the scene."

"In that case, could you drive me back to the motel?"

"If Howell agrees, sure." He wandered over to speak to the deputy.

"Seems your project drew the most destruction." Mike held out a paper cup of water.

I took it and sipped. Too bad it wasn't coffee. "Thanks. That's what I was thinking. Fortunately, I already ordered backup skulls. But that was the last of my clay."

He crouched, pulled on a latex glove, and selected a shattered length of wood. After peering at one end, he replaced it in the exact same angle, lifted a second wood chunk, then repeated the process. "Pulaski would be my guess."

"You think a Mormon firefighter did this?" I crumpled the empty cup and looked for an unscathed garbage container.

"What's a Polanski?" Deputy Young asked, returning.

"Pulaski. A firefighting tool, with an ax on one side and a mattock on the other." Mike took my cup. "Why did you say the unknown subject was a Mormon?"

"Tell me why you're really here, and I'll tell you why I think it's a Mormon."

"Fair enough. How about I take you to breakfast and we can talk about it?"

I didn't want to have breakfast or any meal with Mike. He was far too aware of how he looked. In spite of my best efforts, I felt my breath shorten and a warm flush dart up my neck. "No, thanks."

"I'm not asking you for a date," Mike said. "I wanted to hear your theories."

Heat seared up my neck and face. I turned away and fought for air. The hot flash passed, but before I could grope for something intelligent to say, Deputy Howell marched over with a cell phone pressed to his ear.

"Got it. Right." He dropped the phone into a pocket and looked at me. "Seems we have another problem."

"What's that?"

"Rebekah Kenyon died five years ago."

CHAPTER
SIX

REBEKAH LOOKED SERENE UNDER THE BUZZING fluorescent light. And very dead. I avoided staring at the crimson slash across her throat and breathing in the copper tang of her blood. The white vinyl zippered body bag concealed the rest of her. Thankfully. Once again I thought of my own daughter. She hadn't wanted to go to the Selkirk Academy, and I really didn't want to send her, but Robert was too busy running around being a big-shot author, and I needed her safe and unable to act out until I was done with this job. I'd make it up to her. Somehow.

"We'll be sending her to St. George for an autopsy when the ambulance arrives. We need a sketch of her so we can get an ID," Deputy Howell said. "Can't exactly release a photo with her looking like that."

We were in the back of a funeral home, not the area of low lights, deep-pile carpets, and banks of flowers, but one of cold metal, tile, and nasty-looking equipment. Deputy Howell leaned against a counter across the room, as if he were afraid of catching something from the girl.

"Sure," I said. I'd already sketched her once, but that was just a quick study, and I'd given it to Ethan. "Give me about an hour and a half." Driving in from the Mountain Meadows Center, I'd asked Deputy Young to swing by the motel room to pick up my drawing kit. I placed the bag on the floor and pulled a high stool next to the table holding the body. After removing a pad of Bristol paper, pencil container, and sharpener, I settled next to the young woman and began sharpening my pencils. "So, if she's not Rebekah Kenyon, who is?"

My pencil-sharpening routine seemed riveting to Deputy Howell. "What is that?"

"A lead pointer. Used to sharpen lead holders." I held up the metal object and rotated it. "It holds a 2 mm piece of graphite, which is important for accurate drawing. A mechanical pencil's lead is too small. I can sharpen this to a fantastic point and . . ." Deputy Howell's eyes had glazed over. "So, who is Rebekah Kenyon?"

His eyebrows remained furrowed as he consulted a small notebook. "Rebekah Sarah Kenyon. Died five years ago. Accident, thrown from a horse. I called next of kin, shocked the heck out of them. Farming folks, live in a small town southwest of Provo. Place called Jarom. They had no idea someone had stolen Rebekah's identity."

"Do you have a theory about this Jane Doe?"

"If I did, I wouldn't be having you sketch her, now would I?" Howell began pacing. After a pause, he continued, "Sorry. Not much sleep." He dry-washed his face. "According to Ethan, she enrolled at North Idaho College last year. General studies. Didn't talk much about her background. Said she was home-schooled, which matched up with the real Rebekah. They were taking a class on Western history, which included touring sites."

"Not much to go on."

"Nope. One interesting thing. Ethan seemed to think she was supposed to meet someone on this trip. He clammed up after that, asked for a lawyer."

I nodded and began drawing. "This girl must have known about the real Rebekah."

"Yeah, we're working on that assumption."

I debated on adding that piece of information to my notes. Instead, I drew lines on the paper to align the eyes, nose, and mouth. I couldn't see her eye color or shape, so I used my memory to draw them. After sketching for a time, I stood and stretched.

"Done?" Deputy Howell asked.

"Just need to shade it in. What time is it?"

Howell glanced at his watch. "Nine seventeen."

"I need to talk to Bentley Evans, the director of the center." I tugged out my cell, scrolled through the names, then hit Send. Bentley answered before it rang.

"Yes, what now!" Bentley's voice was practically screeching. I pictured his double chin bobbing with each word.

"It's Gwen. What do—"

"It's ruined, the whole center is a total disaster. It'll take months to rebuild."

"I'm so sorry. I'll collect what I can from there and head home."

"Don't bother to return. You're fired!"

The burn started in my chest and flashed up my face.

"Did you hear me? I said you're fired."

"What? Why?" I clutched the phone.

"I had a staff meeting. The docents said the visitors were hostile and angry after listening to your presentation. One of them probably returned last night and did this."

"But—"

"You were supposed to educate, not antagonize. I told you to stay neutral. And, as you didn't finish your contract, we are not obligated to pay you." *Click.*

I couldn't move. The dial tone buzzed in my ear like an enraged wasp. I dropped the phone into my pocket.

Now I *really* needed that interagency job.

"You okay?" Howell raised his eyebrows.

"Sure. Fine." My hand shook as I picked up the pencil. I'd never be able to shade in the drawing at this rate. "Could you find me something to drink?"

Howell nodded and left.

I closed my eyes and made an effort to concentrate. *Everything happens for a reason. Ha.* I focused on the porcelain face of the younger woman. "So what's your story? Were you hiding from someone? Is that why you took on another identity? If we find out who you really are, we also might find your killer."

My hand steadied, so I picked up a paper stump and blended my pencil strokes. "I shouldn't say this. It sounds self-serving." I stopped drawing. "But if you were the target, your murderer wasn't after me." The body looked like alabaster in the buzzing fluorescent light. "I'm talking to a corpse. Maybe I need to make another appointment with that shrink."

A soft cough.

I started.

Deputy Howell stood by the door, a can of Squirt in his hand, lips pursed.

I grinned self-consciously. Since my divorce eleven months and five days ago, my most meaningful conversations were with Beth, clay reconstructions, dead bodies, or my dog. And now my only daughter wasn't speaking to me.

I sighed and tucked my pencil behind my ear. "I'm done with the drawing. Could I have a copy for my records?"

Deputy Howell handed me the soda and took the sketch. "Hey, this is good. I mean, really good. She looks like she's about to blink." He looked at me. "I forgot to ask, how much do you charge?"

Law enforcement budgets. Too much crime, too little money. "This one's on the house."

"Thanks. I'll get a copy for you." He opened the door to leave just as two men stepped in.

"We're ready to transport the girl to St. George," the first one said.

"You're taking George too?" I asked.

"Yeah. He's already loaded." The second one stared at me. "You're the artist. Doing those sculptures. You gotta hear this. When they bagged George's hands, they noticed he had clay under his fingernails. Any reason he'd be handling your stuff?"

"No. He didn't like the clay reconstructions. Said they gave him the creeps." The whole thing didn't add up. But it wasn't my case—or problem.

The men wheeled Rebekah's body from the room. Deputy Howell left, then returned with several copies of the sketch. "Thanks again. Ah . . . I hate to take advantage of your free services, but would you mind doing something for me?"

"What's that?" I asked, packing up my art supplies.

"I'm going to be tied up here doing interviews and follow-ups. I heard you say that you're going home. You'll be driving right past Jarom, the real Rebekah's hometown. Could you, maybe, take a detour? Talk to her family? Your boss, Dave, said you were good at interviewing. I can tell them you're coming."

"Sure. Glad to help." Now that I was going home early, I could spring Aynslee from the school, call for an update on the interagency job, and see if Dave could find some funds to pay me on Craig's cold case.

Howell jotted the name and address of the family in Jarom on a copy of the sketch, then handed it to me. I tucked it into a file folder, nodded at the man, then left. Deputy Young returned me to the motel to check out.

The maid had already cleaned the room, returning it to its sterile tidiness except for a small amber bottle on the desk. I picked it up. Lorazepam, the drug my doctor prescribed for my anxiety and nausea during chemo, was the tablet I'd taken last night to help me sleep. I must not have returned the bottle to my suitcase.

But I would've hidden the bottle. I didn't need to provide anyone with proof that I was a nutcake.

My gaze drifted around the room, looking for anything else out of place. The top of the desk held books and a clutter of papers. Half-full bottle of water by the bed. Extra shoes in the closet.

I'd left in a hurry that morning.

Opening the dresser drawers, I checked my folded clothing. Undisturbed.

I must have dropped the bottle on the floor and the maid found it. I tugged out my empty suitcase and packed, checking to see if anything else was out of place, a useless task as the maid shuffled my room around daily.

Once I loaded the car, I turned toward Mountain Meadows. I didn't want to come face-to-face with Bentley Edwards, but I needed to retrieve the last of my supplies, assuming any were worth saving.

The sheriff's department vehicles blocked the parking lot, and it took me a few minutes to convince a chunky deputy that my presence was legitimate. I tugged out a yellow no.2 pencil and sketchpad as I entered the building. Sunshine streamed into the room, lighting up the destruction like a stage.

I halted at the entrance, then leaned against the door, my legs feeling like cooked pasta.

Deputy Young spotted me and gave me a thumbs-up that the crime scene team had released my area.

It wasn't until I waved back at him that I noticed I'd snapped my pencil in half.

I spotted Mike almost immediately. The agent had his back to me, hunched over the shattered case where they'd found George's body.

I slipped behind him. "Find anything new?"

He leapt to his feet. "How'd you do that?"

"What?"

"Move so quietly I didn't hear you."

"Practice. Learned it from a friend." I moved closer to the case and picked up a small sign. A piece of glass tore the corner in a ragged line. The whole display would need to be re-created.

Special Report: May 25, 1859. The names of the surviving children:

Joseph and Mary Miller, John Calvin Miller, Nancy Sophronia Huff, Prudence Angeline and Georgianna Dunlap; William Henry and Emberson Milum Tackett; Jane, Sarah Frances, and Martha Elizabeth Baker—

"This place has certainly seen its share of violence." Mike closed a notebook.

I continued to read.

William W. Huff, Christopher Carson, and Tryphenia Fancher; Rebekah, Louisa, and Sarah Dunlap; Felix Marion Jones . . .

"Poor little tykes," I muttered.

"Where to from here?" Mike asked.

"I was . . . sort of fired, so no reason to hang around. I'm going home. By way of Jarom and an interview with the real Rebekah's family."

"Where's home?"

"Copper Creek, Montana. South of Missoula. You?" I turned to look at him, tucking the sign into my sketchpad.

"I'm working out of Salt Lake City." He reached into his pocket, tugged out a business card, and handed it to me. "I offered to run these two cases, but Deputy Howell said he had it under control. I'll finish up here and head back to Salt Lake."

I turned the card over in my hand. A. Michael Brown, FBI. I could hand it back with a "no thanks," but knowing someone with the FBI did have a few advantages. I glanced at him. He had a slight smile on his face. Was the card a peace offering? I gave a quick nod, then raced to my area. It didn't take long to confirm the total destruction of my supplies. I left the mess for Bentley to clean up, then headed to the exit. Jarom was over three hours away, and it was already after three o'clock.

I gave Beth a quick call before leaving the parking lot. "Just a heads-up that I'm on my way home."

"Your daughter will be happy. Your dog will be jubilant, as will I. Life has been rather . . . sluggish without you." I'd met Beth at a gallery opening two years ago. She'd graduated cum laude from Bryn Mawr College, and after a fast-paced career at Microsoft, she'd found Copper Creek boring. Until she met me. "Your work concluded faster than you thought."

"Not really." I filled her in on George and the center.

"I'm so sorry about your friend," she said quietly.

"Thank you."

"Now that you're going to be home, would you be interested in a concert in Seattle next week? I have tickets."

"I'll have Aynslee by then."

"Better yet. I have tickets for both of you. Speaking of your daughter, I received a letter from her."

"What did she say?" I tried to sound casual.

"Her grammar is atrocious—"

"Beth! Please."

"Yes, well, your daughter enjoys the art program and misses her dog."

"Did she say anything about—"

"No. Give her time to adjust. Divorce is hard on juveniles,

especially those in their early teens. I can't wait to see you, and I'll have that research done when you return."

"Wait. I didn't ask you to do any—"

Dial tone.

I tossed the cell on the seat beside me.

The drive up I-15 North was long—filled with irrigated farms, high desert brush, distant baked hills, and windmills dragging water for the thirsty cattle. Occasionally cars or ranch trucks passed me. At one point I thought I saw a blue pickup following me and I slowed down to check, but it disappeared down an access road. I kept looking in my rearview mirror but saw nothing. After stopping for lunch, I spent the time listening to the radio and avoiding my thoughts, which picked away at the scab of my life. If bad things happened in threes, I'd just crossed over into four by losing my job.

The late-summer heat beat through the windows, and I hummed an off-key tune to stay alert. I'd hoped that the work at the interpretive center would put my name out in public again in case the regional job fell through. More work would follow once agencies knew I was back in business. Now I'd need to contact each agency, knock on doors, and pray that no one would hear I'd been fired from my last job.

I found a radio station with a fire-and-brimstone, Southern Baptist pastor. It wasn't until he mentioned Nephi, and the Book of Mormon, that I realized it was an LDS program. Apparently converts to the LDS Church were now coming from the deep South.

"Now, my brothers and sisters, I ask you this: Why did Jesus—"

The speaker was able to get four syllables out of the word Jesus: Jay-eeee-sas-a.

"—in Matthew, chapter six, say, 'After this manner therefore pray ye: Our Father which art in heaven, Hallowed be thy name. Thy kingdom come. Thy will be done in earth, as it is in heaven.' But in addressin' the Nephites, as recorded in Nephi three, chapter thirteen and verse ten, he left out the words 'thy kingdom come.'"

I nodded. *Yep. I stayed up nights wondering about that.* "I bet you're going to tell me," I said to the radio.

"I'm going to tell you, and you listen well. The Jews were in the First Watch. The Nephites in the Second Watch had the ordinances and keys to the kingdom, and when Joseph Smith restored the fullness of the gospel, they didn't *need* to pray for the kingdom to come. It was already here! Now the kingdom of God will go forth with the help of a mighty and powerful one—"

I yawned and snapped off the radio. The man's cadence was making me drowsy again. I blinked several times and twisted my head from side to side. I almost missed my turnoff. The small sign, pointing right, whispered Jarom.

Slowing to the end of the exit ramp, I spotted the discrete arrow informing me Jarom was twenty-three miles away. I glanced at my watch. Five thirty. I'd probably arrive just in time for dinner. The thought made my mouth water. I hoped the town featured a good ole ma-and-pa diner serving mashed potatoes and meatloaf. *Meatloaf with raisins. George's family gathering around the dinner table, warmhearted laughter cocooning their home.* I stomped the gas petal, and the car fishtailed. I slowed and relaxed my jaw.

After a mile, I revised my estimated arrival time. The pavement gave way to gravel, and I slowed to keep from bouncing off the surface. The road climbed, with a small hill on one side and a sharp drop-off on the other. The setting sun was blinding.

The pronghorn antelope appeared directly in front of my car.

I slammed the brakes and yanked the wheel. My car skated across the loose gravel and slid sideways off the road. My knuckles whitened on the useless steering wheel. The embankment steepened. The car skidded faster, abruptly stopped, then tipped on its side.

The earth lunged toward me.

CHAPTER
SEVEN

I CAREFULLY LIFTED MY HEAD FROM THE SIDE
window and rubbed the swelling bump on my temple. Just on
the other side of the glass was a hunk of sagebrush and sunbaked
earth. The seat belt hitched painfully across my neck. I wiggled my toes, then moved my legs to be sure I wasn't paralyzed.
"Ouch." My voice was undamaged.

I unfastened the seat belt, breaking my thumbnail to the
quick, and my foot caught between the pedals and my ankle
twisted. "Ouch!"

Everything that had been loose on the front seat was scattered around me, except—of course—my phone, which seemed
to have wriggled into an unknown crevice. I untangled arms,
legs, and torso, and shoved myself to my feet. All sorts of colorful words ran like a banner across my mind. "Doggone it!" I said
in a loud but quivery voice. Not a satisfactory curse, but I didn't
need to apologize for it should someone be in earshot.

The window was an open skylight above me. I stuck my head out the opening and listened for traffic, but all I heard were coyotes yipping in the distance. *Just royally great.* I'd driven fourteen of the twenty-three miles to Jarom, not passing a single car or farm since turning off the highway. Unless I found my phone, I had a lovely nine-mile hike to town. The small flashlight, one of the many objects that had cascaded around me with the tipping car, refused to work. The line from the movie *Young Frankenstein* flashed across my brain: "It could be worse. It could be raining."

I eyed the sky.

The cell, I soon discovered, had landed on the door underneath me, and when I stood, I'd crushed it into electronic heaven. *Double doggone it!*

After tossing out my purse, I wiggled through the passenger-side window. The car wouldn't be going anywhere without help. With uncanny skill, I'd managed to slide down the only part of the incline that featured a culvert, with a small, concrete retaining wall. The tires caught on the lip of the wall, momentarily stopping my crab-like travel, but the momentum tipped the car on its side so the two right wheels were high off the ground. The front wheel still slowly spun.

The way things were going, after turning in insurance claims on both my car and the plaster casting replacements, the insurance company would drop me. I was a bad-luck maven.

I limped up the bare and dusty rise to the road, grit sliding into my open-toed sandals, my passage dislodging small rocks that clanked on the underside of the car. This was all Deputy Howell's fault. He'd sent me on this backcountry hike.

Yeah, but you'd agreed to go, the reasonable voice in my head reminded me.

Be quiet. I needed quality griping time.

The road was still empty. The blinding sun dipped below the rolling hills, backlighting a line of brown-and-white pronghorns watching me with their deer-like curiosity. With the passing light, the temperature dipped. Nine miles. In sandals. I turned and started trudging up the road. The landscape turned grayish blue, and the sky glowed with gold merging into coral, then lavender. I paused in appreciation. God sure knew how to paint the sky.

The light dimmed and the first stars blinked down coldly. I clutched my purse closer, hugging it for warmth.

A coyote yodeled in the distance and night crept closer. Without thinking, I kicked a small pile of gravel, jamming a rock under my big toe. Pausing to tug it out, I heard a murmur behind me. Tiny yellow headlights popped into view.

With my luck it would be two teens on a killing spree in a stolen car.

I'm in the . . . what? Not the buckle of the Bible belt. Magnetic middle of Mormonism? I hoped it was a farmer returning from town. The headlights grew larger.

Then again, Gwen, you've been working on a Mormon massacre site.

I stepped to the side of the road, trying to make up my mind. Hide or wave them down? I wished I didn't know quite so much about crime. The light blinded me. I cupped my hand to block some of the glare. I'd look pretty darn stupid if I hightailed it off the road now.

I waved my arms.

A van stopped and road dust enveloped me. Only when the cloud settled did the driver roll down the window, but not before

I heard the click of locking doors. The driver was a plain-looking woman with long, braided hair. "Kinda far from civilization. Had an accident?"

I let out the breath I didn't realize I was holding. "Yes, I need to call someone to pull my car out."

She seemed to chew on my words for a moment. In the light from the dashboard, I could see some of the passengers. All were female, with braided hair, wearing matching calico blouses.

"What are you doing here?" she finally asked.

My reason for coming was really none of her business. On the other hand, the night was approaching, the town at least nine lonely miles away, and Ted Bundy's apprentice could be driving the next vehicle up the road. "I don't know if you know the Kenyon family?"

She nodded.

"I have an appointment with them."

"Oh?"

"They know I'm coming. My name is Gwen Marcey."

"Nice to meet you, Gwen Marcey."

Okay, this wasn't getting me a ride into town. "I'm here to talk to them about their daughter, Rebekah."

"But Rebekah's gone. Died maybe four or five years ago."

"Someone took the identity of their daughter, Rebekah—"

One of the girls in the back gasped.

Maybe I had more folks to interview. "Uh . . . and I'm following up on it."

"I'll take you there." She looked in the rearview mirror. "Girls, make room for Sister Gwen."

The van door slid open. A line of white grocery bags declaring *Bee Prepared* formed a small barrier. The girls shifted several bags, creating a narrow passage, and two girls hopped on laps to provide me a place to sit. I paused for a moment, staring at their clothing. What I took for calico shirts were long, pioneer-style dresses. I crawled in, shut the door, and wiggled my adult-size behind between the tiny rumps of the girls. Seat belts didn't seem to be an issue, so I just prayed we wouldn't encounter another pronghorn.

The radio played the same hellfire speaker, now pounding a point about "going forth." It was either a popular radio station or the only station. The girls whispered in each other's ears, shyly glanced at me, and giggled.

"So," I said. "Did any of you girls know Rebekah Kenyon?"

Silence except for the radio. "In these last days, lookin' forward to the Day of Judgment and destruction, where the faithful will return to Adam-ondi-Ahman, and Zion shall flourish . . ."

I folded my hands and stared ahead, trying to figure out what an Adam-ondi-Ahman was.

We finally pulled up to a well-lit, sprawling house at the end of an abbreviated driveway. The woman turned off the radio, pointed, and said, "Prophet Kenyon's."

"Pardon?"

"He's a prophet."

"Oh." I jumped from the van, but before I could thank them properly, they drove off. I sincerely hoped this *was* the Kenyon household or, if not, that at least they had a phone I could use.

The house seemed to squat in the middle of . . . nothing. I strolled toward the front stoop. A small boy popped his head up in the window and cupped his hands around his eyes. I wiggled my fingers at him. Two girls with braids joined him. Then three more boys in denim overalls lined up and peered out. A second window filled with more young children.

The setting sun glinted off a shiny bumper to my left. I squinted and stepped closer. I couldn't see the color clearly, but it was a dark-colored pickup with a king cab. It reminded me of the pickup in the parking lot and the one that may have been following me.

The light gleaming from the house suddenly grew dim. I glanced at the windows. One by one, the curious faces disappeared behind rapidly pulled venetian blinds. I didn't appear to be welcome at the Kenyon household. Before I could check it out, the front door jerked open, and a lean, distinguished-looking man peered at me from under pale eyebrows. His tanned face was free of wrinkles, which belied the mass of snowy-white hair. A short beard trimmed his chin. "You must be Sister Gwen."

I blinked. This was the voice on the radio, the one talking about Adam-ondi-Ahman and Zion, the Jay-eeee-sas-a preacher. Or whatever Mormons called their ministers. I hoped he'd give me the necessary information, lend me a phone, and let me leave without hearing the rest of the sermon.

"Hi, Mr.—Prophet Kenyon?"

The man nodded, examining me as if attempting to read my soul. His intense gaze finally lingered on the small silver cross at my throat. His lips thinned for an instant.

Rack up a cultural faux pas. I'd forgotten Mormons don't wear, or display, the cross.

As he opened the door wider, I surreptitiously tucked my cross into my shirt, then followed him into a living room the size of a hotel lobby. It was tidy enough but filled with well-used furniture representing the decorating styles of the last twenty years. Burnt-orange chairs squatted next to a mauve sofa with teal pillows, all sitting on an avocado shag carpet. The clashing colors briefly took away my appetite.

A lank woman perched on a chair, hand sewing the hem of a dress. Next to her was a plastic laundry basket overflowing with more clothing. She wore the same kind of dress as the women in the van, but hers hung from her bony shoulders like wash hanging on a clothesline. Her white-blond hair was tightly pulled into a braid and her face—void of makeup—looked worn.

"Mrs. Kenyon? I'm Gwen Marcey." I held out my hand.

The woman stared at it as if mesmerized before offering her own. Her hand was callused and limp. *Interview techniques 101: learn the witness's name and shake his or her hand.* Bad idea if handshakes are not part of the culture.

Taking the rocking chair next to her, I smiled. "Thank you both for talking to me. I'm sorry for the late arrival. An antelope drove me off the road."

Mrs. Kenyon paused in her stitching and stared at me like I had fuchsia spots on my nose. I shifted my weight, and the chair let out a mournful squeak. Mr. Kenyon, who sat on the nearest sofa, frowned at the floor. *Establish rapport.* Not established.

"Yes, well, I'll need a tow truck when we're finished." More silence. A pendulum clock *thock-thock-thocked* across the room.

After clearing my throat, I tried again. "I'm so sorry about the loss of your daughter."

Mrs. Kenyon nodded slightly, then bent over her sewing.

"God's will," Prophet Kenyon said. Mrs. Kenyon nodded again.

"Yes, well, uh, do you have a photograph of Rebekah?"

Mrs. Kenyon rose, moved to a bookshelf with cabinets below. Her long dress reached her ankles, exposing an incongruous pair of black-and-white Nike Air Max shoes. I gauged the size compared to the stomped face of my reconstruction yesterday. Maybe. I hadn't seen any fundamentalists at the center, but they could have stayed on the far side of the room.

Mrs. Kenyon rummaged around until she found a single photograph. She handed the snapshot to me. I accepted the photo with both hands, carefully touching only the edges. A pretty girl, about the same age as Aynslee, grinned at the camera. Dappled sunlight lit up her pale-blond hair worn in two braids. I swallowed hard. How would I handle losing a child? I glanced at Mrs. Kenyon. A single tear slipped from her eye.

"May I send this photo to the Washington County Sheriff's Department? Deputy Howell is in charge of the case. He's the one who called you and set up this meeting."

They both nodded. I pulled my sketchpad from my purse and opened it. On top was the list of surviving children from the display in Mountain Meadows. I'd forgotten I'd kept it. I glanced at the Kenyons, but they didn't seem to notice. *Good.* I didn't know how sensitive they would be to seeing a reminder of an ugly chapter in Mormon history. I tucked the sign into the back of the pad, then removed my sketch of the unknown girl and handed it to the prophet. "Would you please look at this drawing and tell me if you recognize her?"

The couple bent over the image, and I watched their expressions carefully. I knew before they shook their heads that the face wasn't familiar to them.

"Was Rebekah's obituary published in a newspaper or—"

"No."

"Did your daughter have much contact with . . . those outside your faith?" I asked, taking back the drawing.

Mrs. Kenyon's gaze flickered for a moment toward her husband.

"No," he said firmly.

"Well, then . . ." I glanced again at Mrs. Kenyon's drawn face and pale lashes, then at the snapshot of the young girl. Same bone structure, coloring, and braided hair as her mother, and wearing the same type of long calico dress, but with one difference.

Rebekah was wearing mascara.

"Did your daughter grocery shop, or ever go to town on her own?" I asked.

"Not alone. She was never alone." Prophet Kenyon looked like he was slurping vinegar.

Poor Bekka. I'd have bolted long ago if constantly surrounded by these people. But she hadn't bolted. She'd died. And our Jane Doe knew it.

"Mr.—uh, Prophet and Mrs. Kenyon, someone either knew Rebekah, or knew enough about her to take her identity. Please help me understand how this could have happened."

The preacher stood and began pacing. "We are being tested."

"I'm sorry, I don't understand."

"The time of Gathering is nigh. Only the chosen, mighty one can lead. Only a prophet." His Southern drawl deepened. "He must prepare the way of the Lord, make His path straight. The visions are coming faster." He jabbed a finger at me.

I dropped my gaze and studied the small notebook in my lap. I had no idea what he was talking about, but whatever it was, he was lying.

CHAPTER
EIGHT

BEFORE I COULD FIGURE OUT WHAT TO DO NEXT, the doorbell chimed. I peeked at Mrs. Kenyon. Her shoulders relaxed for a moment. Mr. Kenyon raced to the door as if he, too, was grateful for the interruption. I cleared my throat. One shot. *Talk to her now.* "My friend, Beth, is a quilter. Do you like to sew?"

She looked at the mound of clothing beside her. "Like? I suppose. The Lord calls us to do our part."

I wasn't quite sure what to do with that. I tried again. "Pretty country around here." *Dumb comment. It's dried-up dessert. How would I know?*

Her eyebrows rose. "I guess."

"I love these wide-open spaces. Can't tolerate the cities."

She leaned forward a bit. "It can get overwhelming. It can *all* get overwhelming."

Somehow I didn't think she was referring to her location. *Push on. Time's almost out.* "I'm from Montana. Living remote like that, I worry about forest fires. Here I assume it would be wild fires. Do you worry about that?"

"I hadn't thought much about it. Several of my . . . the young men around here are on fire crews, so I suppose we're safe enough."

Bingo. Pulaski-wielding, Mormon fanatics. *Eat your heart out, Sherlock Holmes.* I'd give Deputy Howell a heads–up as soon as I found a phone.

Prophet Kenyon stepped into the room and motioned me over. "Your car is ready."

"I don't understand."

"Sister Frances, the woman who picked you up, sent some men to pull your car out of the ditch. She'll drive you over."

"That was kind of her." A warmth spread up my neck, and I hoped it wasn't showing on my face. I'd just been thinking his flock was a bunch of murdering nutcakes. Could a leader inspire both kindness and destruction? His earlier behavior, based on studies and research into deception and lies, told me that Kenyon was concealing something. His physical action, finger pointing, should have come just before his passionate comments about a prophet and visions. Jabbing the air afterward showed he either wasn't convinced or wasn't telling the truth.

"I . . . well, here's my card if you can think of anything else. I'm a reserve deputy for Ravalli County, Montana. The sheriff's number is there as well, if you need to talk to him."

I trotted to the waiting van, slipped into the passenger seat, and nodded at Frances. "Thank you so much. I was prepared to call a tow truck—"

"You'd have to wait a long time to get one." She flashed me a grin. "I wasn't sure if you'd eaten, so I made a sandwich. There's a water bottle next to you."

"Thank you." I unfolded the wax paper to find a slab of homemade bread slathered with butter and honey. The sweet flavor rolled across my tongue. I moaned and she smiled again. Frances—calling her Sister Frances made me think of a convent, not an escapee from *Little House on the Prairie*—loosely held the steering wheel and hummed as we turned down the road.

"That's a nice tune," I said.

"'The Unknown Grave,' by Joseph's last son, David."

So many questions about Rebekah piled into my brain. I had this single chance to talk to her alone, and only nine miles to get answers. "Did you know Rebekah Kenyon?"

"Sure. Everybody knows everyone here. It was so sad when she died."

"Did she have much contact with anyone outside of Jarom? I need to find out who knew her or at least was aware that she died."

Frances scrunched up her mouth for a moment. "Well, we go to town for groceries, get together with our families a couple of times a year, like Pioneer Day . . . but there would be no reason to take someone's identity. That would be . . . a sin or something."

"Okay, maybe someone close to your LDS—"

"We're not LDS."

"Oh. So, what's the name of your church?"

"The First Born Apostolic Brethren in Christ."

I bet she couldn't say that fast ten times. "You're an offshoot of the Latter-day Saints?"

"We are Christ's true church as restored by Joseph Smith."

"Ah, okay, uh . . ." I thought for a moment. "Let's assume that it wasn't a member of your church. Maybe someone living in Jarom that's not a church member—"

"No. We have the Law of Consecration. The church owns all the property in Jarom."

If the church owned all the property, and Kenyon was head of the church, he would have considerable power and control, both being good motives for murder. "Tell me about Prophet Kenyon. What, for example, makes him a prophet?"

She turned her head and gave me a speculative glance. Apparently my face reflected nothing disparaging. "God speaks to him."

I'd discussed a few issues with God myself, but this sounded decidedly different. "Don't you believe God talks to you?"

She puckered her lips in thought. "Yeeeess, but God *reveals* things to Prophet Kenyon. Future events, rules, laws, what people should do or not do. He speaks for God."

"Oh." *Careful here, Gwen.* "What if Prophet Kenyon says God told him something different from the Bible?"

"The Bible's been corrupted over time. It's not accurate."

"What about, say, the Book of Mormon?"

"God can change His mind."

"I see." I looked out the window. "Doesn't the LDS Church have a prophet also?"

She made a *harrumph* sound. "They may call someone prophet, but he doesn't have the keys."

I kept silent and continued to watch the landscape unfold in the beams of the headlights.

"Prophet John Taylor had the keys to the kingdom," she continued. "Prophet Kenyon received the authority through the prophets following Taylor."

She might as well have told me about deriving a formula using pi. "And John Taylor is . . ."

"Was. He died in, I think maybe 1887. He was there, you know."

"There?"

"At the martyrdom. Of Joseph Smith."

Before I could work out this bit of information, I spotted my car. My helpful Mormon AAA crew managed to drag it from its resting place back onto the road. Frances aimed her headlights so I could check out the damages, but before I got out of the car, I pulled out my Jane Doe sketch. "Would you look at this drawing and tell me if you recognize the girl?"

Frances took it, then turned on an overhead light. She pursed her lips in concentration, then looked at me. "God has blessed you with a mighty art talent, Sister Gwen."

"Ah, well, thank you. She . . . Do you know this girl? The one who took Bekka's identity?"

The woman dropped the sketch and covered her mouth with both hands. She closed her eyes, then folded her arms and appeared to be praying.

I wasn't familiar with the social and spiritual customs of fundamentalist Mormons. Had she reacted to my drawing, something I said, or did she simply need to pray at that precise moment? I cleared my throat.

She finished, then fished the drawing from her lap and handed it to me with trembling hands. "It's true, then. Someone from our faith took Bekka's identity. That's so . . . dishonest."

"Umm"—I nodded encouragement—"so, you do know her? The girl in the drawing?"

"No. But you called her Bekka."

"Yes, that's the name Jane Doe went by."

"Only those close to our family knew Rebekah went by that name."

I waited, nodding my head again.

She laced her fingers together, then stared at them. When she finally spoke, her voice was so soft I leaned forward to hear. "Did someone murder this girl?"

"Yes."

"How? How was she murdered?"

"It was pretty . . . bloody."

Frances stared at me, face pale. "Please. I must know. How?"

"Someone . . . they sliced her throat and cut her torso."

She sucked in a breath of air. "Blood atonement." The words came out as a whisper. "We don't share our troubles with the Gentiles. But now there's . . . this." She glanced at me, then back to her hands. "About ten years ago there was a terrible split in the family. Prophet Kenyon, of course, had the keys. But the other claimed he was the one mighty and strong, the true son, and he had the scepter of power."

"This other. What's his name and where is he now?"

Frances rolled her lips together, then covered them with her hand. I pushed for an answer. "Please help me, Frances."

"I've said too much. You need to go now." She turned off the light, then faced forward.

It would seem our interview was over. "Thank you." She didn't acknowledge my words. I slipped out of the van. As soon as I'd closed the door, she sped off.

The car was drivable, though banged up. Before heading toward home, I found my notebook and wrote down her comments. Now all Deputy Howell had to do to find Jane Doe's killer was to look for a mighty and strong fundamentalist prophet without the proper keys who practiced blood atonement.

Whatever that meant.

Sweat ran down Aynslee's back and she shivered in spite of the heat. Car trunks made her claustrophobic, but to escape this stupid school, it was the only way. She'd already waited two days to find an unlocked ride in the visitor's lot. *What time is it?* Their idiotic exercise period lasted an hour, then showers and lunch. They wouldn't notice she'd gone AWOL until the midday head count. By then she should be in Sandpoint, Idaho. She figured the driver would stop to eat, and she could look around for another ride.

She'd been shocked when her mom enrolled her in the Selkirk Academy, a school for out-of-control kids. She wasn't the one acting out. Her mom should have enrolled herself here. Aynslee smiled, picturing her mom in gym class.

The warmth and gentle rocking of the car made her sleepy, and she drifted off, only to awaken when the car slowed, turned twice, stopped, and the engine shut off. She waited until she heard the door slam, then counted slowly to ten.

The lock release seemed as loud as a gunshot. She waited for someone to scream at the noise. Silence. She raised the trunk lid just high enough to slip out.

A family strolled by, and she pretended to be tying her shoe, then stood and glanced around. The golden arches of a McDonald's were surrounded by an enormous parking lot about three-quarters full. She recognized the location. Dave had stopped here when he'd driven her to the school three weeks ago. She was just north of Sandpoint.

Thumbing a lift was asking for the cops to pick her up. She sauntered toward the drive-through, checking out the possibilities. She spotted him almost immediately. Under a dirty baseball cap, the dude had unkempt, wavy hair and a pathetic attempt at a mustache and beard. He wore a faded Deadhead T-shirt. He opened the door and jumped into a rusty Chrysler Cordoba.

Perfect. Her parents, and Dave, would *really* be sorry they'd been so mean.

I had degrees of tired. This qualified as the highest, sort of the Oscar of exhaustion. With the windows wide open, I regularly pinched myself to stay awake and keep the car off the center line. The words ran through my brain like a pagan chant . . . *Provo, Provo, Provo.*

It wasn't all that late, but the combination of the long drive and hitting my head in the crash had taken a toll. As I drew near the city, I watched for an exit promising motels nearby. Finally, an eternity later, I turned off the highway and watched for the most beautiful word in the world: *Vacancy.*

Next to a store catering to survivalists was a budget-chain motel. I opened my trunk to pull out my suitcase, but the results from all the day's adventures had turned the trunk into a junk heap. *Forget it. I'll sleep in my shirt.* Tomorrow I'd rummage through and find something fresh to wear.

Room 210 smelled faintly of cleaning solution but was serviceable. A quick spider check between the sheets and I hopped in. The last thing I remembered was my head sinking onto a clean pillow.

The slamming of motel and car doors woke me the next morning. Soon housekeeping would be adding their gentle nudge for me to get going. The lime-green room featured a Lilliputian coffee machine, two paper cups, white powder pretending to be creamer, and decaf. *Decaf?* Life could be so unfair.

I made a cup of the nasty stuff, then jumped back into bed to get some work done. Using my laptop, banged up but still functional, I started a report on my interview of the Kenyons for Deputy Howell.

Report on interview with the Kenyons, first draft.
I met with Prophet Kenyon and Mrs. Kenyon, or *a* Mrs. Kenyon as I'm not sure . . .

Don't assume there are more Mrs. Kenyons.

[delete, delete, delete]
I met with Prophet Kenyon and Mrs. Kenyon at 1900 hours at their home, 12745 West Jarom Road, Jarom, Utah.

I typed our conversation, double-spaced, then added my concerns.

Prophet Kenyon is unconvinced that his visions are coming closer . . .

Hmm. Maybe that's not the part he's lying about?

[delete, delete, delete]

Prophet Kenyon lied at least once, and may be a person of interest in the blood atonement killing of Jane Doe. You might look into judgment and destruction, Adam-something, Zion, someone mighty and strong without the proper keys . . .

I sounded like an idiot.

[click, move cursor, highlight, delete]

Just send the interview without any conclusions. I uploaded the report, then raised my arms over my head and gave it a *Rocky* send-off. "Da-da-daaa, da-da-daaa." Phone calls were next. I felt like I'd lost contact with the world, not having my cell.

Beth accepted my collect call but didn't wait for my excuse. "Where are you? I tried calling several times."

"I'm at the Budget Stays Motel in Provo." I told her about my car and the Kenyon interview.

"Outstanding! You'll solve the girl's murder, and that older man—"

"George."

"Yes. George. You'll clear up the whole thing."

"No, I won't. I've done my part."

"Don't be boring. On television, the heroine always stays on the case until it's solved."

"Beth, I'm hardly a heroine. And that's television. Reality is that a forensic artist does her part, then turns her work over to

82

the lead detective or deputy. Done. Finished. Anything more is considered the Superman Syndrome."

"That sounds intriguing."

"Hardly. It's a negative term."

"Definition?"

"It's a forensic artist who thinks their contribution alone can resolve a crime. Like a superhero."

"Well, *I* think you're a superhero," Beth said softly.

"Maybe my image will tarnish when I tell you I was fired."

Beth was silent for a moment. "A mistake on their part. Your work at the interpretive center is world class. When you return there—"

"Didn't you hear me? I. Was. Fired. My work's done. My contribution to the case, done. Finished. Completed. Ended—"

"At least your vocabulary's improving."

"Do you always look for a silver lining?"

"Of course. There's a reason for everything."

I snorted. "Yeah. Right."

"At least you're involved in that homicide of the girl. My research—"

"Oh no, Beth. I'm not involved in that case. I'm only helping out."

"Then you don't want to hear about blood atonement—"

"What did you say?"

"The ritual way that someone killed that girl. Blood atonement."

"Frances used those very words! What is it?"

"Only if you make me Samwise Gamgee to your Frodo Baggins."

"I thought you said you were Watson to my Holmes?"

"You're not addicted to opium. Anyway, Brigham Young addressed it in a sermon in 1856. He taught that Jesus' blood was not enough to save you from certain sins. Therefore, it was necessary to kill the sinner and spill his blood."

I shook my head, even though Beth couldn't see it. "That was a long time ago."

"Hardly. Brenda Lafferty and her fifteen-month-old daughter were murdered that way in 1984. The story about her case became a best seller."

"Can you find me a copy of the book?"

"I've already checked it out from the library for you."

"That's great—"

"There's more. Let me read this to you: Place your right thumb under your left ear with the palm of your hand downward. Now slice your thumb quickly across your throat to your right ear—"

"No!"

"Wait. Place your right hand on your left breast and draw your hand quickly across the body before dropping your hand to your side. Finally, slice your thumb swiftly across your body, then drop your hand again to your side."

Goose pimples broke out on my arm. "Make it a knife rather than a thumb, and you've just described the three wounds to Jane Doe's body. Where did you get that?"

"Those actions were part of the secret endowment ceremony in LDS Temples to portray the death penalty for revealing secrets. They stopped doing the motions in 1990, but fundamentalist Mormons still believe in it."

"You've just made sidekick status."

"Do I get a badge?"

"Wear a shiny belt buckle. Listen, I'm going to breakfast, then will check out of here and head home. It's about an eight-and-a-half-hour drive without stops, so expect me later tonight."

"Good. What do you want me to research next?"

"Ah, I don't know. Let me think about it." I hung up and yanked on my jeans but left off the wig, instead putting on my favorite baseball hat with *Titanic* embroidered across the brim. I didn't care who stared at me while I rummaged around for clean underwear in my car.

My pencils were scattered among the dirty clothes, and graphite from an open pencil sharpener turned a pair of white shorts a blotchy gray. I found the art case, then picked through shoes, notepads, sculpting tools, books, and a box of forgotten Girl Scout cookies, plucking out errant lead holders. After righting an empty cooler, I repacked a box of watercolors. Under a tube of Naples yellow was a small plastic container. I picked it up. It was a memory card for a digital camera.

I turned the tiny piece of metal and plastic, about the size of a postage stamp, over in my hand. This wasn't mine.

Like a movie playing across my mind, I saw Deputy Howell grabbing Bekka's, or rather Jane Doe's, backpack, spilling the contents into my trunk and onto the street.

She had a camera.

This might be another important lead for Howell. I'd call him when I got home.

I slammed the trunk shut and started toward my room, then stopped. If someone was watching me, they'd seen me find the card. I glanced around. Other than a family with five carrot-topped children piling into a van on the other side of the motel, I didn't spot anyone. Just to be safe, I decided to check out the parked vehicles. Across the lot, perched almost by itself, was the backend of a deep-blue pickup. Utah plates. Maybe more navy than indanthrene. King cab. I memorized the number, B95 2DT. *I am obsessing on blue pickups.*

I returned to room 210, taking one last peek at the truck. After showering, getting dressed, and choosing an artfully twisted peach scarf for my headdress, I asked the woman pushing the cleaning cart for breakfast suggestions. She jerked her thumb toward the highway and muttered something in Spanish. The pickup was gone.

I drove in the indicated direction, but slammed on my brakes and pulled over when I came to a grocery store named Bee Prepared. I thought about the bags in Frances's van.

I turned into the lot and parked under a tree near a corner. Women wearing prairie-style dresses pushed their overloaded carts to waiting vans. Gathered around the side of the unpainted cement building huddled several groups of teenage girls. Their dresses varied, as did their hairstyles and coverings.

Pulling out my notes from the interview with Prophet Kenyon, I found what I was looking for.

Q. Did your daughter grocery shop or go to town on her own?

A. She was never alone.

Q. Who might know enough about Rebekah to take her identity?

A. We are being tested.

He hadn't answered my questions. Rebekah could have met with other fundamentalist girls while her mom shopped for groceries. And Rebekah's fate would be fodder for these girls' gossip.

One piece of the puzzle fell into place.

After snapping a photo of the girls, I continued the short drive up the road to a strip mall where the Country Inn Cafe snuggled between Camera Corral and Big Eddie's Discount Bakery.

I parked and charged toward the entrance to the cafe, then halted.

Camera Corral. The memory card.

Of course, it wasn't any of my business. I'd send the card off to Deputy Howell the first chance I got.

But a tiny peek wouldn't hurt. No one would know. It wasn't like developing film.

That wouldn't be professional.

It's not your case, not your job, and it will make Beth happy. Someone should have a smidgen of satisfaction.

I diverted to the photography store.

The clerk, a clean-cut young man, strolled from behind the counter. "May I help you?" He seemed fascinated by my turban.

I held up the memory card. "Can you make me a set of prints? Fast?"

"Absolutely. Do you want me to delete the images afterward?"

"No. How long will this take?"

"Just a few minutes."

I nodded. "I'm grabbing breakfast next door, then I'll be back."

"Perfect. Try the huckleberry pancakes. They're the best."

The smell of bacon and buttered toast seduced me when I opened the cafe door. A baby in a high chair was the first to note my entrance. He pointed a yolk-dipped finger at me. His mother stopped chatting and turned to see what had attracted the child's interest. A waitress passed me with a pot of coffee. "Take any seat, hon."

When I sat down at an empty table, a matched pair of tow-headed children rotated in their chairs and gazed at my head until their mother tapped them around.

I should have worn a wig.

After my hair first fell out from chemo, my hairdresser shaved the remaining strands. In anticipation of the inevitable baldness, I'd purchased several wigs and cleverly constructed hats that hid my condition. I found the experience of wearing one of those hats for the first time in public excruciating. I figured everyone knew. I soon got over being self-conscious, finding my naked head more of a cancer banner. *See? I'm a warrior, fighting and winning this battle.* Now I was more concerned about my appearance making others uncomfortable.

The diners finally stopped gawking and returned to their meals.

The pancakes were, in fact, the best. Several people entered after me, each greeted like long-lost family. Apparently this was the local hangout. I felt even more the outsider, sitting alone.

Just as I paid for my meal, a tall, slender man entered the restaurant. He caught my gaze, then turned his head as if searching for a place to sit. As the waitress counted out my change, I watched him through a mirror behind the cash register. The man took a table by the wall, sitting so he faced the door, then stared at my back. Not my turban. Either he had a lot of Sikh friends, or he was watching me. I took a mental snapshot of his features. If he was following me, I'd just mentally drawn him: wavy, burnt-umber hair, narrow nose, deep-set blue eyes, in his midforties. I could draw a composite and turn it over to Dave along with the license plate. *That'll teach someone to shadow a forensic artist. I have a pencil, and I'm not afraid to use it.*

The clerk held my prints up as I entered the store. "I made you hard copies and a CD with the images on them."

I paid for them, then stood at the counter and opened the packet, rummaging through the images. College photos, cowboys, a town, then one I recognized: the Utah visitor's center. My heart thumped faster. Another grouping of images showed the inside of a building. I froze at what I saw next.

I brought the print closer. *It can't be.*

"I need a nine-by-twelve of this one." I held it out.

Moments later I had the enlargement. A glassed-in display case with two faces. One looked almost exactly like my recent reconstruction from Mountain Meadows: the unfinished third man. The photograph showed the same face, although younger and without the scar, and carved from a creamy-looking clay. The resemblance was remarkable.

The clerk nodded at the photograph. "That's a good one, good angle and lighting. I took the same picture about a year ago."

"You've seen this sculpture before?"

"It's not a sculpture. It's a death mask. Of Joseph Smith."

CHAPTER
NINE

A CHILL RAN UP MY SPINE. "WHAT, *EXACTLY*, IS A death mask?"

"A plaster cast of Joseph Smith's face made after the martyrdom. The church owns it."

"Why a death mask rather than a photograph?"

"Photography was pretty new back then, and no one had taken any of the prophet, only this death mask and a profile drawing." The bell over the shop door tinkled and a man stepped through, then held the door for a pregnant woman pushing a baby carriage.

"Excuse me." The clerk moved toward the woman.

I didn't remember how Joseph Smith's death played out, but I was pretty sure it wasn't in Mountain Meadows, Utah.

My reconstruction lay in a million pieces in the trash bin, but I'd photographed it before it was destroyed. The camera was in the car. Right outside. I could have a copy made in seconds.

What good would that do?

Maybe I was the only one seeing a resemblance. I could give both images to Beth to see what she thinks.

And?

And nothing. *Or maybe something.* Jane Doe fainted after viewing my reconstruction. I had to get the memory card to Deputy Howell anyway. Maybe this was also a lead on his case.

I trotted to the car, found my digital camera, and returned to the store. The young man was still waiting on the other customers, so I checked out the new video equipment.

He finished and turned to me. "Yes?"

I turned on the camera, then scrolled through the photos. "Would you please make a print of the last five images on this?"

He nodded and stepped to the back of the store.

I drifted to the window.

The blue pickup perched at the end of the parking lot.

That's it. I rushed out of the store, stomped to the truck, and banged on the driver's window. I froze.

A startled woman in a tan jogging suit squealed and slammed down the lock, then sped off.

Well. That was embarrassing. That poor woman would probably tell her bridge club about the attempted assault by a crazed woman in a peach turban.

I slunk back to the shop, hoping no one noticed. The clerk's expression told me he'd seen everything. He quickly handed me the images, camera, and bill. I paid, reached for the door, then looked at the clerk. "Well, do *you* know the difference between navy and indanthrene?"

Back in room 210, I checked under the bed and behind the bathroom door to be sure I hadn't left anything. As I was about to leave, the phone rang.

"Hello?"

"Gwen. Dave here."

"Dave? What—"

"Aynslee ran away from the school."

I dropped the phone. *No!* Dave's voice sounded from the handset. I slowly picked it back up.

"—so the school called me—"

"When?"

"I just said. Yesterday. Sometime during the day."

"What are they doing to find her?"

"The school waited an hour or two in case Aynslee'd just meandered into the mountains—"

"Aynslee hates the mountains!"

"If you're going to interrupt me . . ."

"I'm sorry. Go on."

"Then they called the private security company they use."

"Okay."

"They spent four hours going to the usual runaway spots. Then they tried to call you."

"My phone—"

"I know. I spoke to Beth. That's how I got this number. They've put out a BOLO."

"A Be On the Look Out may not be enough. Did they get ahold of Robert?"

"No. Your ex is AWOL. Are you having a custody battle?"

"Hardly." I scooped in a deep breath. "The last time Robert stopped by, I asked him to take Aynslee for a few weeks while

I worked in Utah. It turned into a horrible fight. He said her rebellion was my fault. And my problem. He said we were roadblocks in his career . . ." My voice squeaked on "career," and I waited a moment. "Aynslee overheard it. I'm heading home as fast as I can." I hung up, then threw my purse across the room. I would ground that child for the rest of her life.

Assuming they found her.

Driving home, my thoughts hurtled about like popping popcorn. I needed a piece of paper to jot some notes. I reached behind me and found a pad of Cason Mi-Teintes pastel paper with a few remaining hemp-colored sheets. Pricy notes, but I didn't want to stop and rummage for scratch paper in the trunk. I pulled a Sharpie from my purse and opened the pad. Why had Aynslee written to Beth to say she liked it at Selkirk, then bolted the first chance she got? I thumped the steering wheel. *Robert, where are you when your daughter needs you?*

With his latest girlfriend, that's where. A gold-digging, twenty-year-old with big boobs.

Just like you were. Robert's sarcastic voice echoed in my brain.

"That's not true." My face burned anyway. "I wasn't a gold digger. I married you because I loved you."

You married a best-selling author. I was hailed as the next Hemingway.

I snorted. "More like Harper Lee. A single book."

Not anymore. My latest novel has sold millions on Amazon.

"Ha. A self-published e-book."

And I'm getting most of the royalties.

"Some of which I should be receiving. We were married for fifteen years!"

And divorced before I published it.

"I'm not the reason you couldn't write a second book!"

The only thing you did right in our marriage was to be the inspiration for that second book.

"But I'm not neurotic!"

Does anyone care?

Breakfast threatened to come up. I took a deep breath and concentrated on driving. Continuing north, I passed into the potato-growing region of southeastern Idaho. Turning at Blackfoot, I headed toward Highway 93 and the rugged Idaho-Montana border. Traffic receded and I turned my gaze to the photograph on the seat. I was sure that it was just a bizarre coincidence that my sculpture looked like Joseph Smith.

Right, Gwen.

Now Dave's rational voice played in my head. *Maybe it was subconscious projection because you were working on the site.*

"No. I'd never seen the death mask before, so how could I have patterned the face after it?"

I rubbed my neck. Had Jane Doe noticed the resemblance and that's what had caused her to faint? And she was murdered. Did someone destroy the reconstruction to keep others from making that same identification? That didn't make sense. I'd finished most of his face before Jane Doe saw him.

Why hadn't anyone else recognized him?

"Because . . . because no one expected to see the face of Joseph Smith in that location. It's a simple answer, Dave. Viewers would have a sense of familiarity, but not know why. My reconstruction was an older man with a scar, so maybe that made the difference."

But Jane Doe somehow made a connection.

"Maybe she had some kind of special knowledge."

A car horn honked.

My gaze shot to the rearview mirror, then to the speedometer. I was driving twenty miles under the speed limit.

Stopping only for gas and bladder breaks, it still seemed to take forever to get home. With every mile I itched for my phone. Mountains folded in around me, and my car, and my breathing, struggled over the seven-thousand-foot elevation on the Lost Trail Pass between Idaho and Montana.

I also watched for the pickup.

I pulled in front of Beth's immaculate house after dark and dashed to the door, which opened before I could knock. One look at my friend's face told me Aynslee was still missing.

I gripped the porch rail. *They should have found her by now.*

Beth gave me a quick hug, then stepped away to let me in. Her living room featured soothing oyster, taupe, and camel-colored furniture resting on an oatmeal-beige carpet. She'd moved her Lladró figurines to a high shelf in deference to Winston's waving tail. "I've started a prayer chain at church for Aynslee. I know she'll be fine. She's smart and resourceful."

"Thanks, Beth."

My dog burst from the kitchen, threw his full one hundred sixty pounds at me, knocking me to the floor. He planted an enormous foot on my chest and slurped my face with his wet tongue.

"Winston, no! Bad dog!" The Pyrenees paid no attention to Beth's scolding.

I'd whacked my head on the floor, starting up the same headache I'd had after the accident. I used the dog to haul myself up. "How long's Winston been leaping on people like that?"

"I'm sorry. My attempt to train Winston to track was

somewhat unsuccessful. I give him a scent, and he does locate the person just fine. But he's so elated, he just plows right into them. Poor Norm's been trampled four times."

Beth's husband, Norm, wandered into the room. "Good to see you, Gwen. Really good."

I frowned. Coming from Norm, that was practically gushing. "I'm sorry Winston was such a bother," I said.

"Your dog's wonderful." He moved closer and took my hand. "The problem was my dear wife, you see."

Beth started to protest, but Norm ignored her. "Since you left town, Beth's organized my sock drawer by color, checked out, read, and returned sixty-five library books—"

"Thirty-eight," Beth said.

"See my point?" He let go of my hand. "She was just starting a calorie and exercise chart for me to take fishing tomorrow. Now that you're here, she'll . . . ah . . . help you and let me get on with my trip." He frowned. "Unless you'd rather I help you find Aynslee."

"Oh, Norm." Beth gave him a quick peck on the cheek. "That's so sweet."

"Thank you, but you don't need to do that. I know you've been planning this trip for a year," I said.

I turned to Beth. "I'll take Winston off your hands. I need to get home and start looking for Aynslee." Beth didn't look the least bit sorry that my hairy pet was leaving. Digging up her peach dahlias hadn't put him on her favorites list. I scratched Winston's ear. "My friend, thanks so much for the dog care. I'll call . . ." A lump formed in the back of my throat. *Dang it!* My emotions were still raw and unpredictable from the divorce, and menopause didn't help.

Beth laid a warm hand on my arm. "You're quite fatigued. Why don't you leave Winston here tonight, get some sleep, and we'll both look for your daughter in the morning. Dave's doing everything he can. And remember—"

"Don't say it, Beth. Sometimes things just happen." I clamped my jaw shut before I said more. Beth didn't deserve my temper, and she was right. I was exhausted, and four months of chemo had taken its toll on my endurance.

Beth held Winston's collar while I got in the car and headed home. Tucked just off the county road and surrounded by steep, pine-covered mountains, this place had been the perfect retreat for Robert and me sixteen years ago.

My log house was dark and lifeless as I pulled into the driveway and parked. Grabbing only my purse and computer case, I slammed the car door extra hard. The moonlight provided little illumination, and I fumbled the keys at the back door three times before finally unlocking it.

Everything was exactly as I'd left it three weeks ago, down to the single rinsed cup on the drying board and the ratty dishrag draped over the faucet. The room smelled musty. Even though he would have demanded all my attention, I should have brought Winston home. The house would have felt less empty.

I dumped purse, keys, and laptop onto the kitchen table. I needed to send a quick email to Deputy Howell, but my desktop computer was faster than my old laptop. Plus, it hadn't been in a car wreck. Heading to my studio, I paused at Robert's office and flipped on the light. A bare bulb dangled where a Frank Lloyd Wright prairie-ceiling light had once glowed. Art hangers lined the walls, surrounded by tiny scratches from the absent framed awards. Divots scored the creamy-white carpet outlining the shape of amputated furniture.

After softly closing the door, I entered the studio and turned on the computer. While it booted up, I stretched my arms over my head and enjoyed a jaw-cracking yawn. I sat and began to type.

> Deputy Howell, I've recovered a memory card from Jane Doe's camera. I'd like to speak to you about the contents. I also think you might [delete] should do a follow-up with Prophet Kenyon re: split with another fundamentalist group. Check out Bee Prepared grocery in Provo. Did you recover anything interesting from Ethan? [delete]

That's none of my business.

I stood up. "I'll get you the memory card, and I'm done, done, done with Jane Doe, Mountain Meadows, and fundamentalist Mormons." My bedroom was stuffy so I opened a window to cool it down before stretching out on the bed. I would just close my eyes for a moment . . .

Something skittered across my ankle.

I leaped from the bed, whacking at the exposed flesh. *Spider.* I found a shoe and turned on all the lights. It was here somewhere. The thought made me want to slap at my clothing while doing a tippy-toe dance. I spotted the black beast sneaking across the floor. A well-aimed toss and the spider became a skid mark.

I did the tippy-toe dance anyway, then leaned against the wall to catch my breath and wait for my heart to stop pounding. *Stupid.* I'd gone to bed without checking. A thorough search of the bedding assured me it was now safe to sleep. I closed my eyes.

The phone was ringing.

I jerked upright. It took a moment, then my thoughts reassembled. Morning sunshine flooded my bedroom. I lurched for the phone. "Yes?"

"It's Dave. I have good news. We found your daughter. She hitched a ride with a young man as far as Superior before the guy made a pass at her—"

"No!"

"She's fine, but she broke his finger." Dave snorted. "Looks like my self-defense lessons paid off."

"Where did they find her?"

"I-90 heading east. His erratic driving attracted the state police. They picked her up. The academy gave them my number—"

"I'll go get her right now."

"You don't have to. I have some evidence I need to drop off in Missoula. I can pick her up after that."

"Oh." I slowly sank to the bed. "Thanks, Dave. I—" My throat closed up.

"You bet." He hung up.

I drifted down the hallway to the kitchen. The painted eggshell-white cabinets seemed sterile, and the old linoleum needed replacing. I put on a pot of coffee and called Beth to tell her about Aynslee. Before we hung up, she said she'd bring Winston over in a little while.

The coffeepot dinged and I poured a cup, then wandered to the window.

My car door was ajar.

I turned and sloshed the coffee. My computer, keys, and purse were still sitting on the table where I'd left them.

I walked outside and inspected the car. It was dusty and dinged up from the accident but otherwise looked fine. I shut the door, locked up, and started back to the house when something caught my attention at the edge of the yard.

Leaning against a shrub was a carefully folded piece of hemp-colored Mi-Teintes pastel paper.

My heart pounded a bit faster. *It probably blew out of my car.*

But I hadn't torn out any pages. I walked back to the car and glanced into the front seat. The pad of paper was missing.

The dense forest at the edge of the yard formed a deep, Prussian-green backdrop to the brown of the paper. The yard between house and woods stretched before me. Exposed. No cover. Wind stirred the pines across the ridge above me. *I should have brought Winston home last night.*

I stepped toward the lawn, then froze.

Early-morning dew sparkled like sugar frosting on the grass. A trail, clearly defined, led from the driveway to the paper. In another hour the sun would evaporate the damp lawn and the trail would disappear.

I slowly retreated, not turning my back to the watching forest. I bumped into the kitchen door. Only then did I bolt inside.

I picked up the phone and dialed the sheriff, then promptly hung up.

What was I going to say? A folded slip of paper scared me? Someone's spying on me?

They would come in white uniforms. Fit me for a straitjacket.

I raced to the bedroom and retrieved my 9mm SIG Sauer

from the drawer by the bed. It felt solid in my hand. I chambered a bullet. The sound echoed in the silent house.

I found a baseball hat and jammed it over my nonexistent hair. *Stupid time to be vain.*

The kitchen door creaked as I opened it. Gravel crunched underfoot as I advanced across the driveway. Ravens cawed to each other overhead. *Ravens?* They tended to like carrion.

Dead things.

I gauged the distance between me and the stockade of trees. If I ran, I'd be a difficult target. *On three. One. Two.* I flew toward the woods.

The lawn seemed the length of a football field. My goal was a large ponderosa next to the piece of paper. When I reached it, I sagged against the trunk and waited for my heart rate and breathing to slow. I sniffed, but all I smelled was pine. Nothing . . . dead.

Only then did I look down. The paper was folded a bit like a paper airplane.

Or . . . an arrow.

The forest, thinned years ago, allowed young pines to crowd together. About six feet down a game trail in front of me was a second folded sheet.

My pulse took off like a racehorse. I extended my arms in front of me, pistol ready but quivering in my grip, and stepped into the woods. A chipmunk chattered its reproof of my presence. I crept up to the paper, then slowly turned in a circle. The pine branches blocked my view. Someone could be standing right next to me in this jungle and I wouldn't see him. The paper arrow pointed left.

The third sheet rested three feet away.

I wiped my free hand on my jeans, then slipped closer.

A branch snapped on my right.

I jumped, then spun in a circle. A startled deer flipped his white tail at me and crashed off. I lowered the gun and searched for another arrow.

Something glinted to my left. I shifted and it disappeared.

I squinted my eyes to see better, but couldn't make anything out.

I moved toward where I'd seen the shiny object, the pine needles masking the sound of my footsteps. A shape took form. The sparkle was the sun hitting a gold ring. Attached to a finger. Attached to a hand.

Attached to nothing.

CHAPTER
TEN

ROUGHENED BARK SCRATCHED MY SPINE.

Gold flashed. My feet framed a ring.

Lifeless fingers. Dark-rimmed nails.

The hand. Pale. So pale.

I grabbed the pistol from under my rear. Pointed. The pistol wavered, slipped, fell.

A man's hand.

I dried my palms on my outstretched legs. Grabbed the gun again. Pointed, arms extended. The sights wavered, refused to line up.

Someone had propped the hand against a tree trunk.

Roaring, crashing surf filled my ears. *Get control or you'll pass out.*

A pinecone lay on the ground next to me. I set down the gun, wrapped my fingers around the cone's prickly surface, and gripped until it hurt. Squeezed my eyes shut. Opened them.

Sweat dampened my back.

Taking a shuttering breath, I pushed off the ground, then shuffled forward. The hand was real. Exposed bone gave a hint of ivory at the wrist. No blood. The slightest scent of decay. A fly buzzed, then settled on the raw cut. The gold ring twinkled in the intermittent sunlight filtering through the pines.

I looked around for movement. Only a ballet of gnats danced in the dappled sunlight. I was alone. Just me. And a hand.

A hawk screeched overhead.

Assume the killer is still hanging around. I spun, then tore down the game trail. Tree limbs reached for me, slapped my face. A branch snagged my hat. I ran.

The lawn just ahead.

The kitchen benignly welcomed me. I slammed the door and locked it. I put the pistol on the counter, then grabbed a chair to keep from falling. *Oh, Lord. Oh, Lord.*

I snatched the phone. It took both hands to steady the receiver.

The call went to Dave's voice mail. "Call me!" I redialed.

"Ravalli County Sheriff's Department. This is Deputy Harnisch. How may I help you?"

"Ah, Craig, ohmigosh."

"What's wrong?"

"Dave didn't answer his phone."

"Must be out of range. He's picking up your daughter at a rest stop near Lookout Pass."

"I found a hand. No body. Just a hand."

"What do you mean?"

"Just come now!"

"I'm on my way."

I paced the kitchen. Sat. Then stood. Checked the door lock, then the window. If I stood just right, I could barely see the county road. Was that something blue? Was it the guy following me?

It would take Craig ten minutes to get here from town. Faster if he used his lights and sirens.

I inspected my watch. One minute down.

Maybe I could write—no, draw the hand. I moved toward the studio.

What if someone got in the house?

No, no, the house is safe.

You left the door open.

I wiped my sweaty palms on my jeans. There wasn't time. No one could get in.

Are you sure?

I grabbed my pistol. In the silence, the old refrigerator kicked on, masking any footsteps. Sneak around? Charge from room to room, yelling?

Charge.

The bathroom was on my left. I grabbed the doorknob, turned, then kicked it open. *Wham!* It bounced off the wall, then crashed shut. I tried again. Empty.

Robert's office. On the right. "I know you're in here!" The hinges squealed in protest. I shoved the door open with my hip. No one.

Aynslee's room next. Her name written in pink glitter. Door half ajar. *Thump-sssss.* The deep-pile carpeting slowed the door. I plowed through, gun pointed. "I'm armed!" Only dirty sneakers on the floor.

Living room. I darted through, waving my pistol.

Ahead. My studio. I rushed forward, hitting the door with my shoulder. It smashed open. A face on my right! I fired.

The plaster disintegrated into a powdery heap.

I lowered the gun and leaned against the wall. The neck cracked, split, then joined the chalky pile on the floor. I'd just shot my drawing cast of the human face. My ears rang, my nose burned, and I felt like an idiot.

Gravel crunched under spinning tires.

Taking a deep breath, I trooped through the house to the kitchen, then opened the door. "That was fast."

Craig had one hand on his gun. "Uh . . . you want to put that away?"

"Oh, sure." I gently placed my pistol on the counter. "Was anyone parked on the county road?"

"No."

"Okay then." I leaned against the counter. "The first thing I noticed was my car door open. Then I saw a sheet of hemp-colored Cason Mi-Tientes folded on the edge of the lawn."

"You saw some hemp—"

"Pastel paper."

"I don't understand the significance—"

"It was from my car. And I could see where someone had crossed the lawn."

Craig raised his eyebrows but said nothing.

"Let me show you." We walked outside and I pointed, but my hasty retreat masked the original trail. "Well, it's gone, but the paper . . ."

The paper wasn't there. "The wind must have blown it away. Or he moved it."

"He?"

"Maybe the man following me. In the pickup."

"Ah. I see."

"There are more sheets." I crossed to the tree line and pointed out where I'd found the first folded paper. We paused at the spot, and Craig bent down and inspected the area.

"I followed this game trail. The next sheet—" It, too, was gone. I started forward, but Craig pulled me back. "Stay here and keep an eye out. I'll go first." He unholstered his gun and cautiously moved into the forest. The pines quickly closed in behind him.

I listened to his rustling footsteps, straining to hear over the chirping birds. The ravens were gone.

Silence, then Craig called out, "Where?"

My heart sank. The third piece of paper was apparently missing. I followed his voice. "Look for something gold, shiny."

"I don't see any hand."

I joined him and studied the base of the tree. "Well, yeah, I think . . ." I turned in a circle, probing each trunk. Nothing. "It was a ponderosa. I thought it was this one."

"There are a lot of trees here." He walked around the trunk, then checked some nearby evergreens.

I bent down and touched the pine needles. There wouldn't be blood; the hand had appeared drained. The ground looked undisturbed. "Maybe I was mistaken. It must be around here someplace."

We moved apart, each examining the base of different trees. Nothing.

Craig paused in his search. "Maybe your dog—"

"No. Winston's still with Beth."

"Well then . . ." He cleared his throat and reholstered his pistol. "Any ideas?"

"I know what I saw. The road is right over there. Someone parked there. I could barely see something blue. He could have grabbed the paper and hand, then driven off."

"Well . . ."

"Maybe a coyote found it. Or a wolf."

"Or a lion, tiger, or bear? Do you think the critters were thinking about taking up pastels?"

I gave him a withering look, which he ignored.

"How about you and I go inside and talk?" He strolled toward the house without waiting for a response. I followed. We entered the kitchen. "Do you have any coffee?" he asked.

"Sure. There's—" I gasped. My computer was gone.

"What?" Craig tugged out his pistol.

"Somebody came into the house. They took my laptop. It was on the dining room table."

Craig signaled me to the corner of the room, out of sight from the doorway. He pressed against the wall, took a fast look down the hallway, then dashed forward. *Wham! Wham!* The bathroom door fighting back. *Squeak.* The den. *Thump-sssss.* Aynslee's room. Then silence.

I reached for my pistol.

Footsteps clumped up the hallway.

I licked my dry lips and pulled out my SIG.

Craig entered the room, cradling my computer in his arms.

Aynslee chewed an already shredded thumbnail and stared out the cruiser window. *The stupid pig put me in the backseat. Like*

I'm a criminal or something. The car stank of vomit mixed with disinfectant cleaner.

She probably smelled like an armpit as well. Almost two days without a shower. Her hair felt gross.

"The sheriff should arrive any minute." The cop in front of her shifted in his seat.

The friendliness in his voice sounded fake. Probably because Dave was picking her up and he was a sheriff. What was it called? Oh yeah. The thin blue line.

She pulled her feet beside her on the seat, then rubbed some of the dirt off. They'd have to clean up after her. *Good.*

A car door slammed.

Aynslee bit down too hard. The sharp sting of her torn cuticle made her throat burn. Out of the corner of her eye, she watched Dave saunter over.

"Thanks," Dave said.

"Don't mention it." The cop stepped out and opened her door.

She took her time exiting, making a point not to look at Dave. The cop from Superior had agreed to meet Dave at a rest stop, and she studied the park-like setting. The towering bull pines cast deep shadows over the recently mowed lawn. Traffic muttered in the distance, and a wall of evergreens formed a backdrop.

Mom could paint this view.

She shook her head violently. Her mom sent her away. Dad hated her.

"Come on, young lady." Dave took her arm. "You've given all of us a scare."

Aynslee allowed him to escort her to his car. This time she sat in the front seat. *Maybe this will make Mom and Dad remember I'm still here.*

"Your computer was in your studio," Craig said, placing the laptop on the kitchen table.

My jaw tightened and I shook my head. "No. No. I left it in here. Somebody moved it. They came into my house while we were in the woods. Maybe they're still here." I tried to dodge past Craig, but he put out his arm to stop me.

"I checked the house, Gwen. No one is here." He rubbed his nose. "You know, maybe, well, is there someone I can call?"

"What do you mean?"

"First the folded paper, then the hand, the computer . . . I don't know."

I crossed my arms. "Did you, by any chance, read Robert's book?"

He shifted. "My wife downloaded it onto my computer. I started to read it—"

"Craig, that book isn't me. It's fiction. You know me, for crying out loud!"

"I'm not saying I thought about you when I read it. I just know with your cancer . . . your daughter's running away . . . losing your job in Utah . . . you know?"

"I'm not crazy."

"I didn't say you were. Stressed, maybe."

"You can go now. I'm fine. Sorry I bothered you."

"Gwen—"

I walked to the door and opened it.

He hesitated, nodded briefly, then left.

I wanted to slam the door after him, scream, kick the wall. Instead, I shut it quietly, then locked it. Everyone seemed to know about my personal life, and someone *was* trying to play head games with me. I was sure it had something to do with Mountain Meadows and Mormons.

They'd soon find out they shouldn't mess with a divorced, menopausal, bald woman in a bad mood.

CHAPTER
ELEVEN

THE ROOM DARKENED AS INDIGO CLOUDS GATH-
ered outside. Craig had read Robert's book. Who hadn't read
that cursed book?

Someone rang the doorbell. Probably Craig.

I yanked the door open. "What now!"

The FedEx driver's eyes were huge. "Hey, Gwen, I come in
peace." He nodded at a number of boxes he'd stacked on the step
and handed me an electronic tablet. "Sign here."

I took the tablet and signed. "I'm sorry I bit your head off."

"I understand." He took the machine and gave me The
Look—the same one you might give a homeless woman pushing
a loaded shopping cart and muttering about space aliens.

He'd read Robert's book. I cleared my throat. "Nasty storm
brewing."

The man glanced at the sky. "Looks like." He gave me a quick smile and trotted toward his van.

I gathered the packages and moved them to the kitchen. The top box had the return address of Skull-Duggery, Tucson, Arizona. It had been forwarded to me by Bentley at the Mountain Meadows Center. Overnight delivery. Charged to my account.

"You couldn't have just sent them back, you skunk," I muttered.

After looking up the number for Selkirk Academy, I spoke with the after-hours staff. *Good news, Aynslee's been located and is coming home. No, I'm not sending her back. Yes, please send the bills to Robert.* That last item made me smile.

I'd received a flier on homeschooling. I'd call about it tomorrow.

I heard the rumble of a car approaching. I stepped outside as Dave pulled up next to the house. Before he'd had time to shift into park, Aynslee burst from the car and shot past me into the house.

"Young lady, we need to talk—"

Her response was a slammed bedroom door.

"Storm's brewing everywhere." Dave approached, rubbing his neck, then followed me into the kitchen. "Craig called—"

"Was she hurt?" I asked.

"No. Craig mentioned a hand—"

"Are you sure she wasn't hurt? He didn't touch her? Shouldn't we take her to the doctor and have her checked? I'm so going to ground her for the rest of her life."

Dave took away the pencil I was twisting. "Gwen, she assured me she wasn't touched. Tell me about the hand."

I took a deep breath. "I think some Mormons are killing people."

Dave stared at me a moment, then grinned. "Mormons? How about Catholics?"

"What?"

"You know, if your right hand causes you to sin, cut it off? Those Baptists are pretty literal. Or maybe the Muslim community in Copper Creek. Muslims like to chop off hands too."

"We don't have any Muslims . . . You're making fun of me!" I felt heat rush to my face.

"Nah. I could have sworn I saw two suspicious young men wearing white shirts and black ties riding on bikes—"

"Dave!"

Dave stopped grinning, stood, and reached for me. "I'm sorry. I believe you, even if Craig has his doubts. Someone made sure you'd find this hand by leaving you a trail of folded pastel papers. I'm just not following your 'killer Mormon' conclusions."

"Someone planted a severed hand. They made sure I'd find it."

"Where is it?"

"Gone. They moved it."

"You didn't have your camera with you?"

"I wasn't expecting a crime scene," I said dryly.

Dave raised his eyebrows.

I snatched up the cordless phone and dialed. "I'll prove it to you. I know who the hand belongs to. There was clay under the fingernails—"

"Deputy Howell."

"Hi, Deputy Howell. It's Gwen Marcey. Did someone mutilate George's body?"

Silence. "Well . . ."

"Did someone cut off George's hand?"

"How did you know?" Deputy Howell asked.

"I need you to speak with my sheriff, Dave Moore." I handed him the phone.

Dave shrugged and took the phone from me. "Sheriff Moore."

While Dave and Deputy Howell talked, I headed down the hall. I found Aynslee lying on her bed curled around a pillow. I addressed her back. "Young lady, I need an explanation."

"What's to explain? Nothing happened. You found me. No big deal."

"It *was* a big deal. You could have been hurt!"

"What do you care? You sent me to that school because you didn't want to be around me—"

"That's not true and you know it. Look at me."

She continued to stare at the wall.

"I said look at me!"

Slowly the girl rolled over and sat at the edge of the bed. "What?"

"I love you more than you'll ever know—"

"Oh yeah?"

"Yeah. And don't interrupt. You put yourself in the position of going to that academy when you experimented with drugs—"

"I didn't!"

"And"—I waved her protest away—"you stole money from my purse—"

"I didn't!" She stood and made quotation marks in the air. "'In his first novel in over fifteen years, Robert Marcey writes the riveting story of how a neurotic woman—'"

"Stop!" I'd made every effort to keep that vitriolic tome away from her. "Wh-when did you read your father's book?"

"He said I could read it."

"That isn't what I asked. When did you read it?"

"I don't know. Maybe three months ago."

A light went on in my brain. She'd started acting out about then, lying, sneaking out, taking things. Robert's book claimed yet another victim: his own daughter. Heat rushed to my face, and I gulped air until the stress-induced hot flash passed.

"I just want things to be the way they were." She stared at me, hands knotted into fists. "But you're leaving again for Utah, and you're going to send me back to that school."

"I'm not leaving. My job is . . . done."

"Done? But you weren't . . . you mean you got fired?"

"Well. Yes." I hung my head.

"I hate you," Aynslee said softly and lay back on the bed.

"You may hate me right now, Aynslee, but I love you, and I'm doing my best to keep you safe. You will stay in your room until you're ready to apologize to me for your behavior."

"Don't you think you should apologize to me?" she asked. "You promised you'd never leave for a big case again."

I gently closed the door behind me, then waited a moment until my hand relaxed enough to let go of the doorknob. I had promised. But that was before cancer, divorce, and the prospect of finding full-time employment had changed everything.

Dave was hanging up the phone when I entered the kitchen. He frowned at the floor, then glanced up. "Deputy Howell is on his way here to talk to you."

"Why? Can't we talk on the phone?"

"He said he was following up on your email from last night and had to head out to Jarom and Provo today to reinterview the Kenyons. He wants to pick up the memory card in person, interview you, and check out the hand. Seems you were right about George."

"I told you so."

Dave briefly smiled. "I bet you love saying that." He pointed toward my studio. "Would you draw the hand you saw?"

"Sure."

Dave trailed me down the hall and sat in the oversize wing-back chair. I settled at my drafting table, pulled out a sheet of Bristol paper, and sketched. Once I'd finished shading the hand, I drew an enlargement of the ring in the right corner, then held it up. "Done."

Dave stood and took it from me. "Good. I'll fax it to Deputy Howell." He placed the drawing on the computer desk, sat down, and looked at me. "Now, why do you think Mormons are responsible for the murder of Jane Doe and the mutilation of George's body?"

"I didn't say Mormons—"

"Yes, you did."

I stood. "I meant fundamentalist Mormons."

"Same difference."

"No. The Mormon fundamentalists are the polygamists."

"So being married to several women leads you to mutilate corpses?" He folded his arms.

"That's not what I said." I started to pace.

"You're giving me a hand in your yard and polygamist Mormons."

"Forget the polygamy!" I so wanted to kick him.

"Then why bring it up?"

"Can I start over?" I stopped pacing.

"Please do."

"The fundamentalists practice polygamy—"

Dave raised a finger.

"—AND believe in blood atonement."

Dave put up both hands in surrender. "Keep going."

"Blood atonement is a ritual form of punishment for particular sins and I believe, because of Jane Doe's injuries, that she was murdered—"

"So what was her sin?"

"I don't know."

"So how do you connect George's hand ending up outside your house to Jane Doe?"

"I'm not sure."

"You don't know and you're not sure. Gwen, where's that analytical brain of yours?"

"According to Robert, my brain's forever corrupted because of chemo."

"Forget Robert. Connect the hand and Jane Doe."

I took a deep breath. "Okay. Here's my sequence of events leading up to the hand in the woods. Jane Doe was possibly meeting someone on her trip."

"How do you know?"

"Ethan told me. Or rather, he told Deputy Howell."

"Ethan. Now there's an Ethan?"

"He's Jane Doe's boyfriend. I met him at the motel in Fancher. Oh!"

"What?"

"Ethan! The sheriff's department had all of Jane Doe's things except the memory card and whatever Ethan had. Even though Ethan didn't want to give anything to Howell, I told the deputy about it. I also told Ethan to FedEx the items to Jane Doe's parents' house. I only found out later about her stolen identity. What if . . . what if it was something more than just a jacket and paperback? What if she was meeting someone to pass this item to?"

Dave tapped the table with his fingers. "Earth to Gwen. Helloooo? What was she supposed to be delivering?"

"I don't know. Whatever it was, if I'm right, it was important enough to kill her for it. Maybe the item is still at the motel waiting for pick up? And Ethan may be in danger! No. No. He said his folks were picking him up. He's probably home by now. Or back in class."

"I'll take care of it."

"Good. Right. It's not my case." I nodded. "Of course, then George was late for work."

"What?"

"And they've been following me ever since."

"They? Who's 'they'?"

"I'm not sure."

"You don't know, you're not sure, George is late for work, some faceless 'they'—"

"Not faceless. I can draw him! I saw him in Provo—"

Dave threw up his hands and gave me The Look.

He'd read Robert's book. "Dave, I'm not crazy, and if I weren't bald already, I'd tear out my hair right now." I tried to slow my words but they tumbled out. "Jane Doe was delivering something or meeting someone. She fainted at the interpretive center and was escorted back to her motel. If she was meeting George, she'd missed him because she left early and he arrived late. The killer must have been at the center and witnessed her fainting, then followed her back to the motel and killed her. When he didn't find . . . whatever it was, he went back to the center and killed George, then trashed the place looking for . . . the thing."

"Why would anyone assume you had it?"

I chewed my lip, thinking. "I don't know. Someone searched my room, though, because that prescription bottle—"

Dave sat up straighter. "What prescription?"

"Lorazepam," I said reluctantly. "I don't take it often. But if someone searched my hotel room, they'd know I had an anti-anxiety drug, and they'd know I didn't have their treasure."

Dave stared at me.

"So . . . so if they think I still have this item, and if they think I'm taking drugs because I'm unstable, maybe he followed me, waiting to kill me next, scaring me with George's hand to make me feel more crazy . . . or . . . or . . ." I could feel tears welling up. I turned away and struggled to compose myself.

"It's okay, Gwen, just—"

I spun around to him. "Jane Doe is dead." I made a slashing motion across my throat, chest, and bowels. "Like this. Sliced up like a butchered lamb. Up until 1990, this was the LDS's acted-out penalty for revealing secrets."

Dave's eyes widened.

I ticked off on my fingers. "George is dead, throat cut. His hand was cut off and placed so I'd find it. Someone's been following me, driving a blue pickup, Utah license number B95 2DT. I can draw his composite. Someone should follow up on Ethan. I'm not crazy."

The storm broke, the rain pelting against the roof with a volley of oversize drops.

"You said you told Deputy Howell about Ethan, but I'll call him when I get back to the office. And I'll suspend judgment for now on some of your conclusions." Dave leaned against the counter and was silent for a few moments, then took out a notepad and jotted down the license number. "I'll get a tracking dog to see what we can find with the missing hand. We'll test for latent bloodstains. The storm won't help, but we'll give it a try. Speaking of dogs, where's yours?"

"Winston's still with Beth."

"Get him back. You need a watchdog." He picked up the sketch from the table.

"Let me put that in something. I don't want it to get wet." I found a small box that once contained Bristol paper, placed the sketch inside, then put the box in a plastic grocery bag.

"I'll follow up on the license. In the meantime, please stay home. And . . . don't . . . uh . . . share your theories with anyone else."

"What about the memory card?"

Dave rubbed his face. "What memory card?"

"The one belonging to Jane Doe. The one with the photograph of Joseph Smith's death mask that resembles my Mountain Meadows reconstruction."

"Why don't we get to that later. Stay home." He looked at his watch. "I've got to go. You good?"

I nodded. "Go. Call me when you've set things up."

"We'll talk soon."

Dave raced through the deluge to his car and tossed the plastic bag on the seat beside him. After cranking up the heat, he headed toward the highway. On one hand, it did seem as if someone were playing mind games with Gwen, but she seemed obsessed with the whole Mormon thing. Her last comment about Joseph Smith and her reconstruction was bizarre. He should give her a call and ask if she had any meds left over from her visits with the shrink. Traffic was light, so he pulled out his cell phone and scrolled through the numbers until he found Gwen's. Catching a blur of movement, he snapped his head left. The window filled with the towering chrome grill of a careening truck.

CHAPTER
TWELVE

THE STORM PASSED QUICKLY. WATERY SUNSHINE peered through the clouds and cast a jaundiced glow into the kitchen. I picked up the top package from the small stack by the door to carry to my studio. When I turned, Aynslee stood in the doorway.

I couldn't help staring at my daughter. Her long ginger hair fanned out from her face in spiral curls. Her skin alabaster, her figure slender. Her size zero jeans hugged her almost non-existent waist, and a sleeveless T-shirt barely covered her navel. The tiny, silver nose ring was the only hint of her ongoing rebellion. She was beautiful, and I desperately wanted to hug her and tell her that everything would be fine, that her world, and mine, would be the way it used to be. I wanted to lie.

She sniffed, blew her nose, then said, "Sorry."

I debated sending her back to her room until her apology

sounded genuine. I decided to let it go for now. "Do you want to talk about it?"

"I guess."

I put the boxes down and pulled out a kitchen chair, but before I could sit, a car pulled up next to the house. Aynslee rushed to the door before I could say anything and charged outside. I followed.

Beth slipped from her silver Sequoia, followed by Winston. The dog beelined for the nearest tree. Beth brushed the dog hair from her navy slacks, straightened her khaki jacket, then removed her sunglasses and placed them into a leather case. "I had to wait until Norm left for his fishing trip. You know, he really would have canceled it for you."

"I know." I squeezed her arm.

She waved at Aynslee. "Aynslee! I'm so glad you're home. And I must say you look pulchritudinous today."

"I do not!" Aynslee said.

"Oh dear." Beth frowned. "That was my word of the day. It means beautiful."

"Oh." Aynslee shoved a strand of hair off her face. "Mom got fired."

I stiffened.

"I know. She told me."

"Come on in." I stopped and looked at Beth. "You didn't, by the way, see anyone driving a blue pickup on your way over?"

"This is Montana. Everyone drives a pickup. But no, I didn't notice."

I turned. Aynslee shot past us toward the dog. "Aynslee, come into the house and please bring Winston with you. Dave's calling for a tracking dog, and I don't need Winston to muck things up." Winston and Aynslee tussled a bit before she paused, shrugged, and grabbed Winston's collar.

Beth trailed me into my studio, formerly a screened-in porch, occupying the entire north end of the house. Large windows on three sides provided perfect light for watercolor painting, with the fourth wall a floor-to-ceiling bookshelf. I'd always dreamed of being a full-time artist, and Robert surprised me eight years ago with my own room. He knew me so well then that he'd even chosen a functional, melamine-surfaced drafting table and chair and a matching sculpture stand. I would have preferred the warmth of wood now, but I didn't have the funds to replace them. Near the bookshelves, my "thinking spot," a cozy, floral-covered, wingback chair—my addition to the room—invited me to sit for a spell. I crossed to the corner built-in computer desk.

"You must catch me up on this case." Beth took the wing-back chair.

"Well . . ."

"And no holding back. Remember, you gave me sidekick status. Robin to your Batman and all that."

I narrowed my eyes. "You're not doing this so you can wear a costume?"

Beth waved her hand as if wiping away the vision. "Hardly. I have an idea what you'd look like in spandex."

"Ouch!"

"I couldn't resist. Anyway, I love doing research, and I have some interesting facts to share."

"Okay, you start."

Beth crossed her legs and plucked a dog hair off her neatly creased pants. "No, you lead."

I thought for a moment. "I need to make a phone call and update an FBI agent on the events. How about you listen in?"

"Excellent. No duplication of effort."

Aynslee wandered in with Winston. The dog slumped on his bed in the corner, and Aynslee joined him, using the Pyrenees as a large, hairy pillow.

I picked up the phone and dialed.

"Mike Brown."

His voice left me tongue-tied for a moment.

"Hello?" He sounded impatient.

"Oh, hi, Mike. It's me. Gwen. Gwen Marcey."

"Hi there, Gwen. I was just thinking about you."

A warm flush crept up my neck. I turned so Beth and Aynslee wouldn't see. "I've had a couple of things happen that I thought you should know about." I told him about the hand.

A slight gasp made me turn. Beth's mouth was open, and Aynslee sat straight up in the corner.

I nodded at Beth and made a writing motion in the air. Beth opened her purse, pulled out a small lavender pad of paper, and started writing furiously.

I spoke slower so Beth could keep up. I covered the resemblance between my sculpture and Jane Doe's photograph of the death mask.

Aynslee stood and peeked out the window.

"—and Zion, and Adam-on-something, and someone with the proper keys." I finished, then held my breath, hoping Mike wouldn't think I was crazy.

"You think the murders are connected by an unknown object?"

"Yes."

"This might be the break we've been waiting for." He spoke faster. "You need to stay put and lay low until I can put something together. Did you order the skulls recast?"

"Yes, they're here. But Bentley fired me. I'll have to send them back."

"The FBI just hired you to finish the one you think looks like Smith."

I sank into my drafting chair. "What did you just say?" I glanced at Beth and mouthed the words, "He's offering me a job!"

Beth mouthed, "Yeah!"

"Why?" I asked.

"Bait. Maybe we can lure these killers out of hiding."

"Killers? Do you think there's more than one?"

"I don't know."

I glanced at Aynslee. "Are we safe?"

"I'm on my way, but, you know, you shouldn't leave your house."

"But I can't do the reconstruction without more clay. I need to get to the art store in Missoula to buy more."

"No. Don't drive anywhere. I'll get what you need."

"Okay. I'll need about eight pounds of clay to be safe. Oil-based, nonhardening. In a Caucasian flesh color or combination of colors that I can mix."

"Will do. You know, I'm looking forward to seeing this reconstruction."

I shook my head slightly. Mike just said several "you knows." That meant something he just told me was a sensitive topic. What was the man concealing? "Uh . . . Mike, if we're not in any danger, why do I need to stay here? It's really not any problem to get the clay myself."

He didn't speak for a moment. "You should understand what's happening. The ring you saw on George with the flag and wings belongs to a domestic terrorist group called the Avenging Angels. They leave it as a signature of their handiwork."

"Avenging Angels?"

Beth let out a squeak.

"I'll explain when I see you." Mike hung up.

I looked at my friend. "Well?"

"That was what I wanted to tell you. My research."

"I didn't ask you to look into anything."

Beth stood. "I know. But all this started at Mountain Meadows, so I did some research. I came across the name Avenging Angels."

"So—"

"They're responsible for the Mountain Meadows Massacre. Brigham Young's secret death squad."

Dave shoved the airbag away from his face. Blood pooled below him. *Blood?* He shook his head and more blood dripped into the growing puddle. *I'm upside down. Accident.* The seat belt suspended him above the crumpled ceiling of the car. His leg pounded like a jackhammer. Smelling gasoline, he turned the engine off.

"Hey, are you okay?" Cascading dirt and rocks marked the descent of a Good Samaritan. "Hold on. I'm almost there." More dust filtered through the broken window, then two khaki-clad legs appeared. "I called 911. They should be here any minute."

"Thanks." Dave braced one hand above him and reached for the seat belt release. He briefly glimpsed the man's face, then the muzzle of a gun.

I sank into my chair, trying to figure how an eighteen hundreds death squad fit into a present-day series of murders. I simply didn't know enough, and I was heartily tired of looking like a deranged idiot when I tried to explain. I nodded at the desk computer. "Beth, as my new sidekick, I'm officially appointing you deputy in charge of research. I need help so I can present a coherent case when everyone converges here."

"Who's coming?" Aynslee asked.

"Deputy Howell and Agent Mike Brown. Dave's following up on the missing hand and will call in a tracking dog—"

"Winston tracks, after a fashion," Beth said.

"People. And he knocks them down." I glanced at the dozing mound of white fur. "Mike hired me to work on the one skull. I need a few things from the car, then we'll get to work."

"What task do you want me to perform?" Beth launched to her feet.

"Mike mentioned bait. If he's going to make the case that the skull I reconstructed was Joseph Smith, I need to know more about the man. Would you look up where Smith was supposed to be buried? Aynslee, come with me." I called Winston to heel, and we stepped out just as the sun dipped behind the mountains, pitching the valley into cobalt-blue shadows. Winston would be our early-warning system if someone lurked in the woods. Aynslee helped me unpack the car.

"You acted funny when you talked to that guy." Aynslee paused, arms full of boxes of art supplies.

"What guy?"

"Mike." She looked down and then to her left. "Don't you still love Dad?"

A blast furnace scorched my head, and I leaned against the car until it passed. The sweat rapidly cooled me. I shivered.

Aynslee waited until I took a deep breath, then asked again, "Well? Don't you still love Dad?"

"I'll always love your dad because of you. The man on the phone, Mike, is a law enforcement colleague. I don't know him personally. Come on, let's get this stuff into the house."

Aynslee didn't move. Her lower lip pooched slightly.

A breeze ruffled the pines, the branches writhing like black fingers. Winston stopped, sniffed a bush, and gazed toward the trees.

I shivered again. "Come on." I slammed the trunk and called Winston. Aynslee dawdled for a moment, then sauntered behind us. I shut the door and locked it. We moved the unloaded supplies into the studio. "Aynslee, would you bring me the rest of the boxes from the kitchen?"

She nodded. "Yeah, but I'm hungry."

"One thing at a time," I said.

Beth held up a notebook. "This is too strange. Give me a minute. I'm almost done."

"But I'm hungry!" Aynslee said louder, eyes narrowing.

I clenched my teeth, then made an effort to relax. I loved my daughter, but some days I really didn't like her. "Okay. Pull a pizza out of the freezer and preheat the oven. Then move the packages." Aynslee left. "What did you learn, Beth?"

"Teenagers, so challenging." She read a few more moments. "Mmm. Yes. Interesting."

I resisted the urge to throw a pencil at her head. "What did you *find*?"

"You don't have to be grumpy."

"Sorry. As you said, teenagers. Not to mention my own crazed hormones."

"Your request was to find out where Joseph Smith was buried." Beth tucked a stray hair behind her ear. "The first question we need to ask is: Which time?"

"Which time what?"

"Was he interred. My research led me to some Mormon websites. I've cut and pasted some of the pertinent info into a Word document. A mob murdered Joseph and his brother, Hyrum, in 1844, but the Mormon leaders were afraid someone would disturb the remains, so for the public burial, they filled the caskets with sand. They concealed the bodies in the unfinished dirt floor of the Nauvoo. Six months later members of the church unearthed and reburied them."

"Where?"

"That's where it gets very weird." She scrolled down her notes. "Here it is. Let me read you a quote from *Doctrine and Covenants*, one of their holy books."

Beth was beating around that ole bush again. I picked up a lead holder and lead pointer, then began to sharpen the tip. It kept me from hurling the pencil at her.

"'Joseph Smith, the Prophet and Seer of the Lord, has done more, save Jesus only, for the salvation of men in this world, than any other man that ever lived in it.'"

"Okay. So he was revered." I kept spinning the lead pointer.

"By 1928, they forgot where they buried him."

"What?"

"Apparently the Mormons didn't know where he was interred. They *believed* he was laid to rest somewhere on the Smith family homestead in Nauvoo, Illinois."

"You'd think they'd build a shrine over his grave," I said.

"There wasn't *anything*. By the turn of the last century, the place was deteriorating, overgrown, and occupied by tenants."

"Like nobody cared."

"Indeed." Beth massaged her arm, then continued, "The contrast is certainly bizarre. If you read their writings, they adored him, almost worshiped him, but it's as if the Mormons no longer felt him significant enough to mark his resting place."

"Or it wasn't where he was actually buried," I said slowly. "Is there more?"

"Yes, but this was part of what I researched while you were driving home. The Reorganized Church of Latter Day Saints—"

"Sorry. What's that?"

"They now call themselves the Community of Christ. After Joseph Smith's death, the church split," Beth said. "In fact, at one time or another, followers formed more than a hundred splinter groups. The largest segment went to Salt Lake City with Brigham Young. They are technically called LDS. A much smaller flock stayed faithful to Emma, Joseph's first wife, eventually making Joseph's son, Joseph Smith III, their prophet."

"When was that?" I asked.

"I don't know. Is it important?"

"Maybe. Find out. Anyway . . ." I waved my hand for her to continue.

"The RLDS Church-owned homestead was on the Mississippi

River, and the newly constructed dams made the river rise. No one was sure exactly how high the river would go, so after over eighty years, they decided to locate and move the bodies of Joseph and his brother, Hyrum."

"Reasonable."

"Another reason they wanted to locate the bodies was because mainstream Mormons believed Joseph's body was in Utah."

"Really! How did you get that piece of information?"

"From their own church history books, which I accessed online," she said.

My skin entertained a party of goose pimples.

"By 1928, the RLDS Church hired a surveyor, a luminary in their church named W. O. Hands, to find the bodies. The crew began digging on January ninth. They quickly found Emma's body, although she wasn't buried near her marker. Six days and a maze of trenches later, they uncovered two male bodies. They excavated the remains, photographed the skulls, and reburied them, this time in marked graves." She looked at me. "I thought we were getting somewhere until I read that. I guess it's just a coincidence that the sculpture and death mask look alike."

"Think critically, Beth," I said.

"I beg your pardon. I just did."

"No. What do we know for sure? That the surveyor found two male bodies."

"Yes."

"The surveyor was a high poo-bah with the church. Of course he'd believe it was Joseph and Hyrum—"

"Because that's who they were looking for." Beth nodded.

Aynslee checked on the pizza, then turned to the small pile of packages. The top one was from the casting company. The next from an art supply place. Dad said Mom spent too much money. No wonder he left.

She brought the two packages into the studio. "Pizza in ten." Both women nodded.

Aynslee returned to the kitchen for the final load. The smell of melting cheese made her mouth water. A small box lay on its side next to the remaining parcels. She picked it up and was about to place it on top of the packages when she caught the name: Ethan Scott. It was sent from Utah.

Ethan Scott? Did her mom have a boyfriend? Didn't she just say she loved Dad? It made her sick thinking about some dude sending her mom a gift. Dad wouldn't ever want to come home if Mom was seeing someone else. It was a good thing she found this first.

It was disgusting. *Mom is old. And bald. And doesn't have any boobs, even.* Aynslee's face grew warm, and she whispered, "I'm sorry." That was a mean thought. Her mom was pretty enough when she wore her blond wig, and nobody could tell she didn't have boobs.

Aynslee rattled the box. No sound.

Mom said she was fired from her job, but maybe she had a fight with this guy and that's why he was sending her something. What if he wanted her to go back to Utah? *Would I have to go back to Selkirk?* Dumped like a mutt at a dog pound.

Well, if her mom didn't receive it, then she'd stay mad at him. No Utah. No school.

Aynslee dropped the box into the trash.

She walked back to the oven and peeked in. Almost ready. She shifted the final packages into the studio. Beth and her mom were busy talking and didn't even look over at her.

Aynslee returned to the kitchen and her gaze drifted to the garbage can. What if her mom saw the box when she went to throw something away? She plucked it out.

She slipped down the hall to her room. She'd hide Ethan's gift until she could figure out what to do with it.

"So, if they dug up Smith's body in 1928, they wouldn't have conducted any forensic tests," Beth said. "They just looked at the bones, took pictures, and reburied the remains. By the way, what's a Le Fort fracture?"

"I don't know."

"Anyway, if the skull you reconstructed is based on the real Joseph Smith, they could clear this all up by conducting a DNA test, right?"

"Well, the LDS Church and Mountain Meadows Society have access to the bones. They're not going to perform any tests without proof." I rubbed my neck.

Just then the phone rang.

I looked at Beth and walked to the cordless.

"Gwen, this is Craig Harnisch. Dave's been shot."

CHAPTER
THIRTEEN

I CLUNG TO THE PHONE, UNABLE TO SPEAK FOR
a moment. Finally, I squeaked, "Is he . . ."

"Alive? Yeah. Hanging on. They're transporting him to
Missoula," Craig said.

"Wh-what happened?"

"We're investigating. Someone saw his overturned car down
by the creek. Called it in. Dave was unconscious, covered in
blood. Wasn't until they pulled him from the wreck that they
noticed the bullet hole in his head."

"His *head*?" I whispered.

Beth drew near me and placed her hand on my shoulder.
"Who?" she mouthed.

"Dave." I closed my eyes and tried to concentrate on Craig's
voice.

"Anyway, Andrea's with him. Wanted me to call you."

"Dave was here! They saw him. Maybe they thought he had something—"

"Gwen."

"Dave saw the hand! Well, he didn't really see it, but the Avenging Angels did this—"

"Gwen! Stop it."

"The drawing. I put my composite sketch in a box. Maybe they thought—"

"Who is 'they'? You're sounding like a conspiracy nut."

"Did you find a box in Dave's car?"

"No. Listen, Dave has made plenty of enemies just being sheriff. Until he's out of the woods, I'm in charge, and I have my hands full without you going off on some rabbit trail." He disconnected.

Beth pried the buzzing phone from my hand and set it down. *Dave's shot, maybe dying.* A brick formed in my throat. Dave's family took me in when I was scarcely older than Aynslee. He was a brother to me.

"I said, what are you going to do now?" Beth asked.

"About Dave? I could go to the hospital and wait with his wife. But what if my giving Dave the package caused the shooting? That would mean someone is watching this place."

Aynslee strolled into the room drinking a Mountain Dew. She flipped on the overhead lights. "Why are you guys sitting in the dark?"

I raced to the switch and plunged the room back into darkness, then charged from window to window, cranking the blinds shut.

"What?" Aynslee asked.

"Now you can turn on the lights." I rubbed my sweaty hands together. "Sit down and listen."

"That's the buzzer. The pizza's ready." Aynslee sprinted from the studio.

"Don't tell her about Dave. Not just yet," Beth said. "Her world's pretty unsettled right now. Can you contact Robert?"

I shook my head. "If they're watching us, we need help." I picked up the phone and called Deputy Howell. No answer. "I'll try Craig again."

"What are you going to tell him? Mormon Avenging Angels are watching your house? He'll never believe anything negative you say about the Mormons. Or about Joseph Smith. His entire family is LDS."

I blinked. "Really? How do you know that?"

Beth fingered the computer keyboard. "Okay. Confession time."

I slowly selected a pencil and began sharpening. "Go on."

"I joined the Mormon Church when I was twenty-three. I quit a year later."

I tilted my head to show I was listening but continued to work on the pencil point.

"It's a protracted story, but I know how they think. Most mainstream Mormons don't know the real church history. I never did. They are encouraged to read only church-approved, faith-promoting materials. Technically, they've rewritten their own history anyway."

"What do you mean?"

Beth read her notes from the computer screen. "To quote Brigham Young, 'I commenced revising'—note he didn't say writing—'the history of Joseph Smith at Brother Richards' office.' That's just one of numerous examples of Brigham Young admitting he changed history."

"Where did you find that?"

"Ironically, in *History of the Church*. My point, however, is anything you say to Craig will be considered Mormon bashing. You won't find much help in your deputy."

I put down the pencil and sharpener, then picked up the phone and dialed.

"Mike Brown."

"I need help. Someone shot Sheriff Dave Moore. I told Deputy Craig Harnisch, who's in charge of the investigation, about the events at Mountain Meadows, the hand, the possible missing item of Jane Doe's. He doesn't believe me. I don't have anywhere to turn."

Mike didn't speak for a moment. "Things could be accelerating."

"What do you mean?" I switched the phone to my other ear and wiped my damp palm on my jeans.

"Where was Dave when he was shot?"

"He was on his way into town. In his car. Why?"

"Was he alone?"

"Yes."

"Hmm. The assaults on Jane Doe, George, and your sheriff all had one thing in common. No one else was with them. Are you—"

"No. My fourteen-year-old daughter, my best friend, and my dog are here."

"Good. Keep together. Anyone with ties to the LDS Church, or a fundamentalist offshoot, is potentially connected to the Avenging Angels."

"You think the main church is—"

"I didn't say that. I just want you to be careful."

I thought about Craig. And Prophet Kenyon. *Great.* I gave Kenyon my business card. Complete with address and phone number.

"I don't want to talk anymore on a cell phone. I'll be there as fast as I can."

"Thank you."

"Keep your friend with you for tonight, lock up tight, and don't answer the door, no matter who it is, until I get there."

I hung up the phone, then peeked through the blinds. Only my reflection peered back. Someone out there wanted me dead, and glass would hardly stop a bullet. The faceless Avenging Angels were already here, in Copper Creek. They had to be. They shot Dave. They could be right outside—

Winston shot to his feet.

I spun.

Aynslee, mouth full, offered Winston a piece of her pizza. The dog opened his jaws just wide enough for her to slip the tidbit between his teeth, like feeding a quarter into a vending machine.

"What is it?" Beth stared at my face.

Beth. If they knew Dave had been with me, they knew Beth was here. I'd put her in danger. "Ah, can you call your husband?"

She looked at her watch. "I can try, but I suspect his cell is out of range. Why?"

"Well . . ." I glanced at Aynslee, then Beth. She nodded. "I think it would be lots of fun if we had a girls' night."

Beth's eyes narrowed, but she went along with me. "Is that why you wanted me to contact Norm? Not to worry." She turned to Aynslee. "How fun! We'll have a sleepover."

Aynslee stopped eating, shrugged, then gave Winston another bite. "Whatever."

"Please don't feed Winston any more pizza. We don't need him to get diarrhea." I thought about walking the dog outside in the darkness and shivered.

Winston's attention, initially focused on the impromptu snack, waned when the last bit of food disappeared between Aynslee's lips. He drifted over to inspect the pile of supplies we'd unloaded from the trunk.

"I'll need to borrow some pj's—" Beth stopped. "What's Winston got in his mouth?"

The Pyrenees apparently found a canine treasure in my art materials. He was sneaking out of the room, a stained placard protruding from his mouth. I recognized the mounted label I'd inadvertently kept from Mountain Meadows. Winston had removed it from my sketchpad.

Aynslee caught his collar and pried it out. "What's this?"

"Throw it away," I said. "There could be blood on it, so wash your hands. It's from the display case."

"It's a bunch of weird names."

"Those are the seventeen surviving children from the Mountain Meadows Massacre."

Aynslee examined the piece, lips moving. "Eighteen."

"What?"

"There are eighteen names."

CHAPTER
FOURTEEN

I COULDN'T SLEEP. THE WIND BLUSTERED THROUGH the trees outside, branches scraping against the windows. Dave's attack played out like a movie in my overactive brain. I pictured him helpless in his car while a killer took careful aim at his face.

Beth stretched out under a quilt on the living room sofa. I'd checked on Aynslee and found her wrapped around a pillow and snoozing. Only the computer screen illuminated the studio. A jumble of papers blanketed the desk. I'd transferred my notes from the Mountain Meadows break-in, and the interview with the Kenyons, onto a yellow legal pad. I'd added Beth's research into Smith's bizarre burial and the names of the eighteen children.

Tapping a pencil, I scrolled down the web page, stopping to read or jot a note. The grandfather clock in the hall bonged four times before I'd finished. Somewhere in all this information was a key to the Avenging Angels. More importantly, maybe a clue to their next move. I didn't want to hide out the rest of my life until they decided I wasn't a threat. Or in possession of . . . what?

Aynslee kept her eyes shut and pretended to sleep. She waited until her mom had quietly shut the door before rolling over. Moonlight peered through the blinds and formed stripes on the ceiling.

She fingered the package next to the bed.

She should just send the box back to the guy who sent it: Ethan Scott. Write, *No one at this address.*

'Course, he could just show up. Then what? Maybe she could hide it.

She crossed to the closet and pulled out her old school backpack. After tucking the package in the bottom, she stuffed a notebook and T-shirt on top, then slid the backpack under the bed. Not a great place, but she'd move it in the morning.

The faceless man chased me. I ran, but my legs were molasses, slogging through the underbrush. Behind me, his shoes slapped against the pavement, growing closer, closer—

I screamed. Hands grabbed me, and I screamed again.

"Gwen, wake up! It's me. Wake up!"

Beth's voice, then her words, reached me. I opened my eyes. Beth, eyebrows furrowed, stood beside me. On the other side,

Winston pressed against me. The doctor said the nightmares from my last unsolved case would pass. He didn't say when. "Sorry. I didn't mean to wake you."

"I was already up."

I nodded and peeked at the clock. I'd slept four hours. My notes and papers lay scattered on the floor. I bent to pick them up.

"You're soaking wet," Beth said.

"Cancer leftovers. Would you hand me that tablet?"

She passed it to me. "You told me about this. Estrogen positive breast cancer."

"Yeah. Way fun. I've been on antihormone drugs. So, early menopause and night sweats."

She studied my face.

"What?" I asked.

"Just seeing if you're growing a mustache."

"Ha. Very funny. I did buy season hockey tickets and a lifetime supply of beer and beef jerky." I lightly punched her arm. "I'm going to take a shower."

"Good," Beth said. "I've made coffee."

It didn't take much time to shower and get ready. I checked my eyelids carefully. A thin line along the edge promised the growth of eyelashes. Finally. I tugged on my wig, applied a moderate amount of makeup, and followed my nose to the kitchen. Beth had apparently done more than turn on the coffeepot. The worn linoleum gleamed with a new coat of floor polish. I opened the cupboard for a mug and found new shelving paper under the crockery. "You cleaned?"

"I needed something to do. Didn't want to wake you by working in your studio, so I started to alphabetize your spice drawer, but they're all outdated. You need to throw them out."

Before I could think of a suitable response, Winston alerted, then dashed to the door, barking.

My heart sped up. "Hope it's the good guys." I looked out the window.

Mike Brown emerged from a black Chevy Tahoe. Instead of the traditional Hoover blue suit and tie, he wore sharply creased, charcoal slacks, a thin-striped blue shirt, and a herringbone sports coat. He reached into the backseat and tugged out a black garbage bag, then approached the house.

I opened the door and tried not to stare. Winston pushed past me. Mike's eyes widened at the dog. "Hello there." He offered his fingers for Winston to sniff. Winston looked at me for direction. I shrugged. The dog sat and politely offered an immense paw. Mike took it and pumped once.

I let Mike into the kitchen while Winston inspected, then watered, the SUV's tires. I waited until he'd finished his business before calling him back in.

"You must be the FBI agent," Beth said.

"Mike Brown, and yes, FBI. You must be Mrs. Noble."

"Call me Beth."

"Beth. Good to see you again, Gwen. This young lady must be Aynslee."

Hair tangled, still dressed in a nightshirt, Aynslee froze at the sight of the stranger. "Are you—"

I frowned at her. "Who did you think he was?"

She retreated several steps into the hall.

"Well, Aynslee, my name is Mike, and I work for the FBI. I'm here to make sure you're safe, and to drop off some work I'm having your mother do."

Aynslee retreated to her bedroom and shut the door.

Mike shrugged, then handed me the garbage bag. Inside was a second clear plastic bag with a large block of cream clay.

I made a face. "Where did you get this?"

"I . . . sort of borrowed it from my sister's kids."

"You brought me eight pounds of some kind of Crayola clay?"

"Hey, it was all I could find on short notice. They'd bought it for a science project, then didn't do the project. The price was right."

"Well." I looked at the clay again. At least the cream color would be similar to the death mask. I placed the bag on the kitchen table just as my stomach rumbled. "Sorry. Have you had breakfast?" I asked him.

"I don't know why you're offering a meal," Beth said. "You don't have any food in the house, remember?" Beth politely refrained from pointing out I was also the worst cook in Ravalli County.

Mike slowly checked out my kitchen. I tried to see it through his eyes. The decor was too new to be antique, too old to be charming. Avocado-colored appliances weren't back in vogue. I wanted to hurry him into the living room, but it was more of the same, with the addition of dust. He glanced at his watch. "Gwen, how fast can you do the reconstruction?"

"With sculpting neck and shoulders—"

"No. Just the head and maybe neck. Make him younger, thirties, and without a scar."

"That'll speed me up quite a bit. I guess I could do it in a long day. Let me take some notes." I picked up the bag and trotted it to the studio, returning with a sketchpad and pencil. Doodling my thoughts always helped me focus.

Beth sat at the table hanging on Mike's every word. Winston sprawled like a hairy island in the middle of the floor. I joined Beth.

Mike looked at my friend. "Ah, I appreciate you spending the night, Beth. If you need to leave or have work to do, you are free to go."

"Beth is my partner," I said. "I need her here."

Beth's face turned pink. "Thank you," she mouthed to me.

"Okay then. We've tracked the domestic terrorist group Avenging Angels for years." He glanced at his watch. "But haven't been able to infiltrate them, which would make us proactive—"

"Excuse me, but why is that important?" Beth asked.

"If we can anticipate their next move, we can take steps to prevent it. The two murders, Jane Doe and George Higbee, might not have happened if we'd known more."

"So they *are* connected." I sketched angel wings, then a big question mark. "I speculated that Jane Doe might have been meeting George or delivering something. Ethan told me Jane Doe gave him some personal items but didn't say what they were."

"And I think you're right," Mike said. "Deputy Howell sent me a copy of your interview with the Kenyons, Gwen. Nice work, by the way."

I bent my head over my sketches to cover my blush.

"I'm working on the premise that Jane Doe stole something from a fundamentalist group," Mike continued. "Took Rebekah's identity, and went into hiding."

"She stole money? Jewelry?" Beth asked.

"I was thinking more along the lines of something connected to the Mormon Church or Joseph Smith," Mike said.

"The involvement of the Avenging Angels points to a Mormon connection."

Winston flopped on his side and let out a doggie sigh.

"What on earth could be so valuable that people have to die?" I asked.

"A first edition of the Book of Mormon can sell for more than a hundred thousand dollars," Beth said. "Actually, anything written by Joseph Smith would be very valuable."

Mike continued, "Later, for whatever reason, she could decide to sell it or use it for blackmail."

I pictured Jane Doe's kind face. Somehow I didn't picture her as a blackmailer. I circled the angel wings on my sketchpad, then drew an open mouth with fangs about to bite the wings. "I'm not sure I'm buying the blackmail angle. Was she selling it to George? He was just a security guard."

"Yes," Mike said. "But he was in the right place at the right time to meet with Jane Doe and not be suspicious. And he was a Mormon."

"So the LDS Church is involved." Beth scratched her head.

"Well . . ." Mike pulled out a chair, sat, and grabbed my pencil and paper. "Let me illustrate." He drew two circles, then wrote, *LDS Church* in the first circle and *Fundamentalist LDS* in the second. "This is a huge simplification of what could be happening. I'm lumping the fundamentalists into one circle, but there are many subgroups within here, and they don't exactly all get along. Now, both these groups"—he tapped the circles— "could be interested in Jane Doe's treasure if it relates to Joseph Smith." He placed a big *X* between the two circles. "And the main LDS Church and the fundamentalists hate each other."

"Why?" Beth asked.

"Quite simply, each thinks they have the true teachings of their prophet, Smith," Mike said. "So both have a motive to try to gain whatever Jane Doe was selling or delivering."

"Okay," Beth said.

"So we have to look at what happened to the girl and Higbee. It's the fundamentalists who have a recent history of violence, and the Avenging Angels are probably acting as the hit squad for one of those groups." He tapped the fundamentalist circle.

I thought for a moment. "The severed hand? I told Dave I thought placing then removing the hand was meant to make me look crazy."

Mike peered out the window. "There's another message here. Removing George's hand could be a graphic way of saying they see him as a thief, and sending it to you may mean they think you have their treasure—"

"But I don't!"

"And they're watching your house."

I needed to sketch that composite. My gaze shifted to the closed blinds, and I shivered.

"Did you have any contact with Ethan Scott, the boyfriend of Jane Doe?" Mike asked.

"I gave him my card."

"Did you receive any packages in the last day?" he asked.

"Just my sculpting supplies and castings from FedEx. They're in the studio." I jerked my head in that direction. Mike followed me down the hall. The stack of boxes sat in the center of the room and on my drafting table where Aynslee had moved them. I sat on my stool as Mike knelt down and examined each parcel.

"What about the post office?" he finally asked.

"I haven't checked. Why?"

"Ethan was murdered after you left—"

"Oh no!" *Stupid, stupid me.* I assumed his parents would arrive, take him away. And Dave was going to follow up on Ethan.

"Would you like a drink of water?" Mike asked.

"No, no, ohmigosh." Dave was shot, and I forgot about checking on Ethan. He's dead because I forgot.

"—he would have known where to send it."

"What?" Maybe Robert was right about my pickled brain.

"I said if your business card was in his room, he might have sent something to you."

I could never trust myself again.

"Gwen, do you hear what I'm saying?" Mike asked.

"I . . . I think so."

"I'm telling you that the desk clerk spoke to Ethan about shipping something. She saw him in the business center but got busy and didn't notice if he put something in the shipping drop box. I've got someone tracking that lead, but we're running into difficulties."

"I'll call the post office." It took me several attempts to dial. No luck. This seemed to deflate Mike. We returned to the kitchen. I shook my head at Beth, then slumped at the table. "How was Ethan killed?" My question came out as an exhale. I was glad I was sitting.

"Apparently he'd stayed at the motel in Fancher waiting for his parents to pick him up," Mike said.

"He said he was waiting for his folks." My voice was a whisper. "How—"

"The same way as Jane Doe," Mike said.

"Tell me," I said.

Mike coughed. "Throat cut. Gutted."

I prayed his parents didn't find his body. My head buzzed. Whether or not Ethan sent me something, the presence of my business card could have led the Avenging Angels to believe I had their treasure.

"Can you put Gwen into protective custody?" Beth asked.

"Well, Beth, we have two choices. We can sit around and wait for the Avenging Angels to show up, or we can be proactive and have them dancing to our timetable and on our terms. We have to control the game plan here."

"A sting operation!" Beth said.

"Exactly," Mike said. "We need to set several traps and bait them."

"Ooookay." I looked back and forth between Beth's and Mike's excited faces.

Mike looked at me. "You gave me an idea when you told me about your reconstruction's resemblance to Joseph Smith."

"I can't wait to hear this," Beth said.

Mike slipped off his jacket and draped it over a kitchen chair. A Glock pistol rested in a tan leather holster attached to his belt. He paced from the table to the sink and back. "Gwen, didn't you tell me Jane Doe fainted when she saw your reconstruction?"

I blinked. "Yes."

Mike nodded. "Because she thought she was seeing Joseph Smith's actual reconstructed face. So, let's give the Avenging Angels what they want. We'll announce that two unusual treasures are going to be on display: your reconstruction of the face of Joseph Smith and a priceless artifact."

"Brilliant!" Beth said. "Using the bait of Smith's face."

I frowned at Mike. "I see at least four problems with your plan. Whoever destroyed the Mountain Meadows Center knows that the reconstruction is over plaster—"

"We'll announce the actual skull is under the clay," Mike said.

"Problem two: We don't know what the missing object is."

"You could cover something," Beth said. "With a . . . a blue velvet covering . . . and announce it will be revealed on a certain date. Like a grand unveiling."

"Excellent idea, Beth," Mike said. "On to problem three."

I stared at him a moment to see if he was mocking me. "Everyone who's studied Mormon history knows that Joseph Smith was murdered in a shootout in Illinois, not Utah."

Mike's eyes narrowed slightly. "Well then, I guess we'll have to figure out another scenario for how Smith survived and made it to Utah. The more we can focus attention away from you, and your family, the safer you'll be."

Great. My next case after cancer and chemo was to find the unfindable or prove the impossible.

"But do you really think Gwen's sculpture is Joseph Smith?" Beth asked.

"It doesn't matter what I think. That's for the Mormon Church to sort out. What's important is that the Avenging Angels believe it's Joseph Smith and that their treasure is near the reconstruction."

Aynslee, now dressed, drifted into the kitchen.

"So, I'll move on to problem four," I said. "You mentioned displaying the items—"

"What items?" Aynslee asked.

"Never— Uh, my reconstruction." I smiled at her. "Maybe you and Beth could think of someplace where we could display it, someplace where a lot of people would see it."

"That's easy," Beth said. "The Seattle Peace Conference."

Mike nodded. "An excellent suggestion. Massive media coverage."

"The organizers did put out a prospectus for an art show," I said slowly. "But this isn't art—"

"Ha! Have you seen what passes for art lately?" Beth said.

"And the deadline for entry is past," I pointed out.

"I can fix that. The FBI is already involved, with all the religious leaders, politicians, and celebrities attending."

"What's it about?" I asked.

"A putting aside of religious and political differences and celebrating American shared values," Beth said. "Remember I asked you if you would go to an event with me? I have tickets."

Mike nodded again. "Anticipated attendance of over twenty thousand."

Aynslee's curiosity loosened her tongue. "You'll show Mom's sculpture and catch 'em when they try to steal it?"

"No," Mike said. "We *want* them to steal it."

"I don't understand," Beth said.

"We don't want to just catch one or two Avenging Angels. We need to locate all of them." Mike reached in his pocket and pulled out a tiny black object. "This is a GPS tracking device. We'll plant this in the reconstruction. With all those people milling about, we'll make it an easy target."

I sketched a hand reaching for the skull. "But what if they don't take the bait?"

Crunching gravel sent Winston to the door barking. Beth, Aynslee, and I froze. Mike rested his hand on his pistol and peered through the curtains. "Do you know this person?"

I moved to the window.

Robert.

My mouth tasted of ashes. "Yes. It's my . . . ex-husband."

He let go of the pistol and opened the door.

Robert jerked to a halt.

Mike stepped away from the door.

Robert, hair artfully tousled, new porcelain veneers on his teeth, and sporting tanning-booth mahogany skin, entered and paused at the tableau. "Having a party?"

"Dad!" Aynslee launched into his arms.

I exchanged glances with Beth. "What brings you here?" My voice came out high and strangled.

"Hi to you too, Gwen." Robert held out his hand to Mike. "I don't believe we've met. Robert Marcey."

"Ah yes. The author. Mike Brown, FBI." The two men shook hands, then stepped apart. Aynslee clung to her father and seemed oblivious to the building tension.

Starting with Mike's cowboy boots, Robert's gaze slowly lifted, paused at the pistol, then ended at the other man's face. He smirked and winked at me.

I wanted to claw his eyes out.

"Well now," Robert said. "I had a break in my book tour, and I'm moving to a new condo in Bigfork. Thought I'd pick up a few things. Figured you'd still be in Utah." He didn't look at me as he spoke.

Heat seared my chest and rocketed upward. I didn't want Robert or Mike to see my face turn crimson, but I didn't want to run from the room like a spooked whippet. I spun toward the coffeepot and made a show of pouring a cup.

"Actually," Mike said, "that was our lucky break. We hired her to work on a case."

I could have kissed him.

"Really?" Robert's sarcasm permeated every syllable.

"Yes."

My face had cooled enough to casually turn and look at the two men. I wanted to confront Robert about sneaking back to the house when he thought I was gone, but Aynslee's presence made me bite my tongue. "So. What did you need here?"

Robert's eyes slid toward Aynslee, then back to me, making sure I remembered our agreement to not fight in front of our daughter. "I just need to look around. Come on, sweetheart." He headed down the hall, Aynslee in tow.

I turned, dumped out my coffee, and cleaned the grounds out of the coffeemaker, waiting for my heart rate to slow. How blind I'd been those many years ago.

Mike waited until Robert shut the office door. "You'll need to hurry, Gwen. We have a bit of a ticking clock. We'll need to get that sculpture to the conference. We need time to build up publicity. I'll figure out a story for how Smith ended up in Utah."

I thought of Robert's smirk and wink. "I'll do it."

"Do what?" Mike asked.

"I'll come up with a way for Smith to be in Utah. I'll write an exposé to go with the reconstruction."

"Oh, Gwen," Beth said. "Your reputation—"

"Is nonexistent right now." However, my reputation as a nut was clearly established.

"Good," Mike said. "Your credentials as a facial identification expert will lend authority to your article."

Beth looked at me. "But you'll be crucified by the press."

"Mike is right. If we don't come up with a proactive plan, I'll forever be looking over my shoulder." And if the Avenging Angels didn't take the bait, they'd continue to come after me. And my family. My daughter. My friends. I thought of Jane Doe's ripped body, then shook my head. "I have to make this work," I said quietly.

"You know I'll do anything to help you, but why are you so sure they'll steal the reconstruction?" Beth asked.

"If you make the Smith story good enough, of course," Mike said. "Plus the date of the Peace Conference."

"September eleventh," Beth said. "The day the Muslim terrorists attacked the US."

"Yeah." I nodded. "And the date of the Mountain Meadows Massacre."

CHAPTER
FIFTEEN

MIKE RETURNED TO HIS CAR AND BROUGHT IN a black, FBI-embroidered messenger bag. Inside were a laptop, files, and spiral notebooks. He commandeered the kitchen table and immediately booted up the computer.

I moved to the studio. After finding a box knife, I opened the shipment with the skull casting, placed it on my sculpture stand, then slipped onto the drafting chair. Slivers of golden sunlight striped the studio floor through the half-closed blinds. They looked like prison bars.

Jane Doe flickered across my mind. The Avenging Angels showed no mercy. Their holy grail had to mean so much to them that murder was reasonable. I *had* to make both the sculpture, and Smith's presence in Mountain Meadows, believable.

Before I started on the reconstruction, I called Craig.

"I always knew Dave was hardheaded," Craig said. "He

must have ducked at the last moment. The bullet hit his head at an angle, wrapped around under the skin, then exited the other side. He has a bad concussion, fractured tibia, and cracked ribs."

"But he'll live?"

"Yeah."

"Is he awake?"

"Off and on. No memory and no witnesses have come forward. No evidence other than the bullet."

"Can I see him?"

"Not yet. I'll let you know."

After we hung up, I cradled the phone in my hands. The dial tone buzzed at me like an angry wasp. *Dave's going to live.*

I cried. Not a teeny, ladylike flutter of tears. I gave in to a good old-fashioned deluge of boohoos. I hugged myself and rocked until the squall passed, leaving hiccups and snorts. A box of tissues appeared and I tugged out a handful.

Beth gently set the box next to me. "I'm afraid to ask."

"Dave's going to live."

Beth strolled to my desk and made a show of rearranging papers. "Your wracking lament is over Dave's survival?"

"Sometimes a person just needs a good cry." I blew my nose.

"Could seeing Robert . . ."

"That too. He's like dropping a blob of screaming phthalo green onto the middle of a finished portrait."

"Oh. That's bad?"

I grunted and blew my nose again. "So much for your 'everything happens for a reason.' What reason is there for Dave to be shot?"

Beth sat at the desk. "I don't know the answer, Gwen," she

said quietly. "But if in your lifetime you find out why something bad happened, it's a blessing."

"Yeah, okay."

"Do you want to be alone right now?"

"No. We've got work to do." And a strong motive. My life and the lives of anyone close to me.

Beth grinned. "How exciting! My first case. Where do I begin? Do you think it will eventually involve litigation?"

"It is. Yes. Research. I don't know."

The smile vanished. "Why do you always answer like that?"

"I'm teaching you not to ask compound questions." I chucked the tissue into the garbage. "Okay, we need a believable story about how Joseph Smith ended up in Utah."

"I'll start with his death in Carthage, Illinois."

Beth set to work as I rummaged through the supplies for the reconstruction materials. A tackle box held a set of precut tissue depth markers, nothing more than electric eraser refills with inked numbers on one end. I measured the nasal aperture, teeth, and nasal spine, then recorded the numbers. Using a chart designed for a European male, I glued the markers on the casting. We worked at our projects for an hour, the only sounds the clicks of the keyboard and mouse.

Finally, Beth read from the computer screen. "Here's the official account. On June 27, 1844, Joseph Smith was incarcerated—"

"Whoa, stop right there. He was arrested?"

"That would be a logical conclusion, yes."

"Let me guess," I said. "Polygamy?"

"That was an underlying cause. A former member of his church owned a printing press. In his first, and only, edition, he wrote a scathing exposé of Smith's polygamous practices.

In retaliation, Smith had the Nauvoo Legion, his private army, rally. The Legion marched to the newspaper office, destroyed the press, and burned every copy of the paper."

"Ah."

"The non-Mormon residents of Hancock County were incensed at the polygamous behavior and the wanton demolition of property. With the possibility of civil war breaking out in Illinois, the governor called the Warsaw Militia to active duty and asked Smith to surrender and face trial for riot and treason."

"Ah again."

Beth glanced at me and frowned. "He originally fled, but changed his mind and surrendered to the authorities. Smith was incarcerated awaiting trial in the jail in Carthage, Illinois."

"Jail. Do you have a photo?"

"Hold on." She clattered on the keyboard for a moment. "Here. It looks a bit like a house."

I moved so I could see the screen. "This is recent. It looks like it's been restored."

"It has. The Mormon Church purchased it in 1903." She paused. "Rather an odd priority."

"What is?"

"Remember I told you the Mormons forgot where they buried Smith? They acquired this building twenty-five years before they bothered to look for Joseph Smith's body."

I glanced at the plaster skull on my stand.

"Smith wasn't in a cell," Beth continued. "They were in the jailer's bedroom upstairs. Here's a photo of the bedroom."

"Who is 'they'?"

"Oh, sorry. Smith, his older brother Hyrum, Doctor Willard Richards, who was Joseph's private secretary, and John Taylor."

John Taylor. I'd heard that name before. I closed my eyes. Frances, the woman who'd rescued me outside of Jarom, whispered in my ear, *"Prophet John Taylor had the keys to the kingdom."*

"Who, exactly, is Taylor?"

"Eventually he became the third president of the church after Brigham Young. He wrote a large part of the history of the church," Beth said.

"Thanks, sorry for the interruption. Go on."

"Apparently they were quite comfortable. They'd enjoyed a bottle of wine and smoked pipes. An earlier visitor smuggled a pistol into the jail for the Smith brothers. Something called a pepper-box revolver."

The average high school had better security. I resumed my seat at the sculpting stand.

"Now that Smith was jailed, the governor disbanded the Warsaw Militia, but the men were still incensed at the Mormon leader. At about five in the afternoon, the renegade militia surrounded the jail. To hide their identities, they'd blackened their faces with mud mixed with gunpowder."

"Mud and gunpowder? Strange combination."

"Maybe the mud alone wasn't enough."

"Or they wanted an explosive reaction to their disguise." I snorted at my pun.

Beth stared at me.

"Never mind." My mirth disappeared as I pictured the scene. One pistol against a hoard of men looking like demons.

"Hello?" Beth asked. "Are you okay?"

"Yeah. Just thinking."

"Well then. Some of the militia rushed the stairs, shooting wildly."

"Do you have a photograph or diagram of the layout of the jail?"

"Sure." Beth pointed at the computer. I crossed the room and peered over her shoulder. "The stairs and upper hall are open to the floor below." She traced the outline on the screen. "The hall is about three and a half feet wide."

"Hmm." I wandered back to my sculpting stand. "The mob probably had muskets. Lots of noise, smoke, confusion. And in that narrow hallway, the men wouldn't be able to stand close together because of the side blast of those guns. Plus, they have to reload after every shot."

"You're so erudite about guns."

"Yeah. That's me."

"All four men ran to the door to hold it closed, but the latch didn't work. The militia first fired through the closed door. Startled, the men inside leaped away. The second bullet struck Hyrum in the face, and he fell to the floor, dead. Joseph stuck his hand through the opening and discharged his pistol at the men in the hallway. Three bullets found their mark, but three misfired."

"Found their mark? Did Smith kill someone?"

"Let's see. Several sources report two men were killed."

"Okay." I smoothed the clay on the cheeks. "Go on."

"John Taylor was the next to go down. He rushed to the window opposite the door and attempted to climb out. He was hit several times by gunfire, gravely wounding him, and ended up taking refuge under the bed."

"Where are Joseph and Doctor Richards at this point?" I asked.

"Willard Richards stood by the door with a walking cane,

which he used to whack muskets shoved through the opening. Joseph Smith stood beside him."

I pictured the room Beth had shown me. Something tugged at the edge of my brain. "I need to know the exact eyewitness wording for what happened next."

Beth moved the mouse around until she'd found what she was looking for. "About ten years after the murders, John Taylor wrote—"

"Stop there." I paused from my work. "Ten years later? Wasn't Taylor shot and hiding under the bed?"

"Yessss," Beth said slowly.

"Not much you can see from under a bed. We need eyewitness testimony, not hearsay."

"Yes. Right."

"Did Willard Richards give an account?"

"Richards said Joseph ran across the room to the same window Taylor had tried to jump from. He was struck twice by bullets shot from the door. He fell outward, saying, 'Oh Lord, my God!' Richards stuck his head out and saw Smith land on his left side."

I added strips of clay across the frontal bone, wrapping them around the supraorbital process. "Interesting."

"That's not helpful."

"Sorry. Describe Richards."

"Hmm." Beth clicked on the keyboard. "He was substantial, weighing nearly three hundred pounds. Why do you want to know that?"

The elusive thought crystalized in my brain. I stood, wiped my hands on my jeans, grabbed up a sketchpad, and began drawing. "Come here."

Beth joined me at my drafting table.

"Here's the room. The door is here and window here. According to the photos you showed me, a bed flanked the window on the right, and a desk and chair on the left."

"Okay."

"Smith proved that he was armed by shooting at the mob. The mob doesn't know for sure if there's another gun or if Smith is reloading, so they play it safe and poke their guns through the opening. After each volley, the men have to reload. That could take as long as a minute, but more likely, loaded muskets were passed up the stairs. Regardless, we have a time interval. Once loaded, they'd shove the barrels through the opening, and Richards would whack at them with the cane. Probably during the reloading lull, Smith bolted for the window. Richards followed close enough to see Smith land on the ground, right?"

"Correct. He said he stuck his head out as soon as Smith fell."

"There's a bed on one side of the window and a desk on the other, so Richards cannot be standing *beside* the window, he must be behind Smith."

"Okay."

"Look at the angle of door and window. If Richards is close enough to the window to see Smith land on the ground, his three-hundred-pound body will form a pretty good barrier between the men at the door and Smith at the window, unless the bullets are curving around Richards's body."

"Maybe the desk was smaller, and there was room to stand on the side."

"It still doesn't work. That window ledge is what, two feet deep? Smith would have dropped straight down. You can't just peek out, you have to lean on the ledge to see anything."

Beth blinked at my sketch for a moment, then at me. "Richards sustained no injuries."

"That's right. He should have been shot in the back."

Beth nodded. "Richards's version doesn't line up with the physical layout."

"We seem to have more questions than answers." I picked up some clay and added it to the mandible. "What happened next?"

Beth returned to the computer. "That depends."

I looked up from my work.

"Are you ready for this? Starting with Smith at the window, every eyewitness account differed on Smith's injuries: he was shot in the room; he was unharmed when he fell from the window; he was alive when he landed; he was dead. Some say he was propped up against a wall and shot, execution style. He was stabbed with a bayonet. Someone tried to cut off his head but a beam of light—"

"Stop! Talk about overkill." I chewed my lip for a moment. "Skip over the differing accounts on Smith. What happened to the militia and the men in the jail?"

"The Warsaw rebels fled. Willard Richards writes that he was fearful that they'd return, so he dragged the injured Taylor to the next room and hid him under a mattress."

I touched the damaged left bone of my casting, just under the eye. "Was Joseph struck, shot, or otherwise hit in the face?"

Beth quietly read. "Yes. Both Smith and a man on the stairs had facial injuries."

"Two individuals?"

"Yes. Several members of the militia relayed that when Joseph landed on the ground outside the window, a man named Webb struck him in the face with either the end of his gun or a bayonet."

"Who was the second person with a facial injury?" I asked.

"It says here that Smith's bullets struck the face of a man on the stairs."

A quiver went through me and I touched the scar I'd created on the reconstruction. "Yes, yes, it could work."

"What?"

"This injury to Smith's face is the key to the solution. Willard Richards is a doctor, fiercely loyal to Joseph Smith—"

"He offered to die in Smith's place."

"Yes. Excellent."

"Keep going. Please."

"Substitution, that's the answer."

Beth repeated it like a magic word. "Substitution!"

"He would have walked past, perhaps even stepped over, the man on the stairs with the facial injury. Then, think of it, he goes outside and finds not a dead Smith, but a live Smith with the same type of head injury. Richards would know that if Joseph Smith simply disappeared, he'd be hunted down. They needed a body."

"But if Joseph Smith got up and walked away, wouldn't people see him—"

I shook my head. "Not with a big bandage on the cut and his face covered with mud. Folks would assume Smith was one of the militia."

Beth didn't just digest that. She savored it. "And the men supposedly shot on the stairs dropped off history's radar. Substitution would also explain why Hyrum's clothing is still around to this day, but Joseph's is not."

"More than that. With Hyrum's clothing, every bullet hole, every wound can be examined. Without the clothing we are left with the conflicting eyewitness accounts."

Her face sank. "But Joseph only successfully fired the gun three times. The switched body had four bullet wounds."

"Entrance and exit wounds. What happened to the men next?" I asked.

Beth seemed to cheer up immediately. "This is interesting." She hummed under her breath for a few moments. "Joseph and Hyrum weren't wearing their garments that day."

"Huh?"

"Garments. Underwear."

I looked up. "Doesn't that come under the heading of too much information?"

"No. It's like holy underwear. Anyway, they weren't wearing any. Said it was too hot."

"Is that significant?"

Beth shrugged. "Maybe, maybe not. Modern LDS members consider their garments a symbol of their covenant with God and very sacred. It's strange . . ."

"Well, make note of that and go on."

"Joseph's, or whoever's, body and that of his brother were taken to a nearby hotel owned by Artois Hamilton, a non-Mormon."

"Who moved the bodies?" As Beth read for a moment, I mounted the prosthetic eyes, molded the eyelids, and blended them into the cheek.

Beth let out a little squeak. "Oh wow. Conspiracies and cover-up come next. Samuel Smith, Joseph's younger brother, arrived and helped move the two men—"

"That's not—"

"Wait. Samuel died mysteriously thirty-four days later. His family believed it was due to foul play. He was poisoned."

CHAPTER
SIXTEEN

I WAS STILL STARING AT BETH WHEN ROBERT stuck his head into the studio. "I'm taking Aynslee to lunch in town."

"Did Mike say it was safe?" I asked.

Robert's face darkened. "I don't need anyone's permission." He slammed the door.

I could feel a hot flash building. I folded my hands into my lap to keep from mashing the reconstruction. I needed to take my thoughts captive. Anger, bitterness, and revenge wouldn't faze Robert at all. But it could change me into something I'd hate.

"Well," Beth finally said.

"Yeah. I'm sorry about the fireworks." I stared at the drawn blinds, my mind returning to another quiet room, decorated with warm colors and strategically placed boxes of tissue, where I'd tried to pull my fractured life together after Robert left. I sought someone to talk to who wouldn't choose sides, but who would instead listen and give sound advice. I'd heard the counselor speak at my church's cancer support group as a fellow cancer survivor. Her first question surprised me. *Do I feel sorry for myself?* I thought it over carefully. Was that the emotion? When I shook my head, she smiled slightly. Good.

Later, I'd asked her when I would know there was no hope for my marriage. She told me my union ended when I realized I no longer cared. In spite of his cutting words, I did care to keep Robert safe. I'd never forgive myself if Aynslee, Beth, or Robert were hurt or—Lord forbid—killed because of something I'd done. Even if I hadn't really done anything.

Someone tapped at the door.

"Yes?"

Mike entered, carrying a cup of coffee. "I thought you could use this."

I took the coffee and made a show of drinking it.

"I've made some phone calls. It's all set to take the reconstruction to the Peace Conference," Mike said. "How's the research going?"

I was grateful he didn't mention Robert's exit. "So far, so good. We have a plausible way for Smith to have survived." I placed the cup on the window ledge.

Mike sat on the overstuffed, wingback chair. Beth read him the details and our conclusions, then sat back and beamed at him.

"Really?" he asked. "Wouldn't people have recognized him?"

I rolled out a piece of clay while I thought. "Well, in 1844, there wasn't mass media, television, or the Internet. So only those people who actually saw Smith knew what he looked like."

"Weren't there paintings?" Mike asked.

"In his lifetime, only a profile drawing by Sutcliffe Maudsley existed." I applied the clay. "Profile accounts for only a small recognition factor."

"What about this one?" Beth turned the screen so I could see the image.

"No documented history. It was probably painted from the death mask."

"Hmm, we didn't think about that. There *was* a death mask," Beth said.

I touched the cheek where the bone was chipped. If someone hit Smith in the face with the butt of his gun or a bayonet, why wasn't there a mark on the mask? "Beth, I need to know more about the mask's history."

She nodded. The sunlight through the blinds lit up floating particles. A fine layer of dust covered all the surfaces in the studio. Once I finished this project, I'd do a thorough cleaning. Assuming I survived the Avenging Angels.

Mike left, then returned with a small device to imbed behind the mandible. As he handed it to me, our fingers touched.

I jerked my hand away, almost dropping the device.

Mike sucked air through his teeth.

"I'm sorry." I didn't look at him.

The overstuffed chair creaked with his weight as he sat. I was acutely aware of his gaze and concentrated on the emerging face.

My stomach let out a rumble worthy of a locomotive. So much for professional appearances. "Sorry, again." *When was the last time I ate?*

Beth looked up from her work. "I need to prorogue this session. Prorogue. Now there's a nice word . . ."

"Food, Beth," I said.

"Right. I'll scrounge around your kitchen."

After she left, Mike asked, "Does she always talk like that?"

"Yeah. She works crossword puzzles with a pen."

The lips were next. I cut the rectangle of clay and placed it over the teeth.

"When do you expect Robert and your daughter to return?"

"When he wants to." It came out far more bitter than I intended. I paused in my work. I didn't want to talk about Robert, at least not to Mike.

I continued to work on the mouth, splitting the chunk of clay into two halves, then pushed my thumbs upward, creating the upper lip. Soon the smell of something cooking made my stomach growl again. I glanced at Mike.

"It's all right." He smiled and winked at me.

Was he flirting? I resisted the urge to check my wig.

Beth poked her head in. "Lunch."

I charged for the door. Beth had moved Mike's things to a corner of the counter and turned my battered kitchen table into an attractive setting, with placemats and colorful bowls. I checked the clock. After three. I sat down and enjoyed the rich smell of homemade chicken noodle soup. "How on earth did you make this? I didn't think I had any food in the house."

"I found a few bouillon cubes and dried pasta. Under the stack of frozen pizzas, I found chicken breasts and stir-fry vegetables. But you and I are going shopping as soon as this work is done."

"Uh-huh," I muttered. I grabbed up my spoon, then noticed Beth's closed eyes and moving lips. Placing the utensil down, I waited until I heard her soft "amen."

171

As we ate our lunch, we went over the research, looking for holes.

"Sounding good," he said. "What about Smith's wife? She would need to be in on the plot."

"Good point," I said.

"Also"—Mike scratched his chin—"let's think about motivation for those people who would have concealed Smith's supposed death. What about that non-Mormon—"

"Artois Hamilton, the owner of the hotel where Smith's body was supposedly moved. I'm on it," Beth said.

We finished eating in comfortable silence. Except for the tightly drawn curtains, the room felt like home for the first time in a long time.

Beth offered to clean up so I could get back to my sculpting. Mike followed me and took his usual seat. I'd barely started when Winston's barking and the revving of Robert's new Porsche announced Aynslee's return. Her high-pitched voice carried easily into the studio. "That's the coolest car! Will you let me drive it again?"

Aynslee was a master at playing one parent against the other, and now she had a truckload of guilt to dump on both of us. I could almost write her diary entry, titling the page "Neglected Daughter," followed by a dissertation on her successful, but absent, father and self-absorbed, sick mother. I snorted.

"What?" Mike asked.

I'd forgotten he was there. "Nothing."

Robert breezed into the room. "There you are. Do you know where my red leather notebook is? I'm also looking for that alabaster bowl."

The one I'd bought him for Christmas three years ago. Would

he now bestow it upon a girlfriend? I pushed too hard on the clay and distorted the nose. "Look on the top shelf in your office."

Robert left, and I smoothed the clay nose. "Mike, is there any danger in taking this sculpture to the Peace Conference? Is there a chance someone could get hurt?"

Mike coughed. "No. No one knows you're working on it."

"What about Jane Doe, George, and Ethan?"

"They were murdered because the Avenging Angels wanted their missing . . . treasure. Also, the victims were alone. The Peace Conference will be crowded."

"Who's delivering it? It'll have to be hand-carried, not shipped. This clay doesn't harden."

"I'm working on it."

I hoped he would figure out something before we all ended up sliced and diced by a vengeful clan of extremists. "Do you know if the Avenging Angels have committed murder before? You mentioned you'd been following them for years."

"The FBI tracks all types of radicals: the Posse Comitatus, skinheads, the Order, as well as fundamentalist fringe groups. Until Jane Doe's ritual death, we didn't consider the Avenging Angels particularly dangerous."

"Then why were you tracking them at all?"

"Well, actually, the church—"

"What church?" Beth asked, entering the room and drying her hands with a towel. "Have you been discussing something interesting while I cleaned your kitchen?" She sat in the computer chair and picked up a lavender spiral-bound notebook.

I placed a wad of clay on the top of the head and started creating the appearance of hair. "Mike's telling me about the Avenging Angels."

"They regard the LDS Church as the enemy. Technically, I suppose, the head honchos of the church, but we considered their beef a matter of philosophical differences."

"But now someone is dead. No, make that several someones."

"It's taken care of," Mike said. "They're guarded better than the president. Any threat sends them to bunkers, like bomb shelters, under Temple Square in Salt Lake City."

"Bunkers? That's weird."

"Not really. They started out as underground passages to allow the leadership of the church to move quickly and easily between buildings. It didn't take all that much to convert it, and they often have practice drills for safety. The trashing of the interpretative center, for example, triggered an alert."

I paused in my work. "How do you know all that?"

He gave a wry smile. "The FBI hires a ton of agents that are members of the LDS Church."

"Why's that?" Beth asked.

"Their faith keeps them squeaky-clean. No drinking or smoking, let alone drug use. They can pass any background check. When they retire, the Mormon Church hires them, so many of these church security officers were former colleagues. In fact, I recommended most of them for the job. Word gets around."

"How about—"

Robert entered my studio without knocking. "I've looked on the shelf in my office. Why can't you ever put things away where someone can find them? You've always been so irresponsible."

My eyes felt like they bulged from their sockets. The clay squirted between my fingers. My jaw clamped shut. I wadded a hunk of clay, then threw it. The clay struck Robert's forehead.

That felt good.

CHAPTER
SEVENTEEN

ROBERT PUT A HAND OVER HIS FOREHEAD AND opened his mouth, undoubtedly to yell at me, but I was just getting started. The hot flash shot up my chest, and I knew my face would turn beet red. I jabbed my finger at him. "Irresponsible? I'm irresponsible? What about you? You're not some jet-setting playboy, you're a father. And your daughter needs you! I know you don't care what happens to me, but if I'm murdered because of some—some crazed religious group, you'll have a daughter to raise by yourself."

I spun toward Mike, who looked like he'd rather be on the moon. "And you! I don't know what your plan is, but it had better include protection for my family and friend until you catch these guys."

He glanced away from me and rubbed his nose.

"Wait a minute." I rested my fists on my hips. "What aren't you telling me?"

"I didn't say anything," Mike said.

"You don't have to, *pal*." Robert glared at Mike. "She reads body language like a book."

The two faced each other.

Like a headline running across a newspaper, I remembered Mike's words, *"We need to set several traps and bait them."* The first trap would be the sculpture, but what if the feds couldn't catch them? Once the Avenging Angels saw the sculpture and realized the "item" displayed with it wasn't their prize, they'd keep hunting for the treasure. The item they believed Ethan gave to me. I'm the second trap.

But my family had to be far, far away from here. The Avenging Angels watched this house.

I glanced at the drawn blinds.

Mike said transporting the sculpture was safe. If Beth and Aynslee delivered it, they'd be clear of here. "Robert, you're driving this reconstruction to Seattle. You're taking Beth, Aynslee, and Winston with you, and you *will* protect them."

"Hardly. You're not putting that slobbering dog in my new Porsche—"

"You'll leave your precious Porsche here. You can take my car." He stomped from the room.

"And Winston doesn't slobber," I yelled after him.

A creak and bang told me Robert had pulled down the folding attic stairs. I soon heard him thumping around overhead.

Mike cautiously sidled toward the door. He gave me a speculative glance before leaving.

I picked up some clay and settled down on my stool, hoping my busy hands would slow my racing pulse.

Beth cleared her throat. "Not all fireworks occur on the Fourth of July."

Aynslee dashed into the room. "What did you say to Dad?"

I stared at my daughter and then at my friend. The Avenging Angels wouldn't stop until they found their holy grail and took revenge on those who had secreted it away. I stretched my lips over my teeth in what I hoped was a reasonable smile. "Robert agreed to drive you two, the sculpture, and Winston to the Peace Conference. Won't that be fun?"

"Winston?" Beth asked.

"There's no time to find a boarding kennel. He's crate-trained. You can leave him in your hotel room while you attend. I have a folding, nylon mesh crate you can use." I didn't want to point out that Winston was a terrific watchdog.

"Why aren't you coming with us?" Beth asked.

"I'll follow you, but I need to write the press release on Joseph Smith's 'death.' Also, Deputy Howell is on his way here to meet me."

Beth bit her lip, but said nothing.

"Let's go tie up those loose ends to the Joseph Smith story," I said. "We still need the history of the death mask."

She turned to the computer. "Right. And what motivated Emma Smith and the non-Mormon, Artois Hamilton, to remain silent about the actual events."

"Doctor Haller to ER. Doctor Haller to ER," the hospital loudspeaker announced.

Dave poked at the cherry gelatin with his fork. Hospital fare wasn't fit to eat. Plus, for some reason, everything on his tray was red: tomato soup, cranberry juice, and the gelatin. How was that supposed to help him heal? It reminded him of blood.

The doctor said he'd be released in the next couple of days. Dave couldn't wait. The miniature television was too far away to see without glasses, and sleeping for any length of time was impossible. Just as he'd drift off, the nurse would check him, or an alarm blared on the machine next to him, sending his heart rate soaring. Sleep deprivation made him hallucinate.

The voice of the man who shot him—he was sure he'd heard that voice before.

Winston sauntered to his chosen corner of the studio, then curled up on his oversized dog bed. Aynslee joined him, using the dog as a hairy beanbag. "I'm bored. When do we go to Seattle?"

"As soon as I'm finished," I said. "Do you want to help Beth?"

"That's boring."

"Since you're not going back to the Academy, why don't you find that homeschooling flyer we looked at earlier this summer?"

"School's boring."

"Ooookay . . . since you came up with it, why don't you figure out why the official record had seventeen names, and you counted eighteen. There's a book over on the shelf about the massacre."

"Read a book? That's—"

"Boring," Beth and I said in unison.

We worked in silence for a bit before Aynslee stood, then

trudged to the shelf and pulled out the book. She curled up with Winston to read.

"Find anything on the death mask?" I asked Beth.

Aynslee looked up from her reading. "What's that?"

"Before photography was widely utilized," Beth said, "people created plaster castings of the faces of the deceased. James Joyce, Leo Tolstoy, and John Keats all had death masks."

"Who?" Aynslee asked.

"How about John Dillinger?" Beth asked.

"Wasn't he with that old singing group the Mamas and the Daddies?" Aynslee said.

"Mamas and the Papas. No. Dillinger was . . . never mind." So much for her education to date. Something tapped gently on my memory. Before I could focus, Beth spoke.

"We'll talk about literature later, young lady." Beth looked at me and crossed her eyes. "Moving on, I started with the official history of the church. There's no mention of Joseph's or Hyrum's masks. I searched elsewhere. They officially appear in the church archives more than five years later."

"So who made them?" I paused in my sculpting.

"A man named George Cannon was *supposed* to have created the masks, and made the coffins, when they lay in state at Nauvoo, Illinois."

"Witnesses?"

"The quoted source of the casting was a five-year-old boy, Cannon's son."

"Seriously? Just how much do you think a five-year-old understands?" I picked up a wire sculpting tool. "They were supposedly murdered in Carthage at about five in the afternoon. When did they arrive in Nauvoo?"

"Three the following afternoon. They were transported in coffins on an open wagon."

"So the coffins were made in Carthage. And . . ." I wrinkled up my nose. "June. In Illinois. They wouldn't be embalmed. Not to put too fine a point on it, but by the time the two bodies reached Nauvoo, they would be getting rather, um—ripe."

"So their faces would be—"

"Quite distorted. Certainly Hyrum with the bullet wound."

"Interesting. By the way, I found the reference to a Le Fort fracture."

"What is it?"

"Remember Joseph Smith's missing grave? When his body was unearthed in 1929, all the bones of his face were fragmented. The name for this type of facial damage is a Le Fort fracture. A research team from the LDS Church surmised the damage occurred when Smith fell from the window onto his face."

"But—"

"Right. He didn't fall on his face."

"Now we know why no one noticed the switch. Richards smashed the face of the substitute body. So, that means—"

"Yes?" Beth asked.

"Put it together, Beth. The mob struck Joseph in the face, but no scar or injury is on the mask."

"You're excogitating—"

"Don't make me get a dictionary. The only way Joseph's mask could appear without any marks was if it was cast before he entered the Carthage jail."

"He did believe he was going to die," Beth said.

"Right. And he would want his image preserved. Hyrum's face, on the other hand, showed no distortion from decay."

"So Hyrum's face was cast at the Hamilton house before the bodies were transferred to Nauvoo."

"Yep. You know the difference between a death mask and a life mask?"

Beth shook her head.

"Nothing."

Beth stared at me.

"We do, however, now have another witness to the cover-up. If George Cannon made the life and death masks, as well as the coffins for the bodies, that places him in Carthage. What was his motivation for remaining silent?"

Beth glanced at the computer screen. "He was the brother-in-law to John Taylor."

I nodded.

Beth sat up straighter. "Two months later Cannon was working in St. Louis, Missouri. He died under suspicious circumstances. And the family was never able to locate his grave."

CHAPTER
EIGHTEEN

FOOTSTEPS ECHOED DOWN THE HALL, AND MIKE appeared at the door to the studio. Beth and I were still grinning. "What?" he asked.

"I think we've figured out how Smith could have faked his death," I said. "It fits the facts. This could actually be true."

"What about his wife?" Mike asked.

"I was just about to relay that information to Gwen," Beth said. "In order to hide what had really happened to Joseph, his wife, Emma, required two character traits: deception and discretion. She demonstrated both abilities—"

"Oh boy." Mike took a seat in the wingback chair. "I have a feeling the Mormon Church won't like this."

Beth furrowed her eyebrows. "But I researched from their own materials."

I smoothed a hunk of clay hair. "Just because it's true doesn't mean people will like it or believe it."

"Illogical," Beth said.

"You sound like Mr. Spock. Tell me about her lies and secrets."

"Well, Emma *lied* on her deathbed when she said Smith didn't practice polygamy, nor had ever taught it. Yet by some accounts, Smith had over thirty-five wives. He did, however, burn his revelation about polygamy before he died. She kept secret that sand, not bodies, were buried in the cemetery."

"What?" Mike asked.

"Emma thought that Joseph's and Hyrum's bodies might be desecrated by their enemies. Or maybe, knowing it wasn't really Joseph, she wanted to be sure the switch wasn't discovered. Anyway, she had the corpses secretly removed, replacing them with sand."

"What happened to the bodies?" I asked.

"That night at midnight, ten men buried the remains in the floor of the Nauvoo House, an unfinished structure Smith started several years earlier. The bodies remained for six months. Then Joseph and Hyrum were exhumed and reburied—"

"Only to be lost until the 1928 search done by the RLDS. What a twisted story," I said.

"Replacing Smith's body and pretending he'd been murdered was a perfect solution."

"Wait a minute." A melody floated in my brain. Frances, the kind woman who'd rescued me on the road to Jarom. What had she called it? Mike and Beth were silent as I rummaged around in my memory. "Do me a favor, Beth. Look up the words to 'The Lost' . . . no, 'The Unknown Grave.'"

Beth tapped on the keyboard. "Found it."

"Wait," Mike said. "A poem?"

"A song. It stayed with me for some reason."

"Well," Beth said, "according to history, Emma was pregnant when Joseph supposedly died. Her son, David, was born several months later."

"Okay," I said.

"When he grew up, he wrote a poem attributed to the time his father was buried, hidden, in the floor of the Nauvoo House."

"'The Unknown Grave.'"

"Right. The song says no one knows the location," Beth said.

"But if this is referring to the grave's location in the Nauvoo House floor," I said, "then that's wrong because you said that ten men buried him."

"It also says no one would disturb Smith's body."

"Yet he was dug up and reburied six months later."

"This grave is supposed to be green and covered with trees."

"The dirt floor of an unfinished house?" I asked. "Hardly."

"You nailed it, Gwen. It doesn't fit the facts of Smith's first interment. But the song perfectly matches an unmarked location in Utah."

Mike leaned forward. "Why pretend Smith died in the Carthage jail?"

Beth ticked off the points on her fingers. "Smith was destitute, in debt up to his ears, fleeing arrest, and—well—everyone wanted him dead."

"So Emma wanted him dead too." Aynslee looked up from her book.

"I suspect," I said. "Emma loved him, but didn't want to share her husband with a bunch of other women. Maybe she planned to join him in exile—"

"But didn't I read somewhere that Emma remarried?" Mike asked.

"Emma believed they were sealed—" Beth said.

"What?" Aynslee asked.

"Married for eternity." I thought about being married to Robert for eternity. I clamped my jaw tight.

Beth was reading the screen. "Here it is. She married a man named Lewis Bidamon." She hummed quietly under her breath for a moment, still looking. "So, according to this, she might have figured it didn't count when she married Bidamon after Joseph's supposed death. Bidamon was a Congregationalist, not Mormon, and they married on Smith's birthday."

"Just coincidence?" Mike asked.

"Only a drudge would allow her husband to—" Beth glanced at Aynslee. "Ah, well, be adulterous, then take in his mistress and care for his illegitimate children. Not to mention Bidamon was considered a foul-mouthed drunk by those who knew him."

"So Emma and Bidamon had a sham marriage," Mike said.

"There is one other possibility." I rolled out some clay. "When did Emma remarry?"

"Uh . . . 1847."

"Maybe . . ." I tapped my lip. "Maybe she found out Joseph wasn't coming back to her. He married someone else. Maybe even started a new family. So much for their reunion."

"Poor Emma," Beth said.

A chill went through me. I'd looked for a few holes to throw the Avenging Angels off me, and found catacombs in the official history.

"Well," I finally said. "Thanks so much, Beth. How are you doing on your research, Aynslee?"

"I'm bored." She stood, dropped the book onto the floor, and strolled out without a backward glance. Winston trotted after her.

"The dog probably needs to go out." I looked at Mike. "If they're watching, Winston'll find them. Would they hurt—"

"Follow me," Mike said. "I need to show you something." We trooped into the kitchen. Mike had turned my post-lunch kitchen table into a war room, with his laptop computer and notepads scattered across the surface. He brought up a program that showed an aerial photographic map. I recognized the location. My house squatted in the center. "You have only one road going past here." He traced it with his finger as I nodded. "It dead-ends at Copper Creek Lake. No one lives east between here and the lake. Your nearest neighbor is this abandoned farm—"

"It sounds like *you've* been spying on me."

Mike compressed his lips and waved away my words. "I'm just trying to keep you safe. What I'm getting at is there's no reason for close surveillance of this house. They'd stand out like—"

"A moose in pink spandex."

Mike tried not to smile. "All they have to do is watch this road from a safe distance, say, around here." He pointed.

"You're saying Winston can go outside?"

"I'll keep watch." Mike touched his pistol. "Looks like you're about done with the reconstruction."

I nodded. "I get the hint. I'll let you know when I'm finished."

The hall was now littered with boxes of books that Robert had hauled down from the attic. A quick glance told me they were his research materials. Good. That would save me several trips to the dump.

The sun had set, and the only light in the studio came from

the computer screen, bathing Beth's face in a cold, blue glow. I checked my watch. Six thirty. "Beth?"

She jumped. "Oh. You startled me. I found out about Hamilton."

I switched on some lights and took my seat. "The non-Mormon who helped transport the bodies to his hotel after the attack on the jail. Yes?"

"His fourteen-year-old son was in the militia, the youngest member—"

"And could be identified by Willard Richards as one of the killers. Artois Hamilton offered his silence to protect his son."

"A silence he must have kept until Richards and Taylor left with Brigham Young for Utah," Beth said. "In return, the church gave Hamilton the keys to the Temple—"

Just then the window cracked and there was a loud *boom*!

A bullet struck the wall inches from Beth's head.

CHAPTER
NINETEEN

THE FLOOR WAS COLD. WHEN I LOOKED UP, BETH was still sitting in her chair, frozen.

I swiftly crawled to her side. Her body was rigid, eyes wide. I yanked her arm and she toppled sideways, landing next to me with a *thump*. "Ouch," she said.

"Are you all right?" I asked.

"Ah . . ."

"Were you hit?"

"No."

Racing footsteps crunched the driveway gravel. *Pop! Pop!*

My heart thundered. I could barely breathe. The studio had windows on three sides.

Another shot, farther away.

My pistol was in the bedroom. "Move!"

I shoved my friend through the door and into the hall. The

thick log walls would stop bullets. Aynslee crouched by her bedroom, eyes huge in the dim light. Without saying anything, I opened my arms. She dove into them, shaking. The three of us cowered on the floor between the boxes of books.

Robert joined us, sitting cross-legged against the opposite wall. He reached for Aynslee, but she'd buried her face in my shoulder. No sounds penetrated our hiding place. I sweated through another hot flash. The odor mingled with Beth's perfume and Robert's floral aftershave.

Mike. And Winston. They'd been outside.

This was ridiculous. We were crouched like a bunch of feral kittens hiding from a hawk. And this hallway wasn't going to stay safe. Someone could simply kick in my outside doors. Maybe in the past the Avenging Angels attacked solitary targets, but apparently not anymore. I had to get my pistol.

Robert glared at me, as if this were my fault. In a sense it was, but I didn't ask for trouble. I'd done nothing wrong. I signaled him to hold Aynslee, then got on my hands and knees.

"Where do you think you're going?" Robert whispered.

"Take your daughter. All of you stay put." I sprinted to the bedroom door, twisted the knob, slipped through, and dropped to the floor. Only one window in here. I would put bars over them if we got out of this.

The closed drapes kept me hidden, but also prevented me from seeing what was happening. The oak flooring chilled my hands and knees. Dog hair dusted the rag rug by the bed. The dresser drawer stuck, then squealed in protest. I hefted the pistol, checked the magazine.

Winston barked at the kitchen door.

He's alive. Mike?

Beth and Robert stared at my handgun, but neither moved to stop me from edging to the kitchen. Twilight slightly illuminated the butter-yellow curtains. Winston scratched and whined outside.

I crouched and raced to the door. The dog panted and whined again.

Thinking about the pulverized drawing cast, I didn't chamber a bullet or put my finger on the trigger.

Okay. Count of three. Gun ready.

One. Two—I slammed open the door and aimed the gun.

Mike threw up his hands. "Stop! It's me."

Winston plowed past me, heading toward the studio.

I lowered the pistol.

Mike slipped inside, swiftly locking the door behind him.

"What, who—"

Mike leaned against the counter. "Is everyone okay?"

Beth entered the room. "That was invigorating." Her pale face belied her calm words. Aynslee, arms wrapped around her father, stood in the doorway.

"I thought you said the Avenging Angels watched from a distance," I said. "That bullet almost killed Beth!"

"I'm sorry," Mike said. "Winston spotted someone and took off after them. I think they were just checking up on you, and Winston surprised them—"

"They were shooting at my dog?" My voice shook.

"Calm down, Gwen," Mike said. "Backup agents will be arriving soon. No one was hurt. They'll keep their distance now that they know you have a dog, and that he's as big as a bear."

I didn't want to calm down. I wanted my life back. I wanted to be rid of this whole nutty fringe group and their private war against the Mormon Church. I made an effort to relax my fists. "The reconstruction is finished." I turned and headed to the studio, not waiting to see if anyone followed.

The creamy-white clay was almost the same color as the death mask, and the resemblance extraordinary. I'd taped the death mask photo below the face.

Mike remained in the darkened doorway while I approached the sculpture. The image faced the window, and I gently rotated it toward Mike until it was fully lit by my overhead work light.

He didn't move. Only the sharp intake of breath gave away his response. His eyes darted between the photograph and the sculpture. I waited for a comment, but he didn't speak.

"Well," I finally said. "Will this work?"

"Astonishing." He cleared his throat. "I have a glass case to mount it in. Do you need extra clay?"

"I had just enough."

He remained in the doorway a moment longer, placed a small, black object on my desk, then left.

I wandered over and picked up the object. It resembled a garage door opener.

Mike returned a few minutes later with a cardboard box and placed it on the windowsill.

"What's this?" I held up the object.

"Oh. Universal remote. Useful in my job for opening garage doors."

I put down the remote, crossed to the box, and opened it. Inside I found a square, glassed-in display case.

"I think you can screw the sculpture base into the bottom of the case to hold it securely," Mike said. "Then put it back in the box."

I packed the sculpture, now looking like a bloodless disembodied head, and carried it to the kitchen. Beth and Aynslee huddled with Robert at the kitchen table. I placed my work on the counter.

Aynslee jumped to her feet and left the room. Something about her teased at my memory, but I couldn't grasp what it was.

"Gwen, Beth, and Robert," Mike said. "We're going to treat this reconstruction as evidence." He handed me an envelope. "This is a chain of custody form. Also some evidence tape. Would you fill it out and tape up the box? Beth, Gwen'll hand the box to you, so you'll need to sign and date the form. You'll keep the form with the box, and when you hand it over to the agent in Seattle, be sure she signs and takes the form." We completed the paperwork.

"Let's go over my plan." Mike folded his arms and stared at me. His eyes twitched with a suppressed smile. I looked down at the box, ignoring his bulging arms straining his shirt. When I next looked up, he'd turned to Beth and Robert. "Do you have a garage where we can park the Porsche?"

"Yes." I didn't wait for Robert's response.

"Beth, do you mind driving your Sequoia?" Mike asked.

"Not at all. It's quite spacious."

"So then, Robert, Beth, Aynslee, the dog, and the sculpture will leave together. Tonight. Robert, you said you had a motel room in town, so Beth will drop you off and Aynslee will spend the night with Beth."

"I'll need to get my research materials home," Robert said. "And I have an important meeting tomorrow."

"Can't you cancel the meeting?" I asked.

"Hardly. A production company is sending someone to meet with me about making my book into a movie."

I felt lightheaded. I turned around so no one could see my face.

"Right," Mike said. "Tomorrow Beth will pick you up and you'll head to your apartment—"

"Condo," Robert said with irritation.

"—condo in Bigfork to drop off your materials, go to your meeting, then you're heading to Seattle. Here's a phone with my number on speed dial." He handed it to Beth. "Don't hesitate to call if you have any problems. Special Agent Mandy Black will meet you at the conference center and take care of the reconstruction. She's fully aware of the plans. Her number is also in the cell."

"What about you?" Robert asked Mike.

"I have some additional work for Gwen. I'll stay here until it's completed. I'll watch her house tonight, then drive her to Seattle to join you." Mike stared straight at Robert.

Interesting. A dominant stare.

Robert tried to maintain eye contact, then looked down.

Mike turned to me. "Here's a cell phone for you." He winked.

Beth missed the wink, but caught my expression. She stood. "Gwen, could I see you for a moment?"

I followed her into the studio. She closed the door. "What's going on?"

"Nothing." Beth was my best friend. She wouldn't leave if she knew Mike was setting up a second trap with me as bait. All I could give her were half-truths. "By you delivering the reconstruction to Seattle, Mike is free to stay here and watch the house until Deputy Howell arrives. I'll finish the report and email it to the press. Deputy Howell's picking up the memory card of Jane Doe, which is now evidence, and following up on the hand."

"Why don't we all stay and drive to the conference together? You could ship the sculpture."

"As I told Mike, it's soft clay. It has to be hand-carried. Look, the conference doesn't start for a couple more days. I'll join you as fast as I can."

Beth chewed her lip, looking unconvinced.

"Please?"

She finally shrugged. "Let me make some calls first. Then we should be going if we expect our charade to work." She strolled to my desk and picked up a stack of papers. "Here's my research on everything we talked about: Emma, Hamilton, tunnels under Temple Square, Nauvoo, death masks, fringe groups, and so on. In case you need to review anything."

"Thanks, Beth."

Aynslee was oddly silent as she packed, hugging her school backpack like she was afraid someone would steal her T-shirts. Robert made no bones about his displeasure in leaving his precious car. I secretly hoped a hungry raccoon would find the Porsche upholstery a tasty tidbit.

I wrote the article on Joseph Smith surviving the Carthage shootout, then made sure it went out to all the major news sources. With any luck, it would appear in the online locations before morning. Good-bye, reputation. Such as it was.

In a performance worthy of an Emmy, we rearranged the

vehicles, loaded Beth's SUV with Robert's boxes, and loudly said our good-byes. Mike would wait a half hour, then leave as well.

My eyes blurred and a lump formed in my throat as the crimson taillights disappeared. I knew they'd be safe.

I, on the other hand, felt like a goat tethered out for the lions.

CHAPTER
TWENTY

THE NIGHT AIR HELD THE CHILL OF APPROACHING
fall, with the scent of dried pine needles and an occasional whiff
of smoke from a distant forest fire. I usually loved to wander
outside and stare up at the million diamond stars. The words of
the psalmist came to mind, "When I look at the night sky and
see the work of your fingers—the moon and the stars you set
in place—what are mere mortals that you should think about
them, human beings that you should care for them?" When
conditions were right, I could even catch a glimpse of the
northern lights.

Not tonight. I felt like I stood naked on an empty stage, and
someone in the darkened audience had a gun.

After everyone departed, Mike secured the house, double-
checked the windows, and locked unused rooms.

I gathered my notes from the kitchen table, dropped them,

picked them up, then moved them to the studio. After dumping the notes on the computer desk, I paced to my drafting table and started to rearrange the pencils. They slid off the tray and crashed to the floor. I picked one up and threw it across the room.

"Nice throw. Can I help you with anything?" Mike said from behind me.

"No."

"Fine. Then let's go over the plan one more time."

"I think I've got it down," I said dryly.

"Then just humor me. I'll leave so you'll appear to be alone."

"Hopefully the operative word here is *appear*."

"Don't worry. You'll be safe."

I turned to look at him. "Mmm."

"Once I've gotten rid of the SUV, I'll make my way back and watch the house from the woods."

"Along with a stray Avenging Angel."

Mike frowned at me. "When is Deputy Howell due to arrive?"

"He just said he'd call." I picked up a pencil and inspected its tip.

Mike paced to the drafting table and back. "I don't want Howell wandering into our sting. Can you call him?"

"I can try. Cell reception is lousy in the mountains." I dug out his business card, then fumbled with the phone.

Howell answered after the second ring. "Oh, you're there," I blurted out.

"Where else would I be?" he said.

"Sorry, I was just wondering what your schedule was. I mean, when you thought you'd get to Copper Creek?" *I sound like an idiot.*

197

Mike grabbed a sketchpad and pencil, then wrote, *See if you can meet him away from the house.*

I nodded.

"I'll be there in the morning. Maybe nine, ten o'clock," Howell said.

"Good. There's a small cafe on Main Street, on your right as you enter town. Nora's Coffee Shop. I can meet you there."

"Sure."

I disconnected. "I guess you want this meeting away from the house so as not to spook our resident terrorist?"

He nodded. "I have backup agents joining me in a few hours. Tomorrow, when you leave for your appointment with Deputy Howell, Agent Janice Faga will be hidden in your car. You'll wear a jacket that you'll take off and leave along with your keys. She'll return in your car. You'll stay in town until we call you and let you know you can return."

"How do you know this Agent Faga will pass for me?"

"I selected her because of her resemblance to you. She's a very pretty lady."

Heat built in my neck, and I quickly stood and moved to the shelves, pretending to look for a book.

"You didn't really think we'd put a civilian at risk, did you?" Mike asked.

I did, but didn't want to seem so stupid. With my back to Mike, I fumbled with the book I'd just selected. "Don't you need to inform the local department you're running a sting? What if they show up, guns blazing, thinking it's gang warfare or something?"

"Well—"

"Let me guess. Something you've uncovered in your investigation is keeping Ravalli County Sheriff's Department out of the loop . . . Craig?"

I spun toward Mike. He was rubbing his mouth with his hand. A tug on his earlobe, then he asked, "Why do you say that?"

"Three."

"What?"

"Hand on the mouth, pulling your earlobe, and answering a question with a question. No wait! Five, five! If I factor in the significant pause and incorrect verb use, you gave five signs of deception."

"Do you analyze people all the time?"

"No. It's too much work. But I do have, shall we say, an early-warning bell."

The telephone rang.

I dropped the book. "Oh!"

Mike nodded at me to answer.

A muffled man's voice asked, "Is Randy there?"

"No—"

Dial tone. I stared at the receiver.

Mike took the phone from my hand. "They're checking to see if you're here."

Goose pimples sprung on my arms. "I thought they'd wait until morning."

He glanced around the studio, noting the windows. "Yeah. Me too. Outside of the windows, kitchen, and front door, is there any other way to get into the house?"

"Not really."

"Do you have a basement?"

"Crawl space. You can get to it from the pantry off the kitchen. Outside access is through a small door next to the driveway where my car is parked. There are—" I pictured the inky blackness filled with spiders. I hunched my shoulders. The Avenging Angels didn't seem nearly as creepy as those long-legged arachnids. There was a very good reason I wasn't a forensic entomologist.

We moved to the kitchen. I brought a sketchpad and sat at the table as Mike brewed a fresh pot of coffee. He might need the caffeine to stay awake. I was already wired.

He sat across from me. I tried to ignore him. He smelled of spice.

Research would keep my mind busy. I opened the sketchpad and scribbled, *Craig?* Underneath I jotted, *Family in St. George. Was at the center the day of the murder. Very likely Mormon. Arrived quickly when I found the hand. Didn't believe me. Near Dave when shot.* At this rate the entire Mormon population became suspects. All nine million or whatever their numbers.

I sketched Craig's face anyway, adding horns. The sketch didn't look right.

Mike picked up a flyer from the table and turned it over. "Are you thinking of homeschooling your daughter?"

"She found it." I took the paper from him. "Yes. She's had . . . a tough year."

"Do you mind me asking you a personal question?" he asked.

I kept my head down and opened a fresh page. "Depends." At the top of the page I wrote, *Prophet Kenyon? Fundamentalist Mormon. Devoted followers. Liar. Access to Pulaski. Not home when Deputy Howell tried to interview.* My drawing of Kenyon looked more convincing when I added the fangs.

"Why did you only have one child?" he asked.

I turned the page and continued drawing. "Robert. He was more in love with the idea of children than actually raising them."

"I see."

I really didn't want to talk, or think, about Robert. He was a jerk, but he would protect his daughter. *If only to have a living legacy of himself.*

The pencil dug a trough in the paper. I tore it off the pad and sketched a faceless angel.

Mike stood. "I need to get going. Remember, don't answer the door or the phone. Stay away from the windows. I'll be back, but you need to be careful. Okay?"

I nodded.

"Don't follow me outside. Lock the door."

I nodded again, then threw the dead bolt after he'd gone.

Alone.

The house rustled, shifted, and sighed around me. Although the curtains were tightly closed, I had the creepy feeling someone was still peering in.

I backed out of the kitchen into the hall. We'd shut the doors leading to the bathroom, Robert's office, Aynslee's room, and my bedroom. A tiny nightlight gave scant illumination. My footsteps echoed on the cold wood floor as I crept into the living room. The drapes hung straight down. No one hiding behind them.

Burrrumm!

I jumped. The old refrigerator motor burped to life.

This is ridiculous. I am not some scared mouse alone for the first time. I resolutely squared my shoulders and marched into my studio. A cool whiff of air drifted through the blinds from the bullet hole in the window. Bullet. Even though I knew the police should investigate the earlier shooting, I didn't trust anyone but Dave in his department. I found a craft knife, then gently nudged the bullet from the wall. Ballistics would show if this was from the same gun as the one that shot Dave. I searched for a place to keep it, finally dropping it into a box of gray kneaded erasers where it blended in.

Still twitchy from possible prying eyes, I grabbed a couple of sharpened pencils and scurried to the kitchen. I tugged out my notes to go over one final time before turning them over to Deputy Howell. I found my entry on the pickup, Utah license number B95 2DT, king cab. *That's right. The man in Provo.* That seemed a hundred years ago. I was going to do a composite of the possible driver for Dave before he was shot. That's what had teased my brain all day.

Sketching the man would be a good use of my time. I closed my eyes and brought up his image. Even features, wavy, burnt-umber hair, narrow nose, deep-set blue eyes, in his midforties.

I marked out the proportions, then began sketching.

Branches whispered against the window in the evening breeze like tiny fingernails.

I shifted my weight and continued to draw.

The house creaked, the logs shifting as the temperature dropped. The pencil's scratching on the paper seemed loud.

I checked my watch. One twenty a.m. I propped the completed drawing against a stray coffee cup. Yeah. I'd captured his features. I closed my eyes for a moment.

"Wake up, sleepyhead."

Jerking upright, I knocked over a steaming cup of coffee at my elbow. The kitchen glowed with the peach-colored light of morning. *How could I have fallen asleep?* Mike helped me mop up the coffee.

"Sorry," he said. "You were all done in, so I let you sleep." His eyes were red and his face sprouted a day's beard growth.

Most of the coffee landed in my lap, so my sketch remained relatively unscathed. I stood and wiped my soggy shirt.

There was a man in the hall.

The man in my composite.

Adrenaline surged through my veins. I dove for my pistol.

Mike caught my arm before I could reach it. "Calm down. This is Agent Larry Frowick. We met up about a mile from here and entered through the crawl space. Agent Faga is already in place. You'll want to dress and get going so the poor woman doesn't have to spend any more time on the floor of your car."

Agent Frowick nodded at me.

I pointed my finger. "You've been following me!"

He glanced at my drawing. "You're right, Mike. She's better than our own artists."

"Why?" I demanded. "Why were you tailing me?"

"Mike here"—Frowick jerked his thumb at the man—"figured you might be in danger. Took me quite a bit of time to find you in Provo."

"Why didn't you just identify yourself?"

Agent Frowick blinked, folded his arms, and said, "Ah . . . well . . ."

Mike snorted. "Uh, Larry, you've been made. She knows you're about to lie." He turned to me. "You know why."

"Yeah, you're trying to trap them. Figured I'd be a little bait to dangle."

"See?" Mike said to Frowick. "Told you."

I was a mess. My morning breath would kill anyone within five feet, it looked like I'd peed coffee, and for all I knew, my wig was skewed backward. I dashed past Frowick toward the bathroom. A half hour later I emerged as a respectable forensic artist.

Both men rose as I entered the kitchen. "Do you have the cell phone I gave you?" Mike asked.

I held it up. "What if they don't show up? How long do I need to hang around Copper Creek, especially without a car?"

"I'm sure they're here," Mike said. "The chance to thoroughly search your home for their stolen treasure will be irresistible."

I packed an oversize bag with my research, the memory card, notes, wallet, and other useful items. Mike talked me out of my SIG Sauer.

I grabbed a colorful jacket on the way out and watched my house disappear in the rearview mirror.

The trap was set.

CHAPTER
TWENTY-ONE

I WASN'T QUITE SURE OF THE PROPER ETIQUETTE for driving around with an FBI agent crouched in the back of my car. *Do I make conversation?* Ignoring her seemed rude. "Hi. I'm Gwen—"

"Please don't talk. Someone might see your lips moving." The agent had a firm but pleasant voice. "Park out of sight from the street and cafe and leave your purse in the car. You can take your wallet."

"Do you think you'll pass for me?"

"Agent Brown sent me your photo, so I have a wig in the same style as your hair."

I could've provided the wig. I grunted, then concentrated on driving. Downtown Copper Creek featured a rustic series of weathered storefronts, wooden sidewalks, and hitching posts for the occasional cowboy trotting into town. Stetsons and cowboy

205

boots were the standard attire of both natives and tourists trying to fit in.

Nora's Coffee Shop sat on the corner of the block, bustling with its usual morning crowd. I found an empty spot beside the Dumpsters, parked, then removed my jacket. After stuffing some cash into my pocket next to the cell phone Mike had given me, I grabbed up my notes, then strolled into the cafe. I spotted Deputy Howell immediately. Neighbors nodded at me as I passed, and the clatter of dishes and conversation lowered, then resumed. I edged between an eclectic collection of tables and chairs to the back corner. Even though I arrived early for our meeting, Howell must have arrived quite a bit before me. An empty plate sat in front of him with the remnants of syrup and melted butter. His gaze caught mine, gave the tiniest shake, then roamed about the room.

I took the hint and slipped into the next table.

A waitress appeared at my elbow with a coffeepot, filling my cup without waiting, then asked, "The usual?"

"Yeah, thanks, Donna." My stomach hinted loudly that it could stand chow.

Leaning back into my chair, I casually checked out my fellow diners, seeking out any strangers. Only one couple was unknown to me. When Donna placed my toast on the table, I nodded at the man and woman. "I don't recognize those two. Tourists?"

"Nah"—Donna refilled my coffee—"that's my brother's wife's cousin and her husband. From Milwaukee. He's a shoe salesman." She sniffed. "If you ask me, the shoes he sells are ugly. But he makes good money at it . . ."

Leave it to Donna to know everybody and everything. My problem was how to put a cork in it.

". . . so I asked him why didn't he—"

"Excuse me." Deputy Howell snagged her attention. "Could I have my check, please?"

Donna drifted off to write it up.

Howell jerked his head toward the door.

Donna returned and placed Howell's check in front of him, then set half a grapefruit in front of me.

"I'm sorry, Donna, I'll need this to go."

The woman looked annoyed, but swiftly removed my breakfast. Howell dropped some cash on the table and left the cafe without looking at me.

The waitress returned with my food in a white paper sack and I paid her, adding a generous tip.

Deputy Howell wasn't in the parking lot. Traffic was light, and across the street I spotted a beige Crown Vic. Howell was behind the wheel. He glanced at me, started his car, and drove to the traffic light. I strolled in the same direction. He turned right and disappeared. I crossed the street and continued straight. I'd almost walked the entire block before Howell pulled up beside me. I jumped in. "Making sure I wasn't followed?"

He grunted a reply.

We didn't speak for the first few miles as he drove south out of town on the two-lane Highway 93. The jagged peaks of the Selway-Bitterroot Wilderness formed a wall to our right, and to our left verdant pastures held grazing Angus and Herefords. I rolled down the window slightly, allowing the scent of cedar and newly cut grass to fill the car. I finished my cold toast, soggy grapefruit, and lukewarm coffee and brought Howell up-to-date on the events.

"Interesting."

I handed the envelope to Howell. "I'm glad to be rid of the

memory card. You'll find my notes in there."

"Thanks. I'll read them later. How's Dave holding up?"

"Oh. How did you know about Dave being shot?"

"Word gets around."

"Mike Brown's set up a sting operation at my place. Hopefully, with the card gone and a few arrests, I'll be safe."

"So, what do you think is the motive for the Avenging Angels?" Detective Howell asked. "Who or what sparked this whole murderous rampage?"

We were climbing into the mountains now, crossing Lost Trail Pass. Stark, blackened tree trunks poked out of the charred earth, the remnants of previous forest fires. "Well," I said, "this is just a guess, but I think Jane Doe belonged to a fundamentalist Mormon group, a group somehow related to Prophet Kenyon's flock."

"Why?"

"Jane Doe needed to be close enough to the real Rebekah to know she died."

"So, she escaped," Howell said. "Makes sense if she was forced into a polygamist marriage to an older man." He was silent for a moment. "The preliminary autopsy report showed she hadn't been to a dentist and had been pregnant more than once."

"She was so young! If she was eighteen when she entered college last year . . . and she had more than one child . . . oh, the poor girl." I did a little math in my head. Was Jane Doe having babies when she was Aynslee's age? I shook my head and explained my theory about the stolen item.

Howell frowned. "Insurance? Maybe a way to get some money? Fundamentalist groups have a history of barely educating their kids."

"How would she have gotten into college?"

"Obviously she was bright. And resourceful," Detective Howell said.

I nodded. "I think she was going to meet with George. Maybe sell the treasure to the LDS Church."

"And you think the Avenging Angels are killing to get it back?"

"It fits," I said. "I looked it up. The Avenging Angels served Brigham Young as a type of police force, castrating and even murdering anyone in Young's way."

"But that was a long time ago."

"I think they're still around."

We drove a few miles in silence. I thought about the Kenyons. "Frances, a member of Kenyon's church, said their group split a few years earlier. She mentioned something about 'the keys.' Does that mean anything to you?"

Howell shifted in his seat. "Jesus restored the keys to the kingdom and the gospel to Joseph Smith." He reached across me, opened the glove box, and pulled out a thick book, then handed it to me. The well-worn, leather-bound volume held the LDS scriptures.

A chill shot up my spine. "Are you Mormon?"

"Sixth generation." He opened his jacket slightly, and I saw a pin on his shirt pocket. It was an American flag flanked by two eagle wings. He turned his head slowly and gave me a half smile. "I'm an Avenging Angel."

CHAPTER
TWENTY-TWO

MY HEART POUNDED AND MIND RACED. HOWELL drove too fast to jump from the car. The cell phone was in my pocket. *I need to choose my words carefully.* "So, where are we going?"

"We're going to meet the other Avenging Angels. You need to know the truth."

The hot flash tore up my neck, and I turned to the side window. We'd passed into Idaho where traffic was scarce and civilization remote. I scratched my leg and nudged the cell from my pocket. It landed with a soft thud on the seat next to me. I quickly coughed to cover the sound. "I've told you everything, you know. I don't have what you're looking for. I gave you the memory card and all my notes."

"I know."

My face felt normal, but my palms were wet. I twisted in my seat to look at him. The movement allowed me to turn the phone on and slip it slightly under my leg. I made a show of wiping my hands on my jeans.

"Up till now," Howell said, "we stayed off the radar—"

"I hardly think your blood atonement murders are off the radar," I said dryly.

"That wasn't us."

"Oh?" I glanced at the phone, then gently tapped it.

The battery was dead.

I wanted to throw the phone out the window. *Calm, calm. Use your head.* He would have to slow down to turn off this road. I could make a run for it then. I peeked at the door handle. "So if you didn't do the killing, why don't you just call up the FBI and tell them to stop wasting their time?"

"That's not so easy. We decided it would be better to convince you."

"So you kidnapped me?"

Howell's eyebrows rose. "Not at all. Mike entrusted you to me. I just have you in protective custody. Once you've met the other members, you're free to go. I'll drive you back to Copper Creek."

Yeah. Right. "You said I needed to know the truth. So tell me."

Howell's eyes narrowed, and he tapped the steering wheel with his index finger.

We'd reached another pass, and the land fell away on our right to a wide valley spotted with sagebrush and grass. About a mile away, pine-covered mountains rose, still sporting ribbons of snow. A dirt road appeared ahead that crossed the valley to a series of buildings huddled in the trees. Howell slowed and put on his blinker.

I cleared my throat to cover up the click of unlocking the door.

"Well"—he continued to slow—"there is something I can tell you right now."

I reached for the door handle.

"Your door doesn't open from the inside."

I tugged and pushed.

He turned onto the dirt road and jolted across a cattle guard. Thick, choking dust billowed behind us as we pounded toward the outcropping of buildings. Power lines snaked across the valley, holding out a faint hope of civilization. The hope faded as he drove closer. It was a ghost town, the buildings abandoned, rotting back into the earth. He jerked the car left, turning away from the town, and climbed into the trees. The road became mere ruts, tossing the car and me like an angry bronco. Pines caged their branches overhead. One final twist and we reached a clearing. A windowless gray van squatted beside a raw-timbered hunting cabin.

Howell parked next to the van, then looked at me. He had a strange look on his face.

I tried to wet my lips, but found the term *scared spitless* accurate.

He slid from the car, making sure the keys were with him. The trees appeared denser behind the cabin, but could I make it? Howell was armed. The building was closer, but at least one other Avenging Angel could be lurking inside. I needed to factor in that we were probably over six thousand feet high, and running would be more difficult. I bunched my muscles, preparing to spring from the seat. Howell must have anticipated my move. As he opened the door, he blocked it with his body and latched onto my arm with a vise-like grip.

I struggled, but he just gripped harder, yanking me toward the cabin. I took a swing at his stomach, but it was like punching a rock.

"Knock it off."

Before we reached the cabin door, it flew open, and Howell chucked me inside. I tripped and landed on my hands and knees, skidding across the rough floorboards, gathering splinters.

I wasn't going to die like a dog. I jumped to my feet, ready to fight.

Though it was only about a three-hour drive from Copper Creek to the quaint and exclusive resort town of Bigfork, Montana, they didn't get an early start. Dad insisted on stopping at Missoula, then Kalispell, to arrange for publicity events, then that endless meeting with some movie bigwig. It was late afternoon before they finally took a break at the Bigfork Starbucks. Aynslee spotted the headlines as they passed the news stand. *Joseph Smith Found?* Underneath showed a photo of her mom's sculpture next to the death mask. "Dad, would you buy me a paper?" He grunted, then dropped some coins into the slot.

The press cropped the photo, but Aynslee could see her mom's sculpture stand. Mom must have emailed the digital image to the newspaper.

"That was fast," Beth said, reading the headlines over Aynslee's shoulder.

"Seems like a cockamamie idea to me." Dad held the door open.

A long line of commuters waited patiently for their afternoon double-shot, skinny, grande lattes. Aynslee wandered around until she found a couple of yuppies about to leave. A Mac-toting nerd made a move toward the same spot, but Aynslee yanked out a wooden chair and flopped down before he could dibs it. He made a face at her, and she stuck out her tongue, then opened the paper to read. The story posted her mom's article, then went on to viciously attack it, using words like *reckless*, *Mormon bashing*, and *bigot*.

Dad and Beth joined Aynslee, bringing her hot chocolate.

"This is mean," she said.

Beth looked at Aynslee, then bent over the paper. "I was afraid of that. Your mom's getting a lot of heat for her article. Is there anything positive written?"

"Um, I guess." Aynslee continued to peruse the paper. "The reporter is making a big deal about how the Mountain Meadows Massacre and the attack on the twin towers occurred on September 11, and how both involved religious fanatics." She turned the page. "There's an entire center section of the paper about the conference."

"Yes," Beth said. "Religious intolerance and downright bigotry, masquerading under the banner of separation of church and state, is eroding our country and our history. This conference is trying to mend more than the events of 9/11. It's demonstrating that we still have freedom of religion, not freedom from religion." She glanced at my dad. "Sorry. I'll get off my soapbox."

"No, that's interesting," Robert said. "Maybe there's a

possibility of a book in these events." He tugged out a small notebook and pencil, then jotted a few words.

Beth's lips thinned. "Well . . ." She took a sip of coffee and turned to Aynslee. "Let's plan out our day once we reach Seattle. After we deliver the reconstruction, we'll get some rest. I booked a room months ago right next to the conference center. We can go shopping later."

Aynslee nodded. "Are—are we going to be near the water?"

"Right on the water. Did you want to go swimming?" Beth asked.

"Um. Yeah, maybe." She could throw the package in the water. No one would find it then. But what if . . .

"Dad?"

Her dad continued to write.

"Dad."

He looked up. "What is it?"

"Is there any chance Mom will go back to Utah? Or, um, take a job somewhere else?"

"I have no idea."

"If she does, could I come and live with you?"

Dad shifted in his seat, then carefully closed the notebook. "I don't see how. You have school, and I'm traveling." He smiled at her without showing his teeth.

Aynslee studied her nails. Even if she threw away the package, nothing would change. No one wanted her.

CHAPTER
TWENTY-THREE

BLUE-VEINED HANDS CLUTCHED A WHEELCHAIR in front of me. Hunched shoulders held an ill-fitting, taupe cardigan. Deep wrinkles zigzagged across pallid, sagging skin. Lively periwinkle eyes twinkled up at me. The man nodded a greeting.

Behind the man in the wheelchair, a second man with ashen, wispy hair barely covering his shiny head spoke on a cell phone. "Yes. She's here. I think so. We'll call back." Hand trembling, he placed it on the table. His liver-spotted skin was paper-thin.

"Hello, my dear. Please, have a seat." A raspy voice came from behind me. I glanced over my shoulder. Using a cane, a third senior citizen near the door hobbled forward and smiled benignly.

Fortunately, the chair was near my rear end. I sat before my legs could give way.

Deputy Howell helped a fourth elderly man through the

door, then pulled two ladder-backed chairs from a rustic oak table and assisted the gray-haired ensemble to their seats.

"Allow me to introduce ourselves," the man in the wheelchair said. "I'm Merrill Johnson, this fine specimen behind me is Joel McMurdie, your doorman is Alfred Edwards, next to him is John Bateman, and of course, you know Deputy Howell. As you are well aware, poor George Higbee was murdered. We are the last of the so-called Avenging Angels."

My brain scrambled to make sense of it. These men didn't look capable of swatting a fly. Deputy Howell, however, was fit and much younger. He could be the murderer. As the lead detective, he could easily throw the investigation.

As if reading my mind, Howell spoke. "No. I didn't murder anyone. I was at a meeting with the mayor of Fancher all afternoon when someone killed Jane Doe. We worked the case all night until we got the call from the visitor's center."

"Why did you bring me here?" The only furniture in the twenty-by-thirty-foot cabin was a table and six rickety chairs. An unlit river stone fireplace took up the wall opposite the door, and matching tiny windows provided dim light.

"They wanted to meet you," Deputy Howell said.

"So you kidnapped me?" I glared at him.

"Not at all. Remember? Protective custody." Howell gave a short nod to one of the men.

"Mrs. Marcey"—Johnson spoke from his wheelchair—"not to sound melodramatic, but three people died horribly in the past week. You and your family are in grave danger."

I threw up my hands. "You could have told me that over the phone." Mike was cooling his heels back at my house waiting for this geriatric mob to attack. If I weren't so angry, I'd laugh.

"We need you to see us and understand we're not the enemy," Bateman said. "We want to help you."

"Help me?"

"Stay alive."

"Robert, we really have to get this reconstruction to Seattle," Beth said for the millionth time.

Aynslee sighed, sat on her dad's new sofa, and called Winston over. Maybe she should just put in a pizza if they were going to be here any longer.

Her dad put his hand over the telephone mouthpiece. "If I have to be the delivery boy for Gwen, I'm going to at least set up a signing at the bookstore. We'll leave after I'm done." He turned his back on Beth.

Beth joined Aynslee on the sofa and checked her watch. "We're not going to get to Seattle today, I'm afraid." She patted Aynslee on the leg. "Maybe we'll meet up with your mom and deliver the reconstruction together."

"Whatever."

"Hey, don't worry. Everything happens for a reason."

I folded my arms. "I'm having trouble picturing you all as my bodyguards."

"Knowledge is protection," Edwards said.

"Why don't you meet Mike or someone in the FBI and let them see you're not killers."

"Why would we do that?" McMurdie asked.

Answering a question with a question. Hiding information. "I've heard your names before," I said slowly. "All but yours, Detective."

"My mother was a Lee," Howell said.

I stood. "John Doyle Lee." I pointed to each man in turn. "Nephi Johnson, Samuel McMurdie, William Bateman, John M. Higbee, and . . ."

"William Edwards," the man with the cane said. "Very good, Gwen. Yes, we are the direct descendants of the original Avenging Angels."

"The men responsible for the slaughter at Mountain Meadows," I said.

Edwards cleared his throat. "Yes. Well. Since 1857, one member of each family joined this group. We bound together to make sure that killing in the name of religion, especially our Mormon faith, doesn't happen again."

I bit my lip, looking from man to man. They benignly nodded at me. "No," I finally said.

"I beg your pardon?" Bateman said.

"You want me to believe you're some kind of quasi-military force. Not to make too much of it, but you're hardly young, strapping military men. You formed to hide a secret."

"And what secret would that be, m'dear?" Edwards said.

"My story was correct. Joseph Smith wasn't killed at that jail in Carthage, Illinois. He was murdered twelve years later in Mountain Meadows."

I had to hand it to the old men, they covered their surprise well.

Johnson chuckled. "I'm afraid your work at the Mountain

219

Meadows Center and your vivid imagination are letting you believe your work of fiction. I assure you we're here to protect you, not because of any secret."

I hated people who chuckled at me. "So you read my article? It must have been online."

Edwards glanced at Bateman. "No, no, no, of course not," Edwards finally said.

So they wanted to play the deception game. Fine. Edwards seemed the most transparent. His choice of words and body language would answer my questions. I'd look for three or more physical or verbal clues delivered in a timely response. On his first reply, he'd broken eye contact, significantly paused, and given multiple denials. Answer to first question: yes. They'd read the article.

"Are you responsible for the murders? Jane Doe, George, Ethan?"

"No," Bateman said.

True answer. "Do you know who is?"

"No," Bateman said again.

True.

I strolled across the wooden floor to the tiny window, the floor creaking with each step. The thin walls allowed cold air to seep in between the boards. Pine trees pressed against the building's side. The sun dipped behind the mountains, casting the room in shadows.

Howell pulled a glass Kerosene lamp from the mantle and lit it. The room was less stark in the warm glow.

"We're here to help," Bateman said. "We'd like to make you an offer." His gaze flickered to the cell phone on the table.

They claimed they were the last of the Avenging Angels, but someone else pulled their strings. I needed to get my hands on that cell phone and see the last dialed number. "Offer?"

"The FBI can't put you or your family into long-term, protective custody," Deputy Howell said. "We also know you are in grave danger from whoever is behind the murders."

"Who *is* behind the murders?"

"We're offering to hide you," Edwards said. "Until the killers are arrested and you're no longer in danger."

"So you must know why I'm in danger." I glanced from man to man.

They shifted slightly in their seats, but didn't speak.

"What if I helped you?" I leaned against the fireplace. "George Higbee, who was one of you, an Avenging Angel, was killed at the Mountain Meadows Center. That's a fact."

I had their attention.

"On the same day, a young woman with an assumed identity was also brutally murdered. Both had their throats cut."

Edwards glanced at Bateman.

"You, of course, know all of this because Deputy Howell was the investigating officer. Here's my take on all of this. Jane Doe was delivering something to George Higbee." I turned to Deputy Howell. "And you need to tell your colleagues that I'm an expert on deception, so you'd better not lie to me."

Howell stared at me. Bateman and McMurdie crossed their arms and looked down. Edwards shifted, tried to look me in the eye, then examined his fingernails with rapt attention.

So far, so good.

"But George was late to work. And the girl fainted and was

escorted back to the motel. So the transaction didn't happen. Good so far?"

No one moved.

"So, time to be honest. Who was Jane Doe and what was she delivering to George?"

Edwards opened, then closed his mouth.

"Come on, guys. You know I'm in danger. I have a right to know why."

Deputy Howell positively beamed at me. "I told you she was good."

Edwards glanced around, then gave a short nod as if making up his mind. "Yes, well. We don't know who Jane Doe was, but about two years ago she called us. She needed money and had something to sell."

"How did she know to call you?"

Edwards flushed slightly. "That was one of the reasons we knew she was legit. She said she knew our secret. And she had the proof."

"Which was?"

Merrill Johnson started hacking, bending him forward in his wheelchair with a racking, gurgling cough.

I raced to help, but the other men surrounded him, patting, rubbing, murmuring.

I gripped the table, feeling helpless, and looked away from the distressed man.

The cell phone was inches from my hand.

The men were oblivious to me. I swiftly flicked the phone on, tapped the menu, found the last dialed number, and committed it to memory.

Johnson stopped coughing.

I placed the phone on the table, but the screen was on, screaming that I'd touched it. I stepped forward, blocking it from view. "Is . . . are you okay?"

Deputy Howell tugged a cooler from the corner of the room, opened it, and handed a bottle of water to Johnson. "He'll be fine. For now. Water?"

I didn't dare look at the cell phone to see if it'd darkened. "Sure. Yes."

Howell pulled several more bottles from the cooler and handed them around. Edwards struggled with the cap. So much for the all-powerful Avenging Angels. The room was silent as the men drank. I finished mine first and made a show of placing it on the table.

The phone was off.

Heat rushed up my face. I moved to the window where a pine-scented breeze cooled my forehead. "Keep going. Tell me what Jane Doe was trying to sell."

Howell leaned forward. "Proof that Joseph Smith survived Carthage. She was selling the scepter of power. Joseph Smith's journal, his revelations, written between 1844 and 1857, when he was killed at Mountain Meadows."

CHAPTER
TWENTY-FOUR

I SPUN AND PUMPED MY FIST. "I WAS RIGHT! Willard Richards did switch a body with Joseph Smith at the Carthage jail. And the death mask of Smith was a life mask, and was made the night before his supposed death."

"Deputy Howell told us you were intelligent and persistent," Johnson said. "No one figured out the discrepancies before now."

I leaned against the wall and thought for a moment. "This journal, this . . . what did you call it?"

"The scepter of power," Edwards said.

"Mmm." I strolled to the fireplace, then back to the window. "How did you know it was really his journal? There've been some pretty amazing forgeries foisted on the Mormon Church."

McMurdie frowned at Howell. "When Jane Doe called us, she read passages from the journal. The phrasing, the chiasmus—"

"A writing structure where two or more points are reversed or crisscrossed," I said.

Edwards nodded. "It's found in the Bible, the writings of Shakespeare, and the Book of Mormon. Then, of course, there were the prophesies."

"Did they come true?" I asked.

Edwards simply stared at me.

"Okay, fair enough. I put Smith's real history together," I said. "Up until 1844. You can at least tell me this: Why was Joseph Smith on that doomed wagon train?"

The men looked at each other. McMurdie gave a slight nod to the others. Edwards spoke, "That's simple. Joseph Smith was returning for his church."

My heart beat faster. Yes, that made so much sense.

"How did Brigham Young find out that Smith was with the settlers?"

"I wish George were here," Johnson said. "That's the Higbee involvement. John, you know the story best."

Bateman stared at a point in space to my left. "Chauncey Lawson Higbee was an excommunicated Mormon and editor of the *Nauvoo Expositor*, the newspaper Smith destroyed. That's what landed Smith in jail in Carthage. Anyway, there was bad blood between Higbee and Smith. John Higbee, Chauncey's first cousin, was fiercely loyal to Brigham Young. John was present at Mountain Meadows and even rumored to have given the command to kill. Although it's not documented, we believe at some point Chauncey identified Smith as being in that wagon train and sent word to his cousin about Smith's plan."

"The slaughter at Mountain Meadows was about power and control," I said quietly.

"And hatred and greed," Edwards added. "Believe me, with all our hearts, we wish it never happened."

"Why didn't Smith make his appearance known when the wagon train passed through Salt Lake City?"

"We don't know," Howell said. "He may have been ill, or felt the timing was wrong."

"So, are you saying Brigham Young murdered that whole wagon train to make sure Joseph Smith wouldn't take control of the church again?"

No one spoke.

"Okay. You don't have to say it." I moved to the fireplace and took a deep breath. "This changes your history by a hundred and eighty degrees."

McMurdie found words. "Until that girl called two years ago telling us of this book, we'd decided to let the secret die with us. Enough time had passed that all the witnesses were gone, evidence destroyed, history rewritten, and cases closed."

I shook my head. "You guys are in deep doo if this journal shows up."

Howell nodded. "And you are in deep doo if it doesn't. Whoever is killing won't stop until that journal is located."

My pulse raced. That journal was valuable beyond measure to certain people. "You offered to help me, to protect my family. I accept your offer. What happens next?"

The men relaxed. "We'll need to make some phone calls," Edwards said. "Deputy Howell, would you be so kind as to take Gwen outside for a walk?"

"Do you think I could maybe use the restroom first?" Drinking all that water may have kept me from altitude sickness, but my bladder was set to burst.

"Well now." Johnson cleared his throat. "We, uh . . . take care of that before coming here. The restroom, such as it is, is an outhouse."

"I'll escort you," Howell offered, stepping away from the now crackling fire he'd just built.

"Unless I'm under arrest, if you don't mind, just direct me to the outhouse. I am capable of doing some things on my own."

Johnson actually blushed. "Go out the door, turn right, and go around the cabin. There's a trail. The outhouse is tucked on the opposite side of the woodshed. TP is in the bag next to the cooler."

Deputy Howell handed me a flashlight and a navy flannel jacket. The sleeves covered my hands and hung almost to my knees. It felt wonderfully warm. A gun would have been nice, just in case any grizzlies or cougars fancied white meat for dinner, served up with a toilet paper napkin. I turned on the flashlight and slipped from the room. No faces appeared at the window, so I took a fast detour to check the van for car keys. No such luck. Hot-wiring a car wasn't my strong suit.

I trotted uphill toward the outhouse, flashing the light from side to side. Fallen trees, shrubby brush, and stumps of long-cut timber bordered the path. A million stars sparkled in the ebony velvet sky. The chilly breeze held the promise of snow, making my ears ache. One pocket held a clean bandana, which I tied over my head. The flashlight flickered, and I had to bang it a few times against my hand to restore the dwindling amber light. Little illumination came from the tiny window facing the backside of the cabin. As promised, the outhouse was exactly where they said. I pulled open the door and held up the light.

Spiderwebs, like snarled meshwork, crisscrossed the tiny

space. Long-legged arachnids skittered from the light, or hunched down and glowered at me. I almost wet my pants on the spot. I involuntarily gave a shivery spider dance. There was no way in this lifetime I'd ever go in there, let alone expose my nether region to who-knew-what in that inky hole in the ground.

Back to nature. I held the light higher. In the flickering illumination, a grouping of trees huddled to my right. I climbed to the spot. I could still clearly see the cabin, which meant that they could just as easily see me. A quick flick and I was in darkness. From here, it would be easy to find my way down.

I finished and stood. A sound like a woman's scream echoed off the mountains. *Cougar.* The mountains had always been home to me, and I enjoyed the solitude. *How long do they need for their meeting?* I'd given them a boatload to talk about.

I moved a couple of steps uphill and processed the information I'd gleaned from our conversation. I'd need to call the number on the cell phone the first chance I got. Though they claimed they were the last of the Avenging Angels, they still had someone in authority over them or advising them.

They'd also made it clear that the official church stance would remain that Joseph Smith died in Illinois, not Utah. DNA on the excavated body at Mountain Meadows would prove otherwise, but it was far better for Smith to die in a shootout with a Mormon-hating mob than slaughtered by members of his own church.

I waited a bit longer, listening for the cougar or perhaps wolves, hopefully very far away.

Just as I reached for the flashlight, I smelled it.

Stale cigarette mixed with body odor.

I froze, then crouched behind the larger tree trunk. It took me a few moments to find him. The beer belly, covered with a khaki shirt, poked around a tree upwind of me. His head turned and lips moved.

Is he talking to somebody? A radio?

A stick snapped.

I clapped my hand over my mouth. The toilet paper looked like a snowy beacon. I quickly kicked it under a thick pile of pine needles.

The wind shifted, and a soft voice carried to where I hid. "No one has come or gone since I got here. Yeah. Okay. Wait until we're all in position."

Was that behind me? I couldn't tell. I crouched even closer to the ground, pushing more needles around the toilet paper.

Crack!

My heart jumped. My hand held the scream in check.

Beer-gut open fired on the cabin.

Aynslee sneezed. Winston made a fluffy pillow on the back-seat, but his fur kicked up her allergies. She quickly checked her backpack. It rested undisturbed at her feet.

"Bless you," Beth said from the front seat. "So, you're awake."

"What time is it?" Aynslee asked.

"Almost midnight," Robert said. "We're stopping in Ritzville for coffee."

"How long before we reach Seattle?" Aynslee scratched Winston's ear. He rewarded her with a juicy burp.

"Another three and a half hours, not counting stops.

Technically, the conference isn't in Seattle," Beth said. "It's north of Bellevue, on Lake Washington. A new, elegant conference center. We'll have quite the adventure."

"Yeah, well, okay." Aynslee shrugged, then nudged the backpack open. She'd wrapped the package from Ethan Scott in a T-shirt. Maybe she could find a chance to throw it into the lake. No Ethan, no Utah, no Academy.

I burrowed farther into the tangled shrubs, my ears covered against the bedlam of gunfire. Pinpoints of golden light appeared in the flimsy cabin walls as the pounding projectiles struck.

No return fire came from the cabin. I moved my head slightly. *Boom!* That sounded like a shotgun.

Had the men inside ducked the bullets? Somehow I didn't think Johnson, confined to a wheelchair, would move fast enough to avoid the onslaught. Why didn't Howell fire back?

I hunkered down farther, blending with the darkness, allowing only my eyes to move, breathing silently through my mouth. As each shot occurred, I'd shift my gaze and locate the shooter. *One. Two. Three. Four. At least five men. Maybe more in the front where the cabin blocked my view.* Beer Gut approached the structure, passing me without looking.

The light from the cabin expanded, then a *whoosh!*

The building exploded. Fire lapped around the shattered windows.

Dead. They are all dead.

Voices called to each other around me. The killers.

Think. If they find you . . .

The inferno illuminated the woods, turning the pines olive green and orange. My patch of darkness evaporated with the light.

The woodshed in front of me cast a deep shadow, but it was too near the blaze. If I could shift to my left, a line of trees could provide a small amount of cover. *Then what? I'm in the middle of an Idaho wilderness.*

Move now. Worry later.

That seemed like such an easy concept, but I remained frozen.

Go. Now!

I stayed in the shadow of the trees, sliding, creeping, slithering away from the fire. The cover ended. Three quick steps, then another lodgepole. I clutched the craggy bark like a lifeline. No killers in sight. They must be in front of the cabin.

The illumination from the fire lapped at the darkness, sucking up cover, undulating in the shadows. I crouched, scrambled away from the cabin's pyre. If I could swing around the building, I could follow the road to the cluster of houses I'd spotted on the way in. Electrical wires meant that they were less primitive. I might even find a phone.

Whoooosh!

I ducked.

The roof caved in, sending dancing sparks upward.

Oh, Lord, those poor men. They didn't have a chance. They were fathers, grandfathers, probably great-grandfathers. They should have died peacefully in their sleep.

Not shot down and burned.

My nose ran and I wiped the tears streaking my cheeks. The

air was thin, and I sucked it in, trying to get enough oxygen to race to the next set of evergreens.

A twig snapped. A hand gripped my shoulder. A rasping male voice said, "Well, lookie what I found."

CHAPTER
TWENTY-FIVE

AYNSLEE WATCHED THE PASSING HEADLIGHTS, curled up in the backseat with Winston. She'd tried to talk to her dad about the article, but once again he was ignoring her. The more she thought about just running away, the better it seemed. Her dad's book was more important than she was. She'd heard her parents fighting one night and Dad had said they both ruined his writing career. Mom wasn't any better. She said she *had* to take the job, that a motel room in a small town wasn't any place for a kid acting out.

It was a stupid little party where some other kids were doing drugs. No one had even asked her to explain, and instantly, she was a dope addict. Then Mom sent her to that school full of losers.

What ever happened to second chances?

Aynslee buried her face in Winston's fur to hide her tears.

The man gripped my shoulder painfully. I didn't wait for reinforcements. I spun, then slammed my foot into his crotch.

He dropped like a pile of concrete.

I ran. *Keep the cabin behind you. Run downhill.* Branches snapped and broke in my hair, rough bark ripped my skin, loose pine needles skidded underfoot.

Someone shouted on my left.

I ran faster, sucking in thin mountain air. How far did we drive past those buildings?

The ground disappeared under my pounding feet.

I pitched forward over a precipice. I clutched at air, flipped, banged my knees, grabbed at shrubs, slowed, then finally slammed into a scaly trunk.

I lay motionless, trying to breathe.

A flashlight wavered above me, probing the drop-off. "You're sure she ran this way, Sheriff?"

Sheriff?

I edged around the tree until hidden by its trunk, then pulled my knees to my chest. My legs, arms, ribs ached. The thick jacket absorbed some of the fall, but not enough.

A sheriff was responsible for the ambush? Could they have known they were shooting four ancient men and a fellow law enforcement officer? And me?

"We need to find her."

I jerked my head back so hard I smacked the tree.

"Did you hear something?" The flashlight whipped in my direction.

"I didn't hear a thing."

The raspy voice belonged to the sheriff, the one I'd kicked. *Terrific. Assaulting a cop.*

A killer cop.

A snap, then the squeak of leather. "Suppose she's armed like the others?"

"Put your pistol away," the second man said. "Keep looking."

Footsteps crunched above me and to my right.

My heartbeat pounded a tattoo in my chest. Sweat soaked my shirt. *Armed like the others?* It started with a single shot. Had that come from the cabin? Only Deputy Howell appeared to have been armed.

I closed my eyes and replayed the raid on the Avenging Angels. No. Not Howell. The gunfire was near the parked cars. Someone outside the building pulled that trigger. Itchy trigger fingers, expecting trouble. One shot would have started the frenzy.

They must have followed the men up from Utah. Or had they tracked Howell? Did they see me get into Howell's car? Could I have led this batch of good ole boys to the evil Avenging Angels? Were the men dead because of me?

Bile rose in my throat.

Other flashlights now pierced the darkness, flickering between the lodgepoles. They were coming from every direction.

High overhead, orange fireflies darted through the tree limbs.

If I were the bait, that meant they knew I was here. They started that shootout, believing I was inside that cabin. Did I know too much? Was I getting too close to . . . what?

I crouched, ready to spring. As soon as the searching lights retreated downhill, I'd run.

Wait a minute. Fireflies live in temperate climates, not in the mountains at six thousand feet. The pines in front of me became visible, bathed in a copper glow, as a crashing sound grew. Roaring, booming. Thundering hooves. Louder, closer. A mammoth elk tore past me.

I stumbled forward, legs wobbling, arms shoving tree limbs. Two deer, the eyes showing white, bolted after the elk. A locomotive roared above me, turning the trees orange.

The forest fire crested above me.

CHAPTER
TWENTY-SIX

I PLUNGED AFTER THE DEER AND ELK, AIMING downhill. I was hounded by the roar of exploding pines and waves of heat. A black bear caught up, then passed. The hellish light illuminated the ground. Sparks prowled on the breeze, seeking the next lodgepole, landing, flaring to a blaze, sending fireworks skyward.

I ran.

My eyes burned from smoke, my vision blurred. Two raccoons joined my headlong rush. Glancing behind me, the dense smoke glowed orange, silhouetting the pines. A downed tree limb caught me in the shin and sent me sprawling. I crawled to my feet and raced on, ignoring my throbbing leg. *Go, go, go.*

I splashed in water. A small stream, frigid from melting snow, ankle deep. Follow it? The fire lit up my answer. Downed logs crossed over the water's trail. I raced on. My left shoe caught in a snag. *Leave it.*

I burst through a line of dense shrubs. Space opened up. More trees ahead. I'd made it to the road. No longer able to run, I held my burning side, turned, and jogged, still heading downhill. The fire raged behind me.

The vehicle came out of nowhere.

I dodged. Not enough.

My hip felt like a sledgehammer struck it. I rolled up the hood, slid off, hit the hard, packed earth. Air flew from my lungs. Tarred-blackness lapped around my consciousness. I sank into its depths.

Dave's head throbbed in spite of the painkillers. The doctor finally released him from the hospital, but instead of his wife, Andrea, driving him to the station, she'd ignored his pleas and headed home. As she opened their front door, the smell of fresh coffee and chocolate chip cookies greeted him. She'd moved his usual clutter of departmental files from the table by the door. The living room was empty of visitors. *Good.*

He maneuvered his crutches through the door and headed for the sofa, not wanting to tell her how exhausted he was. Or how much he hurt.

She turned on the television. "Want something to drink?"

Dave nodded. He watched for a few minutes, then dozed off. He awoke to Andrea gently covering him with a blanket.

"Oh," Andrea said. "I didn't mean to wake you. You have company—"

Louise bustled in and placed a steaming cup of foul-smelling tea on the oak coffee table. "Now, you just drink this. I made it myself. For healing. Started with dried mandarin orange peel—"

"Stop!"

Louise's eyes widened.

"I'm sorry, Louise." Dave shifted, sending shooting pain down his side and launching the pounding in his head. "Where's Craig?"

Andrea handed him two pain pills and a glass of water. "The doctor said rest. You're not to do any work for at least another week."

"That's right, dearie." Louise patted his arm.

He wanted to dump the tea on her shoes. "I need to know what's going on. I need to talk to Craig and Gwen."

Andrea folded her arms and squinted at him. "You're not talking to anyone just yet. Craig is perfectly capable of taking care of things, and Gwen's checked in on you several times."

Andrea would be leaving for work. He could get to the phone and make some calls.

"Oh no, I know that look on your face," Andrea said. "Louise will be staying here and watching out for you."

The older woman bobbed her head and grinned at him. "You can go back to work in a week."

Dave rubbed his face. *A week could be too late.*

My hip throbbed. My head felt like someone was jabbing an ice pick into my temple. What a crazy dream. *A cabin. Forest fire. Run!*

I opened my eyes.

The stark white ceiling seemed a mile away. I shifted my weight. *Squeak-aa.* Bedsprings? I hadn't heard that sound in years. A musty smell rose from a faded, handmade quilt pulled to just under my chin. I carefully turned my head, mindful of the stabbing headache. A window across the room allowed harsh daylight to bake a rectangular section of the floor. Daylight? How long had I been unconscious? Pushing away the quilt, I discovered I was fully dressed, down to the bandanna still holding my wig in place. Pings and jabs of pain from various parts of my body said move slowly. I gingerly swung my legs from the mattress and sat up. The world spun. "Ooooh." I grabbed the bed and held on. *Don't puke.*

While waiting for my brain to stop spinning, I noted one muddy shoe on the floor. *That's right. I lost a shoe in the woods.* Someone had peeled my socks off and placed a Band-Aid on a cut on my big toe. So, maybe someone doesn't want me dead just yet.

The twirling in my head dwindled enough for me to raise myself up. The room, obviously a bedroom, featured heavy, dark-oak molding. As stark as a monk's chambers, the chalky-white walls held framed photographs and what looked like cross-stitched samplers. A battered table with one drawer sat next to the bed. The room was otherwise barren.

I untied the bandanna, straightened my wig, then slowly stood. I still wore the oversized jacket Howell had given me. My arm burned as I unzipped the jacket, then removed it. Under a minuscule drop of dried blood on my forearm I found an injection site. *Scumbag.* I'd probably been tranquilized. For how long? A quick peek at my hip revealed the granddaddy of all bruises running from my waist to my knee.

The sight made my stomach lurch. *At least nothing is broken.*

I stood and hobbled to the door. Locked. I jerked on the knob a few times just to make sure, then placed my ear against the wood. Silence. The closet was empty. Not even a clothing rod, let alone handy wire hangers. The stark window was without curtains or drapes softening its outline. I limped over and looked out.

CHAPTER
TWENTY-SEVEN

BETH CHECKED HER WATCH. "FOUR THIRTY. TOO early to call anyone."

Dad pulled off the freeway to an all-night restaurant. "We can have an early breakfast. Aynslee, are you awake?"

"Yeah. Where are we?"

"Bellevue," Beth said.

After walking Winston, Aynslee put the dog back in the car and joined them at a window seat. Except to order, no one spoke.

A pot of coffee later and a picked-at breakfast, they were back on the road. Beth finally reached someone on the phone and agreed to meet the FBI agent at one of the loading docks of the convention center. They turned off the 405 freeway, passing under emerald-and-white banners announcing the Peace Conference. Early-morning street vendors hawked glitzy souvenirs. Winston soberly watched out the window, now partially opaque from pressing his nose against the glass.

The street was a cul-du-sac. The convention center, an eight-story, ebony marble structure with copper-tinted windows, loomed on the right, next to a new, partially finished office complex. Ahead was the skeleton outline of an abandoned condo building surrounded by a tottering, plywood barrier. A cream-stuccoed, modern hotel was on the left, directly across the street from the center. A garnet-and-gray uniformed bellman at a curved desk watched them. Beth pointed at the barrier in front of the condos. "Look at the graffiti. Shameful. Makes the whole area look . . . disrespectful."

News vans from Seattle's KIRO, KOMO, KING, Fox News, and other stations with satellite dishes mounted on the roofs, parked at the front of the huge entrance to the center. Newscasters, with microphones in hand, cheerfully addressed their cameramen while a gaggle of tourists watched. Dad followed Beth's terse directions to the side of the building and up to a set of large, roll-up doors.

A slender woman with short, auburn hair, in a navy blazer and khaki slacks, waited next to a metal door. She glanced at her watch as they parked. Without waiting, Aynslee jumped from the backseat, followed by Winston. The dog trotted to a nearby cement wall and hiked his leg.

"A Pyrenees!" The agent's face lit up. "My folks used to have one. May I pet him?" she asked Aynslee.

"Sure. His name's Winston." Aynslee slipped on her backpack after first patting it. Package intact.

With one hand on the dog, the agent turned to Beth. "I'd love to give you a tour, but the building's secured. I'll take custody of the sculpture out here."

Beth removed the box from the back of the SUV and made

sure the forms were properly filled out. "I have tickets, so I'll go when it opens. It looks like this will get substantial news coverage."

The agent gave a wry smile. "It's been a logistical nightmare. Security is beyond tight. Everyone will have their purses and bags screened and pass through a millimeter wave unit—"

"What's that?" Aynslee asked.

"A screening machine. Religious leaders, the ACLU, the Atheistic Society, you name it, are planning on attending or protesting. Now we even have this." She held up the box.

"I hope this works the way Mike planned," Beth said.

The agent shrugged. "We'll place it near the window on the second floor so everyone coming and going will see it. Agent Brown's working on another angle, so we may not even need to display it if he's successful."

"What other angle?" Beth asked.

"He didn't say." Holding the box carefully in her arms, she walked to the door and tapped it three times with her foot. A second agent let her in.

As the door swung shut behind her, Beth turned to Aynslee. "Let's find a dog park for Winston, then see if we can check in to the hotel."

"Here." Dad handed Beth the car keys. "I've done my duty. I'll take a cab. I've got a . . . friend in Bellevue. See you later." He strolled up the street without even saying good-bye.

Aynslee's vision blurred and a lump formed in her throat. Oh, he'd pay big-time for walking away.

I pinched myself. Nothing changed. Coral morning light shone between the soaring pines, casting dappled light across a dirt road. A cedar-shingled roof below me suggested a porch. From the height of my window, I appeared to be on the third floor.

A wagon, burdened with feed bags and pulled by two bay mules, trundled past. The driver wore an Indiana Jones slouch hat, white shirt, and denim overalls. Across the road, a woman hung laundry on a clothesline. Her biscuit-colored, calico dress hung to her ankles and a sunbonnet hid her face. Nearby, a small girl, also dressed in eighteen hundreds clothing, played with a puppy.

I searched for a film crew and additional actors.

The wagon passed from sight, replaced by a man on horseback. I blinked.

The man wore a black suit, silk vest, high collar, and crimson cravat. The woman paused in her laundry duties, and the man tipped his bowler hat to her before kicking his horse to a canter.

Fingers slithered between my shoulder blades.

I need to get out of this time warp. Find a weapon. After crossing to the door, I moved left, carefully examining every square inch of the room. I opened the drawer of the bedside table. Inside was a worn, leather-covered Bible. The cover page noted that it was the Joseph Smith translation. *Well, Sherlock, that eliminates the Amish as kidnappers.* Next to it rested a book of classic Mormon scriptures. I placed them on the bed. A dull pencil, digital thermometer, and calendar—dated two years ago—were the only other contents, and I lined them up on the bed next to the books.

I continued my search. The bed was stripped down to the mattress pad, and the pillow just blue-and-white ticking. Under the bed, dust bunnies hovered and danced around an empty bed-pan. *Charming.* The floor was scarred oak and apparently solid.

A bell pealed in the distance and I stepped to the window. Two more ladies joined the woman hanging the wash, each with an overflowing wicker basket of wet laundry. All three paused and looked up the street.

I heard it too. Laughing and loud chattering.

First came the girls, maybe seventy-five or more, all wearing long dresses and small ivory coverings over their braided hair. The boys followed in a sea of denim overalls, cropped hair, and bleached white shirts. They all appeared to be under ten or eleven years old and each carried a small book. As they spotted the three women in the yard, they fell into an unnatural silence. I counted as sixteen children left the group and entered the house across the street. About the same number disappeared into the house I was in. The rest continued down the road.

School wouldn't have even started this early in the morning. Some kind of children's church service?

I returned to my search of the room, this time checking the items hanging on the walls. A cross-stitch between the windows helpfully informed me, "On earth as it is in heaven." Opposite the bed was a photograph.

I stopped dead, then tried to yank the image off the wall, but it seemed to be secured like hotel art. Printed on inexpensive paper was what looked like a photograph of none other than Joseph Smith. He had a scar on his left cheek and appeared to be in his late forties.

The image was the exact duplicate of my reconstruction.

After a quick trip to a nearby dog park, Beth parked and they entered the lobby of the conference hotel. The receptionist stared at Winston, but made no comment about allowing dogs in the rooms, nor about the early hour. After Beth checked in, she pushed the overloaded brass luggage cart to the elevator. Aynslee and Winston followed. As the door slid open, Winston crowded ahead and buried his nose into the front of an unsuspecting businessman.

Aynslee stifled a giggle and hauled the dog off the red-faced man. At least Winston has a sense of humor. Their room, on the fifth floor, featured white bedspreads with navy trim, not the best color combination for a shedding Pyrenees with grubby feet. Aynslee set up Winston's mesh crate in the corner of the hotel room, then flopped onto one of the two queen-sized beds. Beth unpacked her suitcase, hanging up her clothes by color. Aynslee watched for a few moments, then closed her eyes.

I paced to the window, then back to the bed. My stomach informed me that food had been something well in my past. I rattled the doorknob, then banged on the door. "Hello? Anyone? Hey! Somebody call the police!" Back to the window. Maybe I could get the attention of the women hanging wash. I whacked on the glass. One of the women paused, turned, and stared at the house. I jumped up and down, waving my arms like a crazed cheerleader. She finally seemed to notice my antics. Carefully, she reached for another sheet from the laundry basket, then turned her back on me.

I sank to the floor. Apparently all these escapees from a bad western were in on my kidnapping.

What about Mike? He might wonder where I'd gone. Eventually. Or he might figure I'd headed to Seattle instead of going home. Beth might start calling if I didn't show up. Dave? No. For all I knew, he could still be in the hospital. It was up to me.

Even if I used the small table and threw it through the window, there was still the problem of being three stories above the ground. And I wouldn't exactly find help and shelter once I found a way out.

I pushed off the floor, grunting at the chorus of aches and jabs from offended nerve endings. Once again I circled the room, this time tapping on walls. No hollow thwacks. I ended up by the bed. The calendar had numeric daily entries, obviously for temperature if the digital thermometer was any indication. Birth control? Not with a bajillion children. The opposite then, an ovulation calendar that some woman had used to record her basal body temperature. She'd apparently wanted to know when she was the most fertile. I'd read that in some polygamous groups, husbands wouldn't sleep with their wives unless there was a chance of a pregnancy. *Nice.* Reminded me of a dairy farm, where the cows needed to be constantly pregnant in order to produce milk.

Someone rattled the doorknob.

I leaped to my feet, seeking a weapon, anything.

I dashed to the hinge side of the door. I'd slam it against the person entering the room.

The door swung partly open.

I put my shoulder against the solid oak. *Just a little more. Then push. Hard.*

Two hands appeared holding a tray.

Child's hands.

CHAPTER
TWENTY-EIGHT

THE LITTLE GIRL CAREFULLY BALANCED A TRAY containing a bowl of lentil soup, a scratched plastic cup of water, a spoon, and a paper napkin. Behind her was a woman about my age holding a very businesslike pistol aimed at my midsection.

"You will move to the other side of the room," the woman said.

Any thought of grabbing the gun fled with the look from the girl. She was terrified. She placed the tray on the small bedside table before fleeing.

I took a step away. "Where am I?"

"You'll find out soon enough." Like the women hanging up laundry, my captor wore an ankle-length, calico dress with drab peach flowers on a gray background. She'd French braided her auburn hair, which hung to the middle of her back.

"You can at least tell me your name," I said.

She thought about it for a moment. "Jane."

Plain Jane. It didn't quite fit this woman. Maybe it was the gun, but the word *dangerous* came to mind.

Jane inspected me as if checking out the list of ingredients on a cereal box.

I returned her gaze, starting with her oversized, grubby Nike walking shoes, past the tan anklets, then made a point of staring at her uneven hem. I finally finished my examination by returning to her face. A vein throbbed in her temple and her lips formed a thin line.

"You know it's illegal to kidnap someone," I said quietly.

She worked a muscle in her jaw. "You do not know our laws, for you have not read our books!" She pointed at the scriptures on the bed. "On earth as it is in heaven." She pointed to the needlepoint on the wall. Her hand trembled. "I bind you here on earth, in the name of Jesus." White spittle gathered at the edges of her mouth. "You do not know what's coming. There will be wars and rumors of wars. Then blood, fire, sun darkened. The remnant shall, *will*, be gathered. Zion will be redeemed. Then the kingdom of God will go forth, and the kingdom of heaven. Jesus will return and set up His government through His commissioned holy priesthood, to reign for a thousand years." She backed away from me. "Though you are bound, you have been blessed." She raced from the room, locking the door behind her.

I waited until the blood stopped pounding in my head. *Blessed? That was seriously creepy.* I checked the door, just in case she hadn't shut it tight. No such luck.

The soup smelled like vegetables. I strolled to the bed and sat. What if they poisoned the food? *That's stupid.* Jane could have simply shot me. But what if it had sleeping pills in it? Or drugs?

At least time would pass by more quickly. Someone was bound to look for me. I'd been out of sight for twenty-four hours. Deputy Howell and the other men weren't going to be much help. They were dead.

Thinking about their murders made my throat burn. *Just eat the soup. Get some strength.* I tried a sip. It needed salt. Badly. Any seasoning would have helped. It was as nasty as my cooking.

I finished the meal and sipped at the warm water. I was thirsty enough to drink it all, but somehow I figured they wouldn't be waiting on me hand and foot.

Lunch, or was it breakfast, now completed, I returned to the window. The women had finished their laundry duties. More lackluster calico dresses, denim overalls, white shirts, towels, sheets, and—just visible on the back row—underwear hung on the clotheslines.

Suddenly a group of men and boys poured from the house across the road. They were joined by an equal number of men coming from the front door below me. Smiles, back-patting, and cheerful nods told me whatever the occasion, it wasn't a SWAT team rescuing me. To my right, more men joined the throng and raced down the road to my left.

The men disappeared around a bend. After a few minutes, two buckboards, pulled by mules, followed. I waited, but all the action was out of sight.

The sun beat through the window, heating up the room. I shoved against the frame, but it was firmly stuck or locked. Sweat broke out on my forehead. My deodorant gave up and my armpits dampened my shirt. No sign of an air-conditioning vent. No vent at all.

I gazed around the stark room again. No power outlets.

No light switch.

No overhead light.

Once the sun set, unless someone brought me a flashlight, I'd be in darkness until morning. That was so not going to happen. I hobbled to the bed and surveyed the contents of the drawer. Slim pickings. I opened the Bible. In the center was a place to write family names.

A single name was penned in a flowery hand. *Jane Baker (Smith) 1847–1931.* Below it, she'd written, *Because of the blood of them who have been slain; for they cry from the dust for vengeance upon it.*

Slowly sinking to the bed, I pictured myself holding the blood-stained plaque from the Mountain Meadows Interpretive Center.

Jane Baker was the eighteenth name on the list of surviving children.

Smith not only survived the Carthage shootout, he remarried and started a new family. Jane was ten at Mountain Meadows. She must have appeared much younger or she, too, would have been brutally murdered.

After two years, the US Army located seventeen children. Her name didn't appear on their list of recovered children, only in the memory of the surviving children. She'd remained a captive of the killers of her family.

What would that have done to a young girl's mind? How would it affect, twist, taint her thoughts? The quote below her name gave some insight. *Vengeance.*

I shook my head. How did Jane Baker . . . *Jane?* The name of the woman holding me captive. Coincidence?

After grabbing the Mormon scripture book, I feathered the pages. A few passages had penciled notes in the margins, and a ribbon marked one section. I rechecked the calendar. No additional important dates. Just daily temperature readings.

The pencil was dull. I itched for a sharpener. I twirled it around in my fingers as I tried to piece together the information. *Primitive conditions. Except for the thermometer. Baby making.* I picked up the calendar. The writing jumped out at me.

I stopped twirling the pencil and stared at the lead tip.

Someone wrote the daily temperatures with a sharp pencil point.

But this was a rounded, dull graphite tip.

I jumped from the bed, ignoring the pings of protest from my body. Where? Where? The bed refused to move, in spite of my efforts. I tried the cross-stitch on the wall. Bolted down.

That left the small table. I yanked the drawer out, but it caught and refused to budge. Pushing it back into place, I eased to the floor, lay on my back, and slid under.

The penciled note on the underside was short, but clear.

CHAPTER
TWENTY-NINE

THE WRITER HAD SCRAWLED HER GRAPHITE message deep into the wood with a sharp, angular hand, dulling the pencil I'd found in the drawer.

My name is Mary Allen Smith. I'm seventeen. I've had three children. Nephi, Sarah, Benjamin. They all died. I must leave. God give me strength.

Poor Mary Allen Smith. She would've started having babies at around thirteen. A bit younger than my own daughter. From what I knew about such groups, that age wouldn't have been unusual. Did she actually get away from here?

Thirteen. She wasn't old enough to vote or get a driver's license. Just old enough to become a mother, and to bear the pain of her babies' deaths.

The Joseph Smith photo stared benignly from the wall in front of me. She'd probably stared at that photo every day. Memorized it.

So she'd recognize that face when confronted with the sculpture of it.

Jane Doe was between eighteen and nineteen. The autopsy report said she'd borne children. She'd taken another identity. Run away. Fainted when she saw my sculpture.

It fit. Mary Allen Smith could be the murdered Jane Doe. How did she get away from here? I couldn't exactly ask the gun-toting woman to point out a handy escape route.

The hard floor felt good, a brush of coolness on my back in the baking heat. Maybe I could just remain here, pretending to be unconscious, then spring on the woman when she bent over to check on me.

Assuming she returned.

And I didn't die of dehydration first.

After a few more minutes, the pain from my shoulder and hips became unbearable. I gingerly sat up and reached for the water. A few sips and a new problem emerged. I had to go to the bathroom. Did these demented people really want me to use the bedpan?

They had to have a bathroom or two or six for all those kids. I stood, then limped to the door. *Bang. Bang. Bang!* "Let me out." *Bang.* "Anybody." *Bang. Bang.* "I know you can hear me!"

I continued to kick and pound the door while shouting. No room can be that soundproof. My foot and hand now joined the litany of pain from the rest of my body.

A rattle of the doorknob. "Move to the far side of the room." I moved.

Jane shoved the door open, gun still gripped in her hand. "You are wearing my patience thin. Stop the noise or I'll be forced to tie you up."

"I have to use the powder room."

"We don't have a powder room."

"Bathroom, then. Latrine. Loo. Head. Potty—"

"Under your bed."

She was serious. Bedpans don't flush. In this heat . . . "Look. I won't run away. I just need a real toilet."

"I don't have time for your selfish needs. The Gathering—" Her mouth snapped shut and she was silent for a moment. "Use the chamber pot."

I hoped she'd be the one to have to empty it. A hot flash whipped up my neck and across my face without warning.

Jane's eyebrows furrowed and her gaze sharpened. "You. You're going through the change!"

The change? A giggle bubbled up and I rolled my lips to stifle it. *Yeah. I am changing into a cranky, menopausal toad.* I lifted one shoulder. "Life happens."

Her eyes widened and the pistol wavered. "But that means you're sterile!"

I thought of the calendar and thermometer. Was the purpose of my abduction to provide fresh breeding stock for their tutti-frutti band of nuts?

"I have to call . . ." She backed from the room, locking the door after her.

The original plan probably was for me to die in the forest fire. Deputy Howell's car was parked in front, and Mike will tell people that I was meeting with the deputy. When I'd obviously survived, someone saw the potential of replacing the runaway Mary. If I was correct in what this room was used for, I'd just made myself useless. Now Jane would be told to just get rid of me. *Great.* They were already hidden from society. If they could conceal an entire community, tucking away a single body would be easy.

I pulled out the drawer in the small table. This time it slid completely out. Crossing to the window, I sank to the floor, rested my head against the glass, and looked at the message. My tongue stuck to the back of my throat. I would kill for an aspirin and a tall, frosty glass of water.

I shifted lower, trailing my finger across the wood. No one knew I was here.

A brick settled on my heart.

How many people had died because of what I now know? I would never be allowed to leave here alive. If I could just fly . . .

I read again Mary's epitaph. "I hear you, Mary," I whispered. "You summed up your life in just twenty-five words."

Twenty-five words. I'd begin with my name. I pulled out the dull pencil and carefully inscribed under Mary's words, *My name is Gwen Marcey* . . . Five words. Twenty left.

Mary would have been seventeen, and in that time she'd become a mother three times. I'd lived a lot longer. What had I accomplished? How about I write, *I screwed up?* No. Not completely. I could write, *My daughter hates me.* Aynslee's image shimmered in front of me, hair tangled from sleep. "I love you," I said to the vision.

She nodded. "I love you too, Mom."

The room blurred. That was so easy. Just three words under my name. I still had seventeen left.

I could list my achievements. Awards. Friends. Cases. How I always tried to choose the right course of action. But look where that got me.

Maybe challenges?

I touched my wig. *I survived cancer.* Good, but cancer survivor didn't define me. Maybe changed, honed, focused, strengthened. Not delineated. Still seventeen words to go.

Ambitions? Goals? Marriage? Mary didn't mention her husband. What would I say about Robert? My mind went blank. Seventeen words wouldn't do it. Or seventeen hundred.

Regrets?

That would take an entire novel; a *War and Peace* tome. I could start with letting Jane see my hot flash, which probably signed my death warrant.

I really wasn't any use to anyone.

Not quite. There was someone who could use me if I'd just ask.

Beth always said that everything happens for a reason. I carefully printed the words: *God, I need You. Your will be done. I trust my life, and Aynslee's, to You.*

Sixteen. I had one word left. *Amen.*

I traced the word, then studied the landscape in front of me.

Even if I could find a way out, I had no idea where I was. Idaho? Montana? Colorado? Somewhere remote, with mountains. Not near the forest fire as I could neither see, nor smell, smoke. Big enough to hide an entire colony of misfits. All gathering . . .

I straightened. *Gathering?* Jane had briefly mentioned the remnant gathering, but where had I heard that term before? I closed my eyes and remembered. The drawl echoed in my ears. *"The time of Gathering is nigh. Only the chosen mighty one can lead. Only a prophet. He must prepare the way of the Lord, make his path straight."*

Chosen mighty one. Prophet. *Prophet Kenyon?*

Did these people believe the end of the world was near? Of course, almost every major religion had some form of eschatology. What was this group's particular take on it?

I pushed up, put the drawer back in place, then paced. Moving seemed to hurt less than sitting still.

Would it help my situation to know what they were planning? If they were contemplating some kind of a big whoopty doo, maybe they'd ignore me, at least for a little while. Or maybe the Gathering involved people outside their group. That might draw some attention.

I strolled to the bed and rummaged through the Mormon scriptures again. The place marked with a ribbon was *Doctrine and Covenants*, section 85. I skimmed it, pausing at number seven.

"And it shall come to pass that I, the Lord God, will send one mighty and strong, holding the scepter of power in his hand, clothed with light for a covering, whose mouth shall utter words, eternal words; while his bowels shall be a fountain of truth, to set in order the house of God . . ."

Joseph Smith called his journal the scepter of power. This mighty and strong one needed that book to stake his claim.

Sweat broke out on my forehead. If the mainstream LDS Church gets ahold of this journal, it will disappear, and this group of nuts will be delegitimized.

The urge to use the restroom became too strong, and I pulled the chamber pot from under the bed. No sign of spiders. With my various injuries, squatting was torture.

The temperature in the room was Africa-hot and ripe with sweat and outhouse stench. I nudged the chamber pot with my foot to the closet and shut the door. *Ha.* Now I did have a water closet.

I debated stripping to my undies. That'd cause Jane to take notice. Maybe stand in the window wearing my birthday suit. They'd get the hint I was cooking up here.

The water was almost gone, with no sign of anyone bringing another glass. I took a tiny sip, then finished it off. What was I waiting for? Room service? I wandered to the window in case a convoy of Navy Seals appeared on the road to rescue me. Maybe I could break a window? But that might bring Jane running with that gun.

The only things moving outside were the tops of the trees in a slight current. I slid to the floor and leaned against the wall.

I awoke with a start, my head resting on my arms against the windowsill. The hot room must have lulled me to sleep. Cerulean-blue shadows crept down the mountains. Night would come quickly, and my room would be plunged into darkness.

The rattle of the doorknob sent me lurching to my feet. My foot had gone to sleep, and I moaned as prickly needles stabbed my chemo-damaged toes.

A young woman, obviously pregnant, entered carrying a tray of food and water. What happened to my good ole gun-packing Jane? Maybe now that I wasn't fertile Myrtle, she wasn't concerned with my health. Hopefully this woman was more interested in talking to me. She looked about the same age as Mary Allen, my possible Jane Doe.

"Hello," I said.

The pregnant woman unloaded a bowl onto the small table, then turned and leaned against the door. "You need to eat."

"I will. Thank you for bringing my dinner."

She frowned at me and murmured something under her breath. Whereas Jane's dress was newer and her shoes expensive, this girl wore hand-me-down, faded, ill-fitting clothes. It seems I had come down in position with the group, no longer warranting Jane's attention, but relegated to a wife of lower status.

"I'm sorry. I didn't hear you." I moved closer.

The woman's eyes grew larger and she started to play with the end of her long braid. "I didn't say nothin'. Nothin' important."

"It might be important to me." Another step nearer. "My name's Gwen. What's yours?"

"Esther."

"That's a pretty name. From the Bible, Queen Esther?"

Her attention flew from twirling her braid to looking at my face. "How did you know that?"

I sat on the bed. "I've read the Bible."

She ducked her head and muttered again.

"What is it, Esther?" I asked gently.

"You be smart."

"Smart?"

"Readin' and all."

I blinked, then thought about the children I'd seen earlier in the day. She'd probably been born into this society, both isolated and uneducated. She was obviously old enough to become pregnant, but she'd been kept in childlike ignorance of the world. I needed her help, but I'd have to be very careful. "I'm not so smart. I bet you know something I don't."

She cocked her head like an alert puppy.

"I don't know the name of your group."

"Group?"

"Um, church?"

"Oh. The Remnant Latter-Day Saints of Zion."

I nodded. "See? I didn't know that."

She twisted the braid around her finger and thought about my words.

"I bet you know the names of every single person that lives in this house also."

"But that's easy."

"No. It's something I don't know. So you're smarter than I am about that. Everyone knows some things that others don't."

She nodded her head. "But Adam knows everything."

The name of the leader? "Tell me about Adam."

She let go of her hair and pointed to the bowl of soup. "You eat. Then I can leave."

Okay, Adam was a bad topic. I picked up the dull pencil and calendar, then turned the paper over to the blank side. Quickly I sketched the face of Jane Doe. I could see Esther's feet out of the corner of my eye. She moved closer. Closer. The bed protested as she sat beside me. Bathing seemed to be an option, and deodorant off-limits. I breathed through my mouth and glanced at her face. She stared at the sketch with rapt attention.

"Wow. You're a good drawer."

I continued to shade the face.

"I know her!"

CHAPTER
THIRTY

MY HEART BEAT FASTER. "WELL, NOW, SEE? YOU'RE smarter than me about something else. I don't know her name."

"Mary Allen."

I wrote *Mary Allen* under the sketch and handed it to Esther. The woman furrowed her eyebrows as she studied it. "She were smart. She had books and everything."

I thought about the grocery store in Provo. "Did Mary Allen ever leave here?"

"Oh sure. Sometimes all the way to Provo and Salt Lake City, even."

I nodded.

"She wanted to birth the babies."

"That's a noble calling. What do *you* want to do?"

Esther shrugged. "I do what they say."

"Yes, but what do you *want* to do?"

She grabbed up her braid and tugged on it slightly. Obviously the whole idea of choice was a foreign concept. "Have a live baby."

Live? Not healthy? Strange phrasing. Then again, the girl's grammar was odd.

Finally she let go of her hair and looked at me. "How did you know what she looked like?"

I caught the past tense. "Is Mary Allen gone?"

"She be dead."

Taking a deep breath, I nodded. "I know. I found her."

Her head whipped up. "Found her? But she be dead."

"After she was murdered—"

"Mary weren't murdered. She died birthin'. I be at her funeral."

Now it was my turn to frown. So maybe Mary wasn't Jane Doe. I stood, then paced to the window. "When did Mary . . . die?"

"Two years past." The woman stood. "But . . ." I could see her puzzling over the information. "How come you done this?" She held up the sketch. "You be new, and Gentile."

"Did you see her body?"

"Of course not. The senior wives fix her up."

"Senior wives? Jane?"

"Yah. She done prepared your dinner." She pointed at the food. "Eat. I can't leave till ya do."

I hobbled closer to the girl. This young woman was my only chance. "Look, Esther. Mary Allen didn't die in childbirth. She escaped here after having three children: Nephi, Sarah, and Benjamin. They all died."

"Died? I heard whisperin', woman talk . . ."

"What did you hear, Esther?"

The woman looked at me. "You found her? How she be?"

It took me a moment to work out her question. "Someone cut her throat and slashed her body."

"Blood atonement," Esther whispered through her hand. Her other hand cradled her bulging stomach. "No."

"What did you hear? What did the women talk about?"

"If'n you can't birth live babies, the Lord be angry with ya. You be cursed."

"I doubt very much that the Lord had anything to do with Mary's murder. She must have known what was in store for her. She ran for her life. When she left, she took something, something important."

Esther's gaze drifted to the photograph of Joseph Smith. "But that not be true. She don't drive. None of us drive. No . . ." She waved her hands in the air.

"Driver's license?"

"That be it. She'd be caught."

"Maybe she had help. I don't know how she got away." I touched her on the arm. "She was going to school. She was happy." I held my breath, hoping my words would sink in.

Esther absently rubbed her pregnant belly, then slowly reached for the sketch lying on the bed. She stared at the drawing for a long time, then carefully folded it and placed it in a hidden pocket before looking at me. "The soup be bad."

Aynslee woke from her nap. She hadn't planned to sleep, but when Beth darkened the room and curled up on the other bed,

Aynslee lay down and drifted off. The next thing she knew, Beth was taking a shower.

Winston lay next to her, his head on a pillow. Aynslee scratched his ear, and he sighed. *He* loved her. Her eyes filled with tears and she hugged him. "Winston," she whispered. "What am I going to do?" She thought about her escape from the school and her heart beat faster. She'd been free.

"The day really got away from us, didn't it? We'll take Winston out for a walk, then go to dinner." Beth emerged from the bathroom. "Tomorrow we'll go back to the dog park, then go shopping. Bellevue has some great stores."

"Okay." Aynslee thought about her meager clothing jammed in the backpack. Maybe . . . maybe she could get some really different clothes, maybe stuff to change her appearance. How far was Bellevue from Seattle? She could even disguise herself in the changing room and escape from a back room or something. She'd seen a show on television where someone did that.

I carefully picked up the bowl of soup and transported it to the closet where I dumped the contents into the bedpan. Esther accepted the now-empty dish, nodded her head once, then left. After slowly counting to ten, I peeped through the keyhole. I couldn't see out, which meant the key was still in place. *Thank you, Esther.*

Picking up a page from the calendar, I slipped it under the door below the doorknob. Now I needed some way to push out the key. I folded a second page of the calendar to form a long, thin rod. It took several pokes to jiggle the key loose. The clank of it striking the paper seemed loud. Quickly I slipped the paper back under the door and snatched the key.

If the soup contained something to either kill me or knock me out, Jane would come and check soon. I tugged and pulled at the quilt on the bed so that, with the poor lighting, someone might think I was sleeping.

Light faded quickly as the sun set. I unlocked and opened the door a crack, listened, then peeked. A long hall stretched in both directions, with shut doors on both sides. A window at one end provided scant illumination of the blank walls and austere oak floor. I'd have to go barefoot as Jane hadn't brought me shoes, but my feet were pretty tough. The chemo damage actually made it easier to go without shoes.

Locking the door behind me, I tucked the key into my pocket. That would slow Jane down a bit until she found another key.

I slipped toward the window. Stairs opened to my right. I could barely make out the first few steps. Gripping the handrail, I felt my way down. Occasionally the step would let out a tiny squeak or groan, and I'd freeze. The house was unnaturally silent considering all the children I'd seen enter this morning.

Maybe the house was empty.

I reached the second floor. Another window, another hall, another set of doors. Ahead, yet more stairs. And voices. A bouncing, flickering light illuminated the bottom of the stairwell. I ducked out of sight. Footsteps. No place to hide. *Please, please.*

Two young, female voices, speaking softly. ". . . so I told her it wasn't my turn."

"What did she say?"

I reached for the nearest door.

"She said I had to do it anyway . . ." The light reached the hall. A hand, holding a candle, appeared.

I opened the door and plunged into the room.

CHAPTER
THIRTY-ONE

I WASN'T ALONE. THE ROOM WAS ONYX BLACK, but a faint rustling sound to my right made my neck prickle. I crouched, feeling around for furniture—or someone sneaking up to clobber me.

My nose wrinkled from the onslaught of odors from a chamber pot, dirty clothing, mold, and dirt.

"Is it dinnertime?" The female voice cracked with age.

"Um . . . soon. Jane's . . . preparing it." I slowly stood.

More stirring of fabric on fabric. "I don't recognize your voice."

Great. She could start screaming for help anytime. "I'm Gwen."

"Gwen? Gwen. I don't . . . Are you the new one?"

"Yes. That's right."

The old woman chuckled. "I knew Adam would find a replacement."

I could hardly admit I didn't know who Adam was. Or who she was. "Mmm." I opened the door a sliver. No sounds from the hall. I quietly shut the door and waited for my vision to adjust to the dark. "How are you feeling?"

"The same. But I'm not one to complain. Not at all. A lot of old people like to talk about their aches and pains, but not me. I could make your hair stand on end if you knew the half of it."

"I'm sorry." I opened my eyes. A faint rectangle of a window against the far wall glowed. Next to it stood an old-fashioned wheelchair. At least the woman wouldn't be leaping on me if I said the wrong thing. Of course, she could have a bell or another way to notify someone.

"No, my days are drawing to an end. I'm not sorry. I had my time, had the children, never complained. It was hard but I kept my peace."

"I'm sure you did." The floor was sticky under my feet.

"It's your time now. Time to have children, be a wife." She was silent for a beat. "But being a new bride, you must have questions. All the new brides used to come to me and talk. It helped them, you see. But they don't come anymore. I'm not complaining, you understand. But you'll come back and see me, won't you?"

"I know I'll have many questions, yes." An oversize oak dresser with an oval mirror filled the wall next to me, the surface cluttered with dirty dishes and bottles of medication. I touched the doorknob. "Who takes care of you?"

"Mostly Jane. When she remembers. I know she's very busy, so I don't say anything."

I could just make out mold growing on a plate.

"Are you still there?" she asked.

"Sorry, just thinking."

"I miss teaching the young ones. It was my calling. You'll come if you have questions on scripture? I love to talk about the word. I received the second anointing, you know. Not that I'm boasting, you understand, but as a queen and priestess, I can guide you."

This is how they treat their queens and priestesses?

"Come anytime. I don't sleep much these days—"

"I'm sorry," I said again.

"Jane never whimpered. Not once, even after all they did to her. She was my role model."

"Was? Not anymore?" Was she confused, or was it me?

"She died. Oh. I see." The mattress springs pinged. "I'm talking about Jane Baker Smith. Mother Smith," the old woman whispered. "She was eighty-three when the Lord took her home. Her burning for the Truth blazed until the day she died." More rustling, then a sigh. "Adam has her fire, her vision. He is the fountain of Truth. He will bring vengeance and set in order the house of God!"

I made an effort to shut my mouth. That was creepy. *Okay, okay.* I'd take a chance. "Adam is the one mighty and strong with the scepter of power."

Silence.

Did I blow it? Was she going to start yelling now?

"Of course," the old woman said. "You're blessed to be sealed to him."

I could do without that kind of blessing. Right now I needed more of a "live long and prosper."

"Well, I need to get going—"

"What's today?"

"Uh . . . the day or the date?"

"Date."

I did a quick calculation in my head. "The ninth. September ninth."

The woman made a strange cackling noise. It took me a moment to figure out she was laughing. "Soon. So very soon. You've prepared? Read the section?"

"Yes, ma'am. Section . . . uh . . ."

"Sixty-four, child, sixty-four."

"I'll go reread it right now. Uh, I'm new and get so turned around in this big ole house. Where—"

"The stairs are on your right outside my door. When you reach the bottom, the front door is straight ahead. Unless I'm mistaken, prayers and scripture study are going on right now. I used to lead prayers, you know, but not now. Not for a long time now." She gave a heavy sigh.

"And I can find this prayer and scripture study . . ."

"Downstairs. Third door down the hall. You'll come back to see me, won't you?"

The loneliness in her question made my voice waver. "Lord willing, ma'am. I'll go now and check on your dinner, then join the others for prayers." I slipped from the room. No voices carried up from the ground floor. I paused at the top step. I didn't relish the idea of simply walking out the front door, but wandering around the house looking for another exit could introduce me to a hostile remnant clan member, one that would actually notice I wasn't wearing a long dress and braids.

The steps creaked and rasped under my weight. I tried to breathe quietly, listening for any sign of alarm at my presence.

The stairwell was jet-black. At least I'd see someone carrying a candle long before they'd see me.

The rail ended and I stumbled forward. Bottom of the stairs. Front door straight ahead. Arms outstretched, I moved forward.

Ca-clack! Golden light outlined a door in front of me, widening. I bolted to the hinged side of the opening.

I pressed against the wall as a windup lantern illuminated the hallway. The door swung toward me. A grubby hand emerged, holding the light. "Do you think there'll be any dinner left?" Leather boots clunked on the bare flooring. A slender figure entered, silhouetted in the blue-white illumination.

"Don't know." A second man followed, blocking the light for a moment. Without looking, he reached for the edge of the door, catching it in midswing, and flipped it shut.

They thumped forward, leaving dusty footprints on the bare floor. In the dim, receding light I could see the tattered and filthy bottoms of their overalls.

"Did you see that car?" the front man asked, glancing at his companion.

"Yeah. Neat." They disappeared around a corner.

Car? That sounded promising. I shot out the door.

I paused for a moment on the small porch to get my bearings. Ahead of me, white sheets slapped each other as they dried on the rows of clotheslines. Apparently whatever was going on made the women forget to bring in the wash. Crisp mountain air brought the scent of pine. And millions of stars and a crescent moon dappled the deep-navy sky.

Voices, and bobbing lights, came from both directions toward me. I sprinted across the road and dove behind a dirt berm.

A group of men and boys, shoulders slumped, trudged up the road from the right. Golden light from their lanterns glinted off sweat-cut rivulets running down the grimy faces. Only the half dozen younger boys talked with each other in low voices. "Can't wait to get some sleep . . ."

". . . I've worked since seven this morning . . ."

". . . got out and kissed the ground . . ."

A second cluster of men passed them, heading in the opposite direction. The younger ones sparred with each other: pushing, dodging, mock-punching. ". . . can you believe . . ."

". . . Adam said . . ."

The tired ones were going home to bed, so I'd need to follow the fresh shift of men.

I tried unsuccessfully to wet my lips. I probably shouldn't have emptied the glass in the room.

I waited until croaking frogs, trilling crickets, and gently flapping laundry replaced the murmuring and chattering men, then stood. The bobbing lanterns of the fresh troupe of men winked out as they rounded a curve in the road.

The pregnant woman's words came to me. *Women can't drive. They're not allowed to have a driver's license.* So being female appeared to be a liability.

I turned to the clothes still clipped to the clothesline. Going more by feel than sight, I moved down the hanging overalls until I found a pair near my size. I did the same for a shirt. The last row of clothing looked like long underwear. These must be the holy garments Beth talked about. I'd stick with my own panties. Taking refuge between the hanging sheets, I stripped, shivering in the cool night air.

My specially constructed bra held prostheses I'd nicknamed

Lucy and Ethel. Without them I was flatter than a boy. I removed my wig and rubbed my scalp. My fuzz was only a bit shorter than the young men's closely shorn hair. I never thought I'd be grateful for removable parts.

My pockets contained some cash from when I'd met with Deputy Howell—could that have only been yesterday?—I couldn't see how much I had in the dark.

I tugged on the shirt and overalls, stuffed the cash in my pocket, then rolled my old clothing around the bra and wig. Tucking everything under my arm, I trotted in the direction the fresh group of men had gone. No one carried any bundles in their arms, just the lanterns. I'd have to dispose of my things first chance I got.

Fortunately the dirt road held few rocks to stub against my bare feet. I padded silently for about fifteen minutes, passing large, candlelit houses set back slightly from the road.

I crested a rise. A slight echo carried in the wind and I broke into a limping trot. The road curved right around a stand of pines. Now I could see lights pulsate between the branches and tree trunks, and hear the low growl of car engines.

I left the road and advanced to the tree line, gingerly placing my bare feet on the rough ground.

A line of cars inched along the track leading to the compound. Headlights outlined an overall-clad, silver-haired man in the center of the road waving a lantern and pointing right. The cars turned on a dirt path, churning up thick powdery dust, and slowly passed my hiding spot. A number of young men dressed like me acted like parking-lot attendants, guiding the moving vehicles.

Everyone was singing.

I couldn't catch the words. They floated on the breeze, rising and falling in the slight shifts of wind.

The tiny hairs on my arms prickled.

A pine snag provided a hiding spot for the parcel containing Lucy and Ethel. I pushed them as far under as I could reach. "Good-bye, girls," I whispered. Hopefully I'd be far away before somebody discovered them.

After watching the parade of vehicles for a few moments, one of the clan suddenly peeled off and dashed in my direction. I melted farther into the shadows. He pushed through the branches until he was so close I could've reached over and touched him.

I held my breath.

The sound of a zipper, followed by a stream of liquid and the scent of urine, started my giggle reflex. I pinched my nose and covered my mouth to keep the sounds in. He finished before I could explode. In one part of my brain I recognized the tension release of laughter, but the analytical thoughts did nothing to stop my mirth.

Jane, or someone, would soon discover I'd escaped.

My hilarity evaporated. The young man's impromptu woodland toilet gave me an idea. I cleared my throat, then sauntered from the trees, making it a point to double-check my zipper. After a quick glance, none of the young men paid me any attention. They kept singing. I didn't know the tune, but recognized a few words. *And has made us into Gods and kings: and we shall reign on the earth.*

I stopped abruptly. The words were from Revelation, but had been changed. I remembered Dave's dad giving me my first Bible. My first book, really. Painful memories of my life before that time threatened to surface and I shoved them back. Several young men directing traffic noticed my pause. Trotting again, now in the direction of the cars, I thought about the words. *And has made us unto our God kings and priests.* Not into Gods and kings.

I pretended to sing as I paced alongside a garnet-colored van driven by a smiling man in his thirties. The animated blond woman beside him waved her hands to illustrate some point, then touched his arm. Four matching children were in the back, eyes wide in wonder. A tiny, curly-haired girl wiggled her fingers at me. I smiled back. The entire rear of the van seemed to be loaded to the roof with containers.

Moving faster, I mimicked the arm gestures I'd observed; a cross between a traffic cop at a busy intersection and ground crew directing a commercial jet into a terminal. I caught up to the next car in line, a black Suburban. The couple in this car was movie-star beautiful, with the obligatory passel of towheaded kids in the back. They also seemed to be filled to the gills with boxes. Stopping, I allowed several cars to creep past. All the occupants were young, attractive, Caucasian, with numerous children, and loaded down with what might be luggage.

The dirt road dropped into a large valley surrounded by towering mountains. Ponderosas fringed the natural amphitheater, giving way to knee-high prairie grass, dried to pale yellow.

I jerked to a halt. The cars and trucks split, forming lines, each waiting their turn to enter one of four long, low buildings buried in the earth like potato cellars. The mountains echoed the drum of powerful generators. Electric lights blazed with Steven Spielberg intensity from oversized doors big enough for a semi to pull through.

"You there," a voice called from behind me.

I debated on continuing as if I hadn't heard him.

"Young man!"

Plan B. It would look far more suspicious if I just kept walking. I'd have to take my chance that every face wasn't familiar. I turned.

"Have you been assigned?" he asked me as he caught up.

"Um. Not yet." I pitched my voice as low as I could.

The man consulted a clipboard, then pointed with a pencil toward the nearest building. "Storage one. Help unload."

I nodded.

The man frowned at my bare feet, then jerked his chin at the building. "Get on with you."

After shifting course, I gimped in the indicated direction. I followed a Land Cruiser into the building.

I blinked at the brilliant lights, illuminating the vast interior. Perpendicular to the center unloading space, rows of shelving units reached to the rafters, with neat labels indicating the contents. A cluster of denim-clad men and boys surrounded the Land Cruiser. The driver, a studious man in his thirties with a receding hairline, got out of the SUV, leaving the engine running, and helped his wife from the car. She released six children from the backseat. They huddled next to their mother and stared at the strangely dressed clan. She gently rested her hand on each child's head and gave them a reassuring smile. A local stepped forward and led them out of sight to the right, while another slipped into the driver's seat and put the car into gear. It slowly moved forward, pacing behind five other vehicles in line.

A gangly young man opened the rear compartment. Boxes and large plastic containers marked *Food Supply* filled the available space. Each man stepped forward and received a box or container that they promptly scurried off to the appropriate section of the warehouse. When my turn came, the young man handed me a beige, twenty-five-gallon container marked *Entrées*. I nearly dropped it. Using both hands, I humped the tub to the entrée aisle and jammed it onto a wide shelf.

My lips felt raw, and my tongue stuck to the roof of my mouth. There had to be a water storage area. I watched the action for a few moments, peering between the containers. Once the remnant clan unloaded the food, they returned for more. I slipped between the shelves to the next row, waited until the aisle was empty, then crossed again. I was now keeping pace with the van just in front of the Land Cruiser. Dashing toward the van, I joined a new group of young men. Once again a clan member handed me a container, this time a beige tub of freeze-dried vegetables. I glanced around seeking the correct aisle.

My heart sank. The vegetable row was toward the front of the building. I shuffled in that direction, then ducked into the fruit section. Rotating the container so the contents were invisible, I waited until no one watched, then jammed the squash behind some dehydrated apples.

This wasn't working. Any load could send me in the wrong direction. And it appeared water wasn't something they were storing. I'd spotted water bottles in most of the vehicles.

I needed to drive one of the cars.

No one looked in my direction. I dodged away from the center unloading area toward the outside wall. The bright lights of the center of the building gave way to shadows. Although the open doors kept the exhaust fumes moving, here on the outer wall the air was thick with the stench. Someone had overlooked the minor detail of poisonous vapors gathering in the unvented sides.

That was good. A chink in their plans, an overlooked detail. There would be more.

Dashing toward the front of the building, I soon reached the first row filled with baby food. My heart thumped and breath came in short gasps. Moving food stuff, I was invisible. I grabbed a box filled with jars of split peas and calmly moved to the center of the building.

A mineral-gray SUV pulled forward. I thrust the baby food onto an open shelf, then charged to the car. As the toothy, Donny Osmond clone stepped from the driver's seat, I hopped in.

A broad-shouldered, even-featured young man in his early twenties caught the door before I could shut it. "What do you think you're doing? Who said you could be a driver?"

"Um . . ." I lowered my voice. "Adam. He promised." I held my breath as he glared at me.

After a millennium, the man shrugged his shoulders and slammed the door. I started to breathe.

Slowly, ever so slowly, I crawled forward as the young men emptied the car. An opened bottle of water in a cup holder helped alleviate my thirst. I'd worry about germs tomorrow.

Yet another denizen of the community, holding a clipboard, seemed to be checking off the cars before they exited. I put my head down and watched him out of the corner of my eye.

He didn't even blink.

I drove from the building. I wanted to sing, jump up and down, let out a hearty *woo-hoo*. Instead, I followed the van in front of me up a gravel road. It gradually climbed, then crested.

My mouth dropped. Ahead, lit by headlights, was what

looked like three football fields of parked cars. Not just parked, but jammed together, leaving no room in between to drive out. To my right was a sea of tents.

The Gathering.

CHAPTER
THIRTY-TWO

I PARKED IN THE INDICATED SPOT AND STEPPED out, but before I could make a run for it, another clipboard-toting, gray-haired man spotted me and started strolling in my direction. I didn't fancy being assigned to unload again. He raised his arm and waved at me, and I casually waved back. His wave became an impatient gesture for me to come to him.

A piercing siren from one of the buildings sent him running in that direction, and I used the opportunity to dash between the parked cars. I dove on my stomach between a Trooper and a Dodge Caravan. Prickly field grass jabbed me in the stomach. Dust burned my nose, and I pinched it to keep from sneezing. The horn ceased bellowing. Soon a pair of denim legs and a swinging clipboard marched in my direction. I ducked, slithered under the Trooper, and held my breath. The legs hesitated, then tramped closer.

I clutched the earth and tugged my body between the rear tires. The chilly sod seeped through my clothing, and I clenched my teeth to keep them from chattering. My feet were numb. I inched forward until I could slide my hands into my armpits to warm my frozen fingers.

The legs paused next to the front of the vehicle. If he bent down, he'd see me.

Everything ached: My jaw hurt, hip pounded, and fingers remained icy. My whole body now shivered uncontrollably. He didn't have to find me. I'd freeze to death hiding here.

Finally, an eternity later, the legs strolled off.

I wasn't sure I could move. I wiggled, then blew on my fingers to warm them. On elbows, I slithered from under the Trooper, then used the door handle to stand. My feet seemed to belong to someone else.

After checking for any lurking remnant, with or without clipboards, I peered inside the nearest vehicles. Good news and bad news. The keys were left in the ignitions on most, but they were parked so tightly that only the outer rim of cars and trucks could move, and then only by tiny increments. The first row and corner vehicles held the most promise.

Keeping a lookout for anyone paying undue interest in my snooping, I crouched and limped down the row. Unfortunately, this bunch seemed prone to large families and even larger vehicles. I'd almost given up hope when I spotted an older Toyota Prius.

I slipped into the car. The icy, plastic bucket seat started the shivering again. Pulling my frozen feet up, I chafed them until pain replaced the numbness.

Now I just needed a good story to get out of here, an important reason to be heading away from, not toward, the Gathering. *Okay.* What if I said I had an urgent package for Adam? But who the heck was Adam?

What if I said that, unknowingly, *to* Adam? Or Adam was one of the clipboard-crew? I chewed my lip, watching the stream of cars.

Wait. What if someone couldn't make it? Their car broke down? I could be heading out to pick them up.

As long as a clipboard Nazi doesn't stop me and ask for a name.

I could say Smith. Or Young. Not very creative, but it just might work. I started the engine, put the car into gear, and drove forward. I wanted to twist the heat to high, but it would only blast cold air until the engine warmed. I didn't put on the head-lights until I was clear of the parking area. The kicked-up dust covered part of my escape. To my right, I spotted a dirt track swerving around the buildings. I aimed the car in that direction and turned on the headlights.

I made it as far as the waiting line of vehicles on the far side of the buildings before a middle-aged man in a quasi-police uniform stepped in front of the car. I rolled down my window. "Yes?"

He swaggered over and stared intently at my face. "Out of the car."

The pit of my stomach felt hollow. I could gun the engine and try to make a run for it, but I had no idea where to run. I got out.

"Stand there." He pointed between the headlights. I stood.

Taking a flashlight off his belt, the officer carefully exam-ined the car's interior, then popped the trunk and did the same.

I thought about Esther's odd speech pattern. "There be a problem?" I kept my voice lower and worked to keep it from cracking.

"Maybe. Got a possible runaway. Woman. Short, blond hair. Wearing pants."

He said it as if the pants were pasties. *Great. Jane's called out the dogs.* "Uh, no, sir. Didn't see nobody."

He slammed the trunk closed. "Where ya heading?"

"A family be in trouble. Car's broken down. I be picking them up."

"Name?"

I wasn't sure if he wanted my name, or the family's name. "Smith."

He grunted.

I wiped my hands on my overalls. He'd clearly see my bare feet if he moved any closer. I'd left one shoe in the room. Jane would've noted I was barefoot. *Please, Lord, maybe You could smite the man right now?*

The officer waved me back to the car. I hesitated, unwilling to move. A truck pulled in behind the Prius, and the officer strolled over to speak to that driver. I sprinted to the car, slammed it into gear, and pulled out, turning the heater to high. I was the sole car going in the opposite direction.

The line of vehicles waiting to unload ended just around the first corner. I drove a bit farther and passed under a lit banner. I paused and turned to read it.

Welcome to Zion.

Zion indeed. The families exiting the cars hadn't been wearing the standard attire of The Remnant Latter Day Saints of Zion. They would blend in with ordinary folks. I wouldn't know the good guys from the bad. Any car filled with a family could be clan members heading to Zion.

I was under no illusions with this group. They weren't a bunch of kindly religious folks retreating from society to practice their faith. One or more of them brutally murdered Mary Allen, George, and Ethan. They'd tried to kill Dave. They were behind the murders of the old men and Deputy Howell. They'd kidnapped me. I thought about the lonely old woman confined to her bed, and Mary Allen's pregnancy at thirteen. As far as I could tell, they didn't even treat their own members well.

Safety lay as far away as I could get from them. The license plates of the parked cars represented most of the western states. That didn't help me know my location.

Remote.

Wait. I lived in a remote location. How did all those cars, trucks, and SUVs pass unnoticed by the locals?

The Prius bucked and rolled over the rutted track, then dropped down a series of hairpin turns. When I finally reached level ground, pines and aspen crowded the roadside.

The lane ended.

I stopped.

A dense line of trees blocked the road. Tracks disappeared into their depths. I drummed my fingers on the steering wheel.

It took a moment to realize the trees were creeping toward me. They were attached to a gate, motion-activated from this side.

I slammed the car into reverse. The gate swung to my right.

I let out a breath and drove through. The trees swung back into place. I'd bet each of the Gathering families had some kind of keypad or identification system, as well as detailed directions, to their Zion retreat.

Surveillance cameras?

Ahead, the backside of six oversized Dumpsters crouched in a semicircle. I drove around them to a pull-out, with a dirt road disappearing in both directions. Which way? The stars told me to my right would be heading north.

If there were security cameras, they'd see my hesitation. I was supposed to be picking up a family. I turned north. After a few ninety-degree turns, the dirt road ended at a four-lane highway. Again I turned right.

Two signs brought me up-to-date. I was on Highway 89. Just outside Manti, Utah.

The sun feathered the sky on my right with pale peaches-and-cream. An early-morning delivery truck signaled and turned ahead of me. A city police cruiser going in the other direction drifted past, the officer intent on the road ahead. I wanted to stop for directions, but in my strange outfit, barefoot, and lacking any identification, I'd draw attention.

After breakfast, Beth drove Aynslee and Winston over to the dog park. At first Aynslee thought the stranger was watching Winston. After all, the dog looked like a spirited snowdrift. He was a massive thirty-two inches at the shoulder and weighed more than she did. He pranced around the dog park's grassy open field looking for a pooch to play with. When a golden retriever engaged Winston in a game of tag, the man's gaze remained in her direction. *Maybe he's one of those perverts.*

Mom told her to always be aware of anyone that made her uncomfortable, and he definitely brought goose pimples to her arms. He sat alone on a wooden bench next to the nearly deserted parking area. Aynslee put her theory to the test. She walked over to Beth, watching him out of the corner of her eye. When she reached her, Aynslee stood so she could see him over Beth's shoulder.

He put on a pair of sunglasses.

Ha. Hiding his eyes. Aynslee found an old tennis ball and moved toward the middle of the field, still furtively watching him. Sure enough, his head turned in her direction. She planned to slip away from Beth during their shopping trip. If this creep stalked her . . . But if she took Winston with her, she'd be safe. He'd die protecting her, but she could hardly merge into the Seattle background with a Great Pyrenees. She'd need a new strategy.

Home was north of Utah. I sped on. A helpful sign just outside of Manti informed me I was in Sanpete Valley on Utah Heritage Highway. Salt Lake City lay a hundred and twenty-four miles ahead.

Home would be another eight hours beyond that.

I'd wanted to call Mike from the first pay phone, but the number was on the long-lost dead cell he'd given me. I could try my house, just in case he was still there. Kidnapping across state lines was a federal crime. Plus, I'd found his true "Avenging Angels."

Stopping anywhere in Utah made me twitchy. Someone might recognize the distinct attire of the remnant men and drop a dime to the Zion Gathering. At some point the remnant folks would figure out I'd escaped their compound. They might even find my wig and clothing and put my altered appearance together. They undoubtedly knew where I lived. Hopefully they'd be too busy with their Gathering to try to find me, especially since Jane knew I wouldn't add much to their breeding stock.

I was kidding myself. I was a liability.

Four hours later I reached the potato country of eastern Idaho. Both the car and I ran out of gas outside Pocatello. I'd stuffed two twenties and a five in my pocket before meeting with Deputy Howell, which was enough to fill the tank. The remaining few dollars bought me a burger and soda from the dollar menu at McDonald's. Without shoes, I used the drive-through. The teenage girl at the window did a double take on my appearance as she handed me the change.

I could see a pay phone at the corner of the parking lot, but that would put me in sight of the girl. I drove up the road a few blocks before locating another phone. Parking so the car would partially block the booth, I scurried across the baking pavement praying everything worked. It did, but if Mike was still at my house, he wasn't answering the phone.

I raced back to the car. Home lay four weary hours away.

The LDS Temple in Idaho Falls reminded me that I was still in a region where members of the Remnant Church could live. I stayed on Interstate 15, passing through the wide vistas where cowboys still rounded up the herds of cattle, until just outside of Dillion, Montana, where I turned on Highway 278. All homes, towns, and traffic left behind, I kept alert, watching for deer, elk, or wandering moose that might cross the road. The September sun beat through the windows, heating up the car in spite of the air-conditioning on high. My eyes felt like sandpaper, and the burger was now just a memory.

In less than two hours, I'd be home.

I couldn't just drive up to the front door. The remnant could have someone waiting for my return. Sneaking around might not be the best decision either, as Mike and his fellow FBI agents could still be waiting for the Avenging Angels to pay a visit.

The thought of the old men murdered in the mountains brought tears to my already burning eyes. The road blurred to a gray ribbon. I'd been awake for somewhere around thirty-six hours. I was hardly in a position to make wise decisions, let alone act quickly. I pulled onto the highway, watching for an access road. The visitor's center of the Big Hole National Battlefield appeared on my right. I could park there for a bit, but if I overstayed, the park rangers might get suspicious. Several more aching miles passed before trees again embraced the road. A pullout appeared ahead, and I turned off, continuing into a thick matting of trees, and stopped. After waiting to see if any vehicles slowed to check out the slight stirring of dust from my exit, I slipped into the backseat and closed my eyes.

Telling Beth about the stranger at the dog park would ensure Beth would call her mom and then she'd hover over Aynslee like a worried chicken.

Aynslee rolled onto her stomach and inspected her snaggy nails, then stood and peered out the window. Their hotel was a scant block from Lake Washington, but the black marble convention center blocked the view. The street leading up to the center was below. The news vans were now replaced by a steady stream of cars pulling up to the front of the hotel. Baggage handlers trotted around like so many ants, unloading, ushering visitors inside, and directing traffic.

She picked at a hangnail. Once Beth fell asleep, Aynslee'd have several hours to get away. Downtown Seattle wasn't that far.

A black SUV pulled up to the front of the center. The stranger from the dog park stepped out and glanced around.

Aynslee jerked away from the window.

He strolled to the main doors and rapped on the glass. The woman agent appeared.

What the heck? Was *he* an FBI agent? Did Mom, or Mike, send someone to watch her?

The two spoke for a moment, then the man nodded. He turned and stared at the hotel.

Aynslee ducked behind the drapes. *That complicates things.*

Ultramarine shadows dappled the car windows as I sat up. I'd kill for a cup of coffee, and my breath could be the weapon. I felt like someone took a baseball bat to my body. A glance at the bruise on my hip showed an impressive dioxazine purple with a hint of yellow ochre. I worked my tongue to raise some spit, wishing I'd saved some pop from McDonald's. At least I was somewhat rested.

The lack of traffic allowed me to pull onto the highway unobserved. I couldn't assume some of the clan hadn't been dispatched to search for me, and my home would be the first place they'd look. But without a driver's license, credit cards, and different clothing—not to mention another vehicle—I had nowhere to go. Beth and Aynslee were safely tucked into the masses of attendees at the Peace Conference. Dave would help, but he was still in the hospital when I'd left. Mike would absolutely believe me, but he might have moved operations elsewhere. I'd have to call the Salt Lake field office to get in touch with him.

What if members of the clan worked at the field office? Every car I'd seen waiting in line at Zion looked like your average, clean-cut, Mormon family with their legion of kids. Mike said the FBI was full of Mormons. Would that include fundamentalists?

I had to get home, and I had one advantage. I knew the land around the house intimately.

The sun set and shadows covered the last few miles to the turnoff for the county road leading to my place. Mike had circled the old McCandless farm, about a half mile from my driveway, as a possible surveillance spot. An overgrown logging road cut through the woods just before their farm and circled around behind the abandoned homestead. If I didn't encounter any downed trees, I could almost drive to my own land. The track bumped for several hundred feet before a large log blocked my progress.

A pack of coyotes tested their voices higher up on the ridge, and pines murmured overhead. The densely clean fragrance of cedar told me I was near the stream that crossed the McCandless farm. I was heartily sick of going barefoot.

The crescent moon gave scant light, but it was clear that the McCandless homestead was void of human occupants. After passing it, I studied the area to my right, seeking a glint of metal from the chimney cap. I thought I'd passed my place when I finally spotted it. A game trail wove through a patch of snow-berries in the right direction. I edged forward, moving as silently as possible, listening for any human sounds.

My home came into view.

CHAPTER
THIRTY-THREE

CROUCHING BENEATH A THICK CEDAR, I WATCHED for any sign of life. No light glowed from the windows, and the only sounds came from crickets, a few frogs, and an occasional coyote. I sidled closer, using a pine to block my approach. No cries of alarm sounded.

The house *seemed* empty, that unexplainable feeling that no one lingered in the dark, waiting. Though early September days could be summer-hot, the nights grew progressively colder, and the smell of snow drifted in the air. Taking a deep breath, I strolled to my car, which was parked next to the house. The engine was cold and the hood sported a light powdering of dust. I left a faint outline of my hand on the surface. Someone had locked the back door. My keys rested in my purse, but I always had a spare hidden in a fake, rubber dog poop under the bushes to my right. After retrieving the key, I opened the door.

The kitchen table still had the look of a command center with scattered papers, books, and a notepad, but my laptop sat open in place of Mike's computer. The counter and sink were squeaky clean and a single cup rested in the bamboo dish rack. The same cup I'd left two days ago. Beth had cleaned the kitchen and put all the dishes away. I chewed my lip.

My jacket draped over the back of a chair and my purse rested on the seat. A quick check showed no one had helped themselves to my credit cards. I wandered through the house, my footsteps sounding loud in the silence, peering in each room. The house was dead quiet and deserted.

A slight ripple of unease tripped up my spine. People, strangers, had been in my home while I was gone. They'd touched my things, used my dishes. I hadn't thought about it when I left Mike, Janice, and Larry here, but it made me twitchy now.

My stomach grumbled. I returned to the kitchen where the freezer yielded a frozen pepperoni pizza. I preheated the oven, then trudged to my bedroom for a change of clothing. After taking a clean outfit to the bathroom, I returned to the kitchen to chuck the pizza into the oven. While it baked, I took a hot shower. I didn't own back-up breast prostheses, so opted for a baggy top.

The timer beeped just as I finished, and the smell of melting cheese permeated the house. I stood at the counter and bolted down half of it.

I finally felt human. My bed called for me to curl up under the covers and sleep for a week, but the tiny matter of a crazy remnant showing up at anytime kept me moving.

The too-still house made me itchy. After turning on the kitchen radio to the local soft-rock station, I assembled all the cash I could find, then threw some clean underwear, change of clothing, and a dark-brown wig into a small case. My pistol was missing. Maybe for the best, considering I'd blown away a plaster head, but not having it bothered me.

Revisiting the living room, I opened a few drawers just in case someone had moved the gun. The room yielded no results beyond looking exceptionally tidy. Beth must have dusted before she left.

No. She didn't have time. She left before me. *Odd*.

The ripple, now more of a wave, of unease returned. The living room wasn't just dusted, someone had vacuumed. The furniture was slightly out of place as well. I continued to the studio. It, too, looked clean except for the sculpting stand. A boxwood modeling tool rested on a small hunk of clay.

I swallowed hard. I was sure I'd used all the clay in the reconstruction. I picked up the clay ball and rolled it around in my hand. It looked and felt just like the clay I'd used before. After putting it down, I strolled to the center of the room and slowly turned. Tiny things stood out to me. A hand-thrown pot was in a different place. Watercolor trays were in a reverse order. A basket of spray bottles sat at an angle. On the third shelf, behind the mounting adhesive and varnish, was a spray can I didn't recognize. I pulled it out. Krylon spray paint, the same color as the graffiti at the interpretive center.

My heart pounded faster. I sprinted to the hall closet and pulled out the vacuum cleaner. It contained a new bag.

The bathroom was next. I'd used the shower, and my wet towel hung over the rod. The medicine cabinet was the usual clutter, but the prescription drugs were in the front. A jar of shells from a trip to Florida sat on the tank of the toilet. The fluffy peach cover had a slight impression where the jar origi-nally rested. I removed the shells and pulled off the tank lid. A clear plastic bag floated in the water.

The bag was full of cash.

I left the money and replaced the lid with shaking hands. My mind didn't want to put the pieces together. Racing to the bedroom, I found the same overly tidy results I'd missed. Clothes hung where I'd left them, and my shoes lined up on the floor, but a shoe box behind a wicker laundry basket caught my attention. I licked my lips, nudged the box closer, then removed the lid.

A white pair of newer Nike walking shoes nestled inside, my size, and covered with rust flecks.

I found myself in the kitchen without knowing how I got there. The only clutter in the house had been the kitchen table. I'd thought Mike's notes covered the surface, but the papers were Beth's notes, a printout of the article I'd written on the recon-struction, and a large, leather-bound book of LDS scriptures.

The old woman's voice whispered in my ear, *"Soon. So very soon. You've prepared? Read the section?"*

"Yes, ma'am. Section . . . um . . ."

"Sixty-four, child, sixty-four."

Snatching the book, I ripped through the pages. Section sixty-four. *Doctrine and Covenants.* I skimmed the words until I reached the final verses. They leaped from the page.

". . . the willing and obedient shall eat the good of the land of Zion in these last days . . . Behold, I, the Lord, have made my church in these last days . . . a judge . . . to judge the nations . . . if they are not faithful in their stewardships shall be condemned . . . And the day shall come when the nations of the earth shall tremble because of her, and shall fear because of her terrible ones. The Lord hath spoken it. Amen."

The outline at the top of the page informed the reader that the revelation was given by Joseph Smith, then gave the date and location. The date was September eleventh.

Today was September tenth.

Tomorrow was the day when the nations of the earth would tremble. But where?

Again the words from the outline jumped from the page. *The stronghold in Kirtland will come to an end . . .*

Kirkland.

The Peace Conference was in a suburb of Seattle.

Kirkland, Washington.

CHAPTER
THIRTY-FOUR

THE SOFT VOICES OF ALISON KRAUSS AND Union Station crooned from the kitchen radio, at odds with my racing pulse and thoughts. The song ended with a station break, then a male voice said, "Bringing you news at the top of the hour. The FBI and local authorities advise you to be on the lookout for a suspected terrorist. Gwen Marcey, of Copper Creek, Montana, escaped custody this morning. She's a person of interest in several murders at Mountain Meadows and Fancher, Utah, and is considered armed and dangerous. She is described as a white woman—"

The book dropped from my numb fingers. *Terrorist?*

Terrorists blow up things, kill people. How could I be—

"No. No. No." I clapped my hand over my mouth to stop the mindless chant. Chunks of the puzzle dropped into place as I ran to the studio.

I booted the computer on my desk and paced until it was on. I kept mistyping the words, but finally the website came up. The photo in the center of the page showed a cream-colored block of material. *How can I know for sure?* I picked up a tiny chunk of clay from my sculpting stand. Grabbing up a piece of paper, I put it in the utility sink and placed the clay in the center. After finding a match, I lit the paper and backed away as far as the door.

As the flame lapped at the edge of the clay, it caught fire.

I raced forward and turned on the faucet, blasting the flames with water, then jumped back as the last wisps of smoke drifted upward.

Oil-based modeling clay doesn't burn.

The website photo exactly matched the substance I'd used to reconstruct the face of Joseph Smith.

Mike hadn't brought me child's modeling clay from his sister's kids. He'd given me C-4. Plastic explosives. Over eight pounds. And he didn't hand me a tracking device to plant in the mandible. He handed me a detonator.

Now that reconstruction was at the Peace Conference.

Thousands of other innocent people were there.

And so were Beth and Aynslee.

I yanked the phone and tried to dial Dave. The numbers jumbled in my brain, but I kept punching buttons.

Louise answered. "Moore residence."

"Oh. Louise. I called Dave—"

"Gwen, it's you. Dave's here. He can't come to the phone. Now listen, child, you're in a world of hurt. You need to turn yourself in. This will all get sorted out. It's just a big mistake—"

"Listen to me, Louise, I *have* to speak to Dave—"

"Now, now. That's just not possible. They're getting a search warrant right now for your home. Just sit tight—"

"How did you know where I was calling from?"

"Caller ID. I just know—"

I gripped the phone tighter. If they had a search warrant, I had precious little time. "Louise, a whole bunch of people's lives depend on you. Write down this number." I recited the phone number from the Avenging Angels' cell phone. "Did you get that?"

"Yes, but, dear—"

"Give that number to Dave. Tell him that Mike Brown, the FBI agent, is planning to blow up the Peace Conference tomorrow! The bomb is Joseph Smith—"

"Oh dear. You need to take some of that medicine—"

I slammed down the phone. No time to argue. I had to get out of here.

With his plaster-covered leg propped on the couch in the living room and his patience worn as thin as silk thread, Dave stifled the urge to snap at Louise. "Who was on the phone?"

"Now, Dave." Louise made as if to plump the pillows behind his head.

He caught her arm. "Louise, I'm not an invalid. Just answer my question."

"Harrumph." The older woman sniffed. "If you must know, it was Gwen."

"What did she want?" Getting Louise to talk was like eating broth with a fork.

302

"She was just babbling on about some man and a conference . . . I don't know. It didn't make any sense. Would you like your tea now?"

"Not now. Not ever. Did she say anything else?"

Louise chewed her lip in thought. "Well—"

"Louise!"

"She gave me a phone number."

"Bring it to me."

"I don't—"

"Bring it to me and go make me some tea." Dave tried to smile.

Louise visibly brightened and left the room for a moment, returning with a sheet of paper. "Here you are."

"Now bring me a phone."

"Oh no, I can't do that. Doctor's orders. German chamomile sound good?"

"Lovely." Dave grabbed the paper and waited for the woman to leave. As soon as he heard the clatter of the teapot in the kitchen, he shifted his leg to the floor. The nearest phone was in the hall. He hopped three steps and grabbed the back of a recliner, dragging what felt like four hundred pounds of plaster. The bouncing relit his headache. He waited, caught his breath, then hobbled two more steps and clutched the door frame. Sweat dampened his forehead. The phone was on a small table to his right.

The teapot whistled in the kitchen.

Dave pushed off the door frame and used the wall to brace him. One, two, three slow hops and he reached the phone. He checked the crumpled paper in his hand, then dialed.

"No one is available to take your call. Please leave a message after the tone."

"This is—"

Louise grabbed the handset. "I told you. The doctor gave me strict orders. No work. No business, even on the phone."

Dave wanted to argue, but his unbroken leg felt like spaghetti and his head had a marimba band banging away in it. Leaning heavily on the older woman, he staggered to the sofa. Gwen's problem would have to wait.

The police would arrive any moment, and if I left immediately, my car would be promptly spotted. The stolen Prius probably had an APB on it by now. That left Robert's Porsche. I raced to the hall closet and found one of Robert's jackets and a baseball cap.

My credit cards could be traced. I needed more cash. I tore into the bathroom, pulled off the tank lid, and grabbed the plastic bag holding the money. Cold water from the tank dripped on my foot and I stopped unzipping the plastic.

I was stealing.

Ha! What's stealing when I'm already being framed for murder? I grabbed half the cash. Not bothering to pull on the jacket, I scooped up my purse and bag and charged toward the door.

The papers on the kitchen table stopped me. I shuffled through Beth's printouts from the Mormon Church's website, searching for the article I needed. I could feel the clock ticking away the seconds before the police would arrive. I made it to the bottom of the stack. The page I sought wasn't there. I turned to run when I spotted the corner of paper with the article on Temple Square. I tugged it out and scrawled Dave's name in the margin. It was a long shot but all I could do for now.

I sprinted to the garage. Robert always kept a spare key in a metal box inside the wheel well. I felt around three wheels before locating it.

In seconds I had jumped in the car, jammed the baseball cap on my head, and started the engine. I backed out, spun across the grass to get around my car, and tore down the drive.

Just as I reached the Safeway on the edge of Copper Creek, a long line of law enforcement vehicles passed me, lights blazing, sirens blasting. No one even glanced at Robert's platinum-silver metallic, 911 Turbo.

Louise would've told them I was home. They'd probably cut the sirens when they got close to the house, not knowing the situation. If I was lucky, they'd waste valuable time surrounding the place and trying to talk me out.

I had to reach the Peace Conference before Mike could put his plan into action.

Naturally, Robert had a radar detector. For once I was glad he spared no expense on himself. He even had a custom license plate: Porsche. I sped up Highway 93, slowing down when I reached Missoula. I caught I-90 West without incident. It would take a bit more than seven hours to drive to Kirkland, not counting stops for gas, but I should be able to pick up time by speeding. I'd reach the conference sometime around six in the morning, well before the opening at eight.

Traffic was light on I-90. I tapped the steering wheel and thought about Mike. I'd been the perfect patsy every step of the way. Robert's book, cancer, the divorce, and Aynslee's rebellion left me ripe for manipulation, which was perfect for a sociopath, who can often pass lie detector tests. He must have laughed at my pathetic need for attention.

I punched the dash, then swiped at my damp eyes. *Fool. No wonder Robert left you.*

Once Mike had my trust, I hadn't bothered to ask for identification on the two "agents" Larry Frowick and Janice Faga. They must have been members of the remnant clan. The three of them had all day to search my house for the Smith journal, then wipe away fingerprints and vacuum any stray hairs and fibers that would place them there. The planted can of Krylon would, of course, match the graffiti at the interpretive center, and the rust stains on the shoes would match George's blood. I'd bet somewhere around the place would be a Pulaski. I had no alibi for the time of his murder. I'd been alone in my room sleeping.

Mike would probably try to pin Mary Allen's killing on me as well. I'd found her body and pointed out the motel room the killer had used to clean up. Only George knew what time I'd really left the center.

Mike'd paint a very convincing portrait of me as a terrorist, starting with the near-riot at the center's opening, which he undoubtedly caused by hiring the protesters. He'd probably planted evidence that I was part of the Avenging Angels, which he conveniently pointed out were killers, then sicced the local good-ole-boy law enforcement on the old men in that cabin.

But how did he find the cabin? The old men could have been followed. Or me—*the cell phone!* The cell he gave me didn't work as a phone, but I bet it worked just dandy as a GPS. He'd want to see the results of his handiwork. When I escaped from the burning cabin, Mike found out. Maybe he was even the one to hit me with his car.

Why didn't Mike kill me in the mountains?

I tapped the steering wheel with my fingernail. *Come at it from the other direction.* I ended up in Utah at the remnant compound. Mike must be close to Adam. Or Adam was also at the shootout. Adam talked Mike into letting me become a replacement wife, probably saying that if I were sequestered in a remote location, I'd be forever silenced.

When I reached Coeur d'Alene, I spotted an all-night gas station and minimart. After gassing the car, I squeezed it between a Dumpster and a tow truck. The coffee at the minimart was brown-gray with age, so I doctored it with extra cream and sugar, then grabbed a plastic-wrapped pastry. The sugar would keep me going for a bit longer. The woman behind the counter barely looked at me as she counted out the change.

Back in the car, I slid down in the seat and waited until a Coeur d'Alene patrol car drifted past. When the coast was clear, I pulled back onto I-90. I stuffed the stale pastry in my mouth and washed it down with the bad coffee.

I had to stop Mike and Adam. No one would believe me. All the paperwork, the research on the kitchen table, would point to an obsessed conspiracy nut. I bet my computer had all kinds of new, hidden files that Mike placed there. The C-4 on my sculpture stand would match the reconstruction perfectly. If that bomb went off, I'd be blamed for the slaughter at the Peace Conference. And the possible death of my daughter and best friend.

My stomach heaved and I pulled over. I barely had time to open the door before I threw up.

I stood and walked around until my stomach settled. The interstate was mercifully free of traffic.

When I got back in the car, my hands were still shaking. Hopefully, Dave would make the connection between the phone number I'd given Louise and the printout I'd left on the kitchen table with his name on it, but I couldn't count on it.

I had no idea where Mike's triggering device would be, but I did know exactly where the detonator was. I'd have to get to the Peace Conference and yank that detonator from the Joseph Smith reconstruction.

I'd have to prevent that bomb from going off by myself.

CHAPTER
THIRTY-FIVE

THE DOORBELL RANG, FOLLOWED BY THE LOW murmur of voices growing louder as Louise and the visitor came down the hall.

"The doctor told me—" Louise said.

"I don't care." Craig briskly entered the living room. "Dave, I just came from Gwen's place. The FBI is serving a search warrant—"

"I heard." Dave shoved himself into a more upright position on the sofa.

Craig ran his hand through his hair. "Looks like she just left."

"Oh dear." Louise entered the room behind Craig. "I told her to stay put."

Craig turned to the woman, a vein throbbing in his forehead. "You called her and warned her we were coming?"

"She called here." Louise looked back and forth between the two men. "I . . . I—"

"Do you know where she's gone?" Craig asked her.

"No," Louise said.

Craig stared at her a moment longer, then turned to Dave. "It doesn't look good for Gwen. Her kitchen table was covered with all kinds of Mormon materials. And this." He held out a piece of paper tucked inside a clear evidence bag. "Your name is in the margin in her handwriting. We're hoping you can come up with something."

Dave took the paper and struggled to pronounce the name. "Ra . . . me . . . youp . . . tom?"

"*Rameumptom.* It's the name of an LDS online magazine," Craig said.

Dave skimmed the article, then shook his head. "Sorry. I have no idea why my name is on this." He handed the evidence bag back to Craig.

Craig's cell phone rang. "Deputy Harnisch." He listened for a moment, then his gaze drifted to Dave.

Dave's stomach lurched. Whatever Craig was hearing, it wasn't good for Gwen.

I turned off I-90 and headed up the 405 through Bellevue. Traffic was light at six in the morning. The Kirkland Convention Center, a sprawling mass of marble and glass, was easy to spot. I slowly cruised for a parking spot before pulling into a hotel's subterranean lot across the street from the center. The parking garage was full, but I snagged a spot by waiting for another car to leave.

By the time the conference opened, it could be too late. Adam, or Mike, would set off the device as soon as the dignitaries and crowds were in attendance. I left my itchy wig on the seat, tugged on a pink sweatshirt and baseball hat, slipped from the car, and dashed up the ramp, avoiding the elevator, which would dump me in the lobby.

Hiding behind a concrete pillar, I checked the road. The only movement was a piece of paper twisting in the lake-scented breeze. Surveillance cameras hovered on the street lights. I trotted out of the garage and aimed for the alley between the center and an unfinished office complex. *Just an early-morning yuppie jogger.* From a distance, no one could see my shoes weren't running sneakers.

I didn't pause, but continued down the alley, seeking a way into the center. The glossy facade and cheerful banners in the front gave way to industrial cinder block and concrete on the lower section, with tinted glass above. I tried each door, but all were locked. Part of the convention center extended over Lake Washington. No access on this side of the building. I stopped at the water's edge. Navy-green waves slapped at my feet. If I could get the detonation device from behind the jaw of the sculpture, I could chuck it into the lake.

The sun glinted through the Cascade Mountains behind me, tinting the lake's ripples with rose. I checked my watch. The conference doors would open in a little over an hour. Short of scaling the walls, I had no way into the building, and with a warrant out for my arrest, I could hardly sweet-talk my way through the front doors.

I'd have to put on my brown wig and join the first of the participants.

Aynslee woke early. Shopping bags covered the chair beside her. The trendy store she and Beth had shopped at yesterday had a huge selection of shirts and jeans, and with Beth's help, she'd tried on a half dozen outfits. The fitting rooms had no outside exits, and Beth hovered like a hummingbird near a feeder, so Aynslee had decided she'd just have to wait until the Peace Conference.

Sometime during the night, Winston snuck back on the bed and now sprawled across most of the surface. His head rested on three pillows.

Beth stirred. "Good morning, my Peace Conference crony. Today's the big day. Doors open at seven and the conference begins at eight."

"I'll need to take Winston out for a walk first."

Beth sat up. "I took the liberty of ordering room service for our morning repast. It should arrive—"

Knock. Knock. "Room service."

Beth jumped from the bed, tugged on a maroon floral silk robe, checked the peephole, then opened the door. Aynslee grabbed Winston's collar to keep him from checking out the waiter's crotch. The man placed a large tray on the table in the corner, handed Beth the bill, then nodded and left after she signed it.

The scent of bacon and fresh bread drove Aynslee from under the covers as soon as the door shut. Winston joined her, rested his head next to the tray, and stared intently at the plates.

"Is that dog salivating on our breakfast?" Beth asked.

"Mom says he's doing more of a Vulcan mind meld, you know, *feed the dog, feed the dog.*" Aynslee picked up a piece of toast, then noticed Beth was praying. She closed her eyes until she figured Beth was finished, then opened them. The toast was gone and Winston was licking his chops.

"Speaking of your mom, I wonder why she hasn't called." Beth opened the phone Mike had given her. "Well, that explains it. The battery's dead. I'm sure she's on her way here."

Just admit she doesn't care. Breakfast no longer looked appetizing. "I'm taking Winston for a walk."

Beth pursed her lips. "I'm not sure that's safe—"

"If you were a bad guy, would *you* want to challenge him?" Aynslee pointed at the dog. "I have my ticket. If I'm not back by seven thirty, I'll meet you by Mom's sculpture."

"I'll want you back here as soon as possible."

"I'll try, but Winston doesn't like anyone watching when he does his business. Don't worry, I'll be as fast as possible. The band Neutral Stench plays at ten."

Beth wrinkled her nose.

"They're great." Aynslee pulled on a pair of jeans and red T-shirt, then grabbed her jacket, backpack, and Winston's leash. "Chill, Beth, we'll have a great day."

"You're right." Beth smiled.

Craig dropped the cell phone into his pocket. "Well." He cleared his throat. "I know Gwen's like family to you—"

"What is it?" Dave asked through stiff lips.

"Doesn't Gwen have a 9mm SIG Sauer?" Craig shifted his weight.

"Yes."

"The FBI just found a boatload of cash in Gwen's bathroom. And two bodies in the woods near her house."

I waited at the entrance to the alley, watching the street come alive. Cawing seagulls floated like kites through the sapphire-blue sky, and the aroma of popcorn, hot coffee, and baking rolls wafted from the food vendors up the road. No Parking barriers blocked the front doors, men in gray coveralls spread red carpeting from the entrance to the street, and the news vans from Seattle's stations parked in the surrounding unloading areas. A few well-dressed spectators settled into a ragged line on the sidewalk. Farther up the road, police were placing roadblocks.

Distant flashing lights grew closer, a patrol car and a pair of motorcycle cops, followed by a limo. More police cars with flashing strobes followed. The black stretch car pulled up to the red carpet, energizing the news teams. Two men in navy suits stepped from the car and immediately started scanning the area, followed by a woman wearing gold wire-rimmed glasses, her hair a neat cap of curls, and her dress made of ivory silk. The woman waved at the cheerful crowd, then moved toward the press.

The first of the high-profile attendees had arrived: the vice president of the United States.

While Aynslee waited with the dog, she watched the action on the street from the window next to the elevator. A shiny black limo dumped some guys and a woman in front of the center while two more limos turned toward the loading dock in the back where Beth had delivered the reconstruction. Big muckety-mucks, apparently.

No sign of the creep who'd followed her yesterday.

The conference looked fun. Maybe she could go for a few hours, then run away later in the day. She could enjoy the bands and maybe get the autograph of the lead guitarist, Travis Judge. Then she could throw away the package, maybe hitch a ride to Seattle with someone, and be gone even before her mom arrived.

The elevator was taking forever. Aynslee gave up and headed for the stairs.

Enough people milled around for my presence to pass unnoticed. I jogged calmly across the street. Once I retrieved my wig, I'd join the waiting line. I wish I'd thought to bring a camera. No one looked twice at someone taking photos.

I reached the bottom of the ramp when a hand snaked out and grabbed me.

I bit my lip and tasted blood. Before I could scream, a gun barrel rammed into my side.

"Don't say a word," Mike whispered in my ear. "Or you're dead."

CHAPTER
THIRTY-SIX

DAVE GAVE UP ON SLEEPING BY FOUR A.M. HIS fumbling out of bed woke his wife. She helped him to the kitchen and made coffee before returning to her much-deserved rest.

He stared out the window, watching the sky turn gray, his thoughts racing. No way had Gwen murdered two people. That was an absolute certainty. Then who had? Dave tried to remember their last conversation, just before he drove away and was shot. Nothing. His memory remained a blank. Had she told him someone might be framing her? That she was in danger?

The phone rang.

Dave's hand jerked, spilling coffee down his arm. Who would be calling so early? The news wouldn't be good. He picked up the receiver. "Sheriff Dave Moore, who's calling?"

"Sheriff?" an elderly male voice said. "Sheriff of where?"

"Ravalli County, Montana. Who is this?"

"You called me last night. How did you get this number?"

"Tell me your name, then I'll tell you how I got your number."

The man was silent for a moment, then gave his name.

Dave couldn't speak for a few seconds, trying to put the pieces together.

"Hello? Are you still there?" The voice rose in irritation.

"Uh, yes." Dave cleared his throat. "Gwen Marcey, one of my reserve deputies, had your number. She wanted me to call you."

"Did she say why?"

"No, she's . . . no."

"Did she give you anything?"

Dave described the article with his name in the margin. "Does any of this make sense to you?"

"Yes. Where is your deputy now?"

"I don't know."

"Find her."

Aynslee opened the stairwell door and stepped into the packed lobby. A man in a charcoal suit turned from three other businessmen. "What kind of dog is that?"

"Pyrenees."

The man grinned. "Bet you could ride him like a horse."

"Whatever."

A girl in pigtails and yellow shorts stroked Winston's head. Her mother guided the girl away with a firm pressure on her shoulder. "I wouldn't want to feed him."

A small boy with spiky hair and missing front teeth hugged Winston's neck and kissed him on the muzzle. The Pyrenees gently waved his tail.

Aynslee just wanted to get outside. "He's gotta go to the bathroom. Okay?"

She tugged the reluctant dog to the door and entered the street in front of the convention center.

A small crowd clapped around a steel band beating out a calypso tune while a snowy-haired man and a woman in a polka-dot dress danced like they could read each other's minds. The scent of baking bread, fried bacon, and coffee filled the air. A line of twelve first graders, six per side, walked toward the center, children holding on to a center rope with a teacher at each end, forming an engine and caboose. Two men wearing long black dresses and white collars waited in line for tickets behind a woman in tight jeans and tighter shirt pushing a baby carriage.

Girl and dog trooped past a street vendor with brown dreadlocks squatting on a blanket. "Come on, missy, get yourself a necklace!"

Aynslee shook her head and kept walking. Winston slowed to check out an open guitar case holding a few crumpled dollar bills, then greeted the wrinkled man with long gray hair crooning some old folk song.

Like fish swimming upstream, Winston and Aynslee sidled around several young families, a pod of giggling teens, two clowns making balloon animals, and a middle-aged women's group wearing *Mothers for Peace* T-shirts.

Winston spotted the grassy patch at the end of the street and sprinted toward a tree.

My mind raced with alternatives. Screaming would indeed be the last sound I made. I was a wanted woman, and he'd make a good case that I'd tried to escape. I tugged my arm, but he dug his fingers into my flesh.

The pain brought tears to my eyes.

He marched me across the underground lot, passing close to Robert's Porsche, and we climbed stairs that brought us to the street. A river of people poured toward the convention center. Mike slipped the gun between us and under my sweatshirt, then strolled forward.

Two teenage girls wearing halter tops and shorts passed, each texting on their phones, oblivious to the early-morning chill. A curly-haired man in a mime outfit and riding a unicycle wove through the chattering horde. Several monks with shaved heads and saffron-colored robes meandered, bobbling to an unheard rhythm. I tried to catch someone's eye, but Mike jabbed the gun deeper into my side and pulled me closer. Steel drums kept time with our steps.

No curious glances came my way, no concerned inquiries.

Once clear of the stream of convention-goers, he forced me toward an eight-story skeleton structure. A tattered sign claiming the Osprey Condos would open soon was partially covered by a foreclosure notice. My feet barely touched the pavement. We walked through an opening in a graffiti-covered barrier, passing out of sight from the street. Gravel, trash, and a few straggling weeds lay between the barrier and structure. The stench of a dead animal floated in the air. If he shot me here, how long would my body remain undiscovered? We were only a handful of yards from the crowds, yet it seemed as if we were totally alone in this godforsaken stretch.

He maintained a purposeful stride. The solid barrier ended at a chain-link gate. He opened it and shoved me toward the soaring, glass-fronted office complex under construction.

He'd have to let go of me to open that door. I could make my move then.

As if reading my plan, at the door he spun me so I faced him, then punched me in the stomach, driving all the air from my lungs.

I doubled over, gasping. My legs collapsed.

Mike caught me before I fell, then shoved me against the building's side. I slid down. He grabbed me again and yanked me through the open door. I tried to breathe as we dodged long sheets of plastic, raw beams, and stacks of two-by-fours. Dust burned my nose. Mike dragged me up a set of stairs. My knees banged on the raw concrete. I grabbed for the railing. Air trickled into my heaving lungs. The stairs seemed to last an eternity.

We stopped climbing. Mike hauled me down a long hall, turned left past a bank of elevators, then opened a solid mahogany door and shoved me into a room.

I faced him, one hand holding my stomach, the other outward toward him. Any gunfire wouldn't be heard from the street.

I didn't want to die. "You won't get away with this. Those two agents, the one that followed me and—"

"Janice and Larry?" He grinned. "The police will find their bodies neatly laid out near your house. Along with your pistol."

My legs suddenly wouldn't hold me. I dropped to the floor. "I thought they were part of your remnant group—"

"They were. And real FBI agents as well. Loyal to the end. Sacrificial duty, as it were." Mike's expression didn't change. Killing people he knew evoked no visible emotion.

I wasn't going to die curled up on the floor like a dog. I struggled to my feet.

He pulled a ziplock bag from his pocket, crouched, and slipped a black object onto the floor without touching it. His gaze never wavered from me. "You've seen this before, Gwen."

"You left it on my desk." I stared at him. "It's not a universal remote."

He jabbed his finger at something behind me.

I looked.

CHAPTER
THIRTY-SEVEN

WINSTON TOOK HIS SWEET TIME SNIFFING THE patch of grass behind the hotel. Aynslee leaned against a tree and pulled out the package from her mom's boyfriend, Ethan Scott. She might as well open it. Fumbling a bit, she finally unwrapped the box. Inside was an ancient, leather-bound journal.

Weird. She opened it. Written in faded ink on the inside cover were the words *Joseph Smith, Jr., New Revelations from God.*

She slowly turned the book over. *Joseph Smith.* That was the guy Mom had Beth look up on the Internet. Something to do with Mom's work in Utah.

Not a gift from a boyfriend.

A warmth flushed her face.

Mom had acted strange since returning from Utah. She'd shut off the lights and closed the blinds in the studio. She'd made Beth spend the night. And she'd stayed behind instead of coming to the Peace Conference. Mom wasn't trying to get rid of her. She was afraid.

But Mom is never afraid.

Aynslee's hand trembled.

No one knew she had the book. She could just throw it away.

Or do they? The guy in the dog park was following her. He knew she was at the hotel. He was connected to the FBI.

She jerked her head up and looked around again. No one seemed to be watching her. For now.

Ideas bounced around like Ping–Pong balls. She could call home. Say she was sorry. Mom would understand. For Pete's sake, it was just an old book.

An old book that some bad people wanted.

Her legs felt like rubber, and a chill went up her spine. What had Mom and Beth said about Joseph Smith? She couldn't remember. Flipping through the yellowed pages, she paused to read:

November 6, 1852

I know these things by the words of Jesus.
The Angel of Desolation will hear the wicked
And stop their hearts,
Yea their evil hearts.
But to those who hear the anointed one
Know the words of one mighty and strong.

This was seriously weird stuff. She needed to show it to Beth. She'd know what to do.

In front of me, a wall of glass overlooked Lake Washington. Across the alley, convention center windows showed an ocean of people slowly wandering, forming eddies, waving to each other, and pausing to point at my reconstruction mounted on a display stand.

The bomb.

I jumped to my feet, raced to the glass, and pounded with my fists. "Get away! It's a bomb!"

"They can't hear you. Or see you. That's one-way glass."

I stopped pounding and faced Mike. My gaze dropped to the black object. A hot flash surged up my neck.

"I can see the light of understanding on your face, Gwen. Yes, a detonator. One you handled, covered with *your* fingerprints. You'll be the one blamed for the bombing. Your name will be right up there with Timothy McVeigh and Osama bin Laden."

The bomb would kill hundreds, if not thousands, and blow out the side of the building. The force of the blast would destroy the glass wall in front of me. They'd find me in the rubble, along with the detonator.

But if that were the case . . . in order for that plan to work . . . my body couldn't have bullet holes in it.

A glimmer of hope seeped into my brain. Maybe I could reason with him, delay him if he had a timetable.

He shifted slightly and readjusted his earpiece. His impeccably cut navy suit, starched white shirt, and maroon tie screamed FBI.

"Won't the other agents be suspicious? You did arrange for the reconstruction to be put on display."

"Larry did. He's in no position to point a finger."

What about his other identity? "You don't want to kill all those people. You're a member of the remnant. Maybe a prophet." I stumbled over the word *prophet*.

He lifted his chin slightly. "Not *a* prophet. I'm *the* prophet."

"*The* prophet? I thought Adam was the leader."

"I am."

"*You?*"

"My full name is Adam Michael Brown."

The blood drained from my face, leaving me faint. I put out my arms to steady myself. He'd been there all along. Mary Allen's murder. Then George. Ethan Scott. "So you cut off George's hand?" I stared at him.

He waved his arm as if swatting at a fly.

"You shot Dave," I said softly. He'd been in the mountains, surrounding the old men. He'd *started* the shootout. He'd transported me to Zion. "Why are you doing all this?"

"I'm fulfilling the prophecy. Joseph's name being, 'had for good and evil among all nations, kindreds, and tongues.'" Mike's voice rose. "The gospel was returned, and the keys restored, but the church has fallen away, as the scriptures stated. You were there. You saw Zion gathered and flourishing upon the hills. They await the cleansing. They have brought their rich treasures to the children of Ephraim."

I pictured the huge food storage buildings in Zion. "All those families coming together in one place?"

Mike nodded. "'For behold, the day cometh that shall burn as an oven, and all the proud, yea, and all that do wickedly shall burn as stubble; for they that come shall burn them, saith the Lord of Hosts, that it shall leave them neither root nor branch.'"

My skin prickled across my shoulders. "Burn? What—"

"Before the Lord destroyed Sodom and Gomorrah, He removed Lot and his family."

I looked at the reconstruction across the street. "And this is your idea of God's destruction?"

"'Fear God and give glory to Him; for the hour of His judgment is come.'"

I pointed. "But *you* created that bomb!"

He shrugged.

"And all this is in preparation for . . . ?"

He opened his arms to form a cross and chuckled. "The second coming of Christ, of course."

The hairs on my arms stood. "You figure blowing up a bunch of innocent people will send an invitation to Christ? Hey, Jesus, come ooon down!"

"'The destruction of the wicked. Christ will rule with His holy priesthood for the millennium.'" The words were memorized, delivered in a sing-song voice. He gave me a sardonic grin.

"You don't believe any of it, do you?" I said slowly.

"No. But *they* do." Mike waved one hand in the air. "They are truly sheep in need of a shepherd." He leaned against the wall. "Do you know how wealthy the Mormon Church is?"

My face felt numb, my mouth unable to form words.

"They rake in billions. Every year," he whispered, then glanced at his watch. "I've enjoyed our little chitchat, but it's almost time—"

"Time for what?"

"In two minutes, I'll call in a bomb threat in a parked car. The police will use dogs to sweep the cars. I, of course, have been in charge of security arrangements—"

"Ah. Perfect. Who knows better about—"

"—safety than a domestic terrorism expert?"

I was going to say, "Fanaticism than a crazy megalomaniac," but changed my mind. Who knew what kind of response I'd get if I poked at his obsessions.

"I made sure at least one of the bomb dogs was cross-trained for drugs," he continued. "Then placed marijuana in a van. The dog will respond. Security measures implemented."

"The vice president has Secret Service agents. They'll pull her out—"

"That's why this is a perfect location. Essentially a dead-end street. Water on one side. They'll conclude the safest place will be in the conference center for now."

"Snipers posted on the roofs—"

"Ah, yes. A good time to be politically correct, don't you think? Snipers aren't friendly. Their appearance wouldn't look good at a peace gathering." He checked off on his fingers. "Threat noted. Lockdown on the conference. No one in, no one out. Call in the bomb unit. Before they can figure out it's nothing more than a bag of marijuana, time will be up. On the hour, *boom!*"

"But what will mass murder achieve?"

Instead of answering, he studied the peach fuzz on my head. "Everything always works out for the best." Mike leveled the pistol at my midsection. "I never lose." He leisurely pulled a pen out of a breast pocket, then leaned over and used the pen to click a button on top of the detonator. He straightened, then backed from the room, closing the door between us.

I charged to the door and turned the knob. *Locked.*

The detonator, a black box the size of a deck of cards, now

flashed with a digital readout of glowing crimson numbers rapidly winding down.

A hot flash raced up my throat and burned my face. Sweat dampened my shirt. I turned. My gaze darted from the detonator to the bomb across the street. After wiping my hands on my pants, I gingerly reached for the mechanism.

What if my touching it sets off the bomb?

I froze.

He had it in his pocket. If it were motion activated, it would have gone off already.

Gently lifting the object, I turned it over in my hand. On the back was a screw-down cover over a battery compartment. If I had the right tool, I could open it and remove the batteries.

But it could be booby-trapped. Set to go off if I tampered with it.

The red numbers counted down. 20:00 . . . 19:59 . . . 19:58 . . .

Aynslee tucked the book into her backpack and headed for the hotel entrance. She'd drop off Winston in their room, then find Beth.

Sirens in the distance grew louder. Winston perked up his ears. She stopped. Two police cars roared past, lights and sirens blaring, then stopped in front of her and blocked the street. A uniformed officer jumped out and held up his hand. "Sorry. Road closed."

"Why?"

"Bomb threat."

"But my friend's at the conference—"

"You have to stay away until we've cleared the area."

Cops are all pigs. She'd find another way in. She trotted up the block, then turned right. She was out of sight of the cop. She could go through the hotel from the parking garage. A metal fence with horizontal bars enclosed the garage, with the floor a six-foot drop below. Aynslee slowly scanned the vehicles next to the wall until she found what she was looking for: a pickup truck parked backward.

She slipped through the bars and jumped, landing lightly on the metal surface. Winston hesitated, then followed, causing the truck to bounce with his weight. After unlatching the tailgate, she leaped to the concrete floor, Winston hot on her heels.

Red, white, and blue strobes alternately lit up the walls.

She sucked in a big breath of air. *Okay, get going.*

Hunched below the line of cars and trucks, she worked her way to the side of the building nearest the conference center. The wall was lower on this side, barely three feet high. She'd almost made it when Winston jerked to a stop and raised his tail on alert. She gazed in the same direction he was looking and spotted the dog.

A black German shepherd. At the other end of the leash was a cop.

Aynslee crouched and waited until the dog and cop moved away, then crept to the wall and peeked. Up the street to her right was a second bomb dog, a yellow lab. The dog was sniffing a van. Suddenly the dog sat.

Aynslee knew what that meant.

The dog had found the bomb.

The sound of distant sirens penetrated my brain. *Police.* Mike's plan had gone into effect. I ran to the glass. Whatever was happening, I couldn't see it from my angle. I banged and screamed, but no one was looking in my direction.

I circled the room. Obviously this was to become some kind of boardroom or meeting room. Now it was empty, with concrete floor, raw drywall, and open electrical fixtures in the ten-foot ceiling. A large mirror reflected back my image from the wall on my left. I rapped against the mirror, producing a hollow sound.

My heart beat quicker. The mirror wasn't hanging on the wall, it was built in. I pushed my finger against the glass. The reflection touched my finger without a gap. Cupping my hands to exclude light, I peered into the glass. Faintly I could see a room on the other side.

A one-way mirror.

The mirror was above waist height, too high to get any leverage to kick in. I spun and checked the room, seeking a rock, brick, hunk of concrete, framing hammer.

Empty space mocked me.

Giving up on the mirror for now, I hammered the door and then moved on to the drywall. I kicked the brittle surface until a section crumpled. Quickly I grabbed chunks of the dusty material and threw it behind me. On the other side of the wall was metal sheeting.

I sat back on my heels. *What?* I closed my eyes and pictured the building's layout. *The elevators.* He'd dragged me past a line of elevators. I stood and returned to the window, thumping it with my heel, hoping it would break.

I stopped and leaned my hot forehead against the glass. Across from me, people navigated around the sculpture. They moved, breathed, talked, laughed, loved—not knowing they were doing it all for the last time.

Beth stepped next to the sculpture.

Oh, sweet Lord.

I renewed my screaming and battering the glass. My vision blurred. I tried another area, then charged around the room, kicking, yelling, pummeling the walls with fist and body.

I found myself in the center of the room, gasping for breath, fists knotted by my side.

Mike said he'd detonate the bomb at the top of the hour. I checked my watch. I had fifteen minutes.

CHAPTER
THIRTY-EIGHT

AYNSLEE GRABBED WINSTON'S RUFF AND TUGGED the dog away from the wall. Ducking below the cars and SUVs, she finally paused and leaned against a green van.

How safe was she? What about Beth? She'd seen photos of the Oklahoma City bombing. Where could she go? Chewing a thumbnail, she rummaged in her brain for an answer.

Winston whined.

"Shh, boy." She stroked his ear.

Winston whined again, then tugged his leash. At least the dog had a plan. Maybe she could call Beth's cell phone from the hotel room. She strolled toward the entrance, but Winston refused to move.

"Heel."

The dog remained motionless.

"Winston, no!"

The Pyrenees turned to face her, then backed away, tugging the leash. Aynslee shrugged and followed the now-trotting dog. They passed through a line of vehicles.

The dog stopped, yanking her arm backward.

A gray 911 Turbo Porsche, vanity Montana license plate: Porsche.

Her dad's car.

She whipped in a circle, looking for her father. *No*. Dad drove them in Beth's car. The Porsche was parked here because her mom had driven it. "Mom?"

Quiet. The police were on the street. That FBI guy was looking for her.

She took the big dog's head in her hands. "Winston. Find Mom. Find!"

Winston's tail rose over his back and he wheeled to the car, sniffing it carefully. Swiftly he trotted toward the exit ramp, but before they arrived, he reversed direction.

"Find Mom, find."

The dog headed toward a set of stairs. At the bottom, Aynslee peered out of the garage opening.

Two police cars blocked the street in front of the conference center. Three officers stood by the patrol cars, staring at something out of sight.

Dog and girl charged across the road. Winston, sniffing the ground, veered, now aiming at a blue barrier with a foreclosure sign and lots of spray-painted graffiti.

The dog yanked her through an opening, then raced faster,

head up, across a smelly, garbage-filled lot. The growing *whop-whop-whop* of a helicopter echoed off the spooky, abandoned building beside them. Aynslee glanced up. The lettering on the helicopter's side read *King County Sheriff's Department*.

Aynslee and Winston came to a chain-link gate. Winston impatiently jumped against it. Locked.

I paced, thinking. Mike planned each step, but he also took advantage of opportunities as they presented themselves. He murdered his own fanatical followers. Covered his tracks. Framed me as the one responsible.

He avoided answering my question, though. What would mass murder achieve?

Power and control. Revenge. Yes. But something more . . .

Try a different track. What did anyone attending the conference do to deserve death?

They didn't do anything. Mike has a bigger plan.

I shook my head. Right now it didn't matter. I had to get out.

I picked up the detonator and hefted it in my hand. *Think like Mike. You don't want Gwen to remove the batteries, so screw down the cover. The detonator would need to work—*

Power and control. Revenge.

No. It would need to appear *to work if they find it in the rubble after the bombing.* Just in case he couldn't switch it with the real detonator. The one in his possession.

I pictured his glee as he thought of me sweating bullets, staring at the crimson numbers counting down on the fake detonator, wasting time trying to get out or get help.

He'd use the real thing in—I checked my watch—twelve minutes.

I took a giant breath, held it, and threw the device as hard as I could at the mirror.

A starburst crack appeared in the glass.

CHAPTER
THIRTY-NINE

I PICKED UP THE DETONATOR AND THREW IT AGAIN. The mirror shivered. Jagged lines radiated outward.

Taking off my shoe, I smashed it against the surface.

The first small shards fell into the room. I struck again, harder. A small hole opened. Razor-edged shards covered my feet. *Bang!* I belted the mirror.

The mirror shattered. Slivers of glass peppered my face. I slipped on my shoe, tucked the detonator in my back pocket, and pulled off my sweatshirt. Drops of blood freckled the material. Wrapping the sweatshirt around my arm, I broke away the remaining pieces on the bottom of the frame.

I would have to crawl over the waist-high edge. Stretching the sweatshirt as wide as possible, I raised one leg over the bottom ledge. My bruised hip screamed in protest. My ankle scraped across a remaining glass shard, gouging a deep cut. Ignoring the sharp, new jab, I slid over the frame. The splintered mirror crunched underfoot.

Nine minutes left.

I bolted from the room and ran to the stairs, taking them two at a time. The unfinished lobby stretched before me, plastic sheeting gently waving in the air, the street ahead. *Get help? Try to convince the police that I am not a murderer or terrorist?*

No time.

I charged to the side door Mike had dragged me through earlier. I slammed it open and leapt through, then froze.

Aynslee and Winston gazed at me from the other side of the chain-link gate.

Eight minutes.

"Mom!" Aynslee screamed over the thumping of an overhead helicopter.

I sprinted, scrambled up the side of the gate, and dropped to the ground. Winston launched himself at me, knocking me backward into the wire. "Down, Winston! Aynslee, did you see Mike? Quickly!"

"No. Mom, I—"

"No time, sweetheart. Take Winston and run. Run away from the convention center."

"But—"

I pushed the dog down. "I have to find Mike. He's a really bad person." I looked at my watch. Seven minutes.

"Maybe Winston can find Mike." She pointed. She had a leather book in her hand.

"What's that?" I asked.

"A creepy book. Ethan Scott—"

I grabbed the book and flipped it open. A signature. *Joseph Smith*. Mike's scepter of power. He'd have handled it.

But so had a lot of other people. *Leather holds scent longer than metal.* "Give me the leash."

Aynslee handed it over.

"Winston, find." I held the book to the dog's nose.

He sniffed for a moment, then looked around as if confused.

Mike *had* to have gone through this gate.

Winston spun and dashed toward the raw outline of the Osprey Condos.

Six minutes.

CHAPTER
FORTY

WINSTON CHARGED ACROSS THE VACANT LOT, dodging piles of trash, old tires, and broken glass, toward the gloomy interior of the abandoned structure. The bare concrete surfaces amplified the helicopter's thumping blades. Daylight surrendered to cold, shadowy dimness. I stumbled over a rotting sleeping bag left by a homeless squatter. Aynslee, following behind, grabbed my hand. The dog leaped ahead, pulling us deeper into the interior. I couldn't see my watch. The seconds ticked off in my head.

Winston twisted, then plunged up a set of almost invisible stairs. I tripped and sprawled on the hard surface, rapping my knee so hard that tears flooded my eyes. Winston didn't slow, his momentum pulling me up and onward. My knee stiffened, and I released Aynslee's hand and used the metal handrail to keep up with the dog. We reached a landing. Winston kept going. Two stories. Three. My breath came in sobs. Seconds gone. Minutes.

We stopped climbing and raced forward. The helicopter's pounding thudded like my own heart. Ahead, dusty light beat back the darkness. I could finally see orange plastic netting forming a flimsy barrier around the exterior.

Cement dust made me blink.

Mike appeared.

He stood behind a half wall of concrete. He raised his right arm, aiming the detonator toward the conference center. His other hand reached for the button.

I released Winston's leash.

Mike half turned toward us. Winston didn't slow. Mike reached for his gun.

I screamed, my voice drowned out by the helicopter.

Mike pulled out his pistol, aimed.

Winston jumped on him, driving him to the floor.

I couldn't hear if he'd pulled the trigger. I kept running. All I could see was Winston and Mike's legs thrashing underneath. A flash of blue steel appeared by Winston's neck. I kicked, sending Mike's pistol flying.

The detonator! Frantically I spun about, searching.

Mike grabbed my cut ankle, his grip slipping on the blood. He dug tighter using his fingernails and pulled.

I fell hard, elbows abrading on the rough surface, cement dust filling my nostrils. Rolling and kicking at the clinging fingers, I pushed away.

The hand loosened, then let go.

I lunged to my feet, still looking for the detonator.

Mike shoved Winston away and stood. The dog tried to get

up, failed, and collapsed on his side. A red stain spread at his shoulder.

Adrenaline flooded my veins. My vision narrowed.

Mike faced me, his jaw a granite block, veins throbbing in his forehead.

The copter's thumping diminished.

A figure shot past me, landing beside the prone dog. Aynslee's wail of anguish rose above the sound of the retreating helicopter. I jumped between Mike and my daughter. I felt my lips pull back into a snarl, my hands clenched into fists.

Mike's gaze transferred to something to my left. I risked a glance. His pistol.

We both dove for it. I was closer. I grabbed it, rotated, and swung the weapon. His fist caught me alongside my head and a million sparklers went off.

I dropped the gun, stumbled backward, then fell, landing next to Winston.

Mike snatched the pistol, whipped it around, and fired. The bullet tore through my side, ripping clothing, peeling skin from ribs. A legion of rattlesnakes bit me. I clamped my teeth together to hold in the scream.

Mike raised the gun, now aiming at my head.

"Wait!" Aynslee stood, tears streaming down her deathly pale face. "Don't kill my mom." She stood between Mike and me, holding the journal like a shield in front of her.

I couldn't breathe.

Mike stared at the book and licked his lips. "Bring it to me."

I put my hand down to brace myself and touched something cool. I risked a glance. The detonator was under the dog's tail. I looked at Mike.

The book riveted his attention. Aynslee edged closer to him.

I moved my hand near the device, watching Mike.

He motioned Aynslee closer.

Grabbing the detonator, I slipped it behind me.

Mike snatched the journal. "Go sit next to your mom."

Aynslee scurried to my side. A soft thump of Winston's tail told me he was still alive. Aynslee buried her face in my lap.

Mike held up the book. "See? I told you. Everything always works out for the best. I never lose."

He again took careful aim at my head. The gun barrel was an onyx tunnel.

"Stop!" A bullhorn of a male voice rang out. "Put the gun down! Do it now!" Four uniformed officers charged into sight, their guns trained on Mike.

"Cops." Aynslee sat up. "The helicopter! Hey, that man shot my mom. And my dog!"

Mike raised both hands. "It's all right. I'm FBI."

"Very slowly, put the gun down," the officer repeated.

Mike complied, gently placing the journal next to his firearm.

"Now step back and get on your knees with your hands behind your head."

One officer approached Mike, kicked his firearm farther away, and handcuffed him.

"Careful of the book. You'll find identification in my jacket," Mike said.

One officer gingerly checked Mike's pocket, pulled out a wallet, and flipped it open. "Sorry, sir. We—"

"Just uncuff me. I was about to arrest Gwen Marcey, wanted for murder." He nodded in my direction. "Killed two FBI agents."

Four pistols now rotated to me.

Aynslee stared at the men. "Mom didn't kill anybody."

"Put your hands where we can see them." The older cop glared at me.

I extended both arms, palms outward.

Mike's gaze sharpened on the device in my hand. "Careful! That's a detonator."

"Put it down, lady." The officer licked his lips.

With one hand, I placed it next to me.

"Push it over here. Gently!"

I slid it toward the officer.

"I'll take it from here." Mike picked up the detonator, retrieved his pistol from the ground, and pointed it at me. "See, Gwen? I keep telling you. Everything always works out for the best."

"Not quite." I tried to ignore the warm puddle of blood forming under me. "Beth says everything happens for a reason."

Mike shrugged.

"I left a message and phone number for Sheriff Dave Moore before coming here," I continued. "The phone number the Avenging Angels called just before you had them murdered. Dave should have called it by now. He knows everything."

"You have the right to remain silent," Mike said.

"Do you want me to cuff her?" the older cop asked.

"I've put some things together since," I said.

Mike spoke louder. "Anything you say can and will be held against you in a court of law."

Two officers glanced back and forth between Mike and me.

"I kept coming back to power and control." I glanced at each of the officers.

"Get to your feet," Mike said.

"Sir," one of the officers said, lowering his pistol. "Do you want us to call an ambulance? She's bleeding pretty good."

"She's fine." He raised his pistol. "You have the right to speak to an attorney . . ."

"You'll be the one needing an attorney," I said.

"Shut up!"

My voice was getting weaker. "What would you gain by killing all the people at the conference?"

Two of the officers shifted until Mike was in their sight.

"The only way you'd get power and control over the Mormon Church was to take over the leadership. How did you phrase it? 'Rule with your holy priesthood,' with your scepter of power."

"If you cannot afford an attorney, one will be appointed for you." Mike rotated the pistol toward Aynslee, then back to me.

The world grew fuzzy around the edges. "You told me the details." Every breath burned like salt in my wounds. Aynslee touched my hand, and I briefly smiled at her. "You had to destroy the power structure of the LDS Church." I addressed the cops. "The bomb he created for the Peace Conference—"

"Shut up! Shut up!" Mike waved the detonator.

"Hey, careful with that thing," the older officer said.

"When his bomb," I continued, still looking at the cops, "in the Joseph Smith's reconstruction blew up, he'd create a specific threat that would send the LDS hierarchy to safe bunkers under Temple Square in Salt Lake City."

"I said shut up!" Blood drained from Mike's face.

"The security guards you recommended to the LDS Church placed, what? Another bomb? Sarin gas?" I pointed at the book. "With all the leaders dead, you'd become the Prophet of the

Mormon Church. Complete power and control." I looked at the cop. "You have to warn them . . ."

The cop aimed his gun at Mike. "There was a bomb threat in Salt Lake this morning. They found explosives. No one was injured."

The officer nearest Mike grabbed for the detonator.

Mike pushed the button.

Nothing happened.

"Wrong detonator." I held up the real one and smiled. "You lose."

CHAPTER
FORTY-ONE

AYNSLEE CLUNG TO ME, AND I GENTLY STROKED her hair. "Sweetheart," I whispered. "I have to go now."

Aynslee slowly released me and stepped away. The travelers at the SeaTac airport rushed past the corner where we hovered, racing toward security. "You'll have a wonderful time going up the Inside Passage to Alaska with your dad." I briefly removed my oversize sunglasses and smiled at Robert. "Your dad made sure he booked you a—what did you call it?"

"Neptune suite," Robert said reluctantly.

"Ah, yes, a suite. Your ship doesn't leave Vancouver until tomorrow, and I know you didn't pack enough in that backpack, so your dad will take you shopping at Nordstrom's." I smiled again. It was so much fun to see Robert have to part with some of that royalty blood money for his daughter.

"What about school?" Aynslee asked.

"I've ordered the homeschool books, and we'll start on it when you get home."

"I love you, Mom." Aynslee hugged me again, careful of my bandaged side.

"I love you—" Emotion seized my throat, preventing anymore words, so I simply kissed the top of her head, picked up my carry-on, and nodded to Special Agent Patricia Pfeiffer. She whisked me through a side door to the waiting plane.

Agent Pfeiffer shook my elbow. "Mrs. Marcey? We're almost to Salt Lake."

I rubbed my eyes and shifted in my seat. *Bad idea.* My stitched-up ribs protested the move. The jet's landing gear thumped into place and the jet touched down seamlessly. Agent Pfeiffer placed a restraining hand on my arm. "Please stay seated until everyone's left. I don't want anyone to spot you."

I nodded. Even though Dave's phone call led to the discovery of a bomb set to explode in the tunnels under Temple Square and prevented Mike from wiping out the LDS leadership, the FBI were being cautious. They had no way of identifying Mike's followers. With his charismatic leadership, direct lineage to Joseph Smith, and Smith's journal, Mike could have remnant members anywhere.

Then, of course, there was the small problem of the remnant in Zion. I seemed to be the only person who knew of its exact location. And I wasn't sure I could find it again, nor was I sure I wanted to. I just had this nagging feeling that there were still some loose ends.

"Can I make a phone call while we wait?" I asked.

"Sure."

I dialed Beth's number.

"Gwen, you have a very bad dog."

"You've said that before. Now what has he done?"

"After I picked him up from the vet, Aynslee and I took him to the hotel where he proceeded to snatch the steak I ordered from room service and swallow it in one gulp."

I tried not to laugh. "He deserves it. How is he?"

"The vet said he'd have a slight limp, but otherwise he's fine. He's crated at my hotel room. Norm's home from his fishing trip and invited you to a fish fry."

My vision blurred and I swallowed before asking, "When are you driving home?"

"Tomorrow. I'm still at Nordstrom's with Aynslee and Robert."

"And . . . ?"

She let out a small snort of laughter. "Robert's platinum card is taking a hit, but I think he's making a real effort to be a dad. Aynslee is walking on air."

I cleared my throat. "Mmm."

"One last thing," Beth said. "I don't know how much they're telling you—"

"Assume little to nothing. I've been in seclusion since Mike's arrest."

The agent looked as if she'd grab my phone. I turned slightly so she couldn't reach it without gaining the attention of the departing passengers.

"The FBI arrested three security guards connected to the plot. Mike's been charged with the murder of the two agents found at your place."

"Good." But with that memory, maybe I'd sell the house.

In the end, I had no trouble retracing my escape from Zion. SA Pfeiffer, joined by Deputy Oakes of the Sanpete County sheriff's office, emergency vehicles, and a host of FBI agents, followed my directions. Oakes was an immense man, at least six foot six, with massive shoulders and kind eyes. He spoke sparingly as we traveled, but he'd brought me bottled water and a thermos of coffee.

All that remained of the tent city and vast parking area was flattened grass. In another few weeks even that would be back to normal. The huge food storage buildings held empty shelves and dust. I could see why the structures hadn't been discovered by searching airplanes. They'd covered the roof in a thin layer of earth and tangled grass like giant root cellars.

I rubbed my arms and thought about the remnant. They'd been lucky. They were drawn in by Mike, a charismatic leader, but unlike the followers of Jim Jones or David Koresh, the remnant survived. They had left this hidden enclave and gone back to their homes. Perhaps they now waited for a new prophet, a new leader to guide them.

Prophet Kenyon refused to help authorities in their investigation, but Frances decided to leave the First Born Apostolic Brethren in Christ Church and was providing the link between Kenyon's and Mike's groups.

We continued up the road into the small town. For the first time in daylight, I saw the house where I'd been held captive. The porch was smaller than I remembered, the house bigger.

No children played in the road. The clotheslines were

empty. A puff of wind stirred baby-powder dust, and a red-tail hawk drifted on an updraft. Tangy cedar perfumed the air. The only sound was the crackle of police radios.

Deputy Oakes waited beside me, leaning against the patrol car, while the agents searched the other boarded-over buildings. The house in front of us was the last to be cleared.

A deputy approached the front door with a crowbar, prying the wood off with a loud screech. The agents forced open the door. Their boots thumped on the uncarpeted hallway and into the downstairs rooms. "Clear!"

"Clear!"

"Clear!"

My gaze drifted toward the window of my room. A face stared back at me.

My heart skipped a beat. "There's somebody inside!"

Deputy Oakes radioed the warning and then moved me so I was behind the patrol car. I strained to hear any sounds from inside the structure. The breeze kicked up, whispering through the trees, sending golden aspen leaves flying.

Deputy Oakes's radio crackled and he acknowledged the indecipherable message. "They want you inside. It's safe."

I trudged after him, my feet reluctant to once again enter. We mounted the stairs and turned a corner. It was the old woman's room. The door stood open. The room smelled of pine cleaner. The dresser gleamed with fresh polish, and starched white curtains fluttered at the windows.

Esther, the young woman who'd helped me escape, stood by the bed, clutching her pregnant belly. She relaxed when she saw me. "Ya came back."

"Yes."

She smiled. "Ya ax me what I wanted ta do. I done thought about that."

"I'm glad you did, Esther."

"I wanted ta take care of folks. That's what I wanted ta do. When they said they was leavin, they was gonna leave without her." She nodded at the old woman in the bed. "That weren't right. She be Adam's mom."

"His mom?" I asked.

"Sure. That's why she be alive past birthin years. She be The Mother. But when they left, she woulda died." The young woman paused, then went on. "So I took care of her."

My eyes blurred and I blinked. "But no one knew you were here. You can't drive. You don't have a phone . . ."

Esther pointed. "She says you was comin' back."

The old woman was propped in bed with a host of snowy-white pillows. "I told you, child. Lord willing, she'd return."

"Yes, ma'am," I said.

Esther reached into her pocket and pulled out a piece of paper, then offered it to me. "You wrote her name: Mary Allen. Mother said she'd learn . . . uh . . . teach me to read."

I took the sketch from her. "Mother said teaching was her calling." The drawing I'd done of Mary Allen had been folded many times and smudged from grubby fingers.

Two EMTs appeared with a stretcher to transport the old woman. I stepped into the hall, leaned against the wall, and thought about the nagging, unfinished feeling I'd had. What if I refused to help law enforcement find this place? Or simply couldn't find it again?

Beth's words echoed in my brain. *Everything happens for a reason, Gwen.*

351

I looked at the sketch of Mary Allen. The young girl's death started me on this path.

No. Before her murder. I wouldn't have met her had I not been in Utah in desperate need of a job. If Robert hadn't divorced me.

A voice whispered in my mind. *Go further back.*

I slowly climbed up the stairs. The dingy hall on the third floor carried numerous footprints of the fleeing remnant members. Pausing, I touched my wig. Cancer came before the divorce, robbing me of my breasts and hair.

But the effects of cancer allowed me to pass for a boy and escape from the remnant.

I walked down the hall. The room where I'd been held captive was on my right, door open. I entered.

The bedding was missing, and the drawer was yanked from the small bedside table. I lifted it and sat on the bed. My words were still inscribed below Mary Ellen's, *My name is Gwen Marcey. I love you.*

Aynslee and I had said those words before she'd left with her father. I swallowed hard.

But it was Aynslee's rebellion that caused her to steal Joseph Smith's writings, blocking it from falling into Mike's hands.

Cancer, divorce, rebellion, escape, death, shooting . . . all combined to prevent a third massacre on September eleventh.

God, I need You. Your will be done. I trust my life, and Aynslee, to You. Amen.

Beth was right. Everything happens for a reason.

AUTHOR NOTE

AFTER READING THIS STORY, THE FIRST QUES-
tion most folks ask is where does fact end and fiction begin? The
simple answer is that fiction is woven between historical and
forensic facts. And I found the research riveting.

As a forensic artist, breast cancer survivor, and Great
Pyrenees owner, I wrote of what I knew, but I couldn't say
exactly what started the Mormon slant of the story. Possibly an
article on the Internet about a Le Fort fracture found on Joseph
Smith's skull. His *skull*? That led me to an obscure book written
by the granddaughter of Hands, the man who dug up the bodies buried in Nauvoo. I'd been thinking about drawing his face
from the skull, but the illustrations in the book showed too little
information to work with, but it got my mind working.

With the only known documented image of Joseph Smith
being a profile drawing and the death mask, I followed up on
their origins. My research got more and more interesting.

A vague idea took shape. I had visited the Little Bighorn

Battlefield in Montana. An interpretive center was built on the site with reconstructions of some of the men's skulls on display. Mountain Meadows, a very real place and a very real event, had little to show of the massacre. There had been three settlers formally buried on the location. What if . . . what if a forensic artist reconstructed those long-dead faces? And what if Joseph Smith's was one of the faces reconstructed?

Then I had to look at how Joseph Smith died. Several LDS members created an online reconstruction of the Carthage jail, and I purchased their findings. I also bought a score of books on the subject. My husband and I had spent years creating storyboards for courtrooms that showed the possibilities for different crime scenes. I simply applied the same approach. The good news for me was the different eyewitness accounts. For every difference, it allowed me to come up with an alternate explanation. The truly eye-opening information was the death of two of the men involved, the handing over of the keys of the Temple to a non-Mormon, Emma's actions, missing clothing, the poem by David Smith, and the comment in the LDS Church history about the rumor of Smith's being buried in Utah. There was so much more I could have used but left out to keep the tension high.

I used materials written by the LDS Church, the Community of Christ, historians, and survivor accounts. If you are interested in the materials and sources of my work, I invite you to visit my website at www.CarrieStuartParks.com. There you can sign up for my newsletter and keep up with Gwen Marcey's next adventure.

One final note: a special thank-you to Carter Cornick, FBI Terrorist Unit (ret.), for his input and suggestions. Dinner coming.

Blessings,
Carrie

READING GROUP GUIDE

1. The prologue opens with a fictionalized eyewitness account of a real event: the Mountain Meadows Massacre. At Mountain Meadows, 120–140 unarmed men, women, and children were killed. Had you heard of this event before? If so, where? If not, why do you think this is not a widely known piece of American history?

2. In chapter one, Gwen notices a CTR wristband on one of the agitators. "Choose the right" is taught to young children by the Church of Jesus Christ Latter-day Saints as a reminder to make wise choices in their lives (and that God will bless you for doing so). The Christian version is "What Would Jesus Do?" Compare and contrast these two different sayings. In chapter twenty-nine, Gwen is trying to sum up her life. She thinks, *I could list my achievements. Awards. Friends. Cases. How I always tried to choose the right course of action.* Reflect on this.

3. In chapter two, we are introduced to the theme of "every-thing happens for a reason." Beth, in chapter fifteen, adds ". . . if in your lifetime you find out why something bad hap-pened, it's a blessing." Have you found this to be true in your own life? Why or why not?

4. Gwen is carrying a lot a baggage in the beginning of the story: just two months from her last chemo treatment for breast cancer, double mastectomy, hot flashes, lost income and position, divorce, and guilt over her daughter. How does she handle these setbacks at first? Does this change by the end of the book?

5. Gwen and her husband, Robert, are divorced. What things can you point to that each of them could have done dif-ferently? Would you recommend that they make different choices where Aynslee is concerned?

6. Gwen encounters several groups in this story: Prophet Kenyon's "The First Born Apostolic Brethren in Christ," Adam's "The Remnant Latter Day Saints of Zion," and main-stream members of the Latter-day Saints Church. What seem to be the differences between them? What is the same?

7. Beth is Gwen's positive friend, supporting her and help-ing her at every turn. Is this what Gwen needs during this tumultuous time in her life? Why or why not?

8. Reflecting on Prophet Kenyon, Gwen thinks, *could a leader inspire both kindness and destruction*? What do you think about that? Can you think of any examples?

9. In chapter eight, Frances, a member of Prophet Kenyon's

flock, makes the comment, "God can change His mind." How would you respond to this if you'd been sitting there?

10. Aynslee runs away from the school, and then thinks about running away from her parents. Is that what she really wants? How do her actions show her real feelings?

11. While locked in Mary Allen's room, Gwen attempts to sum up her life in twenty-five words. If you were to do the same, what twenty-five words would you choose?

ACKNOWLEDGMENTS

I'D REALLY LIKE TO THANK THE WHOLE WORLD for this book: thankyouthankyouthankyou . . . oh wait, that might take more time than I have, especially if I want to finish the second book of this series. So, specifically I'd like to thank Frank and Barb Peretti. You both believed in me from the start. And you sat through *years* of my painful growth as a writer. Frank, thank you for your humor, kindness, gentle suggestions, and not-so-gentle cries of horror at times at what I wrote.

To my husband, Rick, and your endless "Are you done with that novel yet?" Yes, darlin', I'm finally done. I love you for waiting. A grateful and appreciative thank you to my agent, Terry Burns of Hartline Literary Agency. You believed in the project and took the chance. A big thank you to Amanda Bostic, Editorial Director, who made me feel as if I were coming home at Thomas Nelson from the very start. Thank you, Natalie

Hanemann, for your spot-on editing. How could I have made *so* many mistakes? Thank you, Jodi Hughes and Laura Dickerson, for all your hard work and caring.

I wish to send out a great big hug and thanks to the folks who helped with this book—some of you without even knowing how much you helped. Dave and Andrea Kramer, Larry Frowick, Bentley and Aynslee Stuart, and the rest of my great family. Scott, hang tight. Next book. Thank you to my critique group with their bloody, red pens: Steve, Steve, Steve, Pat, Carol, Bruce, Carrie, and Joyce. Thanks to all my forensic students for providing suggestions from your vast pools of knowledge, with a special thanks to Craig Faga and Cris Harnisch. Thank you, Kerry Woods, Lori Bishop, Michelle Garlock, and everyone else who provided much needed insights as beta readers. Thank you to Winnie, Maria, Bonnie, Munchie, Tawney, Woodruff, and all my beloved Great Pyrenees over the years for providing the template for Winston.

Mom and Dad, I wish you could have been here for this. You were such inspirations. I miss you every day.

Finally, and most importantly, thank you to my Lord and Savior, Jesus Christ. To You goes all glory and honor and praise.

Carrie Stuart Parks
Philippians 4:8–9

An excerpt from *Playing Saint* by Zachary Bartels

PROLOGUE

THIRTEEN YEARS AGO

DANNY SAT QUIETLY IN THE PEW AND WAITED for his exorcism.

It wasn't scheduled, but it would happen. He would make it happen. He'd been down this road countless times before—enough to know that all the elements of the equation were present here this morning. He would be *delivered*; at least that's what they would call it. He'd probably fall to the ground and writhe for a few seconds. He'd own the moment, milk it a little.

The prospect failed to thrill him. It had become banal, like waiting to be called in to the dentist's office, flipping through ancient, dog-eared magazines, or sitting at the DMV, fiddling with that little numbered tab of paper, willing your turn to come. And yet, a certain dampened twinge of excitement persisted. Not butterflies in the stomach. More like a tingle of expectation somewhere deeper.

Which was fine. Stuffed full as it was with meat and grease, his stomach would not accommodate butterflies. Danny was a trim, young man and usually ate little, but on these special Sunday mornings he always felt inexplicably compelled to stop at some rural greasy spoon and eat until he felt a bit queasy. It was like that old maxim about a pregnant woman eating for two. How many was Danny eating for now? He'd lost count.

And he had no choice but to continue feeding Them, to carry on with increasing momentum down this road, all the while pretending that he didn't know the truth: at the end of the day, he would be the main course.

ONE

DETECTIVE PAUL KETCHAM DID NOT NEED TO flash his gold badge at the patrol officer covering the door—they knew each other on sight—but he did anyway. He liked the way it felt. He also enjoyed ducking under yellow crime-scene tape, but there was none here to duck.

"Let's get some tape up," he barked at the officer. "Press'll be here any minute. We don't need them contaminating the scene."

The house on Lane Avenue had lain vacant for nearly a year. Squatters found the body three hours earlier, and hoping to collect a reward, made the call to the Grand Rapids police. There was none to collect, so now they waited for the local news affiliates, thinking they might get some TV time in lieu of monetary remuneration.

Ketcham entered the spacious living room, noticing the hardwood floors and early twentieth-century leaded windows.

It was clear that the house had once been beautiful, despite the years of neglect and the shirtless corpse lying in a pool of blood.

"Hey, Paul," called Corrinne Kirkpatrick, descending the curved staircase. "I've been here twenty minutes already. I can't remember the last time I beat you to a scene. Did you have to do your paper route?"

Like Ketcham, she was a senior detective with the Major Case Team. They weren't partners—there was no such official pairing in their unit—but they had been building a mutual respect and interdependence for the better part of a decade. Corrinne was the only person on the force who dared to call him Paul. To everyone else he was Detective Ketcham, save to his superiors, who simply called him Ketcham.

In her midforties, she was almost ten years his senior, which somehow wound up as a source of ribbing in both directions. He also dished out frequent digs about her boyish haircut and severe pantsuits—both of which she took as compliments.

"This is already looking too familiar," he said, approaching the corpse.

The young man looked to be in his late teens, his dark hair shoulder-length, his skin pallid, and his throat cut from ear to ear. On his forehead the number 666 had been applied in a dark red-brown. His chest bore a large five-pointed star in the same substance.

"Pretty uninventive," Corrinne observed with some disappointment. "I still give creativity points for painting on the guy with his own blood. But the star and the 666 are a little nineties, am I right? It's just like that corny movie; what was it called?"

"Hm? I don't know. I don't watch movies." Ketcham ran a hand through his thick hair and squatted down for a better look.

"It's definitely our guy, though. Same technique, same detail—looks like a pretty fine paintbrush. That didn't make the press, so we can rule out some copycat inspired by the headline."

"Nothing related to playing cards either. I guess they'll have to come up with a new name for the perp. The Blackjack Killer doesn't fit anymore."

"Yeah. Maybe the Pentagon Killer."

Corrinne shook her head. "A pentagon isn't a star. It's a five-sided shape, like the building in Washington."

"Pentagram?"

"Yeah, maybe. Anyway, this changes the profile altogether. I don't think I'm jumping to conclusions when I see some definite religious overtones here. That's new."

"Hm." Ketcham scribbled some notes in a pocket-sized spiral notebook. "And if we're not dealing with playing-card imagery, the whole thing about expecting four victims is out the window too."

"That was pretty thin anyway. I think Channel 6 came up with it. My real takeaway here is that our whole 'new gang' theory is probably off base. Gangs rarely employ Satanic rituals and symbolism, am I right?"

"I wouldn't think so." He rubbed his chin. "This whole thing is off. Two victims in two days. Ritualized killings. Looks like the work of a serial killer, but I'd expect another girl in that case."

"Why is that?" Corrinne folded her arms.

"Oh, save the feminism. We're talking about a murderer here. Guy's slicing people up; I doubt he cares whether his choice of victim is politically correct."

"And why exactly does the killer have to be a man?"

"If you're trying to advance the cause, I think you're doing it wrong." He turned his attention back to the body. "What have we got on the victim?"

She perused her own notepad. "His name is Benjamin Ludema. He was a senior at Central High. No arrest record. We're waiting to hear back from a school representative. I'd like to interview all of his teachers tomorrow morning."

"Yeah, that's good. Let me know if you need help."

"Now that you mention it, I was hoping you two might have some classes together. Are you friends with any upperclassmen?"

"Funny stuff." He pointed to the design on the boy's chest. "Did the lab ever confirm that the blood from yesterday's image was the victim's?"

"Type matched, but we're still waiting on DNA confirmation. I wouldn't stand on one leg until it comes in. I'll make sure they do the same tests on young Ben here, with a few unique samples."

"What's your guess at time of death?"

"Definitely within the last four hours. I'd be real surprised if it were any earlier."

"Sheesh. Killing for the devil on Sunday morning." Ketcham shook his head. "What's the world come to?"

"I know what you mean. In my day all the Satanic murders happened during the work week. Between this and all the churches getting tagged, this town's really throwing in with Beelzebub."

He gave her a chuckle. "Those two vagrants out there waiting to give a statement?"

"No, they've been handled. Pretty much worthless."

Ketcham was beginning to sweat. It was early October and

still too warm for the lined trench coat he wore. "Techs should be here soon," he said, checking his watch. "You mind babysitting while I start the paperwork?"

"Of course the woman has to do the babysitting."

"You're a regular Gloria Steinem, you know that?"

———

The story continues in *Playing Saint* by Zachary Bartels, available October 2014.

ABOUT THE AUTHOR

ANDREA KRAMER, KRAMER PHOTOGRAPHY

CARRIE STUART PARKS IS AN AWARD-WINNING fine artist and internationally known forensic artist. She teaches forensic art courses to law enforcement professionals and is the author/illustrator of numerous books on drawing. Carrie began to write fiction while battling breast cancer and was mentored by *New York Times* best-selling author Frank Peretti. Now in remission, she continues to encourage other women struggling with cancer.

Visit her website at www.carriestuartparks.com
Facebook: CarrieStuartParksAuthor
Twitter: @CarrieParks